What the critics are saying...

"Water Crystal is a fast-paced, futuristic tale.... This is one story that never lets the action falter.... The passion that flares between Angelo and Bianca is the epitome of erotic romance. Their scenes blend outstanding sexual heat with a welling of emotion." - *Fallen Angels Reviews*

"...the action never stops and the adventure is just as high." - *The Romance Studio*

Anya Bast

Water Crystal

Ellora's Cave
Romantica Publishing

An Ellora's Cave Romantica Publication

www.ellorascave.com

Water Crystal

ISBN # 1419953001
ALL RIGHTS RESERVED.
Water Crystal Copyright© 2005 Anya Bast
Edited by: Briana St. James
Cover art by: Syneca

Electronic book Publication: June, 2005
Trade paperback Publication: October, 2005

Excerpt from *And Lady Makes Three*
Copyright © Anya Bast, Nikki Soarde, Ashley Ladd, 2005

With the exception of quotes used in reviews, this book may not be reproduced or used in whole or in part by any means existing without written permission from the publisher, Ellora's Cave Publishing, Inc.® 1056 Home Avenue, Akron OH 44310-3502.

This book is a work of fiction and any resemblance to persons, living or dead, or places, events or locales is purely coincidental. The characters are productions of the authors' imagination and used fictitiously.

Warning:

The following material contains graphic sexual content meant for mature readers. *Water Crystal* has been rated *E-rotic* by a minimum of three independent reviewers.

Ellora's Cave Publishing offers three levels of Romantica™ reading entertainment: S (S-ensuous), E (E-rotic), and X (X-treme).

S-en*suous* love scenes are explicit and leave nothing to the imagination.

E-*rotic* love scenes are explicit, leave nothing to the imagination, and are high in volume per the overall word count. In addition, some E-rated titles might contain fantasy material that some readers find objectionable, such as bondage, submission, same sex encounters, forced seductions, etc. E-rated titles are the most graphic titles we carry; it is common, for instance, for an author to use words such as "fucking", "cock", "pussy", etc., within their work of literature.

X-*treme* titles differ from E-rated titles only in plot premise and storyline execution. Unlike E-rated titles, stories designated with the letter X tend to contain controversial subject matter not for the faint of heart.

Also by Anya Bast:

And Lady Makes Three (Anthology)
Autumn Pleasures: The Union
Blood of an Angel
Blood of the Raven
Blood of The Rose
Ellora's Cavemen: Tales of the Temple III (Anthology)
Ordinary Charm
Spring Pleasures: The Transformation
Summer Pleasures: The Capture
Winter Pleasures: The Training

Water Crystal

Dedication

To my Aunt Carol who reads my books anyway. Your support means more than I can say.

Chapter One
Earth 2075

Bianca sat on the floor of the crumbling building where she'd taken shelter. Her solar-powered lantern cast a dim light, bathing the bleached walls of the room in an eerie glow. Old rusted pipes, which at one time actually transported water, protruded from the ceiling. A bolt of lightning illuminated the broken-out windows and thunder boomed. Rain pelted the roof and leaked in through the cracks in the walls.

She tipped her canteen back and caught the last drops of purified water on her tongue. Closing her eyes, she savored the liquid, and then let the canteen drop to the side. That was the last of the water and soon she'd run out of sector credits. On the border of Sector Thirty, at the last water vendor before the Wastes, she would buy one more canteen full and a bath. That would take care of the rest of her credits and would have to last her until she made it home to Sector Twenty-Nine.

A bead of perspiration trickled down her temple, and she wiped it with the back of her hand. She stood and walked to one of the broken windows to catch a breeze, carefully staying away from the green-tinged rain that fell through it. It was one of life's little ironies…to be completely surrounded by water and unable to consume any. Thunder boomed again, and the wind gusted from the opposite direction, blowing rain onto her T-shirt and pants before she could jump away.

"Shit!" Her voice shattered the silence of the room and startled her. She had to change her clothes now. The freysis could not be allowed to stay against her skin for any extended period of time. Yesterday she'd been caught in the rain briefly, before she'd been able to find decent shelter. Her freysis level was probably pretty high right now. She couldn't afford any more exposure. The hydrologic cycle had spread the bacteria everywhere. It even fell from the clouds.

Cursing herself for her negligence, she crossed the room, shedding clothing along the way. She pulled a spare pair of pants and a long-sleeved, baggy shirt from her sack and shrugged them on.

The master crystal, the booty from her break-in at the Water Company that afternoon, was secreted in a small black velvet sack. She found it and looped the bag's string around her neck, letting it hang heavy between her breasts. The only thing driving her now was the need to get the crystal back home to Melvin. He wanted to reverse the freysis poisoning, and the crystal played a key role.

Bianca spread her clothing out on the floor. Water activated the freysis, but the bacteria were harmless when dry. She laid down on her bedroll, making sure her pistol was within easy reach. The Guardians from the Water Company would never find her now that she'd traveled past the border of the Center. However, that didn't mean she was out of danger.

She closed her eyes and listened to the relentless pounding of the rain on the roof. Rain was how her twin sister Calina had killed herself. She'd gone out into the gardens at the Water Company one afternoon when it was pouring and had let the freysis soak her. She'd stayed out there until the bacteria had poisoned her blood.

Bianca swallowed hard against her already dry throat. Still, she couldn't cry. She'd tried to make the tears come, but they just wouldn't. She knew it wasn't only from dehydration. She hardly felt anything now but anger...and numbness. Numbness was like an emotion, too, since she felt it almost constantly these days. Maybe that was a blessing.

Bianca had worn Calina's dress and jewelry when she'd stolen the crystal. To obtain them, she'd made Calina's quarters her first stop as soon as she'd breached the Water Company. Finch had given both expensive items to her sister, and Bianca had burned them at the first opportunity. It had been deeply satisfying, as if she were destroying Calina's fetters.

Placing her hand over the pouch, she rubbed at the velvet material. She fisted it in her hand and squeezed her eyes shut. The crystal would to go a long way toward making things right. She'd make Finch pay for what he'd done to Calina.

* * * * *

A fine tremble ran up Angelo DiMarco's spine. He halted his mount outside an abandoned building that read Hayworth Seed Co. on the side in faded lettering. There was nothing special about the structure. It was just one more dilapidated building in a whole ocean of them. Same broken windows. Same forced-in front door. But he could feel the heat of another person in there, radiating out and into him. A magnified presence.

"Stop," he said quietly to Dell, the Guardian of Order who traveled with him.

Dell reined up beside him. "What is it?"

He jerked a thumb in the direction of the building. "We need to search this place. I think she's holed up here." They'd been tracking a thief from the Center for the past three days and it hadn't been an easy trail. Once anyone traveled beyond the borders of the Center, it was a hardship experience. Perhaps they'd just found their fugitive and could head back home.

"How the hell do you know?" asked Dell.

Angelo didn't answer.

"Well, how do you know?"

His jaw locked. He was unwilling to explain. Sometimes he just knew where people were, where they were going. People told him he had a sixth sense for it, but he didn't like that explanation.

Dell stared at him for a moment, his glossy black hair falling into his angular face. He laughed once, short and bitter. "Whatever, man, you're the captain."

They swung down off their horses and entered the building. Darkness, along with the scents of must and humidity, enveloped them. Crumbled drywall and broken glass littered the floor beneath their feet, and old rusted pipes hung from the ceiling. These days piped-in water was luxury reserved only for the extremely wealthy and those in their inner circles. Angelo motioned Dell to the right, then drew his alter-gun and ascended the stairs.

At the top was a large open room. A human-shaped bundle lay on a bedroll in the center of the floor. At one end was a toss of silvery-gold hair, the same unusual color as that of Calina, his boss' deceased wife. His grip tightened on the handle of the alter-gun. Jackpot. The thief was Calina's twin sister. He couldn't see this woman's face from where he stood, and he didn't have a clear shot at her head. He needed to get closer to use his alter-gun, which, if flipped to its current setting, would only knock her unconscious. Aloysius Finch, his boss, had told him to take her alive.

Carefully, he removed one foot from the top stair and placed it on the floor of the room. She made no sound, no movement. He brought his other foot up and took two steps forward, hoping that below him Dell also made no noise.

She sighed in her sleep and turned over, throwing one arm wide. He froze, waiting for her to settle in again. He listened for her breathing to return to a steady pattern. When it did, he took another step. The floorboard beneath his foot squeaked. He glanced down.

Fuck. So much for stealth.

He heard a rustle and the distinctive sound of a pistol being cocked, the slide of metal on metal and a click. He looked up. She was on her knees with a gun pointed right at his heart. Jesus. He'd finally crossed paths with someone who moved faster than he did. She held a 9-mm pistol in her hand. It was an antique, but still entirely capable of ripping a path straight through his heart.

"Drop it." She jerked her head, indicating his alter-gun. "If you move to shoot, I'll get you first, and I use honest-to-God bullets in mine. I hear they hurt."

He hesitated for a moment and then dropped the alter-gun to the floor with a clatter.

They regarded each other warily. More than the pistol she leveled at him took him aback. Now he understood why everyone who'd come into contact with Bianca Robinson on her little flight to Out-Center had remembered her. She wasn't easily forgotten. He'd seen a picture of her twin, Calina, but this woman had a far more feral kind of beauty. Her hair hung past her shoulders in a tumble of gold and shades of silver-blonde. It framed a face with exquisitely molded features and clear blue-green eyes. Her skin was tawny and her hair tousled. She looked like a wild thing with the face of an angel. Women like her were as rare as pure well water these days. No, you never forgot one. Right now, that pretty face was set in hard lines of determination. He didn't doubt she'd use the gun.

He took a step forward before he realized he'd done it. "Look, I won't hurt—"

Before he even finished his sentence, she squeezed off a shot. It whizzed past his head, making his ears ring. The smell of sulfur and hot metal filled the air. "Whoa! I'm not going to hurt—"

"I meant to miss that time. I won't mean to miss next time."

Dell pounded up the stairs, drawn by the sound of gunfire.

She trained her weapon in Dell's direction. He came off the top step, his alter-gun aimed at her head. She fired. The bullet grazed his shoulder and embedded itself in the wall behind him.

She tried to fire again, and the gun clicked, empty. Dell leveled his alter-gun at her, a smile of anticipation on his face. She dropped and rolled, obscuring Dell's aim.

Angelo brought his alter-gun up and searched out the woman's crown, but she moved too fast. She rolled onto her feet and went for the window. He took a couple of shots in desperation. Christ. They were three stories up and the only thing to cushion her fall were the jagged concrete ruins of the street below.

"No!" The word ripped from his throat as he watched his quarry dive out. Angelo ran to the window with Dell fast behind him.

Another narrow roof stretched about four feet below the window she'd dove out of. It was completely hidden until you came right up to it. Jesus...had she even known it was there? The woman pounded across the roof now, headed straight for the window of an adjoining building. Leveling his alter-gun, he trained it on his moving target and squeezed the trigger. He hit his mark and she went down.

He scrambled out the window with Dell behind him and approached her. She lay facedown where she'd fallen in a jumbled heap of oversized gray shirt. It made her look small and innocent. But the word innocent definitely had nothing to do with this woman.

"Sleeping like a baby," said Dell. He knelt down and flipped her to her back. He whistled low. "If it's possible for this one to be better-looking than her twin, she is."

Angelo wasn't listening to Dell. His attention was riveted on the woman's forehead, where blood welled and made a crimson trail down the side of her face. He knelt and took her chin in his fingers, tilting her face in his direction to get a better look at the injury. "Dell, do you have a canteen on you?"

Dell unhooked the water canteen from his belt and handed it over. Angelo uncorked it and wet the edge of his shirt.

"Hey, that's the last of my pure-water," Dell protested.

Angelo quelled his companion's words with a stormy look and drew the dampened part of his shirt over the gash on her forehead, wiping the blood away. The wound wasn't too bad, but she'd have a hell of a headache when she woke up.

He spotted the velvet sack around her throat and felt the contents—the stolen crystal. He broke the sack's string and put it in his pocket.

Angelo slid his arms beneath her and lifted. She felt light and warm against him. "Let's get inside and bandage her head. I smell more rain on the way."

* * * * *

Bianca woke to the sound of rain. Blasted rain. Blasted, undrinkable, murdering rain.

The second thing she noted was that her head pounded out a staccato rhythm in time to the rain hitting the roof. She groaned, brought her hand to her forehead and touched material. Someone had wound it around her head.

"Take it easy."

A low, rumbling voice met her ears. It wasn't Dell. She knew his voice.

She risked a glance and saw the brown-eyed man sitting beside her. He didn't look at her. He was too busy loading her bullets into the cartridge of her gun. She watched his actions covetously.

Earlier, when he'd surprised her, she hadn't recognized him. She thought she knew all the guardians in the Water Company's employ, but she didn't know this one. When she'd seen him before, for the briefest of moments, she'd thought maybe he wasn't working for Finch at all. He wore a dark blue, short-sleeved shirt and a pair of tan pants, not the uniform of a guardian.

He had a powerful build, and he looked threatening because of it, but there was something that offset his physical appearance in those chocolate-brown eyes, a kind of deep, unbelievable kindness. It was disconcerting to her. How could someone who worked for Aloysius Finch be kind?

And earlier, that warm gaze had made her miss the shot she'd taken at his head. Now, eyeing her gun, she really wished her aim had been better.

She caught herself trying to catch his gaze again and shook herself out of it, telling herself not to be a fool. Most of the kindness in this world had disappeared with drinkable rainwater. Anyway, she'd lay money it was his shot that had taken her down and gashed her head open. The bastard.

Her hand made its way to her chest. The crystal was gone. Something resembling despair settled in the pit of her stomach. It couldn't have been despair, though. She didn't feel things like that anymore. Hell, she didn't feel much of anything anymore. Still, the loss of the crystal was devastating. She'd just taken it three days ago. It had been her biggest, most difficult acquisition ever, and by far the most important.

She dropped her hand to her lap. "You got what you came for. Why don't you leave me alone now?"

"'Cause Mr. Finch wants the thief as well as his stolen property," Dell said from across the room.

Of course he does. Of course he wanted her when she was the spitting image of Calina. Bianca slowly pushed herself into a sitting position, wincing at the pain that shot through her head and shoulders.

She eyed the rangy, black-haired man. He stood across the room, leaning against the wall. Dull anger rose within her, made a coppery taste in her mouth. "Dell," she acknowledged in a flat, expressionless voice. His shoulder was bandaged where her bullet had grazed him. Satisfaction made the edges of her mouth curl up.

"How do you know who I am?" asked Dell.

Bianca laughed. "Dell, if Calina knew you, so do I. Oh, yes, I know you." She smiled and winked at him. "I know you only too well, darlin'."

Dell had the good grace to look nervous for a moment. He pushed off the wall, then leaned carelessly back against it and pulled a mask of cool arrogance over his face. A slow smile spread across his mouth. "Well, I may have known Calina, but I don't know you." He walked toward her. "Maybe we should remedy that."

Bianca stiffened.

The brown-eyed man sprang to his feet. "Back off, Dell." He leveled her pistol at Dell's chest and cocked it. Bianca noted with interest that he'd chosen her pistol and not his alter-gun, which wouldn't inflict damage if set properly.

Dell didn't move. He just stared at the brown-eyed man. Bianca thought they looked like a couple of wolves with their hackles raised.

Dell threw up his hands. "All right, all right! No need to get all serious on me. I was just kidding around, Angelo."

"Right," muttered the man called Angelo. "I know your reputation. You will keep the Covenant of the Order, Dell, and you most definitely will keep the Guardian's Code when you're working with me."

Angelo drew the cartridge from the pistol and expelled the bullet from the chamber before replacing it. He slipped the pistol back into his waistband, nestling it at the small of his back. Bianca noted exactly where. She had to. She needed to get it from him somehow. The seriousness of the situation was not lost on her. Her firepower, not to mention the damn crystal, had been taken from her. She was a prisoner of two guardians and on her way to the Water Company in short order.

None of these things could be allowed.

"Dell, why don't you go downstairs and amuse yourself for a while," said Angelo.

A slow smile bloomed on Dell's mouth. "Well, if you wanted some privacy, you just had to say so."

"Get the fuck downstairs now," said Angelo through gritted teeth.

"Whatever you say," he muttered. "You're the captain." With an insolent swagger, he made for the stairs.

Angelo knelt and dug around in his pack. He pulled out a nutro-wafer and a canteen of water and handed them to her. "My name is Angelo DiMarco. I'm a—"

"Guardian of Order. Finch's muscle," Bianca said with a tired sigh. "I know." She placed the wafer on her tongue. Most lived on Sector-provided nutro-wafers. Those lucky enough to have jobs and credits could buy meat and vegetables from one of the few vendors that had livestock that were raised freysis-free, and grew produce on purified water only. Nutro-wafers had the taste and consistency of a piece of burlap, but had all the vitamins, minerals, carbs and protein to keep her alive. She washed it down with the water and closed her eyes as the cool liquid ran down her dry throat.

Once, before the Kirans had poisoned Earth's water with the freysis bacteria, good food had been plentiful and it had been safe to dance outside in the rain.

"You are our prisoner," he continued. "We're taking you back to the Water Company for the crime of theft,—" he hesitated, "—and impersonation of Calina Robinson."

She laughed at the last charge and he ignored her.

"Mr. Aloysius Finch will decide your fate when we arrive."

She could only imagine what that would be. "How did you track me, Angelo?"

"I have a knack for it."

Bianca raised her gaze and her eyebrow. "A knack for it? You found me four days' journey out from the Water Company. You tracked me through the goddamn cement jungle of Sector Thirty. I had a million places to hide. You tracked me even though I zigged and I zagged and I left no trail. I'd say you have far more than a knack for it. Your tracking skill is damn near preternatural. Come on, how'd you do it?"

"We got a couple of lucky breaks. People remembered they'd seen you."

"I've come into contact with exactly three people since I left the Center. You couldn't have found me that way."

A muscle in his jaw twitched and he averted his gaze. This seemingly innocent subject angered him. That was most interesting. "Then believe I have more than a knack for it and drop it," he answered in a gruff voice.

She threw her hands up in a gesture of surrender. "Whatever you say. You're the one with all the guns. Consider the subject dropped." For now, at least. "So, you're working for Finch, huh?"

"I was recently summoned to the Water Company. I kept the peace in Sector Thirty-One before that. I haven't been working for Mr. Finch for very long."

Bianca almost laughed. Kept the peace? She wondered if this man realized he worked for the most bloodthirsty and destructive creature to walk planet Earth since the Kirans contaminated the water. He probably didn't. Aloysius Finch was practically a god to most people in this area. He was the man with the life-giving water, in a world where water was all around and none of it could be consumed.

She took a long, appraising look at her captor. This man was a breed she'd never encountered before, a strange animal. He seemed to have some kind of twisted, misplaced sense of honor. This man was nothing like Dell. No, Angelo seemed to be one of the rare few who actually believed there was an order that merited guarding. Poor, silly man.

Suddenly, she didn't know if she wanted to smack him upside the head for his wide-eyed naïve view of the world or cover him with her body and consume every last fiber of his being. She could use a little of what he was in her life.

One thing was for sure. She'd never met a man like him and that made him unpredictable. She didn't like that. Overall, this man could be a good thing for her or a very bad thing.

But there was one thing that made all men predictable.

Bianca wondered where his limits lay in that regard and how fast and hard she could push them. She thought about the pistol tucked into his waistband and the different ways she could get her hands on it.

As a general rule, Bianca didn't like men, and she sure as hell didn't like sex. She'd had it once...if you could call it that. She wasn't sure you could when she'd never consented to it. All Bianca knew was that it hurt—both inside and out.

Despite that unpleasant experience, she'd learned that the promise of sex could get a man to do pretty much anything she wanted him to do. It was like magic. You showed some leg, maybe a little more, and bingo, you got what you wanted. It could be a dangerous business, though. The perilous line lay in the offering of it without actually having to fulfill the promise. Despite that danger, and regardless of whether or not she liked to use them that way, her face and body had become necessary tools for her survival. In this ravaged world, you used every advantage or you died.

She could protect herself. Melvin had taught her self-defense, and she never hesitated to use it. But since Calina had died, Bianca had lost the urge to protect herself at all. It didn't matter what happened since her heart was missing. Without her heart and with her soul twisted up so badly, really, who cared?

Despite her dislike for men, this one fascinated her and made her pussy twitch just a little with mild interest. He was as good-looking as they came, broad shoulders, muscled chest and narrow waist. Yeah, he probably made the hearts of most females go pitter-patter. He probably didn't have any trouble at all filling his bed. That would make him confident, maybe even a little arrogant, and would make what she was about to do even easier.

She got to her feet slowly, gritting her teeth at the pain in her head. Sizing him up like a hunter examines its prey, she advanced on him, head cocked to the side, smile playing about her lips. Strong arms met broad shoulders and below that was a smooth, muscled expanse of chest tapering to a narrow waist. His dark-brown hair was tousled; a glossy hank of it had fallen over a dark eye.

Yes, he was strong, much stronger than she was. He'd be hard to handle if she couldn't control him, but she could defend herself even against a man such as this. If she played her cards right, she was still the hunter and he was the still the prey. In any case, Bianca sensed that he would never hurt her, never force her to do anything she didn't want to do, no matter how mercilessly she teased him.

And she fully intended to tease him.

Maybe she could tease him right into losing his composure. Maybe she could get him to let his guard down...maybe even enough to get her gun back.

Apparently wary of her intentions, he backed away from her as she approached. She hesitated. He'd hold a loaded gun on his partner without blinking, but he shied from an unarmed woman. That was curious.

She took a few more steps toward him. He backed up and his head connected with a pipe that protruded from the ceiling with a painful-sounding thunk. She stopped in the middle of the room, her smile fading. Man, this was discouraging. He wasn't going to be an easy one. Where was the confidence of an outrageously good-looking man at whose feet likely swooned dozens of women a day? Frustrated, she put a hand to her hip and cocked her head to the side. Apparently, the regular, direct approach just wasn't going to work. She quickly tried to think of ways to get him to touch her.

Remembering the pistol had no bullet in its chamber, she feigned a near faint, putting her fingertips to her temple and teetering on unsteady legs. When she collapsed, she had no doubt he would catch her...and he did. Strong arms wrapped around her midsection and held her in midair. She used her legs to pitch herself into him while he was off-balance. He fell backward, and she went with him. She ended up right in his lap. One of his hands splayed back behind him, the other wrapped tight around her waist.

Oh, it couldn't be more perfect.

She wound an arm around his neck and pressed her breasts against his chest. "Thank you," she whispered, looking up at him through the veil of her lashes.

Every muscle in his body went rigid. Every single one. She smiled slowly and nestled her ass down on his highly impressive erection. God, all men were predictable when it came to their response to a woman. She sighed a little and shifted her rear in his lap again and felt his body answer her swiftly. Under her hands and against her breasts, she felt his breathing and heart rate quicken. She spread her hand flat against his chest and then slid it slowly down over the solid muscle, feeling his left nipple under the material of his shirt. Biting her lip as hard as she could without drawing blood, she tried to be immune to the feel of him. She drew her hand toward his back…toward her pistol.

His eyes were on her lips, she noted with amusement. Thank God he wasn't immune to her. She wet them, letting him see her tongue steal out for the briefest of moments. Then she tipped her face toward his, lightly rubbing her mouth against his. Simultaneously, her fingertips brushed the butt of the gun.

Just as she grabbed for it, he pushed her off his lap and onto the floor. She landed with a thump and he got to his feet, taking the shiny steel glint of the pistol tucked in his waistband, and any hope she had of escape, away from her.

"I don't kiss thieves," he said.

Well, at least he didn't realize what she'd really been trying to do. She cradled her head in her hands. Her reply was clipped. "Yeah, you just work for them."

"What do you mean?"

She sighed. She couldn't really blame him. She hadn't known what a monster the Water Baron was either until her sister had died. After all, it was through Finch's generosity that there were pure-baths available throughout Sector Thirty. Finch even gave free water to the poor and downtrodden masses from time to time. Everyone thought he was really great guy.

"I know you probably won't believe me, Angelo, but Finch is a sinister man. He's greedy and vicious. He took my sister when she was just sixteen and kept her a prisoner until she…um…escaped."

"I thought Calina was Finch's wife."

She made a snorting sound. "Yeah, she was. She was forced to be his wife."

"Hold on now. You broke into the Water Company with no problem and stole a damned Kiran crystal right out from under Mr. Finch's nose. If your sister had been kept there against her will, why didn't you just go break her out?"

"I didn't know she was there until she died. I didn't know anything that had happened to her until that exact moment."

Angelo looked at her in disbelief. "What are you talking about?"

Good question, she thought. Too bad the answer was so unbelievable that she'd lose all her credibility with him. What was she thinking? She didn't have any credibility with him.

"All right, you asked for it." She laughed. It was short and bitter-sounding to her own ears. "Since Calina and I were twins we shared things, you know?"

"Yeah, sure."

"No. I don't mean dolls and stuff. I mean we shared a mental link." She glanced up at him to see how he was absorbing the information. He looked down at her with an expression of rapt attention. "One day, she, Melvin and I—"

"Melvin? Who's Melvin?"

She scowled at the interruption. "Never mind. Not pertinent to the story. Anyway, Melvin, Calina and I came into Sector Thirty for supplies. Calina became separated from us. The next thing we knew, a hovercraft was speeding away and Calina was nowhere to be found. I lost my heart that day."

"I'm sorry."

"Yeah, well, it happens. You can lose your wallet, you can lose your mind and sometimes you can even lose your heart. The deal is, I still was able to communicate emotionally with Calina from time to time. I knew when she was happy, sad or terrified, but I never knew where she was or what had happened to her. Then, on the day she died...I saw it all. I saw everything. I saw her walk into the garden in the rain. I felt the freysis seeping into her skin and blood as though it was me." Her voice trembled and she swallowed hard.

She paused and glanced up at Angelo to gauge the expression on his face. Stone. Stoic.

"Go on," he said.

"When she finally died, when her soul finally left her body, I became bombarded with images, emotions and the knowledge she'd gained throughout her life. It was like she passed through me, and all her memories clung to me. Right before she died she felt so calm, so happy...see, because she knew she was free. When she finally left, I went numb, and let's face it, I've been that way ever since."

"Jesus."

"Yes." Bianca drew a shaky breath. "So that's how I know all about Aloysius Finch and even about Dell. Trust me, they aren't nice people."

"Why didn't your sister go the Guardians of Order to protest her imprisonment?"

She frowned. She honestly didn't know why and it had perplexed her for some time. Her sister had been a calm, peace-loving child, light to her own dark, but even Calina would've fought Finch. She had no memories of Calina fighting and it was still a mystery to her. "I don't know," she said with an air of defeat.

"Hmmm... I hope you realize how hard a story that is to swallow."

"Yeah, I do." She laughed. "I almost don't believe it myself."

He smiled. "It's especially hard to believe coming from the little con artist that just tried to seduce her gun right out from under me."

She closed her eyes briefly. Damn.

"So I guess you don't want to hear how bad Finch really is?" she asked.

"No, I think the time is over for bedtime stories. It's time to sleep now."

"Sleep? I slept all day long."

"Well, it's time for Dell and me to sleep, then. It's time for you to stay put and be quiet."

She spotted a spent shell casing on the floor and picked it up. She rolled it back and forth between her fingers wistfully.

Angelo walked over to his pack, knelt and rummaged through it. He came up with an old, rusty pair of handcuffs.

She flicked the casing to the floor and shook her head. "Oh, no. I'm not wearing those things. Those cuffs are so old they're liable to give me tetanus or something."

"They're not going to give you tetanus."

"How do you know?"

"Look, it's either the cuffs, or I'll use the alter-gun on you again and delta you out for the night."

Bianca instantly raised both her wrists to him. She hated that alter-gun.

Angelo slapped the handcuffs on one of her wrists and yanked on them gently, forcing her to stand. He led her over to a long pipe that protruded from the wall and cuffed her to it. After carefully checking her bedroll, she guessed for weapons, he gathered it up and laid it on the floor beside her.

"Sit," he ordered.

She sat down on the bedroll and he knelt in front of her. As he unraveled the bandage around her head, she could feel his breath warm against her cheek.

He threw the material to the side and examined her wound. "The bleeding stopped. It should be better by morning." He drew a thumb across her forehead, under the gash, with a gentleness that seemed at odds with his physical strength.

She closed her eyes and enjoyed the feel of his touch. Funny enough, it wasn't even an act. She really did enjoy it. Maybe she was trying to absorb some of his goodness.

He removed his hand and she opened her eyes. His gaze was strange and intent, tinged with curiosity. She held that gaze for a few moments, but it was too intense, and she looked away.

Trying to make her tone light, she said, "You could always reconsider your rule against kissing thieves and—"

He grunted, rose, and headed toward his own bedroll. "Get some rest, angel-face. We travel at morning's first light."

Great.

Chapter Two

Angelo looked down at the little thief with the fast-moving tongue. She was sprawled on her bedroll, looking uncomfortably warm in her long-sleeved shirt. Thick strands of her sunlight-colored hair were fanned out around her head. She looked so innocent while she slept. It was a marked contrast to when she was awake and her mouth was moving with that tough, practiced, know-it-all air of hers.

It made him want her even more than he already did. Yesterday, when she'd feigned her little faint in order to take her pistol back, she'd made his cock hard just by the feel of her heated body against his. A multitude of images had ridden him hard when she'd been in his lap. He'd imagined peeling off her T-shirt and cupping her small breasts in his hands, licking her nipples into stiff little points. Angelo had imagined pulling off her pants and seeing if her pussy tasted as good as he thought it might. He'd love to make her come that way, love to have her body tightening in ecstasy. Her moans filling the air and his name issuing from her lips would sound so good. It had been a long time since he'd enjoyed that particular pleasure.

Angelo fisted his hands and fought away the desire to send Dell out of the building for a while. Angelo could tease her awake right now and she'd welcome it. He could pull off her pants, spread those lovely, long legs and ease his aching cock into her tight pussy. She'd love it. Angelo would bet money that this woman was a fiery hellcat in bed. Just the way he liked them.

He fisted his hands, letting his gaze take in the rise and fall of her breasts. It had been so long.

He gave his head a sharp shake to clear it of the temptation and gave a low, long whistle to wake her. He watched her rouse. She looked up at him in that drowsy, just-awake way. What he saw in her at that moment unsettled him. He didn't see the hard, jaded woman of yesterday. In her unguarded eyes he glimpsed pain and deep despair.

As she came awake a bit more, he actually saw the veil cover her eyes, a mask slide over her features, transforming them. Her eyes got that long-lidded, bored look and she smiled her little smile — like she had some secret she wasn't giving up. That smile of hers never reached her eyes.

This naked flash of her took him off-guard. He realized then just how much illusion was a part of Bianca Robinson.

She stretched languorously and looked up at him with feigned innocence. "You're staring at me, Angelo," she said in a low, sleep-roughened voice. "Finally decide you want to live on the edge and break a rule? Hmmmm? You want to kiss a thief?" She licked her lips and let her gaze travel up his body. "You should know that I'd let you do a whole lot more than just kiss me."

Behind him, Dell was packing up their gear. Angelo heard him chuckle.

Still jarred by what he'd seen in her, he clumsily fished in his pocket for the key to her cuffs. "We don't have time for games. We need to travel." He located the key, walked to the pipe and knelt.

He felt her free hand on his arm, running up the curve of his biceps to his shoulder. Her breath warmed his skin. He dropped the key, cursed and picked it up. She drew her hand down to his thigh and slid it up toward his hardening cock and he dropped the key for the second time.

"Christ, she's playing with you like a kitten with a mouse," said Dell.

Angelo really didn't need the commentary at this point. He concentrated on unlocking the cuffs. When he finally had them undone he took her free hand from his thigh with a little more force than he'd meant to use and slapped the other cuff around her wrist. He glanced at her and caught a flash of discomfort in her eyes.

"Sorry," he muttered.

"No problem, Angelo." She smiled. "I like it when you touch me."

She didn't realize just how badly he did want to touch her. With her soft skin and the curves he'd felt under her baggy clothes the day before, she made him want to break every rule of the Guardian's Code of Honor. He wanted to rip her pants off, ease her legs apart and fuck her until she screamed. Angelo could only imagine how good she'd feel. But no matter his fantasies or the temptation she posed, he could not do that, would not do that, and he had to spend the next two to three days with her practically joined to him at the hip.

Christ.

There was something about this woman that made her want her, something that had him imagining all kinds of carnal things. The fact she'd allow him to act out the fantasies he was having about her made it all the worse.

They ate and took care of their morning hygiene. The Essential Providers, the people who governed the Center, had gained power and wealth because they'd manage to develop things like toothpaste you could use without water. Thanks to them, it was possible to maintain acceptable levels of cleanliness with a limited amount of pure-water. Dell went downstairs with the packs and began to ready the horses for traveling.

Bianca brushed her hair as best she could with the brush from her pack, but it still looked messy when she was done, like a man's fingers had combed it through. Angelo had to stop himself from imagining it was his fingers that had done it. He wondered how it would feel to plunge his hands into that fall of sunlight, pull her head back, lay a line of kisses down her throat, maybe lightly nip at her exposed collarbone.

He gave his head another sharp shake. Goddamn it, what was wrong with him?

"I need to change my clothes," she said, handing the brush back to him so he could repack it. "It's too hot to wear this long-sleeved shirt all day long."

Her words snapped him from his daydream. He shook his head. "You can't change your clothes with your hands cuffed, and there's no secure place to put you uncuffed"

"You could always stay in here with me and turn your back," she suggested sweetly.

Minx. He smiled and narrowed his eyes. "I'm not going to turn my back on you for a second."

She shrugged and smiled. "Fine, then watch me while I do it. I don't mind."

Images of Bianca taking her shirt off in front of him flooded Angelo's mind and spurred him forward. He took her by the upper arm and pulled her to the stairs. "No, it's time to go. You'll have to wait to change your clothes."

"All right, all right. No problem, Angelo, just don't break something in your rush to get me downstairs." Just as she finished her sentence, she stumbled. He caught her before she pitched headfirst down the stairs.

He steadied her, balancing her on a stair several steps above him. It made her eye level with him. Her eyes were blue sometimes, at other times more green. Most of the time they seemed to be a combination of the two colors, swirling together, unable to decide on the shade they wanted to be. Now those eyes were watching him intently, more blue than green.

He inspected the gash on her forehead. There was bruising around it, but it looked like it was healing well. He drew his thumb beneath it, as he had the night before, feeling her skin — smooth and warm. Her eyes drifted closed.

"Does it feel better now?" he asked.

Her eyes flew open. "What?"

"Your injury, does it feel better?"

She smiled. No secret smile this time. No mocking or bitterness. It was dazzling, but it still didn't reach her eyes. "Yes, much better."

He led her down the rest of the stairs, through the ruined door of the building and into the morning sunlight. Not a cloud in the sky. They would make good time without the threat of rain. Abandoned buildings lined the street, their broken windows looking like jagged teeth and empty eyes. Weeds flourished in the cracked pavement and vines climbed the sides of the structures, reaching toward the sky. The alien bacteria in the water actually made the vegetation thrive, oddly enough. Made plants grow green and wild, didn't hurt most animals…yet murdered humans.

The Kirans, an alien race, had tried to steal Earth out from under humankind by poisoning the water with freysis. The sun on their own planet had been close to complete death and they'd chosen Earth because it could sustain them, although they needed a certain type of bacteria in the water to survive. The bacteria had used the hydrological cycle of moisture and evaporation to spread throughout the planet. The act had spurred a war between the Kirans and the surviving humans. A war the humans would've lost had it not been for a virus that had ripped through the Kiran population, leaving only a fraction of them alive.

Something moved on Angelo's left. He and Dell both turned toward it, drawing their laser guns in the same instant. A deer stepped out from behind a building, spotted them and froze in fear. Angelo relaxed, but beside him, Dell took aim.

"No," said Angelo. "Let it live, Dell. Some things ought to be able to," he finished in a mutter. Shooting the deer wouldn't be anything more than target practice. The Kirans had engineered the freysis bacteria so that it would attack only human DNA. As a result, mammals, birds, fish and reptiles could metabolize the bacteria, but it made their flesh inedible to humans.

Dell lowered the gun and shot him a look of contempt instead.

Angelo left Bianca to go around his horse and tighten the cinches on the saddle, keeping her always within view. He and Dell had their alter-guns ready to fire if she made any move to flee.

He watched as Dell brushed near her, seemingly to get to the other horse. He came closer than was needed and Bianca took a step back, flinching away from him.

"Awww...come on. You're not interested in playing with me like you do Angelo? I make a really good mouse." He leaned into her, leering.

Angelo came around the horse, toward Dell, but Bianca was faster. She caught Dell fast and hard in the solar plexus with her elbow.

Dell grunted and bent over, his hand to his stomach. He looked up at her through the fall of his black hair. His eyes glowed undisguised hatred. He straightened slowly. Angelo could tell it pained him to do it.

"Dell, you deserved it," said Angelo. "Now get the goddamn horses ready."

"Yes, sir," he said, with a thread of sarcasm in his voice. He hobbled off to finish his job.

Angelo watched him go. Dell was one of a troublesome coterie of Finch's guardians who seemed to have no respect for him. Since Angelo was new to the Water Company, he hadn't yet proven himself in the eyes of some of the men. He understood he had to earn their deference, especially since he'd been called in from another sector, and had been promoted over the heads of many who'd expected to get the position of captain. Dell probably resented him for that, but he was pushing that resentment a little too hard. That was going to have to change...soon. At first, Angelo had been dismayed that Mr. Finch had ordered Dell to go with him, but maybe he could get the recalcitrant guardian to fall in line on this trip.

"I take it you don't like Dell very much," Angelo said to Bianca.

"You take it right. Doesn't your stupid Code of Honor say something about protecting the prisoners in your care? Keep him away from me, Angelo."

"You look pretty capable of taking care of yourself. I think it's Dell who needs protecting."

Upon hearing the comment, Dell fixed him with a steely gaze.

Bianca shivered. "Just keep him away from me."

Dell whistled. "You might look like Calina, but you're nothing at all like her."

Pain flashed in her eyes and she looked away. "Yeah, well, she was always the good one. Look what being good got her."

Dell mounted his horse, still holding a hand to his solar plexus. "So, I guess you'll be riding with Angelo, since you don't seem to have any aversion to touching him." The words dripped with acid.

She brushed a stray hair out of her face and answered him with a sweet smile. "I don't mind touching you either, Dell, as long as it's to cause you pain."

Dell opened his mouth to reply but Angelo quelled him with a look.

Angelo tipped his head to the sky and sniffed the air. "I think the rain has finally passed us by." He lowered his gaze to Bianca. "It's a good thing too, because you don't even own rain gear." He glanced at her boots. "At least you have the right kind of footwear."

"What? Did you go through my pack?" she asked, outraged.

He had and he'd seen she was truly impoverished. She had little clothing with her, one empty water canteen, a couple credits and two broken nutro-wafers. It still perplexed him. She seemed like she had all her senses, for the most part anyway. So why hadn't she taken credits or valuables from Finch? Instead, she'd taken some useless Kiran crystal, a trinket left over from the war. A memento Finch kept to remember his father, the man who'd originally discovered the enhydros and how to use the trapped liquid inside them to purify water. The crystal she took wasn't even an enhydro.

Why the hell had she risked her life for it?

"There wasn't much to go through. I'm surprised you've stayed alive this long," he replied.

She flashed white teeth at him. "I have an aptitude for it."

Angelo placed his hands around her waist, trying his best to ignore the heat and the feel of her under his hands, and helped her onto the horse. She felt deceptively fragile. "That is more than apparent, angel-face," he replied.

* * * * *

The first thing Bianca did when Angelo's arms came around her to take up the reins was catch her breath. Her pulse quickened as she was enveloped in his maleness. He smelled like man, with a trace of soap, and the rich leather of the saddle and shoulder holster. His chest pressed up against her back and the strength of his arms encircled her and she actually felt safe…*safe*. How incredibly strange.

This man did things to her libido that no other man had ever done. Hell, he actually made her pussy sit up and take notice whenever he was close to her. Like now. She'd thought her cunt had died a long time ago, gone as numb as the rest of her. Teasing him was no chore, that was for sure.

She settled against him, molding her body to his. It felt right, as natural as breathing. She closed her eyes. "Hope you don't mind," she said, sighing a bit.

"I don't mind at all." His deep voice rumbled against her back. "I think you need to be touched. I think you haven't been touched enough in your life."

Bianca made a scoffing noise. "Believe me when I say that's not true." She couldn't keep the bitterness from her voice. Those were memories she didn't want in her mind's eye right now. Not while she was actually enjoying the feel of this man against her.

"No, I don't mean that kind of touching. I mean touching with no strings attached, the kind of touching that doesn't put demands on a person. Touching merely for the pleasure of it, not because it will get you something you want."

Bianca had no retort or reply. She was quiet for a long while, letting his words sink in. Finally, abruptly, she spoke. "Who the hell do you think you are? You don't know what I need! You don't know anything about me! I don't need—" She heard Angelo laughing and it halted the flow of her words. She twisted around to look at him. "What?"

"Guess I struck a nerve. You don't even realize you're telling me I got it right."

She made a low noise of frustration and sat up straight, putting as much space between them as possible.

Angelo put his hand to her abdomen and pressed her back against his chest. The heat of him bled through her clothing and seeped into her skin. "Come on now, Bianca. It's all right. Relax."

It was the first time she'd heard him use her name. He'd called her angel-face but not Bianca. Her name issuing from his lips was oddly satisfying.

She lapsed into silence and undid the top buttons of her shirt. It was hot. Dell dropped further and further behind them until he was finally out of earshot. Maybe he was hunting more innocent deer. She decided it might be a good time to try and reason with Angelo. With every step they took back toward the Center, her anxiety mounted. The weight of the crystal laid heavy on her mind. She had a responsibility now.

"So what do you think Finch will do with me?" she asked.

"That's none of my concern," he answered. "I'm just the delivery man."

"Do you think he'll sentence me to death?"

"For stealing an ordinary Kiran crystal? He can't sentence you to death for something so paltry. It's against the New Covenant of Order. The Covenant says you can only sentence criminals to death when they've committed a capital offense—murder, disruption or contamination of the water supply or theft of an enhydro crystal."

"Ah, yes, disruption or contamination of the water supply," repeated Bianca. "Wouldn't it be great if we could purify massive quantities of water? If we could somehow use the hydrological cycle to reverse the bacterial poisoning?"

"Fairy tales. Useless dreaming. Finch has a limited number of enhydro crystals and an even more limited number of purification machines. The water can only be purified in small quantities. Otherwise all the enhydros will be used up."

"What do you think will happen when all the enhydros are gone?"

She felt him shrug. "That won't happen for a long time, but when it does, the inevitable, I guess," he said. "If we can't find a way to purify the water without them and we can't find sources of natural pure-water then—"

"What if I told you it's possible to purify the water without enhydros?"

"I would ask you how you know anything about it."

"Do you remember our conversation yesterday?"

"Oh, yeah, *that*."

She sighed deeply. Obviously, she'd never be able to convince him she was telling the truth. She chose to remain silent.

"Would this fantasy of yours have anything to do with why you took a worthless crystal from the Water Company when you had any number of other valuable things to steal?"

Angelo asked finally. "Because, I'll tell you, Bianca. I've been wondering a lot about that."

Inwardly, she sighed in relief. Maybe she had a chance with him after all. "What do you think would happen if massive amounts of water could be purified? I'm talking huge quantities of it all at one time. So much of it that we might be able to get running water to flow through pipes and right into people's homes. What do you think that would do to the Water Baron's wallet?"

"I guess it would hurt it. It would make purified water a readily available thing."

"What if I told you there is a master crystal that would do all this, and that Finch knows about it but does nothing with it because he fears a loss of power and money."

"Is that what you're telling me?"

"Yes."

"And this is the crystal that you stole? The one he kept out in full view of all the world?"

It probably was hard to swallow. Finch had hidden it in plain sight—in amongst his Kiran crystal collection. Bianca sighed. He didn't believe her. "Calina was the only other person who knew about it. She was like his confessor or something. Since no one else knew about it, he treated it as though it was an ordinary crystal. He figured that in this case, being out in the open was the very best hiding place for it."

"Uh-huh." He sounded highly skeptical. "How does this magic crystal work anyway?"

"Umm—well…I'm not sure exactly. Melvin will know how."

"Okay." He was humoring her. She could hear it in his voice.

"I know. It sounds crazy, doesn't it?"

"Uh-huh."

Bianca brought up another sigh from the depth of her soul. "There's a lot of craziness in this world."

"Tell me about Melvin."

Bianca stiffened. There wasn't much she could reveal about Melvin, especially to a Guardian of Order. She would have to tread carefully. "He's not that interesting." Wow, had she just told a whopper. "Like I said, he raised us. He used to be a scientist before the war, I think."

"Really? But he knows all about Kiran crystals, huh?"

Fear rippled through her. "Really, there's not much to tell. Calina and I were orphaned when we were eight and we struggled in the Out-Center on our own until we were about fifteen and Melvin found us. He brought us to Sector Twenty-Nine to live."

"Oh, I get it." Disgust laced his tone.

"No! Yuck! It was never like that. He's like a foster father, only without the father part. He's not a lecher. That's all. End of uninteresting story."

"Uninteresting? I wouldn't call it that. I happen to know a little about Sector Twenty-Nine. There's lots of survivor Kirans hiding out there."

Bianca swallowed hard and kept her tone light. "Yeah, well, prove it. There are lots of humans out there too. Everyone knows the only way you can tell a human and a Kiran apart is by freysis toxicity testing."

"No," he said. "There are other ways Kirans are set apart from humans. They age slower and heal faster. Their IQs are higher. They use more of their brains and different parts of it than humans do. None of those things are obvious to the eye but they're still differences."

Dell had drifted back toward them and was now listening to their conversation with an air of interest. Bianca eyed him warily.

"Yeah, Angelo, you can find any Kiran or track any human within a fifty-mile radius, can't you?" Dell cut in. "That's why

Water Crystal

Mr. Finch brought you to the Water Company, made you captain. Isn't that right?"

She felt Angelo's muscles stiffen. "I'm a good tracker. That's one of the reasons, yes," he replied.

"Well, what's the matter? Most guardians enjoy hunting Kirans. You sound as if you don't like it." There was a note of teasing in Dell's voice.

Bianca cut in. "They don't have anywhere to go now. Their planet's sun is burned out. If we hunt them down, kill them or lock them away, are we any better than they are?"

"So, little girl, we should just let them share our planet?" asked Dell. "After they tried to cleanse us right off the face of it?"

"I think we have to let the past be the past and face the future. Not all the Kirans are bad. That's like saying all humans are good." She raised her eyebrow at Dell. "And we know that's not true, don't we, Dell? Life isn't that black and white."

"What is black and white is the fact the Kirans tried to kill off the humans and they failed," said Angelo. "That presents a problem for them, doesn't it?"

This was not something Bianca wanted to linger on. It was time for a subject change. "Melvin is very old," she cut in. "He won't survive long without me there to take care of him."

"So, I should let you go right now and give you back the crystal that's going to save mankind," replied Angelo caustically.

Nope, he didn't even come anywhere close to believing her, and he never would. She was going to have to find some other way to get herself out of this mess and back to Sector Twenty-Nine. That wouldn't be easy with a Guardian of Order on her trail who had a nose like a bloodhound.

Her thoughts ran to his broad shoulders and strong chest, the feel of his thumb tracing a line on her forehead. At least he'd be fun to play with until she could find a way to escape. Maybe she could still tease him enough to cause him to let down his guard.

She settled herself against him with a little sigh of contentment, snuggling into his chest and drawing a lazy finger down the tensed muscles of his forearm. Black hair dusted the back of his capable-looking hands. She gave a small, deliberately sexy-sounding little moan of relaxation and felt his cock get hard against the small of her back. She smiled. "Oh, no, Angelo, I don't ever want you to let me go," she purred suggestively. "You can hold me as close as you want to."

Bianca smiled. That shut him up.

Chapter Three

Bianca sighed and shifted her weight against Angelo's chest. He noted her restlessness. Her long legs dangled over the sides of his horse and her cuffed hands lay limp in her lap. Everyone was fatigued, so soon they'd stop for the night. They wouldn't make it past the southern border of the Center today. Already the skies were darkening and it didn't pay to travel at night. Not in Out-Center where the Flot picked off unwary travelers.

The Flot had their own culture, their own rules and their own guns. They set themselves apart from those in the Center and refused to live by the governing body of law Mr. Finch and the Essential Providers had constructed.

The sound of hooves on concrete echoed down the deserted streets as they passed crumbling buildings on either side of the wide road. Most of the windows were broken and it made the structures look like they had jagged and shattered teeth. Every once in a while decaying pieces of furniture stood in the center of the road, the ripped and decomposing fabric stained slightly green by freysis. Weeds had overtaken this part of the city, growing from every crack in the pavement. Most of Center and Out-Center, which had previously been called Chicago, literally was an urban jungle.

In Out-Center there were inhabited areas amidst long stretches of abandonment where damage to the city was especially bad. During the war, mankind had destroyed its own infrastructure in an effort to rid itself of the Kirans. It had been akin to a man trying to tear out his own veins, since the Kirans had deeply embedded themselves in human culture by then, and had been outwardly undistinguishable from humans. The initial part of the Kiran conquest had gone on far longer than humankind had realized. As the Kirans had readied themselves to poison the water, they lived on Earth for a century, blending in.

Out of the corner of his eye, Angelo saw a shadow move between the buildings on their left. He drew his laser.

"What was that?" Dell whispered, taking his laser from its holster.

"I don't know. An animal. Flot, maybe," Angelo answered.

"They're one and the same." He urged his horse to a trot. "I'm going on ahead a little."

"The Flot aren't so bad. They're just trying to survive like everyone else," said Bianca.

"The Flot are bad because they don't want to play by the rules," answered Angelo. "They're out here, running around with no law. They kill and steal without consequence."

She huffed out an exasperated breath. "And people in the Center don't do that?"

"Mr. Finch and the other Essential Providers are trying to create a society where lawlessness doesn't happen." The Essential Providers produced things like Nutro-wafers, clothing and food grown on freysis-free water. They formed the backbone of the government in Sector Thirty. Aloysius Finch was unofficially the leader.

Angelo slipped the laser back into his holster. He didn't sense any threat around them. Usually he could feel it if there was another person near.

Bianca snorted. "Right. More like they're trying to create a society where the only people who can steal and murder without consequence are themselves."

He let out a sharp breath. "This isn't worth arguing about, Bianca."

"You'll see, Angelo. When we make it back to the Water Company, you'll see how Finch bends the rules to suit his own desires."

"Maybe if you spend some time in the Center without stealing things, you'll see what potential it has. We're starting to heal from the war. We're starting to recover from what the Kirans did. We might be able to build something truly great on the ruined foundations."

"You really believe that, don't you?"

"It's the only thing I believe."

"It's funny how we can sometimes blind ourselves to the truth when we want to believe in an illusion bad enough."

"I'm not blind, Bianca."

"I have my doubts about that. Oh, I think you're well-intentioned. You serve Finch because through him you think you're serving the greater good, but you're still blind. That blindness originates from one of two different reasons, or maybe a combination of the two."

He sighed, but allowed her to go on.

"One, you're either too new to the Water Company to have seen Finch's corruption." She glanced over her shoulder at him. "How new to the Water Company are you?"

"I've been there three weeks."

"Mmmm. Or two," she continued. "You're driven by something else that causes you to see his deceit without truly seeing it. Maybe you have some kind of strong need to create a better society, and so you rationalize the corruption."

His control slipped and his voice rose. "Are you crazy? There's nothing going on at the Water Company beyond Aloysius Finch trying to raise a society in the ashes of war. And if you think for a second—"

She laughed.

"What?"

"Guess I hit a nerve, huh?"

Angelo took a deep breath. "We're doing the best we can to survive the freysis."

"Until the enhydro crystals run out, you mean."

"We survived the Kirans trying to steal our planet. We'll survive when the enhydros run out."

"You have so much faith. I wish I had something to blindly believe in," she said quietly before lapsing into silence.

Bianca's unease was a palpable thing. He could understand her nervousness, but she had to know her punishment would not be dire. Her true crime lay in the breaching of the security at the Water Company. She'd slipped the guards a syntho-sleeping draught and cut some alarm wires to initially gain entry. Once in, she'd taken advantage of the fact that the techs hadn't deleted Calina's face from the building's computer system and had used the facial recognition keys to gain access to where she needed to go. But she was Calina's twin and Mr. Finch seemed to have genuinely loved his wife. Because of this, Angelo doubted he would punish his own sister-in-law very harshly.

It had to be Calina's death that was causing Bianca to act so crazy. Or maybe Bianca was just plain crazy to begin with, because to break into the Water Company and pull a stunt like she had—that took either a whole of chutzpah or insanity. She'd broken past the formidable security system, and then breezed right past Mr. Finch dressed up just like Calina, with her hair done and even wearing her twin's jewelry.

Since Mr. Finch hadn't known Calina had a twin sister, Bianca had been long gone before he'd gathered his wits. It'd taken Angelo two days of pounding pavement and interrogation to discover who the doppelganger had been. Angelo wanted to ask her how'd she'd done it, but now was not the time for an interrogation.

They traveled on, and no more shadows flitted between the buildings. Only the sounds of the horse's hooves echoing, the creak of leather and their own breathing filled the silence.

They caught up to Dell and he fell in beside them. "Didn't find anything. It was animal, maybe."

Angelo sighed. It was time to find food, a bath and a bed. "To Hank's, Dell?"

"Hank's," he agreed.

"Who's Hank?" asked Bianca in a low voice. Suspicion threaded the words.

"It's a hotel. We'll be able to stay the night there, get a drink and even some real food," answered Dell.

"They have music there," said Angelo.

"Music? Really?" The suspicion faded into excitement. "I hear music sometimes when I come into Sector Thirty," she continued. "People will stand outside on the street and play instruments they've made, even sing sometimes."

"This music is in the form of a thing called a jukebox. Hank's has the only working jukebox in the Sector," said Angelo, wanting to encourage her interest. A happy Bianca was a far less troublesome Bianca. "He's kept it in excellent repair."

"A jukebox, yes, I've heard of those," she answered. "Melvin tells me sometimes about what the world was like before."

The closer they got to the southern border of the Center, the more people they saw. This part of Out-Center was inhabited by a mixture of both Flot and those considering themselves under the jurisdiction of the Water Company and the Essential Providers.

Angelo guided his mount down a street that was tidy compared to the rest of the Out-Center. A group of children playing on the street looked up curiously at them when they passed. Sounds of conversation drifted down from occupied apartments. An old woman hobbled down the street, a bag of purchased goods in one claw-like hand.

They turned a corner and Hank's came into view. It had been a bar and flophouse before the Forty-Year War and had miraculously survived almost intact. It showed wear and tear, of course. All the remaining buildings in Sector Thirty did now. The war and the passage of time showed in chipped stone and discolored paint. The stress of their environment was apparent in the inexorable dissolution of cement, where the bacteria in the rain ate away at it slowly. Solar panels adorned the roof like the wings of a crow.

When Angelo lifted Bianca from the horse, she slid down the length of him. Her breasts pressed against his chest and her stomach brushed his pelvis. She managed to hook her cuffed hands around the back of his neck and draw his head down toward hers.

Damn, he was like a deer caught in a hunter's line of sight. Their breath mingled. Her eyes were shiny and curious, a swirl of blue and green. She didn't know she was playing with fire. She thought she was safe—that he wouldn't take her up on her invitations. She thought he was so dedicated to the Guardian's Code of Honor that he'd never breach it. This was all a game to her, a way to pass the time.

She had no idea how hard she was pushing him.

She didn't know how long it had been since he'd imposed celibacy on himself, a celibacy that had nothing to do with the Guardian's Code. It had been a long time since he'd fucked a woman, and lust coiled within him like a snake ready to strike. It wasn't that he wanted to be celibate. He simply had to be. It didn't change the fact that he wanted her.

God, how he did.

It made him wonder about her. Either she simply didn't care what happened to her, or she was a complete innocent and didn't understand the seriousness of the games she played. Maybe it was both.

His eyes focused on her lips, full and stained a healthy pink. She caught her bottom lip between her small white teeth and he felt his body tighten and his cock harden—a familiar feeling since he'd met her. Her mouth widened into that smile that never reached her eyes and the spell broke.

He ducked his head and twisted away from her, only to come up to Dell's satisfied smirk. "If it was me, I wouldn't be running," said Dell.

Water Crystal

Angelo took Bianca by the arm and led her toward the entrance to the bar. "Good thing it's not you she's targeting, then. Because if you touch her in any way that isn't completely decent and in keeping with the Guardian's Code—" he stopped, turned and smiled with wolfish anticipation at Dell, "—I'll take your fucking head off." If Dell gave him any excuse, he'd do it with pleasure.

"Not to mention he'd have a bad dick injury," Bianca said. She bit her lower lip and eyed Dell speculatively. "Umm...provided I could hit a target that small."

Dell made a sound deep in his throat and took a couple of menacing steps toward her. Angelo stopped him with a firm hand to his chest. "See to the horses, Dell, and try to ignore her."

"Can we gag as well as cuff the little bitch, Angelo?" Dell asked. "'Cause—"

"Just see to the horses and bring in the packs." Angelo led Bianca away.

"Do you guys always talk about a lady as though she's invisible?" she asked.

"Never," he answered lightly, allowing her to draw her own conclusion.

Bianca's body went tense and she shot a gimlet glare at him. She probably had a whole stream of not very nice things to say to him all ready, but if so, when he pushed the door open to the bar, they died on her tongue.

Tables and chairs were scattered throughout the dimly lit establishment. A long bar dominated the left side of the room and a small dance floor, along with the famous jukebox, took up the right side.

The bar's patrons, mostly male Out-Center—which meant some of them were probably Flot—and mostly with their eyes trained on Bianca, sat around sipping Hank's Special, a homemade alcohol. Angelo didn't know how they made it and he didn't want to know.

Dell walked in behind them with their packs in hand.

"Angelo. Dell." Hank, a tall, red-faced blond-haired man came up to them. He wore a broad smile of welcome that made his blue eyes crinkle at the edges. Hank nodded at Bianca. "I see you're working."

"Hi, Hank," said Angelo. "We're on our way back to the Water Company and we need to bathe and get some supplies. We also need two rooms for the night. We'll make it back to the Company tomorrow." Bianca stiffened beside him. Yes, they were making good time. She probably hadn't expected them to move so fast. But when you had horses it made travel a lot quicker.

Hank scratched his head, looking back and forth between Angelo and Dell. "Well, I can do the rooms and I can do the supplies, but we're due a water shipment so I can't do the baths."

Bianca groaned.

Hank turned and held two fingers up to a woman behind the bar. "Your rooms will be ready in a while."

"I need to change my clothes, now, this second," said Bianca. "I've been traveling in this long-sleeved shirt all day in the heat. I can't spend another minute in it let alone *a while*."

"All right," said Angelo. "Dell, you take Bianca to the bathing room. There's only one door, and there aren't any windows for her to use to escape. Guard the door. I'll go with Hank and get some supplies. I know better what we need, and I don't want to waste any time with that tomorrow morning."

"Whatever you say, Captain DiMarco," Dell said with a hint of sarcasm. He dropped the packs to the floor and guided Bianca toward the bathing room.

"Dell," Angelo called after him. "Remember what I said about keeping the Code, especially the part about your head."

Dell grunted and turned away, dragging Bianca with him.

* * * * *

Bianca watched a storm descend on Dell's face as soon as he turned from Angelo. He gripped her arm and led her out a doorway off the right side of the bar, down a hallway to another doorway, and unlocked her cuffs.

He pushed her through the door and tossed her pack to her. "If you're not out in exactly two minutes, I'm coming in after you." He shook his head and a ghost of a smile passed over his thin lips. "And believe me, little girl, you don't want that." He shut the door.

No, she didn't want that. She didn't trust Dell at all. She knew things about him that could get him killed, and now, because of her own big mouth, he knew she knew those things. She'd let it spill after Angelo had apprehended her that she knew who Dell was and what he'd done.

She shed her clothing, for a moment reveling in the cold cement floor under her bare feet. It was a typical bathing room. Several large tubs dominated the room, separated by privacy walls.

When Bianca was dressed, she shoved her clothes into her pack. She reached for the door at the same time Dell banged it open. He stalked toward her, murder in his eyes. She backed away from him.

"You think you're not going to get hurt out of all this, don't you?" Dell narrowed his icy gray eyes. "Well, guess what? I'm on to you, and I will hurt you if I have to. So, you tell me, just how much do you know about me, little girl?"

She choked down a bitter laugh. She shouldn't tell him a goddamn thing, but ever since she'd laid eyes on him, she'd wanted to tell him everything she knew. Anger rose up in her, almost choking her with its intensity. She spoke before she could stop herself. "I know all about you and Calina, but you know that already, don't you, Dell? I know Finch is impotent and was never able to consummate his marriage to my sister. I know you seduced her with the more pleasant of your two faces."

Dell didn't move a muscle. She could feel his hot breath on her face and it was enough to sour her stomach.

"I know you seduced her, made her think you really cared about her," Bianca continued. "You gave her hope, let her think you'd take her away and then you let her languish there at the Water Company."

Dell made a menacing noise deep in his throat, but she couldn't stop the flow of her words. "You took Calina's virginity when Finch couldn't. You shared her bed over and over when he couldn't. Finch would've sold all his enhydros to do the things with Calina that you got to do."

She dropped her gaze and looked up at him through her lashes. She smiled, trying to taunt him. "Finch will probably have you killed if he finds out about it." She shouldn't have said it. She knew she shouldn't have. But to be able to threaten this man who'd helped destroy her sister was too much of a lure.

Dell looked distracted, like his mind was turning the situation over and over, trying to find a way beyond it. When he finally spoke his voice was cold, calculating. "You're really lucky Finch sent Angelo to pick you up. 'Cause if it was only me..." he trailed off softly. He reached out and touched her cheek. "Since I slept with your sister, it's a little like I slept with you, isn't it?"

She reached up, caught his fingers and bent them back in one smooth movement. He gasped in pain and swore.

"No, it's nothing like it, because I'm nothing like my sister." She pushed past him and raised her hands. "Come on, cuff me up. I want to go back to the main room, and get the hell away from you."

Dell looked at her balefully, holding his wounded fingers. "Hell no, I'm not going to cuff you. If you run, I get to shoot you. And you know—" his eyes darkened and his voice deepened, "—it would be so easy to mess up the settings on that alter-gun."

Okay, so running was definitely out of the question. Bianca realized then that she probably wasn't going to make it back to the Water Company alive, but that was all right. All she had to look forward to there most likely was lifelong marital imprisonment by Finch. She was the perfect replacement for Calina, after all. The only thing she regretted was Melvin. She'd miss the old coot, as unpleasant as he was sometimes.

Bianca shrugged. "Fine, don't cuff me then." She turned on her heel and walked out.

When she breached the entrance of the bar, every male eye in the hot, stuffy room turned toward her. Angelo's were not among them. She guessed he was with the hotel owner. She glanced around the room and her eyes came to rest on what had to be the jukebox. She walked over and stared down at it, trying to figure out how it worked. Discolored tabs of paper declared the titles of songs she'd never heard. She punched a button at random. Music poured from the speakers. It made her stare at the thing in wonder. This music had such a polish to it. It was nothing like the music she'd heard in the Sector before. It was a conglomeration of instruments she didn't know the names of and was slow, mournful.

The music got into her blood, spoke to her intimately somewhere near her core. She tipped her head back and closed her eyes and let the sound wash into her, through her, filling up a hollowness deep within.

* * * * *

Angelo pushed the door open to the main part of the bar with Hank in tow. "We will also need...three...extra...water canteens...*Holy Christ.*"

Bianca swayed near the jukebox, dancing to the music that poured from it. But it wasn't just dancing, nothing as innocent as that. She moved in a way that made every muscle in his body go taut as he watched her. She'd closed her eyes and she moved in a highly suggestive way to the music. Her hips thrust back and forth and she rotated her pelvis in a way that screamed sex.

The old faded pants and too small T-shirt she'd changed into hugged her curves closely, revealing every little detail. Graceful hips arched out from a slim waist. Small breasts strained against the fabric of her T-shirt. It wasn't hard to imagine what she'd look like without any clothes on at all. It wasn't hard for Angelo to imagine her beneath him as he sank his cock into her balls-deep and lost himself in soft, wet heat. He clenched his fists, causing his fingernails to dig into his palms. Every other man in the room was probably imagining the same fucking thing and that was dangerous...

Christ. She might have the face of an angel, but she had the body of a—

"Angelo, close your mouth. You're drooling all over the floor."

He dragged his gaze from Bianca to Dell, who'd come to stand near him. Vaguely, he noted that Hank had moved back to the bar. Dell held a glass with two swallows of Special in it. He swished the clear liquid around in the glass idly.

Angelo gestured toward Bianca with an open hand. "How could you let her do that?" he asked. "She's the goddamn center of attention. She'll be attracting every man in the room like bees to nectar."

Dell gave a short laugh and gestured in her direction. "Awww, look at her, man. How could I *not* let her do that?"

Angelo looked back at Bianca. Her eyes were still closed and she seemed unaware there was anyone else in the room. The music held her swaying form as close as he did in his fantasies.

"You want her," Dell stated matter-of-factly. "You want her so bad you can taste her. So why don't you take her?"

Angelo glared at Dell. "I don't exploit or take advantage of the prisoners in my care, Dell."

"Mr. By-The-Book," muttered Dell. "You wouldn't even take her if she was willing, Angelo? She seems more than willing to me."

Angelo stared at him for a long moment before responding. Dell had just practically admitted he'd rape a woman if he felt like it. He was a disgrace to the uniform he wore. "Not even if she was *willing*. Not even if she begged for it. Not while she's in my protection."

Dell shook his head. "You're hopeless, man."

Angelo ignored and turned. He crossed the floor toward Bianca, acutely aware of all the gazes fixed on him. He placed his hands on her shoulders in what he hoped was an authoritative way. She opened her eyes and smiled. Then she moved close to him, brushing her breasts against his chest and pushing her hips against him.

He gritted his teeth against his own arousal, tamping it down with a sheer force of will. "Bianca, you have to stop this *now*." His voice was far harsher-sounding than he wanted it to be. "What do you think you're doing?"

"I'm making you squirm, Angelo," she purred. "I enjoy testing the limits of your honor." She moved his hands from her shoulders to her waist and he let her. She flipped her hair and it brushed his upper arm like a silken veil, sending a wave of desire rolling through him.

He wanted to reach up and let that hair slip through his fingers. He imagined what it would feel like to have it brush across his bare chest, how she'd feel sliding over him, skin on skin slick with sweat. It had been so long since he'd been with a woman. What he missed most was not the release, but the intimacy of a woman's skin against his, her breath warm on his lips, the small sounds she made in pleasure as he thrust his cock into her with long, hard strokes. He wanted to step into that dark fantasy, press her up against the wall, bury himself inside her and take her in front of every person in the room.

He stifled a groan. "I have limits, you know. So does every other man in this room who hasn't seen a beautiful woman in a long time. You're testing everyone's honor. Fuck. Stop, *stop* moving." Angelo tightened his grip and she finally went still. He let out a short breath of relief.

"You think I'm beautiful?"

She suddenly sounded unsure of herself, shy even. He held her gaze. It didn't seem feigned. He almost laughed. Didn't she know? "God, Bianca, yes."

She blushed a little and that surprised him. This woman was a mystery to him. Right when he thought he had her pegged, he found he didn't. She looked away. When she spoke again, her voice had that bored sound to it again. "Yeah, except you're forgetting one thing. You're probably the only man in this room who actually has any honor."

"If you know that, why are you doing this? Don't you care what happens to you? Don't you care that your actions are constantly putting you in danger?" God, he wanted to shake some sense into her. He wanted to make her care.

She looked up at him through the fringe of her ginger-colored lashes. "Not really. No, I really don't."

There it was again. There was that pain, that damned vulnerable look in her eyes. That hurt and vulnerability went straight down into the core of her. No mask she donned could cover it. No act she put on could hide it. And it was an act. It was all an act. Angelo would lay credits that there was no one in the world who really knew Bianca Robinson. Perhaps her sister had.

Fine. He'd have to care enough for the both of them then.

Then he realized that something very important was missing. He stepped away from her. "Where are your handcuffs?"

Bianca shrugged. "Dell told me he'd shoot me with his alter-gun set to kill if I ran. That's a pretty good deterrent."

Angelo made a frustrated sound.

"You don't trust me at all, do you, Angelo?" she asked.

"Have you given me reason?" he responded heatedly.

She sighed. "Guess not, but I haven't really given you reason not to trust me, either."

Angelo raised an eyebrow. "First you tried to shoot my head off, and when I took your gun away you tried to steal it back," he remarked dryly.

"Oh, that," she said with a dismissive wave of her hand. "You would've done the same if you'd gotten yourself into a predicament like mine. I would have gotten away if it hadn't been for your preternatural tracking skills." She tipped her head to the side in an inquisitive gesture. "I never did get a good explanation for those, either."

Angelo pushed away from her and glanced toward the bar. Hank caught his gaze and motioned. Their rooms were ready.

"Come on," he said. "You'll stay in my room tonight so I can keep my eye on you."

"You can keep more than just your eye on me if you want to, Angelo," she teased. "Like your hands, your mouth…"

God, if only she knew what he was imagining right now.

Chapter Four

Two narrow beds and a nightstand between them were all that decorated the tiny hotel room. A small bathroom, now virtually useless without running water, stood to the left of the door. Bianca knew there would probably be a single meager pitcher of pure-water in there, a bowl, some glasses and a few towels.

She brushed a stray tendril of hair from her face. The room was stifling.

Angelo closed the door behind them and locked it. He slid the key into the pocket of his pants and dropped the pack in the opposite corner, well away from her.

She went to the only window. They were on the fourth floor so Angelo shouldn't object to her opening it. It wasn't like she could fly, no matter how much she wished she could. She unlocked the window and tried to slide it up. It wouldn't budge.

"Don't bother. It's painted shut," he said behind her.

Bianca hit her palm against the bottom sill in frustration. The heat in this room was going to strangle her.

She turned from the window and sucked in a surprised breath. Angelo had removed his shirt. She watched as he balled it up and tossed it into the corner. His hands went to the top of his pants and he began to unbutton them.

Had she misjudged him so badly? Bianca made a low sound in her throat. It was not from fear. She was far past the point of caring what happened to her. No, this sound came from deep dismay. It came from the possibility that Angelo might not be the person she believed him to be.

Was he as two-faced as Dell then? The thought chilled her to her toes. With a start, she realized that if Angelo wasn't the man she believed him to be that the one thing driving her, the crystal, wouldn't matter to her. Nothing at all would matter anymore. In a sudden realization that made her heart pound, she knew that even though she thought him naïve, she admired him. She envied him his ideals and honorable dedication.

He looked up at her. She imagined she must be white as a sheet. His hands came away from the top of his pants. "Bianca." He put his hand out as though she was a wild animal he was trying not scare away. "I took my shirt off because I'm hot. I'm not going to take all my clothes off and I mean you no harm."

Her entire body relaxed.

He looked at her with a strange expression on his face. Cocking his head to the side, he smiled. "You act like you've never seen a man stripped before." His tone was curious, with a subtle note of teasing.

She turned away to hide her blush and chipped at the white paint of the windowsill in what she hoped was a bored way. "Of course I have."

"Uh-huh."

She turned back toward him. He walked to the opposite corner of the room to collect his shoulder holster, where he'd dropped it on the pack. He'd meant to take his pants off, she was sure, but he'd left them on so she would feel more comfortable. They hung low on his hips with the top couple of buttons undone. The sight of him caused her body to respond. Her breath came faster and her pussy flared to life. Strange what this man could do to her.

Her gaze raked his muscled back and her breath caught in her throat. Deep, angry-looking ridged scars crisscrossed his back. Walking toward him before she could stop herself, she reached out and touched one of them. He flinched from her fingertips as if burned. "My God. What happened to you?"

He turned and brushed past her, shoulder holster in hand. The scars wrapped around his side like a snake to lie across his stomach. "It's a complicated story and it happened long ago," he said. He'd tried to make his tone light, but an undercurrent of pain was all too audible.

"Angelo—"

"Listen, why don't you lay down and try to rest a little?"

He didn't want to talk about it. That made sense. She was his prisoner after all, not a friend. She moved toward her own bed.

"Against my better judgment," he continued. "I'm going to leave your cuffs off, but know this, I sleep very lightly. I will hear you if you try something."

The sound of bedsprings creaking filled the room and Angelo made a low groan of satisfaction—the sound of a tired man who'd just fallen into heaven.

She looked at him and fell into heaven herself. He had his eyes closed and his arms thrown over his head. Smooth muscle rippled over the expanse of his chest and arms. A light dusting of dark hair tapered into a treasure trail that led down his stomach, past the waistband of his low-slung pants. She thought about where that trail led and felt her cheeks flush.

What would it be like to touch his chest, to lick it? God, what would it be like to wrap her hand around his cock, to feel it sliding inside of her? Would she like feeling possessed by this man? Her pussy felt damp and slightly swollen and her breasts felt heavy and sensitive. Her body seemed to be screaming a *yes* to that question...and she liked the idea of it.

Something long cemented inside of her began to crumble and break free. For a moment she felt him all the way through her. It wasn't just his body that overwhelmed her, but his whole being. It was his sense of honor and commitment to ideals, no matter if she agreed with them or not. It was his sensitivity and protectiveness—everything about him that she lacked in her life.

Water Crystal

He opened his eyes and looked up at her. "Are you all right?"

"I-I'm fine."

"Try to sleep. We've got a long day ahead of us tomorrow." He closed his eyes again.

She wondered how she and Angelo would hit it off if she weren't a thief in his eyes and therefore residing a notch below rat defecation in his opinion. She wondered, if the situation was different, if he'd like her, maybe even would want to kiss her. Maybe he'd even want to confide in her about his scars.

She blinked. It was nice to fantasize about could-have-beens, but she had to deal with reality, and the reality was she had to get free of him. If she didn't, Dell would find a way to kill her before they reached the Water Company and the master crystal would never be used.

Her gaze slipped to his pants. She might be able to slide her hand into his pocket and get the key if he fell asleep. His pack lay in the corner of the room. She was sure her crystal was in there. He'd placed her pistol under his pillow. She could forget about getting her hands on that. But if she could get the key and the pack it would be enough.

He let out a deep breath, making his luscious chest rise and fall, and she slid her gaze down the length of him. Never in her life had she reacted to a man this way. Just the sight of him made her entire body go alive with awareness. The thought of running her hands down his body, stroking his cock, feeling him thrusting inside her made her pussy throb with desire. Just once she wanted to feel his chest rubbing against hers as he sank himself inside her. Just once she wanted to feel his breath on her throat and lose herself in his strength. Bianca laid down on her bed and shut her eyes, feeling the heavy arousal of her body. Dampness coated her pulsing cunt, making her grit her teeth at her sudden surge of yearning for him. She squeezed her eyes shut and thought of everything and anything but Angelo's body and how curious she was about what it be like to sleep with him…and she didn't allow herself to drift to sleep.

* * * * *

A swath of moonlight cut through the room. Angelo's breathing sounded deep and even from where she lay on her bed. Bianca got up as quietly as she could and crossed the short space between them. His face lay in shadow and moonlight kissed the length of his body, coating him in molten silver.

Damn. She swallowed hard. What right did this man have to be so fucking good-looking? He was a hazard to womankind, or at least to her.

Moving her hand down in one smooth motion, she touched the top of his pants. She remembered what he'd said about sleeping lightly, but she had no choice. She had to take the risk. He shifted in his sleep and she froze, waiting for him to settle in again. Once he did, she slipped her hand into the pocket that contained the key. Her fingers closed on it at the same time his huge hand wound around her wrist.

She tried to wrench away from him, but his grip was like steel. Pulling away from him, she attempted to use her free hand to pry his fingers from her wrist. She fisted her hand around the key. In a fit of irrational desperation, she swore she would not give it up. Bracing her legs on the floor, she tried to wrench herself away from him.

He sat up, smoothly swung his legs over the side of the bed and caught her other wrist with almost no effort. Inexorably, he drew one wrist to wed with the other. A sound of complete desperation escaped her. Now he held both wrists in one of his hands. She struggled and pulled backward. He wrapped one arm around her waist and yanked her off-balance, pulling her down against him so she knelt on the mattress, straddling him.

"Open your hand, Bianca. Give me back that key *now*."

She squeezed her fist even tighter. Another sound of despair came from somewhere deep within her.

"Give it up, Bianca," he said in a voice like velvet.

She struggled and he held her firmly against him.

"Bianca," he said again, close to her ear. "Come on, stop fighting and let it go."

She went limp. Her will left her with a silent whoosh. It was no use. With a sob, she opened her palm and he released her wrists. The key fell onto the bed beside them, glinting silver in the moonlight. He scooped it up.

He'd managed to put her in a very intimate position and she felt completely vulnerable. He held her tight around her midsection, and showed no signs of relinquishing her. She shifted on his lap, and felt the hardened length of his cock against her suddenly damp sex. He made a sound deep in his throat at her movement. She stilled instantly, her breath coming faster. Her nipples were like two pebbles on her breasts. Every breath she took scraped the material of her shirt over the sensitive peaks.

Something down deep stirred with the knowledge of his arousal, and how she was positioned against his hard and ready cock.

She closed her eyes. God, she wanted him. For the first time since that unpleasant time back home, she wanted a man.

Her breath came shallow, and it wasn't because she'd been fighting him or because she'd failed in her escape attempt. She knew that if she wanted to, she could have him now. All she had to do was move a little, brush up against him, and he'd tumble her down onto the bed beneath him, Guardian Code of Ethics be damned.

His mouth drew close, hovering not far from hers. Warm breath teased her lips, sent a shiver up her spine. Her clit pulsed. Could he tell how turned on she was? She put her hands against his chest and pushed away from him a little. "Angelo?" She couldn't keep her voice from quavering. Sexual teasing was one thing. This was real.

And it terrified her.

He stilled and closed his eyes and locked his jaw. He slid his hands to her waist and slid them under the bottom of her shirt to rest on her bare skin. She could feel the cold metal of the key sandwiched between his palm and her hip. He let out a sharp breath of air. "Damn it, Bianca," he growled. "You're baiting me hard, too fucking hard. You're going to end up in a lot of trouble one of these days."

The thing of it was, this was the one time she'd hadn't been trying to bait him at all. She whimpered deep in her throat in a mixture of fear and hard, sharp desire. If he tossed her down on the bed right now, she'd let him do anything he wanted to her.

Tense silence reigned for a heartbeat. Angelo rubbed his thumb over her skin. Back and forth, back and forth. Bianca hissed out a breath as her clit seemed to get bigger and more sensitive. It was like he caressed it instead of her hip and the sensation was tipping her straight into a place where she wouldn't be able to hold herself back from him.

Abruptly, he lifted her off him. She had to sit down on the opposite bed. Her knees felt weak. He pushed himself up off the mattress. He shook his head and dragged a hand back through his hair, pacing back and forth between the beds. "God, Bianca, you are something else. Remember what I said about having limits? Being locked in this room with you is causing mine to be breached fast and hard in a couple of different ways. You might be a thief. You might be a con artist. But you still affect me in the way a woman affects a man."

He grabbed the pack from the corner, pulled out his handcuffs, stuffed the key into it, and then threw it with force to the head of his bed. He walked toward her, handcuffs dangling from a finger.

"What are you doing with those?" she asked. As if she didn't know.

"I would like to get some sleep," he growled. "I won't be able to do that if I have to worry about you all night."

"I won't—"

"Give me your wrists."

"I promise I won't—"

Anger flashed through his dark eyes. "*Wrists.*"

She held out her hands and he slapped the cuffs around them.

"Get on the bed and lay down in a comfortable position."

She hesitated a moment and he narrowed his eyes at her. "Don't make me do it for you," he said. She wiggled back onto the mattress and lay down, keeping her gaze on him. He took her in from her head to her feet and a muscle worked in his jaw. He knelt on the mattress and leaned over her, cussing under his breath. Her heart skipped a beat, and her mind created a multitude of carnal images that had her breath coming faster.

He eased her arms over her head and secured the cuffs to the headboard. When he'd finished, he lingered over her, looking down into her eyes. "What's your story, Bianca?" he asked softly. "You tease, you tempt, you almost push me past my limits of control. Then you get all innocent and scared." He cocked his head to the side. "You fascinate me."

Her fingers found and grasped the spindles of the headboard. "Touch me," she murmured. "Angelo, touch me, please."

He stilled, every muscle in his big body going rigid. "Bianca..."

"I know you want to and I want you to do it. For the first time in a very long time, I want..." She trailed off and turned her head away from him, ashamed of her admission. "Please," she whispered, nearly sobbing. "Please put your hands on me." Bianca closed her eyes, readying herself for heartbreaking rejection.

He did nothing, said nothing for several heartbeats. Then she felt his hand high on her waist. The warmth of his palm bled through the material of her shirt and into her skin. He just kept it there, not moving. She closed her eyes at the contact and sighed in contentment.

"Fuck," he murmured.

He slid his hand up and covered her breast. His palm just lay over it unmoving, cupping it. Her breath came fast, every inhalation rubbing her stiff nipple against him. Her sex felt warm and heavy. Her pussy was wet, wanting and anticipating contact. She swallowed hard as he caressed her breast tentatively, teasing her nipple. Bianca bit her lip and shifted her hips in delicious agony. Hot desire seemed to fill her from her pussy upward.

Angelo seemed to bring to the fore all of her pent-up and buried desire, all her sexual curiosity and her neediness to explore it.

"Fuck it," he murmured again, a bit louder. He pushed her shirt up to her neck, exposing her breasts, and made a low, strangled sound in the back of his throat. He cupped one and kneaded it gently, tweaking the nipple between his thumb and forefinger, and closed his sensual mouth around the other.

Bianca gasped and arched her back, offering her breasts to him. God, nothing had ever felt as good as his tongue on her, laving and licking over her pebbled nipple. The sensation of it shot lust straight to her groin, made her writhe on mattress in fervent desire for more. She looked down at his dark head bent over her. The muscles of his shoulder and upper arm worked as he petted and caressed her other breast. Bianca doubted she'd ever seen a more erotic sight.

She moaned and shifted her hips restlessly. He stilled, drawing a ragged breath, then resumed driving her insane. She gripped the spindles until her fingers went bloodless. God, she wished she could touch him back. Her pussy felt needy, empty. She whimpered low in her throat and shifted her hips on the bed again, wanting to spread her thighs for him but resisting the urge.

He broke away from her breast and dipped his head, resting it on her abdomen. He let a soft curse loose before he trailed his hand down and cupped her swollen sex through her pants. A breath hissed out of her at the contact.

He lifted his head. "Relax, Bianca," he said in a low, strained voice. "Just relax."

Through the material of her clothing, he found her clit and rubbed the flat of his thumb against it. Pleasure skittered up her backbone and spread out. She pulled against the cuffs, making the metal bite into her wrists. "Angelo," she gasped.

He found the seam of her pants and pressed it against her clit, rasping against the needy bundle of nerves. Angelo groaned. "You're so warm against my palm," he murmured. "I bet you'd feel so damn hot and sweet around my cock. Fuck, I want you."

"Then peel off my pants and take me," she answered breathlessly.

He let out a little frustrated-sounding growl and pressed and rotated his thumb against her clit. "Just come for me, Bianca."

She shattered. A sensation like she'd never had in her life exploded from her clit and enveloped her body. She arched her back, pressing her pussy against his hand, and pulled on the handcuffs until it bit into her skin. She cried out as the waves washed over her and she felt her underwear drench.

Angelo stared down at her, watching her pant after the first climax she'd ever had in her life. Her chest heaved from it. Her mind reeled. "Angelo, oh, my God," she breathed.

He made a low, strangled sound, then let out a string of curses and his fingers went to the button and fly of her pants. She closed her eyes and bit her lip as he eased them down her legs, taking her underwear with them. He pulled her shoes and socks off and discarded all her clothes on the floor. Cool air bathed her flesh.

Apparently he'd changed his mind about not wanting her.

He stared down at her, every muscle in his body appearing rigid. He fisted his hands at his sides.

"Angelo?" She couldn't keep the note of concern from her voice.

"Spread your legs for me," he commanded in a barely controlled voice.

After a moment's hesitation, her breathing coming fast and harsh in the quiet room, she drew her knees up and spread her thighs. A tremor seemed to run through Angelo's body as he stared at her aroused, glistening cunt. Her clit throbbed under his perusal as though he touched her.

"Bianca, Goddamn it." He shook his head. "You have no idea what you do to me." His voice shook. "You have no idea how fucking hard you push me and how dangerous that is."

"I just want you to touch me." She closed her eyes at the breathless sound of her voice. "I need for you to touch me."

She needed him to bring her back to life, to reach into all that cold, emotionless wasteland inside her and make her feel again. Her voice broke. "*Please.*"

Another tremor racked his body. He descended between her thighs, slipping his hands under her ass and lifting and spreading her. At the same time, he lowered his mouth to her pussy.

Bianca's air left her in a *whoosh* of surprise. She hadn't expected this. Not his skillful tongue on her. Not the enthusiasm with which he seemed to pursue the task, or the groan of pleasure that erupted from his throat.

"Open for me more," he growled from between her thighs.

She spread her thighs further apart and he pressed his thumbs to her labia, parting the folds completely. He licked as far back as he could get his tongue, over her anus. It made her jump and she let out a soft noise of surprise. He speared his tongue in and out of her cunt, mimicking sex. Her body tensed to climax.

His lips drew on her labia, massaging the folds. "You taste so fucking good," he groaned. "Are you going to come for me?"

"Yes," she gasped.

He dragged his tongue over her, finally finding the aroused nub of her clitoris. He laved over her clit, teasing it with the tip of his tongue.

She shuddered and moaned, lost in a sea of ecstasy. He continued to play with her clit, and Bianca could feel the bit of flesh grow larger, engorging with blood, readying itself to climax. Back and forth he licked it, focused on one goal…to hear her scream.

He eased a finger up and rubbed the entrance of her pussy. Her hips bucked and she closed her eyes. Yes, she wanted something inside her. He slipped his finger into her drenched cunt and drew it slowly in and out.

Bianca pulled on the cuffs above her head at the onslaught of sensation. Her climax hit her like a train. Her back arched and she cried out as it washed over her body in overwhelming waves. He snaked his tongue in while her climax racked her body and stuck his tongue up into her cunt. He thrust in and out as deep as he could, lengthening her orgasm.

"Angelo, Angelo," she whispered over and over as she came down from her climax. Her hands relaxed on the mattress above her head and she closed her eyes, breathing heavily.

Ah, God. Sex could be good, couldn't it? It could be unbelievably good.

After the waves had passed, Angelo backed away from her and sat on the edge of his bed. He lowered his head into his hands. His breathing sounded harsh in the suddenly quiet room.

"Fuck," he swore under his breath.

"Angelo?" she asked softly.

Instead of answering, he got up, spread a throw blanket over her and pulled her shirt down. Then he laid down on the bed, using the pack as a pillow. He didn't look at all comfortable. "Get some sleep," he said heatedly.

Bianca closed her eyes, her cheeks warm from her embarrassment at how she'd begged him to touch her. "What about you?" she murmured. "Don't you need, er…"

He turned over, so his back was to her and punched his lumpy "pillow". "I'm fine," he said in a ragged voice.

She swallowed hard and waited a few moments before speaking. "Angelo, I need to take that crystal into Sector Twenty-Nine. You have to let me go." Her voice shook.

A scoffing sound escaped his lips.

Her words came out in a rush. "I'll never get back to the Water Company alive anyway. Dell is going kill me before we get there because I know things about him that can get him in deep, deep trouble with Finch. That's probably a good thing, anyway, because if I do make it back to the Water Company, Finch will probably just use me as a surrogate Calina." She pressed the heel of her hand to her eye in an effort to drive away her sudden headache. "I'll be imprisoned there for the rest of my life, enduring his sweaty gropes and being punished for his impotence."

He said nothing.

"Look. Fine. I don't matter, but that crystal does. It has to be put in the hands of someone who knows what to do with it. Deliver me to Finch if you have to, but take that crystal to Sector Twenty-Nine. It's just a worthless rock, anyway, right?"

Angelo sat up and came to her. He cupped her cheek in his hand. She closed her eyes and sighed at the feel of his callused fingers rubbing her skin. "You do matter, Bianca. Even if you don't think you do. I understand that you're disturbed by your sister's suicide. You hope to rationalize your theft of the crystal by creating this elaborate fantasy—"

Her eyes flew open and she jerked away from his hand. "No!"

"Let me finish. I also understand that within you there is a basic goodness, a bright light shining way down deep that you don't recognize. I sense that you're not lying to me. Or, what I mean is, you don't *think* you're lying to me."

Bianca narrowed her eyes at him. He'd just thrown a bucket of cold water on her desire for him.

"These things will be taken into consideration when we make it back to the Water Company. I will personally ensure that your punishment is not dire."

She laughed. "You're not going to have a thing to say about what happens to me once I get the Water Company. *If* I get to the Water Company."

"As the Captain of the Guardians of Order, I do."

She made a small, helpless sound. "Oh, Angelo, you are about to be educated swiftly in the ways of Aloysius Finch. I almost feel sorry for you."

"Bianca, I give you my word. I will keep you from harm, all right?"

She sighed. "Yes, Angelo, all right," she said in defeat.

* * * * *

When she woke in the morning she found that in her sleep he'd released her wrists from the headboard, but they were still cuffed together. She groaned and struggled up. Careful to keep the blanket from revealing her nakedness, she swung her legs over the side of the bed and watched as Angelo slid his arms into his shoulder holster. Last thing she wanted was to be reminded of how he'd touched her the night before.

How she'd begged for him to do it. Her cheeks burned at the memory.

She watched him, remembering first his hands on her body and then what he'd said to her afterward. The latter helped her pull on a cold demeanor. "So we're back to the cuffs permanently, huh?"

He just grunted at her.

"Intelligible words would be nice."

He muttered something under his breath, then said, "After what you pulled last night? Do you even have to ask?"

She blushed. She remembered all too well what she'd pulled last night, though she doubted they were talking about the same incident. "Did you forget my need to brush my teeth and hair? You've already taken care of your own little necessities, I presume."

"Yes, I have, and no, I didn't forget. I simply don't trust you with your cuffs off."

"But you can't deny your prisoner basic grooming. That would be cruel and unusual punishment, against your precious Code of Ethics, wouldn't it?" It had been an attempt at humor. Apparently, she wasn't funny. He said nothing, simply continuing to secure his holster. Wow, he was in a bad mood this morning, though she couldn't blame him. He'd gifted her with a respite from her all-consuming Angelo-lust. He hadn't received any relief at all.

She tried for a dazzling smile. "Come on, I want to look really pretty for Finch."

His mouth twisted into something resembling a smile. She was shocked. A genuine smile hadn't crossed his lips since she'd met the man. "I'll bet," he said. He fished the key from his pocket and unlocked her cuffs. Then he extracted the items she needed for her morning toilette and a change of clothes and handed them to her.

After Bianca had availed herself of the small amount of water in the bathroom pitcher to wash up and brush her teeth, she raked the brush through her tangled hair. Angelo stood watching with interest as she pulled and tugged without mercy. Finally he stepped forward and with a gesture of agitation, plucked the brush from her hand.

"You're going to make yourself bald," he said. He guided her to the bed. She sat and he drew the brush through her hair in long, gently even strokes.

She closed her eyes at the touch of his hands on her head. "What are you, an expert at brushing women's hair?" she asked.

"Yes. I have three sisters and a mother. That makes me an expert."

"All living?"

"Yes."

Bianca whistled low in admiration. "Having a family that big these days is a true…accomplishment." She let her words trail off and roll into a contented sigh. His fingers deftly worked all the tangles out of her hair and made her scalp tingle with pleasure.

"Tell me about your family," she managed to push out between sighs.

"Not much to tell. They live in Sector Thirty-One, just on the border of Thirty. I'm the youngest. They're not all alive. My father died while my mother was pregnant with me." Sector Thirty-One used to be known as Wisconsin, Bianca recalled.

"I'm sorry."

"Don't be. I'm glad I never met him." He threw the brush into her lap. "Finished," he said. It appeared his father was not an agreeable subject, just like the subject of his tracking ability and his scar.

"What about your parents?" he asked.

Bianca looked at the floor. "They were killed when my sister and I were young. I don't remember them very well."

Angelo stood looking at her in silence. "When's the last time you were happy, Bianca?"

She looked up at him sharply. What a question. She smiled as bright and big as she could. "Me? Oh, I'm happy all the time. Haven't you noticed? My life is a laugh a minute."

He grunted, picked the cuffs off the bed where he'd tossed them and slapped them on her. Then he went still for a long moment, looking at her with an intensity that made her pulse speed up and her mouth go dry.

"Your hair always looks mussed, angel-face, even when it's brushed," he said.

She thought for a moment he was going to reach out and touch her face, but he got up instead. He scooped up the pack and motioned to her. "Okay, come on. Time to travel."

"You mean time to die."

"Bianca, I swear I will keep my eyes on Dell at all times, all right? I will never again leave you alone in his care."

He was humoring her, the bastard. She made a low sound of frustration and rose. "Let's just go." She brushed past him and went toward the door.

They went down the stairs and into the bar. Dell leaned against the doorframe at the entrance and watched as she entered the room. She absorbed Dell's cold gaze for about three seconds before having to look away.

He was going to prevent that crystal from getting to where it needed to go and there wasn't much she could do about it.

Chapter Five

Angelo sat straight up in the saddle, alarming Bianca. His arms tensed around her. "There's something—" he started.

Laser fire shot past the nose of the horse, coming from a cluster of buildings to the left. The animal shied and bolted to the right, and Bianca screamed and grabbed the pommel. Angelo gained control and dug his heels in, trying to guide the horse behind a building while drawing his own laser.

They were in the middle of a wide street, about an hour's ride from the border of the Center. It was desolate stretch; just animals and Flot resided here.

Laser fire ripped through the air again. This time it almost hit the horse's head. The beast reared and dumped both Angelo and Bianca off the back. Bianca landed hard on her butt, causing the air to whoosh out of her. The horse bolted down the street. Helplessly, she watched it run away, its tail waving in the wind. Panic that had nothing to do with the immediate threat ripped through her.

The crystal was in the saddlebag.

Dell drew his laser and returned fire. Angelo bolted to his feet, yanked her up by the arm and pulled her behind the nearest building. Dell followed, dismounted and tied his horse to a fire hydrant.

"Goddamn Flot," muttered Dell before he disappeared around the side of the building with his laser in hand.

Angelo glanced around and focused on an old, rusty railing along the steps of one of the buildings and dragged her to it. He yanked on the railing, testing its strength, and then cuffed one of her wrists to it. "You stay down in the shadow of the doorway, out of the way," he commanded.

She nodded, focused more on the direction the horse had bolted than on Angelo. A stream of laser fire hit the adjacent building, burning a hole in the concrete. She let out a startled scream and looked at him with wide eyes.

"I swear to God, Bianca. If you find a way to run, I'll find you and I won't be happy."

She nodded again. She believed him.

Angelo disappeared after Dell, leaving her alone. She hunkered down at the base of the building to wait it out. Soon, she heard voices that were not Angelo or Dell's. She bunched herself up into the shadowed entryway of the building in an effort to make herself invisible.

"Come on, one of their horses is over this way." Two figures came out from between the buildings across the street from her. They were young, probably not over seventeen years old and possessed the lean lankiness that comes with that age. Both had light brown hair. She shrank back, out of their line of sight. They might be young, but they were still Flot.

One went to Dell's horse, untied it and took its reins in hand, leading the beast back toward the street they'd emerged from. The other one scanned the area and caught sight of her. She tried to hunch down further.

"There's a little trapped bird." He projected his voice loud enough for her to hear. He left his friend and came toward her. His friend hesitated, glancing around nervously, then followed with the horse in tow. Bianca got to her feet, readying herself to kick at them if they drew near enough.

"You're a prisoner of the big men, aren't you," the first one stated upon seeing her handcuffs. *Big men* was sarcastic Flot slang for the Guardians of Order.

Christ, they were geniuses. "Guess the cuffs give me away, huh?" she sneered.

"Should we take her prisoner, Gannon?" asked the one with the horse.

"Nah, Corvin. Any prisoner of theirs is a friend of ours."

Water Crystal

Gannon aimed his laser at the base of the railing and fired. Bianca jumped to the side in surprise. The metal melted and gave way. He ceased fire and wrenched the railing the rest of the way off, and Bianca slipped the cuff down over the edge of it and was free. The cuff hung from her wrist like a clunky bracelet. She wouldn't ignore any opportunity for escape, regardless of any threat Angelo may have made.

"Where did you get the laser?" Bianca asked him. Normally, the Flot were strictly gun-toters. The poor used guns because they were old and inexpensive; the guardians used lasers and alter-guns. It was simply the way of it.

He smiled at her with pride, showing a row of straight white teeth. "A long, but good story. We don't have time for it. Now fly away, little bird, before they come back."

He turned and led the horse away. Corvin followed.

What an abrupt change of luck. She thought of Angelo and actually regretted parting ways with him. She shook her head. Christ, she must be insane, just like he thought she was.

She stared down the street, suddenly bereft. Damn! This was the perfect opportunity for her to run and she didn't have the crystal. Her freedom didn't matter without the crystal. She set her jaw, knowing she had to find it.

Bianca started to run in the direction the horse had gone. Laser fire ripped through the air behind her and she hit the ground. Looking behind her, she saw Dell come around the side of the building. He'd caught Gannon in the shoulder and the boy was on the ground. The telltale smell of charred flesh from the wound the laser made filled the air, gagging her.

Corvin dropped the reins of the horse and ran. Dell gave chase, disappearing down the opposite street. Gannon writhed on the ground, holding his shoulder and yelping in pain.

She stood and hesitated for a moment, torn between making a run away from Dell, toward the crystal and freedom, or back to the injured boy.

Crystal that could save the world or injured boy about to die by Dell's hand?

Goddamn it!

The boy made a strangled sound and that decided her. She ran to him.

The ripped material of his shirt revealed burned and mottled flesh. Laser fire was horribly painful, akin to being burned with a stream of fire. A person with a flesh wound like this could get a nasty case of laser fever if it wasn't treated properly.

She knelt beside him, although she had no idea what she could do for him now that she was here. He reached out and grabbed her hand. "I...have salve...in my left...pocket," he struggled to say. "It will...numb the wound."

She slid her hand into his pocket and extracted a vial of white lotion.

"Spread it...on the wound and it will ease...the pain," he instructed her slowly through clenched teeth.

She uncapped the vial and put some on her fingers. Then she placed her hand above the red, weeping wound and positioned it this way and that, unsure of how to do it without causing the boy more agony.

Without warning, something wrenched her back away from him. She fell onto the street, small rocks and pebbles dug into her palms and soiled the salve. The vial flew from her hand and bounced on the pavement. Dell loomed over her with his laser drawn. "Well, how perfect is this?" he drawled only loud enough for her to hear. He pointed his weapon at her chest and she cringed, readying herself for the blast.

Gannon grabbed Dell's leg with his good arm and bit him in the calf. Dell yelled, tried to step away from him, and toppled to the street. In the process, he dropped his laser and Bianca kicked it out of his reach. Dell growled low and grabbed for her ankle. She backed away from him quick, like a crab on her hands and feet.

Dell and the boy struggled. Bianca watched with horror as Dell plunged his fingers into the boy's wound and dug in. Gannon's screams rent the air then went silent as he passed out.

Now free, Dell scrambled to recover his weapon. Bianca got up to run, but Dell was on her in a second. His fingers curled into her hair and yanked hard, drawing a scream from her throat. He pushed her to the ground and stood on her handcuff. She tried to wrench herself free and only got searing pain shooting around her wrist and down her arm as a reward.

"I'll take care of you in a minute, little girl," he promised.

He raised his laser and leveled it at the boy. Bianca lay on her stomach, one arm paralyzed by the hold he had on her loose cuff. Wrenching her shoulder until it brought tears to her eyes, she twisted so she lay partially on her side and could draw her feet up to the level of Dell's calves. It was a desperate last-ditch effort.

"Stop!" came Angelo's order. "Don't fire, Dell!"

Dell didn't move, didn't lower his weapon.

Laser fire tore through the air, grazing Dell in his already wounded shoulder. The same shoulder connected to the arm and hand that held his weapon. The laser flew from his grasp and he went down on his knees with a grunt, releasing his hold on her cuff. Bianca scrambled back and away from him.

Dell grunted in pain and slapped a hand to his shoulder. "Goddamn, Angelo, you hit me!" he roared.

Angelo walked toward them. A middle-aged man who had the survivalist look of an Out-Center Flot walked beside him. He had long blond hair and wore a shirt ripped at the collar. A couple days' worth beard marked the man's face.

"When you don't follow my instructions, I have to do things like that, Dell."

The man with Angelo went straight to the boy, knelt and shook him. Gannon came to with an agonized groan. "Gannon, I told you I didn't want you pulling stuff like this anymore," said the man in a voice that mixed worry and intense anger together. It was the voice of a father.

Bianca laughed out loud—part genuine amusement and part massive relief of stress. A couple of kids misbehaving had caused all this.

"Get up, Gannon," the man ordered. "Come on, you deserved the wound." Gannon turned his gaze to Dell and it became hard. "But you didn't deserve to be executed when you were unarmed." He paused for emphasis. "Good thing *that* didn't happen."

Bianca got up, retrieved the vial and gave it to the man. "Thank you," he said, noting her dangling cuff with a pointed glance. Small lines drew tight around his eyes and his shoulders looked hunched with tension. If he was Flot, he probably wasn't very happy to be surrounded by guardians right now.

Hell, neither was she.

He turned to Angelo. "Thank you for preventing him from taking my son's life. He meant no mortal harm to you. He simply—"

"Meant to rob us."

"I have repeatedly told Gannon not to engage in these activities and he has disobeyed me. He is young and rebellious, and—"

Sarcasm laced Angelo's voice when he spoke next. "Well, he doesn't have the best of role models now, does he?"

The man was quiet for several long moments. "Harsh times sometimes call for harsh measures. I don't always approve of what my community mates do, but we punish those who disobey our rules. We have a system to deal with lawbreakers. I want you to know that." He paused. "But it does not reflect favorably on you to judge us all by the actions of a few."

Angelo's lips twisted as though amused by the man's words and he gave him a withering look. "Sure," he said under his breath. Then louder, "Your community mates wouldn't have to steal if you came into the Center and lived under the rules of the Water Company. Mr. Finch has created a viable society that you thumb your noses at."

The man flinched as though struck. Like the very idea of living in the Center pained him. "I have reasons for not wishing to do so."

"I should arrest your son and his friend. I should take him back to the Water Company with us," Angelo replied.

A tense silence followed. The man's hands tightened protectively on his son's shoulders.

"However, I will not because of what Dell has done here this day," said Angelo. He turned his eyes to Dell who still lay on the ground holding his shoulder. Dell returned Angelo's glare. "No one should be executed when they are unarmed and without a proper judgment of guilt or innocence."

"My thanks to you. I will ensure he is punished myself," said the man. Bianca could tell by the man's body posture and tone of voice that the deference to Angelo was costing him a lot of pride.

"Just make sure he doesn't try anything like this in the future," answered Angelo.

They stood looking at each other in tense silence for several moments. Finally the man extended his hand. "I'm Quint."

Angelo did not shake his hand or offer his own name.

Gannon and Dell were both on their feet now, eyeing each other warily. "What did you do to Corvin?" asked Gannon.

Quint withdrew his hand from Angelo and gave Dell a sharp look.

"Nothing—" Dell waved his good arm in a dismissive gesture, "—punk ran too fast. He got away."

Quint and Gannon looked relieved.

Bianca felt Angelo's warm, firm grasp on her upper arm. She looked up at him, irritated. "I'm not going to run."

"Then why aren't you cuffed to the railing where I left you?"

"Gannon freed me. Look, I swear I won't run with you standing right here."

He smiled at her. "You'll have to forgive me for not trusting you."

She pointed at Dell. "He just tried to kill me, Angelo."

That now familiar look of disbelief spread across his face. She resisted the urge to cringe.

Dell shook his head and laughed. "She's got an active imagination, Angelo. I'll give her that."

"I swear! He almost shot me with his laser. If it wasn't for Gannon, I'd be a whole lot dead right now." She turned to Gannon, who leaned against his father. "Isn't it true?"

Gannon shook his head. "I'm sorry, I didn't see anything." His lips spread in a weak smile. "You should have flown when you could, little bird."

Angelo's grip on her upper arm tightened.

"I swear I'm telling the truth, Angelo!"

"Dell doesn't have any reason to want to kill you. Mr. Finch would have his nuts if he did that and he knows it. But all the same, I believe that you believe—"

"That I'm telling the truth," she finished for him bitterly. "I'm caught in a nightmare."

Dell pushed past Quint and Gannon, going toward his horse. He fished a vial of fire salve out from his saddlebag, and then led the horse down the street. "Come on, let's go."

Bianca watched Quint and Gannon head down the street in the opposite direction.

Angelo and Bianca walked down the cracked and broken sidewalk, following Dell. They skirted a large chunk of the pavement that had collapsed, as if the soil beneath had turned to powder. She stared down at it as they passed. So, it was happening here too, not only in Sector Twenty-Nine. She hadn't seen the phenomenon anywhere around the Center until now.

Water Crystal

Dell fell into step beside Angelo, leading his horse by the reins. Angelo released her arm. Quick as a striking snake, he slammed Dell up hard against the side of a building. "You ever try anything like that again, Dell, and I'll aim for a vital organ. Do you hear me?"

Dell's face contorted in pain. He grunted. The vial of fire salve hit the pavement. "Yeah, sure, I hear you, Angelo."

Angelo slammed against the wall again, pinning him there. Dell's feet just skimmed the ground. It was clear then to her, and probably to Dell too, just who would win if they ever chose to fight.

"What did you call me?" Angelo asked in a low voice full of threat.

"Ange—er—captain."

Angelo stared at Dell for a few more tense moments and finally released him.

* * * * *

Angelo found his horse down the street munching grass. He ensured the crystal remained in the saddlebag and helped Bianca to mount.

"Who was that man back there?" she asked. "The blond Flot."

"Quint? He is leader of the Flot in that area of southern Out-Center. I've seen him before, but always at a distance." Angelo sighed. "I'll give him this, the Flot in that area are more controlled than in other areas of Out-Center."

"So what's your problem with him?"

He shrugged. "He's Flot." Did he need another reason? They refused to play by the rules and made it harder on everyone else.

He settled in behind her and she eased back against him. He wished he didn't enjoy her closeness, but the truth was he loved her weight against him and the way her soft hair brushed his arms every so often. Maybe it was simply that he'd been a long time without a woman, but he loved that every time he wound his arms around her to pick up the reins, she gave a contented sigh. It was such an unaffected response that he doubted she was even aware she did it.

The night before had been the closest thing to torture he'd ever been subjected to. Feeling her soft breasts and tasting her hard nipples had been bad enough, but her hot little pussy against his hand, even through the material of her pants, had nearly sent him over the edge. His cock hardened now at the mere memory of the soft noises she'd made when he'd touched her and how she'd shattered so sweetly in climax. She'd come easily for him, in complete unjaded innocence. She'd seemed surprised by the whole experience.

There was no way she was the experienced vixen she pretended to be. No way in hell. It was an act.

They were near the border of the Center now. If they pushed, they could make the Water Company by nightfall. Once they were there, Bianca would no longer be in his care. That thought came with a surprising pinch of regret. Even if she did tease him to within an inch of his life.

Bianca was a pain in the ass, there was no doubt about that, but she was also vibrant, alluring, mysterious and definitely not boring. The only predictable thing about this woman was that she was unpredictable.

He wanted to make a smile reach her eyes, to chase the pain from those blue-green depths. He wanted to make her laugh just once, but he didn't have the slightest idea how to do that. Hell, he couldn't laugh himself.

She was a fighter. He hoped like hell that fight wouldn't leave her when they made it to the Water Company and all her fantasies dissolved in the bright light of the truth. The thought of Bianca's pain and vulnerability coming to the fore and eclipsing her vibrancy gave him pause.

He'd considered letting her get a hold of the crystal and allowing her to escape. What would be the harm? It was a just worthless crystal and she was no threat to anyone, except maybe herself. But the truth was, she had broken into the Water Company, drugged the guards, damaged the security system, and stolen a personal item of the most powerful man in the Sector, while rubbing his nose in his grief over his recently deceased wife.

No, Bianca had committed crimes and as much as it pained him, she needed to be punished for them. He could not allow her pretty face and intriguing personality to sway him from the duty he had to the people of the Sector. Above all, the people of this planet needed culture, structure, and society. Those things began with law and order. It was his job to see they were upheld, as difficult as it would be for him to see this through. It was his duty, his responsibility, because of who he was and because of the blood that ran through his veins.

Angelo spotted the border of the Center ahead of him and slowed the horse's pace.

That responsibility could be delayed somewhat.

Chapter Six

No formal barrier, fence or wall separated the Center from Out-Center. Only the notable presence of patrolling guardians and great increase in humanity marked their passage into civilization.

Angelo gave a sigh of contentment. He was home.

Small businesses dotted the sides of the street, having taken up residence in some of the lesser-ruined buildings. During the last five years, workers commissioned by the Water Company had restored many of the war-damaged structures. Through his generosity, and the implementation of social programs, Aloysius Finch was single-handedly responsible for much of the society the survivors now enjoyed.

People walked along the cracked sidewalks, some hurrying to get somewhere, others seemingly just out for a stroll. An old woman with skin the color of smooth coffee tottered into a pure-food shop, helped by an elderly Caucasian man with a shock of white hair. A young couple strolled down the street hand in hand, talking and smiling.

Other people were astride, traveling to their various destinations horseback. Upon rare occasion, a solar-powered vehicle chugged down the road. They were small and not very attractive, but Angelo thought with time they'd become the norm.

"Captain Angelo," greeted one of the border patrollers with a nod.

"Carlos," Angelo responded. Carlos was a good man, dedicated to his job. He wore the dark blue uniform of the Guardians of Order well, unlike Dell.

"Catch any smugglers lately, Carlos?" called Dell.

"We caught Flot trying to get some flamethrowers into the Center yesterday."

Dell clucked his tongue and shook his head. "Crying shame, those Flot. They just don't know when to give up."

The guardians spent a lot of their time confiscating illegal armaments. Every inhabitant over the age of sixteen was allowed one firearm. Usually people carried handguns, pistols or rifles. They were cheap and easily accessible. Less often they carried lasers or alter-guns. But everyone wanted what was forbidden, of course, so illegal weapon smuggling was a problem.

He'd prepared himself to rebuff Dell's inquiries about why they were traveling at such a slow pace but Dell hadn't complained. Angelo couldn't deny it, he wasn't anxious to give up Bianca's company. During the trip, he'd wondered often how he and Bianca would've gotten along if she hadn't been his prisoner. Maybe they could've been friends, maybe even more.

When it was apparent they were in the Center, Bianca gave a deep, resigned sigh. He felt the rise and fall of her body against him. She'd lapsed into an uncharacteristic silence, broken only by the occasional verbal jab at Dell. Angelo thought perhaps she sensed they were getting closer to their destination.

Dell finally broke the silence. "We could push it a little faster and make the Water Company, Angelo, but I thought maybe we could stop for the night. We're all tired and need to bathe."

Bianca straightened to attention. "Do you want another shot at killing me before we get to the Water Company, Dell?"

"Bianca, come on," Angelo said.

Dell gave a short, snorting laugh. "God, little girl, you are crazy, aren't you?" His comment was accompanied by the motion of his index finger circling in the air about an inch from his left ear. "Craaazy."

She slumped back against Angelo's chest.

Angelo thought Dell wanted to get back to the Water Company as soon as possible to be shed of his and Bianca's company. Dell didn't hide his dislike for either of them, after all, so Angelo was jarred by his suggestion. But he wasn't going to question it. Another night alone with Bianca sounded great, even if she was a pain in the ass.

"Yeah, Dell," Angelo answered. "I think stopping would be a good idea. What do you think, Bianca? Are you in a hurry to get to the Water Company tonight?"

"Hmmm…which evil to expose myself to? Possible death at the hands of Dell, or perpetual imprisonment at the Water Company by an impotent madman?" She sighed dramatically. "Choices. Choices." Sarcasm dripped from every syllable. She shrugged. "What does it matter? We can stop for the night, I guess."

"Great," said Dell. "There's a place up the road called—"

"The Phoenix," Angelo finished for him.

"Yes."

* * * * *

Bianca scrutinized the tall, wide building as they approached. The Phoenix was much nicer than Hank's. It had obviously been a grand hotel in its day. It hadn't retained its former glory, although it tried. Large solar panels dominated the roof and gleamed in the late afternoon sun. Parts of the building itself were crumbling from bomb damage, and many of the windows were still broken. Whole, unbroken panes of glass were difficult to find these days.

They gave the horses to an employee and walked inside. The furniture in the lobby was faded and ripped. A half-shattered chandelier hung from the vaulted ceiling, and water-damaged and faded yellow wallpaper covered the walls. But, for all that, the place looked clean and comfortable enough.

The clerk greeted them and opened a ledger for them to sign. Angelo secured a room key and left Dell at the desk to get his own.

"I ordered baths for both of us. Do you want to take yours now?" Angelo asked Bianca.

She kept her eyes on Dell with intense wariness. He hadn't stopped eyeing her since they'd arrived. She could almost hear the wheels in his head clicking, trying to figure out how to get her alone. "Uh, listen, Angelo. I don't care who takes their bath first. All I know is I don't want to be left alone."

"Bianca," he said in exasperation.

She smiled and brushed herself against him. "Come on, I'll help you wash your back...or something."

"No, that's not going to work."

"Even though you wish it would."

"I resisted you last night, so I guess that's not true." What a lie.

She made a scoffing sound.

He gave an irritated sigh. "Look, you take your bath first, okay? Then I'll lock you in the room and take mine."

She looked at Dell. He leaned on the counter against his uninjured left side, one booted foot crossed over the other. He talked to the hotel clerk, but his eyes were on her. Angelo had his back to him. "No, that wouldn't be good, Angelo."

He took her by the shoulders and made her look away from Dell and at him. "No one will harm you, Bianca, I swear it."

She felt the heat of his hands bleeding through her shirt onto her shoulders. She looked up into his earnest, if infuriated, face and then over at Dell once more. A slow smile bloomed on Dell's mouth and he winked at her.

She guided her gaze back to Angelo. "I think you believe you can protect me—" Angelo groaned and released her, "—but

I also believe you don't fully understand all the elements at work in this situation."

"All right, I give up. Let's go up to the room and drop this stuff off." He indicated their packs on the cracked marble floor beside them. "You'll bathe first and I'll guard the door. Then we'll figure out what to do after that, all right?" Angelo led her up the stairs.

When Bianca glanced back at Dell, she saw a look on his face that said she'd be dead by morning.

*****

Angelo led Bianca down for her bath. The bathing room was in what used to be the dining room. The tall windows lining the walls were boarded up because of a lack of glass, and two rows of six tubs each stood in the room, partitioned by five-foot privacy walls. He scanned the room looking for ways Bianca might escape while he left her to bathe. Only one door led in and out of the room. That was fortunate. He could guard it from the outside. But the boarded-up windows gave Angelo pause.

The room was empty save for the two of them. Steam billowed from the surface of one filled tub. To its right side stood a shelf containing shampoo and soap. On the other side stood a rack of large towels.

Angelo uncuffed her and turned to leave, but hesitated at the door. "Let me check the boards on these windows, Bianca." He went around the room, making sure the windows were nailed tight enough that she couldn't pry them off.

"I'm not going to try and escape," she said.

He turned and gave her a look of disbelief. "After what you pulled at Hank's, am I supposed to believe that?"

"Angelo, I swear. I'm much safer with you than without you at this point."

"I agree with you for the first time since we met."

"The water's getting cold," she complained.

Water Crystal

"Just give me a few more minutes, okay?"

She gave him that sly, secret smile that was fast becoming her trademark. That smile meant she was up to something. "Well, if you won't leave me alone, I guess I'll just have bathe with you in the room."

Before he had a chance to protest, she unbuttoned her pants and sent them sliding down her legs to pool at her feet. Shapely calves flowing into strong, beautiful thighs met his view. Above that was a peek of blue material under her shirt, blue cotton with tiny, faded red roses.

She kicked her pants away with one slim foot and the smooth muscles of her legs rippled. He couldn't look away from her. Damn, he couldn't even move. There it was again—that tightness in his body, settling in his groin. He hated that she had such power over him. He hated it even more that she knew she had that power over him.

Her hands went to the bottom of her shirt, as she prepared to slide it up over her head. Her flat abdomen came into view.

His paralysis broke and he went to her in four fast strides. He caught her hands and pushed them down, forcing her shirt back into place. She looked pleased with herself. Too damned pleased. She knew that she had the upper hand, and that she could bring him to his knees if she tried hard enough. He knew it and so did she.

Playing with fire, that's what Bianca loved to do…but she could she handle the inferno once it was started? Angelo doubted it. Maybe it was time to turn the tables. Maybe it was time to push her buttons and reveal the truth at the same time.

Winding one arm around her waist so she couldn't step away from him, he caught her chin in his fingers and tipped her face to his. "Are you going to be ready for me, Bianca, when I finally call your bluff?"

She looked uncertain for a moment. That same raw look of innocence wounded crossed her features. A fake smile flickered across her face. "Bluff? What do you mean?"

He drew his thumb over her lower lip. It was soft and smooth. He couldn't help but think about how her mouth was going to feel under his, so lush, warm and wet.

"This is what I mean." He lowered his face toward hers, and he felt her stiffen.

"Look, I'm sorry I teased." She snaked her hand between them. Her palm pressed against his chest. "This is a bad idea, Angelo," she whispered so low he almost couldn't hear her.

He nodded his head slightly, his intent gaze on her lips. "It's the worst idea I ever had." He drew his hand from her chin to the base of her spine, and then pressed her into him while his mouth descended on hers.

Her lips were unmoving at first and then her body relaxed, curving to fit him perfectly. Her mouth moved under his, returning his kiss with a sudden urgency. He coaxed her lips apart and let his tongue explore within.

Her hands came up tentatively, fluttering against his arms as though she was unsure what to do with them. She finally curled the fingers of one hand into the hair at the nape of his neck. The other she pressed tight against the back of his shoulder. It almost seemed as though she was willing more of him against her.

Her tongue found his and moved against it artlessly. Her inexperienced strokes simply served to stoke the fire that was already burning hot and high within him. All his resolve about staying celibate dissolved like sugar stirred into water at the press of her lips and tongue against his.

He brought a hand around and cupped one small breast, brushing his thumb back and forth over her erect nipple through the material of her T-shirt. She moaned deep in her throat and arched into him. Reveling in the feel of her taut breast pushing against the thin fabric, he pressed his hard cock against her so she could feel what she was doing to him, and how much he wanted her.

Water Crystal

She pulled away a little, gasped, and looked surprised for a moment. Then she smiled and sealed her mouth back on his with a new urgency.

He found the edge of her T-shirt and pushed his hand under it to caress the skin of her lower back. She felt firm and warm. He let his hand roam down, finding hot, aroused pussy and cupping it. She'd creamed nicely for him. He could feel the dampness through the thin bit of material. He wanted to push aside her underwear and slide his finger up inside her but he resisted. He wanted so much more than she was going to be able to give him. His body ached with the desire to lower her to the floor and help her discover all the ways a man and woman could find pleasure together, because for all her teasing she didn't know.

He'd been right all along about her. The truth of it was in her kiss. It had been in her innocent desire the night before.

When his body shook from the need to explore the creamy folds of her bared sex, he eased his hand down her thigh and slid between them.

Bianca made a low, satisfied sound in her throat and spread her legs to give him better access. He pushed the material away and dragged his fingers over her sex. He shuddered, remembering how good she'd tasted the night before, how sweetly she'd shattered for him not once, but twice.

Angelo slanted his mouth over hers and hungrily sank his tongue into her hot mouth over and over, trying to consume her. She whimpered against his lips and his cock twitched.

He teased and stroked her clit until her breath came faster and her body tensed, then he slid first one finger up inside her hot little cunt, then added a second. He worked them in and out of her, still kissing her deeply, until her interior muscles spasmed and her cream gushed out as she came. He caught all her soft cries against his tongue. It hadn't taken long to make her climax. She seemed hot and eager for sexual experience.

She groaned deeply into his mouth, catching and gently dragging his lower lip between her small white teeth. Angelo's whole body shook. He was so fucking close to throwing her down and fucking her until she couldn't see straight.

But he couldn't do that.

And she wasn't ready for that anyway.

Suppressing a groan of frustration, he released her and backed away.

He looked at her and couldn't help but smile. Now who had the upper hand? It had nearly killed him to get it, but he'd savor it while he had it.

* * * * *

Bianca felt him break the kiss and back away, but she couldn't move. She stayed there with her head tipped up and her eyes closed—in warm, honeyed shock at the fire licking its way up her spine. Her sex tingled from where he'd touched it. She wanted more of the same.

Ever since his mouth had covered hers she hadn't been able to think. She hadn't been able to form one simple, coherent thought. All she'd been able to do was feel him. She was amazed to realize that she liked being kissed by him. Liked it a lot. Maybe she even liked it too much. A flicker of fear moved through her, something she hadn't felt in a long, long time. She opened her eyes. "What-what about your rule against kissing thieves?"

"Bianca, you make me want to break every damn rule. Anyway, I did a whole lot more than that last night, didn't I?"

She shook her head, feeling stunned. "No. This is different. You didn't kiss me last night." The kiss they'd just shared felt far more erotic and intimate than what he'd done to her the night before and her body thrummed from it.

He shrugged. "A kiss can tell you a lot about a person. It was an experiment. I wanted to confirm something about you and I have." He looked satisfied with himself and that made Bianca suspicious.

"What?"

"You're a virgin," Angelo said.

Shit. "No," she said, looking away from him. "No, Angelo, I'm not." She knew there was tenseness and sorrow threaded through her voice, but she couldn't help it.

He remained silent for several long moments. She glanced up at him. Yes, he knew what she meant. That was good, because she really didn't want to say the word.

"Who was it? When did it happen? Could we find who did it?" Angelo fired off questions.

Bianca smiled. He was first and foremost a Guardian of Order. She looked away to hide her hurt. "His name was Adam. It happened years ago, when I was sixteen. My wounds are healed for the most part."

She paused. Angelo had gone motionless and silent, but his body language said everything. He fisted his hands at his sides and hunched his shoulders forward, his gaze intent.

"I trusted him," she continued. "That's what hurt the most, that betrayal. But he's long gone now. The people of my community in Sector Twenty-Nine banished him when they discovered what had happened. So he was punished in a way." She laughed. "Calina and I were homeless in the Out-Center for seven whole years and managed to avoid that. Then just a year after finding a supposedly safe place, it happened. I guess I let my guard down." It was so dangerous to let her guard down. It always got her hurt.

Funny that she felt able to talk about this. She'd never discussed it with anyone before. She didn't know why she felt safe divulging this information to Angelo—her own damned prison guard. "I was young and I didn't really know what was happening at first. When I finally figured out what he wanted, I couldn't stop him from taking it." She shrugged in what she hoped he took for a gesture of carelessness. "It was over pretty fast—"

"You're so flippant. You discount the seriousness of his crime."

"Oh, come on, Angelo. You can't possibly be so naïve. Do you actually think a woman can live in this world and not get mistreated from time to time? It's impossible. Anyway, what's the value of my body?" She shrugged. "It serves me because it's a tool. It has little worth beyond that."

He took her by the shoulders and forced her to look at him. "You listen to me, Bianca. You, you, are like rare gold in a city made from lead. You are worth so very much more than you believe yourself to be."

Tears flooded her eyes. He sounded like he meant it. She couldn't remember the last time she'd had tears in her eyes. She thought they'd dried up long ago. When was the last time she'd cried? Oh, yeah, she'd cried when they'd taken her sister. She dashed them away, ripped herself from his grasp and turned so he couldn't see her face.

"That's one man's opinion," her voice was rough with unshed tears. She gave a short, bitter laugh. "And no offense, Angelo, but you're one hell of a strange kind of a man." Her voice sounded harsh. "Now, are you going to let me bathe, or what?"

He paused and drew a breath. "I'll be guarding the room." He walked away and she heard the sound of the door closing behind him.

Bianca stripped off the rest of her clothing and got into the bath. Troubled and distracted, she dunked her head under the water, and started to wash. She scrubbed her hair and skin until they glowed, then dunked herself under to rinse off. When she breached the surface of the water, she came nose to nose with Dell.

Chapter Seven

A scream bubbled up from within her. Dell clamped a hand over her mouth before she could birth it. "Shh, little girl. We don't want big, bad Angelo coming in right now. I hid in here after we checked in." He let a smile bloom on his thin lips. "I've been waiting for you," he said in a low voice that promised violence.

Bianca thought of Angelo. The door was at least a good fifteen feet away. He probably wouldn't hear her struggling, but she had to try. She thrashed and tried to pry Dell's hand from her mouth. Dell brought his alter-gun up from the side of the tub and leveled it point-blank at her forehead. She stilled, letting her hands drop to the water.

"It's set on null, little girl. Just so you know. I press this trigger and you'll end up brain-dead." He said it with pleasure clear on his face. "I saw you and Angelo kiss. It was so sweet, so sickeningly sweet. You baring your soul." His eyes flicked down at the bathwater, now thankfully clouded with soap and shampoo. "And the rest of yourself. Yeah, I saw that, too, little girl. Made my cock hard."

She tried to bite his hand, but it was clamped too tightly over her mouth.

Dell narrowed his eyes at her. "I think drowning might be a fitting end for you."

Bianca knew what he meant to do. He'd stop most of her brain wave function with the alter-gun. Then she'd slip into the water and drown—clean, no signs of struggle.

"After all, your sister killed herself," he continued. "Why shouldn't you kill yourself too? With all that anguish in those pretty eyes of yours, Angelo will probably believe it. I'll just help you out a lit—"

Bianca brought the flat of her hand up hard and fast and hit him in the sensitive part of the underside of his nose, the self-defense Melvin had taught her coming to the fore automatically. He grunted in surprise and pain and let a stream of curses go. His right hand went to his nose, now coursing blood. His left hand, the one with the alter-gun, gripped the side of the tub. The weapon hung from his limp fingers. He was far more concerned with his nose at the moment. She snatched the alter-gun.

She pointed the weapon at him, her hands shaking. There were four buttons on the back of the gun and no trigger that she could see. She didn't have the slightest clue how to use the thing. How the hell did you shoot it? Dell looked at his empty hand and then at her. His countenance darkened with intent and he smiled slowly. He probably knew she couldn't work the goddamn thing. She did the only thing she could think of—she threw the weapon as far across the room as she could.

Bianca opened her mouth to scream, and Dell pushed her below the surface of the water. Bianca flailed her arms and legs, her fingernails seeking desperate purchase in any bit of Dell's skin she could find. She pushed up against him, and managed to breach the surface of the water. Her lungs took in a greedy gulp of air before he pushed her back under again. She fought against him, and he restrained her as if she were no more than a child. He held her there until she felt lightheaded. Thinking fast, she suppressed her panic and let herself go limp. As she'd expected, he loosened his hold, assuming she was gone.

She focused her strength in one final burst. This time when she broke the surface, she sucked in a lungful of air and let it right back out in a scream. He pushed her back under again. This time she had no reserve of air. Her chest felt as if it would burst and she was on the brink of passing out. Her eyes and throat stung. She opened her mouth and gulped in water.

All of a sudden, Dell released her and fell face-first into the water onto her legs. Then strong hands pulled her up out of the water and lifted her out of the tub. She coughed and tried to draw air into her burning lungs at the same time. Through her blurred vision, she saw Angelo. She wrapped her arms around his neck like he was a life preserver.

He laid her on the ground. She rolled to her side and lifted halfway up, bracing herself with her arms as she coughed and heaved. Angelo pulled Dell from the tub and threw him down with force. He fell like a rag doll and made a wet thump when he landed on the floor in front of her. His head hit with a painful-sounding crack.

Angelo grabbed a towel, knelt beside her and enveloped her in it. Then he sat on the ground and drew her into his lap. Strong arms held her close. All the emotion she'd felt when she'd been held under the water—all the emotion she'd kept pent-up inside since her sister had died—spilled forth. The numbness thawed inside of her in one intense rush, leaving deep furrows of raw feeling in its wake. The tears came like a summer flood, hot and heavy. Her whole body ached from her sobbing. She let it wash over and through her. Angelo caught every drop of it as it poured out of her.

Finally, her tears slowed and eventually stopped.

"You told me he was going to try and kill you and I didn't believe you," Angelo sounded stunned. "I didn't think he had any reason to try." He shuddered. "God, I'm glad I got in here in time, Bianca."

"Yeah, me too. How did you know?"

"I heard you scream."

She gestured at Dell "Is he? Is he—uh—"

"My alter-gun was set on delta. He's unconscious."

She brushed a wet tendril of hair from her face. "How long until he wakes up?"

"I'd say five or six hours based on how the gun was set."

"Do you believe me now, Angelo?"

"Yeah, I'm beginning to, Bianca. We'll—" he drew a deep, measured breath, "—we'll need to talk more and decide together what to do."

She sighed, smiled and relaxed against him. Maybe the crystal would get to Sector Twenty-Nine after all. She suddenly felt like everything might be all right. Maybe it was the fact that Angelo no longer believed she was living in a fantasy world, or maybe it was simply because his arms felt safe. Whatever the reason, hope was something she hadn't felt in a long time. She could become accustomed to the sensation. "Get dressed and we'll talk," he said.

Reluctantly, she pulled herself away from him and stood, securing the towel around herself. "What about Dell?"

They both looked at the unconscious man. Blood pooled on the floor from his nose and there were long, bloody scratches on his arms and face from where she'd marked him with her nails. The bandage that had been wrapped around his shoulder had come loose and she could see the two wounds had reopened and were bleeding. Angelo stood, pulled a pair of handcuffs from his pocket and secured them around Dell's wrists. Then he turned and looked at her with dark, hooded eyes. "I'll deal with Dell when he wakes up," he said in a voice that had gone dangerously low. "I have a few questions for him."

Bianca gathered her clothes and went around one of the privacy walls to change, feeling self-conscious all of a sudden. She'd been ready to tease Angelo to hell and back before he'd kissed her. Now things were different. Now she felt shy, exposed. Bianca examined the reason behind that abrupt change and didn't like what she found. She cared about Angelo, cared how he reacted to her, and cared how he viewed her. The fact she cared about him changed everything.

Angelo walked toward the door. "I'll meet you in the lobby." The door closed behind him.

Bianca dressed and went for the door, but then remembered Dell's alter-gun and went back. She picked her way around his prone body and walked to the far side of the room where it lay on the floor. She tucked it into the waistband of her pants. Angelo would want it back.

* * * * *

Angelo walked down the hallway toward the lobby, his mind whirling. How much of what Bianca had told him was true? He needed time to sort things out, time to determine exactly what was happening.

He needed to take a closer look at that crystal.

He walked through the lobby's entranceway and stopped short. Finch stood in the center of the room underneath the half-broken chandelier. Seven guardians, all carrying holstered lasers, surrounded him.

There were few other people in the lobby at this hour, but the ones who were there stared openly at Finch. He was the Water Baron and as his nickname suggested, near royalty in Sector Thirty.

Finch spotted him right away. "Angelo," he called, walking over to him. The guardians followed at his heels like well-trained dogs. "I placed the hotels in the Center on alert for you and Dell. They notified me when you checked in. Where's the woman?"

Not where's the crystal, but *where's the woman*.

"Angelo, I really think we should—" Bianca came down the hallway toward him, tucking in her shirt. She looked up and her voice trailed off. She went completely motionless, her hand still poised mid-tuck. Her hair hung in sodden strands around her suddenly pale face.

Finch's eyes went wide. "Calina," he breathed.

Bianca took a step backward. Angelo hoped she wouldn't run. There was nowhere to go. The bathing room was a dead end.

Angelo put up a staying hand when Finch took a step toward her. "She's not Calina. That's Bianca, her sister."

Finch brushed past him as though he hadn't uttered a word. Bianca backed up against the wall and Finch followed. He reached out a hand and laid his palm against her cheek.

Fear spread across Bianca's face, followed swiftly by a more familiar and dangerous expression. *Anger*.

She reached up with surprising speed and force, grabbed Finch's wrist and twisted it around his back in an arm wrench. Finch's flabby muscles gave little protest. He let out a surprised cry and went down on his knees. She stood behind him, his wrist in her firm grasp. With her free hand, she pulled something that had been tucked into the waistband at the small of her back and put it to Finch's head—Dell's alter-gun. There was a collective gasp from the hotel patrons in the lobby.

When she spoke, her voice shook. "It's set to null."

Angelo stood stunned, breathless for a full heartbeat. Every last guardian drew and trained their lasers on her. The soft whirring sound of them all powering up at once filled the surprised, still air. He drew an uneven breath. "Hold your fire," he ordered.

Finch bellowed in pain...and humiliation, Angelo was sure. There was no way Bianca could know how to use that alter-gun. She was bluffing. Even if she wanted to pull the trigger, she wouldn't know how to do it. Anyway, Angelo highly doubted she had murder in her. If she'd wanted to kill Finch, she would've done it when she took the crystal. So what was she trying to accomplish? She had no hope of escape with so many guardians here. Likely, sheer fear motivated her right now.

Angelo scanned the area. All seven guardians looked confused. Many of them were glancing at him for guidance. "Captain?" queried Morgan in a tense voice.

Angelo extended a hand, his palm out in a staying gesture. "Hold your fire, all of you. Lower your lasers." The guardians complied and Angelo let out a breath of relief. "No! Don't lower your lasers! Get her off me!" yelled Finch.

Water Crystal

The lasers went back up.

"Bianca, let him go," Angelo said.

She looked at him sadly. "No, Angelo, I can't. I can't let him have the crystal back, don't you see? I can't end up imprisoned like my sister."

"No, you won't end up imprisoned like your sister. You're going to get yourself killed instead."

Pain flashed across her features and she glanced away. When she looked back at him, her gaze was steady. "So be it."

A shudder ran through him. The thought of laser fire searing her skin, of having to pick her wounded or lifeless body up off the floor was too much to bear. "Bianca, let him go," he repeated in a voice made thick with fear.

She shook her head, an expression of fierce determination on her face.

"Shoot her with your alter-gun on delta, Angelo," ordered Finch.

Angelo didn't move. If he shot her with his alter-gun, she'd be taken to the Water Company.

"Angelo, you either delta her or I'll have the guardians shoot her with their lasers. I will override your authority. You know that."

All the guardians steadied their weapons as if to fire. One twitchy trigger finger and… "No!" ordered Angelo in the most commanding voice he could manage. "Goddamn it, hold your fire!"

"Shoot her, Angelo!" bellowed Finch.

He pulled his alter-gun out. "Bianca," he said in warning.

Her eyes went wide. "Angelo, no, please don't do it."

"You're giving me no choice." Angelo raised his alter-gun and pointed at her. His hand didn't shake, but coldness clenched his stomach.

He held her gaze…and fired.

Chapter Eight

Bianca lay on the floor where she'd fallen, her midriff bared. Finch reached over and carefully smoothed the edge of her shirt down. Then he hefted his substantial bulk up from his kneeling position on the floor. Raymond, one of the largest guards, moved to aid him. "Don't help me, you buffoon." He snapped his fingers and indicated Bianca. "Help her. Pick her up."

Raymond lumbered over and scooped Bianca up into his arms. The alter-gun she'd been holding slipped from her lax fingers and fell with a clatter to the floor.

"Be careful, Raymond. My God," Mr. Finch said quietly, running a finger down Bianca's cheek. His voice trembled. "She's like Calina come again."

Angelo let the alter-gun hang limp from his fingers. It had all happened so fast. Bianca had stood there holding an alter-gun on the most powerful man in the Sector and she'd had a look in her eye that said she wasn't going down without a fight. The thought of laser fire searing her flesh had scared him so much he'd almost stopped breathing. He'd had to delta her. He'd *had* to do it.

He rubbed his eye with the heel of his hand. The look on her face as he'd pulled the trigger would haunt him. He'd done what he felt he had to do to keep his word to her—to protect her. But, fuck, she'd looked like she'd thought he was betraying her.

"What the hell is going on, Angelo?" Finch came within a breath's space from his face. "Where is Dell and why wasn't the woman handcuffed? Why was she wielding a weapon?"

Water Crystal

Angelo didn't provide an explanation. He walked past Finch, toward the bathing room. "Follow me." He pushed the door open and Finch followed, along with the other men.

When they entered, Finch eyed Dell who lay on the floor, sopping wet from the waist up. His nose had stopped bleeding, but a pool of blood had formed on the floor in front of him.

Finch extended a hand toward Dell and made a sweeping gesture. "What the hell happened here, Angelo?"

Angelo shook his head, as if waking from a dream…or a nightmare. "Dell tried to drown Bianca in her bath. I stopped him."

Finch stalked up to him until he was an inch from his nose. He was shorter than Angelo by a good five inches, so Finch had to tip his head up to meet Angelo's gaze. "Was Dell in here while she was naked?" He narrowed his eyes. "Were *you* in here while she was naked?"

What the hell did that have to do with anything? Dell had tried to *kill* Bianca. Finch was missing the point. Angelo blinked. "Her state of dress was not an immediate concern, sir. Her life was of more importance."

"I will determine what is of importance." He turned and motioned to Raymond. "Come, Raymond, let's go. Angelo, you take care of getting Dell to the hovercraft. Get it done quickly. I want to be back at the Water Company as soon as possible."

Angelo watched them leave, still in shock. The other guards stared at him, awaiting orders. He cleared his throat, but his voice was still hoarse when he spoke. "Morgan, Christopher, gather up Dell and take him to the hovercraft."

"Yes sir," said Morgan as he and Christopher each took a side and picked up Dell under his shoulder blades. They dragged him across the floor toward the door.

"James, you will stay here tonight. Tomorrow morning, bring our horses back to the Water Company. I need to leave on the hovercraft with Mr. Finch." He needed to stay as close to Bianca as possible. "The rest of you board the hovercraft now."

He left the guardians to execute his orders. Angelo gathered their packs from the room, gave his key to James and walked out to the street where the hovercraft had landed.

The silver hovercraft looked like a large helicopter without the propeller. They were designed to dock with a larger ship and it was said some still hovered unmanned out in Earth's orbit. He walked up the gangplank and entered the craft.

All the hovercrafts the humans now possessed had been confiscated from the Kirans after the war. In Sector Thirty there were twenty — all owned by Essential Providers. Finch himself owned ten. Before the Forty-Year War, they had been spotted often as UFOs.

He ducked his head through the doorway and saw Finch sitting in one of the comfortable reclining chairs scattered throughout the passenger area. The craft had a small galley, a bathroom and an emergency freysis shower — something Finch had installed. The craft even came complete with a bed that slid out of the wall at the proper voice command. An entryway off the back of the passenger area led to the cockpit.

Raymond laid Bianca in a chair. Her head was thrown back and her still wet hair cascaded down the back of the chair almost to the floor. Dell lay draped over the chair opposite her.

Angelo sat beside Bianca.

"Do you have the crystal, Angelo?" Finch asked.

His heart stopped beating for a full moment. He glanced at Bianca, then at the guards who lined the sides of the cabin. Now was not the time for heroics. He needed to be smart about how he handled this situation. Finch could easily override his authority with the guardians. Angelo might endanger the crystal, Bianca and himself if he tried to retain it.

"I have it," he answered.

"What are you waiting for? Give it to me."

Angelo fished it out of his pocket and handed it over.

Finch instructed the pilot to take off. It wouldn't take them long to reach the Water Company.

Finch's eyes settled on Bianca. "God, Angelo, I have to hand it to you. You're the best tracker I've ever seen. You've outdone yourself this time. Outdone yourself!"

Angelo swallowed hard. *Outdone himself*. Christ, that was for sure. Not only that, he was undone as well. Emotions pushed and pulled at him so hard he couldn't even see straight. It felt like his whole world had exploded. Bianca had been telling the truth the entire time about everything. He'd suspected that when Dell had attempted to kill her, but he'd known it for sure in the moment Finch had reached over and covered Bianca's midriff where her shirt had ridden up. That one gesture had been so telling. He'd done it as though she were a possession.

Angelo felt like he'd slipped into some strange alternate reality. Nothing was as he thought it was. He'd wanted so much to nurture and protect the budding society Finch and the Essential Providers created. Now he realized that something was going terribly, terribly wrong with that.

"What punishment do you have in mind for her, sir?" Angelo asked.

Finch pulled his gaze away from Bianca. "Punishment? Oh, well, I don't know yet. I suppose I'll wait and see when she wakes up. Perhaps I can reason with her." He smiled. "Maybe we can come to an understanding, she and I."

"An understanding about what, sir?"

Finch remained quiet, as though he didn't know how to respond. "Well, her sister was my wife, you know. She feels I'm responsible for her suicide, I'm sure. That's probably why she gave me that scare when she stole the crystal, to make me pay in some small way for the wrongs she perceives I did Calina. I must take that into account when I'm deciding her punishment."

"I see," said Angelo.

"You know, maybe I'll let her off completely. She is my sister-in-law after all, isn't she? Maybe she'll want to stay at the Water Company with me. You never know, do you?"

Something in Angelo's gut twisted. "No, you never know, sir." Letting his gaze slip to Bianca, he shuddered. He would find a way to make this right. He eyed the other guardians in the passenger area. He would just have to bide his time until he could figure out a way to do it without endangering Bianca or the crystal.

Angelo looked out the window to his left. The Water Company was a miraculously undamaged stretch of architecture that lay close to Lake Michigan. It was dark outside, and the lights from within made the building glow.

Angelo knew if it had been daylight, he would've been able to see the myriad solar panels attached to the building, supplying the extensive amount of energy needed to run it. It was a piece of the past. A piece of the world before the freysis poisoning and the Forty-Year War.

They landed on the hovercraft's landing pad on top of the building. Angelo took it upon himself to carry Bianca off the craft. He didn't want anyone to touch her but himself and he didn't want to be parted from her now. As he walked across the landing pad, he saw the expanse of Lake Michigan in the distance, glittering in the moonlight.

They entered the building and took the elevator to Finch's office on the fiftieth floor. Angelo laid her on the rich green brocade couch in the center of the room. Finch placed the crystal on the edge of his desk.

Raymond and Morgan stood sentry in the back of the room. Angelo glanced at them. Shooting the guardians with his alter-gun set to delta wasn't an option now. The room's computer would react automatically to any shots by setting off an alarm and locking the door.

The Water Company's central computer knew who was in each room at all times. When an alarm sounded in one room, the facial recognition scanners for the rest of the building instantly changed the accessibility for each of the persons in the room. Essentially, all persons in the room where the alarm had gone off became prisoners until the guardians sorted things out. Every room, elevator and stairwell contained scanners. After the computer changed a person's accessibility, there was no way out.

When Bianca stole the crystal, she'd managed to bypass some of the computer's security by cutting outer alarm wires, but she hadn't shut everything down. That was next to impossible. In his initial investigation, he knew that the techs had not erased Calina's face from the database and Bianca had used that to her advantage. But when she'd lifted the crystal, the room alarm had gone off and she'd still made it out of the building.

How?

"You may leave now, Angelo. I'm sure you're tired and are in need of rest."

"I'm fine, sir."

Finch turned and studied him for a moment. "I appreciate your devotion, but really, you may go."

Angelo hesitated, his eyes flicking down to Bianca. His best bet lay in a clever manipulation of Finch at this point. Angelo couldn't allow Finch to lose trust in him, to suspect him of anything untoward.

He had to leave her.

"Angelo, are you worried about the woman?" He laughed. "My God, you are devoted to your job, aren't you?"

"It's simply that normally prisoners are brought to the holding cells in the lower part of the building, Mr. Finch. This is somewhat, uh, irregular."

"Well, the prisoner is somewhat irregular, isn't she?" he snapped. "She's my sister-in-law. I'm not going to throw her in a cell while unconscious, am I? When she awakens, I will talk with her. It's that simple. So, Angelo?"

"Yes, sir?"

"You are dismissed."

"Yes, sir."

Angelo took a last glance at Bianca and then at the crystal. He'd get them both back.

He would.

* * * * *

"Stay away from me, Finch! You fucking stay away!"

Calina's twin had backed herself into the corner of the room. Finch couldn't bring himself to call her Bianca yet, even though he no longer nursed any illusions about her being exactly like Calina. She had none of her twin's delicate tameness. Everything about her showed a dark and feral personality, but those flaws could be easily remedied. She looked like Calina and that was enough.

They'd stripped off her ratty clothes and wrapped her in one of Calina's pink silk robes. Her now dry hair hung long and tangled over her shoulders and in her face. She was a mess. That also could be remedied.

He hadn't been the one to undress her and put the robe on her. There were female servants to perform such tasks. She would have to be courted by him before he could see her undressed. He wished it that way. That's how it had been with Calina as well.

An expensive vase whizzed by his head and crashed against the wall behind him.

He'd just have to do a lot of courting.

"Now, now, don't agitate yourself." Finch cast an arm wide, indicating the room. They were in his private chambers in the Water Company, one of the finest areas of the building. It was richly decorated in dark woods. Thick carpet covered the floor. There was even a fountain here, running with pure, drinkable water.

Delicate unbroken china from the days before the poisoning adorned the shelves. Unfortunately, Bianca was remedying their state of unbrokenness at the moment. A fine china cup went whizzing past him and nearly took Raymond in the throat. It crashed against the wall. Finch winced.

"Look around you, my dear. Here you have everything you could ever want." He held a hand out to her like she was a wild animal he wished to offer food. "Please, calm yourself."

Bianca picked up the mate to the first vase and took aim. "If you think I can be seduced by possessions, you've got a big surprise coming." Her eyes looked past him and rested on the two guardians who flanked the door. He saw her brain working, trying to figure out a way past them.

"You're a rare gift, sent from the heavens above. You're like Calina come again. I truly did love your sister, you know." He gazed at her, swallowing hard. "And I-I could love you as well. I could keep you here in the circle of my adoration, in a cloud of luxury. You'd never want for anything."

She made a scoffing noise. "You don't know anything at all about love, Finch. Cardinal rule, you don't imprison those you love." She heaved the vase at him. He ducked. It crashed against the bookshelves behind him.

"You blame me for your sister's death, is that it?"

She looked at him like he was crazy. "You forced her to stay here, Finch. You took away her freedom. You took away all her choices, you impotent monster. Of course I blame you."

Finch drew his hand back with a gasp at the word *impotent*. He cast a quick look back at the guards. They looked uncomfortable. They looked the way people look when they've received information they really didn't want. "How do you know about that?" he whispered fiercely.

She smiled and laughed. It sounded brittle. "Oh, Finch, you'd be surprised at how much I know." She waggled her eyebrows and gave him a bitter smile. "About a lot of very personal things."

Minx.

"Should I continue to talk about your sexual prowess? Or should I talk about the crystal? I know all about that, too."

He took a few menacing steps toward her in order to shut her up before he realized he didn't know what to do with her. He motioned to the guardians. They stepped past him, going to her. She twisted away from them and skirted the couch. They caught her and each took an arm in their meaty grasps.

She struggled against them. "What? You don't want me to talk about the crystal? Why not? It's such an interesting topic," she taunted.

He sighed. He'd hoped it wouldn't come to this but she was giving him no choice. "Put her down the Oubliette."

She went very still. Confusion and fear clouded her eyes.

Ah, something she didn't know about.

The guardians pressed her down onto the couch. Raymond took the syringe gun that had been lying on his desk. At the sight of it, she began to struggle again. They forcibly extended her arm. She kicked and bit, but they managed to set the needle to her upper arm and shoot the drug into her. That was the worst of it. By the time she needed another dose she'd be tame as a kitten and simply roll up her sleeve.

He walked over to her and looked down.

"What did you give me?" Already her eyes were going droopy. In the beginning he'd also drugged Calina, but with not nearly as much of the drug. Eventually he'd been able to wean her off it and she'd been tame and docile as a housecat, her will broken. He suspected her twin would need a bit more, and maybe for a longer time period. The stronger ones did.

"Those Kirans. They knew so much about the human mind. They knew how to alter brain wave patterns and how to mask memories, even distort them and create whole new personalities. This drug is theirs," Finch explained.

She shook her head and looked at him blankly. The drug was already starting to work. He wouldn't have to worry about her divulging any sensitive bits of information now.

"You'll go down the Oubliette, and we'll forget about the old you," he continued. "Together, we'll create a new you. A nicer, more compliant you."

Chapter Nine

Dell lay with his cheek pressed against a cool cement floor. He opened his eyes and groaned at the brutal pain shooting through his head, his nose and his shoulder. Gingerly, he pushed himself to his back and groaned again. Squinting at the bright light glaring from the bulb in the ceiling, he knew immediately that he lay in a holding cell in the jail at the Water Company.

Something hard and fast connected with his solar plexus. His breath left him in a sharp, soundless gasp. He grunted in pain, curling over into himself. Shutting his eyes, he waited for the nausea to pass.

When he could, he opened his eyes again, expecting to see Angelo standing over him, ready to take his head off. Instead, Aloysius Finch's face blurred then came into focus.

"Mr. Finch," Dell rasped.

Raymond, one of Finch's heavies stood behind him. Dell knew he'd been the one who'd kicked him.

"What's going on, Dell? I come to the Phoenix and find you down, felled by Angelo. He says you tried to kill Calina's twin." He knelt down, which required true effort for a man of his girth. "Is this true?" he asked in a cold tone.

Dell heaved himself into a sitting position, trying to clear his muddled thoughts. He didn't say anything.

Finch motioned and Raymond stepped forward, grabbed him by the front of his shirt and started to drag him away.

"Wait!" Dell yelled. "Let me explain what happened!"

Raymond stopped mid-yank.

"Better be good, Dell. Better be really good," Finch said. "I didn't want the twin harmed. I'm not pleased with you right now, not at all."

"I wasn't trying to kill her sir, just threaten her," he lied.

"For your sake, I hope so." Finch stood and tapped Raymond on the shoulder and he dropped Dell back to the floor.

He drew a shaky breath. "What matters more, sir, the crystal or the woman?"

Finch pursed his lips in consideration. It surprised Dell. He'd expected him to say the crystal right away. If he said the woman mattered more, Dell's fate would be sealed, and it wouldn't be pretty. "She seduced him and he fell right into it," Dell spewed out. "She convinced him to take the crystal and run."

Finch went silent. He just stared down at him.

Dell thought fast, his mind seemingly turning over a hundred different possibilities in a split second. "The only time I could get her alone was when she took her bath. I just tried to scare her, sir. Make her think twice about running with the crystal." He chuckled. "Angelo thought I was trying to kill her."

Finch narrowed his eyes at him.

"I never would've hurt her, sir." He shook his head. "Never. But this one's nothing like Calina. She's not so sweet or pliable. It takes strong measures to bring this one to heel."

"You're saying this girl corrupted Angelo?"

"They were going to take the crystal and run, sir!" Dell exclaimed.

"You're saying she convinced him to run off with *my* crystal? Angelo was going to steal *my* crystal?"

"Yes, sir."

Finch turned away from him and motioned to Raymond. "He's lying. Lock him up until I figure out what to do with him."

Raymond lumbered over to him and grabbed him by his shirt again. "No, Mr. Finch! I'm telling you the truth, I swear to God!" he shouted as Raymond dragged him toward the door.

"There are two flaws in your story, Dell," Finch called after him. "Number one, Angelo isn't corruptible. Number two, if he fell so hard for this girl why didn't he help her escape? Why did he delta her? Answer me that, Dell!"

* * * * *

He'd had no choice.

Angelo kept telling himself that over and over. Seven guardians with lasers meant he'd had no choice. But how he wished now he'd tried something, anything, to get her out of there.

He picked up his glass, took a drink of water and then mechanically lifted his fork to his mouth to take a bite of puresteak. The rare, expensive delicacy tasted rotten in his mouth. He couldn't enjoy it. He couldn't enjoy anything now. His gaze rested on Bianca at the end of the table, where she sat next to Finch.

They'd dressed her like Calina and scented her with fragrant pure-oil, a very costly commodity. She'd smelled lightly of hyacinth when he'd brushed past her before dinner. She looked like a porcelain doll, untouchably beautiful, sedate and fragile. Her untamable hair had been tamed, caught up in a sleek twist on the back of her head and held with one long hairpin topped with a pearl.

She looked nothing like Bianca. He suspected she looked a whole lot like Calina, however. Angelo also suspected they'd drugged her, although with what he wasn't sure. That was the only explanation for her continued state of calm. There was nothing in her eyes—only gentle, vapid emptiness. Every time she looked at him, his stomach muscles clenched.

Angelo pushed his plate away. He wasn't hungry. Finch sat on her left, smiling at her adoringly.

Had the world gone madder than it normally was? Did no one else think this was strange? Did no one else wonder about the drugged woman at the end of the table, dressed up like her dead twin and treated like a mere doll?

Angelo glanced down the long table. The Essential Providers were there along with their spouses, and some of the other high-ranking guardians. They laughed. They talked. No one seemed to wonder why the woman at the end of the table had no will of her own, no spirit, no fight. No one wondered or no one cared.

It was a dinner in her honor, a celebration of Finch finding his sister-in-law. They all whispered that he'd probably marry her. After all, who could say no to the most powerful man in the Sector? Who could turn away the luxury Finch could provide? And wasn't Bianca so sweet, so much like Calina?

Angelo's hand tightened in anger around the fabric napkin that lay on his knee. Over the last two days, he'd gone over a million different escape possibilities and had not yet settled on the one he would execute. All of them were high risk. How had Bianca gotten out of the Water Company undetected when she'd taken the crystal? He had puzzled over this for hours and had no answer. He wished he'd asked her.

Guilt flooded through him. How could he have not seen the possibility of this? Why hadn't he believed Bianca sooner? If he had, none of this would be happening. They'd be far from here, in Sector Twenty-Nine, doing what was best for the human survivors. His actions, his own thick-headedness and inability to see Finch as anything but an honorable man, had put them all in jeopardy. His own blindness had put Bianca's life at risk.

"Angelo, show Miss Robinson to her room, please. I believe she is growing fatigued," said Finch.

He practically fell over the chair in his haste to get up. Finch patted her hand, kissed her cheek. Love glimmered in his eyes — the twisted love of a man hopelessly inured in illusion.

Bianca rose from the table. She looked at Angelo with dull eyes and drew her arm through his, setting her hand on his forearm.

He led her away, out of the room and down the hallway. "Bianca?"

She gave him no response.

"Bianca, please, at least acknowledge me. Tell me you hate me, something, anything." He led down the corridor, leading her back to her chambers, what had been Calina's chambers, actually. The silk of her dress brushed against her legs as she walked, making a susurrus of sound.

She stopped at a large window and looked out over the city. "I feel so strange. I feel like nothing at all matters...numb." She turned and looked up him. Her normally bright and clear blue-green eyes appeared cloudy. "I was supposed to do something, wasn't I? It seems like there was something I meant to deliver to someone. Something very important." She shook her head. "But I feel...fuzzy. I just can't remember."

"The crystal, Bianca. You wanted to deliver the crystal to Melvin in Sector Twenty-Nine."

"Oh, a crystal? Really? How pretty." She turned from the window and continued down the hall. "I like it here. There are so many nice things. Don't you like it here?"

"Not anymore."

She stopped and looked up at him. "Why not?"

"Because it's not the place I thought it was. Bianca, you don't remember anything that happened within the last few days?"

Her brow furrowed as though she chased a memory and couldn't quite catch the tail of it. "I remember being kissed, I think."

Angelo didn't know why he did it, but he couldn't stop himself. He pushed her back against the wall and let his mouth cover hers. Pressing himself against her, he wrapped his arms around her unresponsive body and kissed her as if trying to breathe the memory back into her, the fight back into her — or draw the goddamn drug out of her. He didn't know which.

He let his hands come up and find the pin that held her hair up in the sleek twist. He tugged it out and let it fall to the floor. Her hair came down past her shoulders in a tumble of silver-blonde, sending up a cloud of hyacinth scent. He let his hands comb through it, mussing it. He stifled a groan.

God, he wanted the old Bianca back, full of fire and vulnerable strength.

* * * * *

His hands were strong on her back, his lips warm, sliding over hers like hot silk and then parting them and going within, tasting her, possessing and consuming her. She let him do it because it was nice…interesting. It made places low down in her body tighten and become wet. His kiss made her nipples hard and her sex ache and feel empty.

Mr. Finch's kisses never did that.

She felt her hair come down and made a concerned noise. Mr. Finch wouldn't like that and she wanted Mr. Finch to be pleased with her.

The man released her and stepped back. He wore an expression that was something close to desperation. Shouldn't she know him? He seemed so familiar.

Bianca had a nagging suspicion this all meant something. She just wasn't sure what. She felt folded under a hundred woolen blankets. She couldn't think clearly. Every time she followed the trail of a thought, it morphed into another totally foreign one. Lost in the labyrinth, she pushed forward with all her might, trying to break through the layers.

She stepped back and lowered her head, suddenly dizzy from the force of the effort. The man reached out to steady her. In a rush of recognition she knew him. She looked up. "Angelo?"

Emotions passed over his face like fast-moving clouds, leaving hope in their wake. Then, as suddenly as it had come, the recognition disappeared. She frowned. Hadn't she just known who this was? Who was Angelo anyway?

"Yes, Bianca. I'm Angelo. Remember the crystal? Remember Melvin? Remember Dell? Remember Calina?"

"Calina. That name is familiar."

He placed a hand at the small of her back and led her quickly down a corridor and through a set of double doors that led to the terrace gardens. There was a grave here, in the corner of the walled area. She'd been here before and had seen it. She knew they were high above the ground here. The pure-garden Mr. Finch kept had been amusing. She'd been even more amused by the fact that it was on the fortieth floor. It had seemed so decadent—a whole private garden kept on purified water only.

The man forced her to the ground in front of the grave. He knelt by her. "She was your sister, Bianca. She was your twin."

Unexplained sadness bubbled up from somewhere deep within her. She reached out and traced the name on the headstone. The granite was rough under her fingertips.

Calina. That was a name she should remember.

Bianca pushed up with new resolve through the layers of confusion. Through a sheer force of will, she cleared the heavy fog from her mind. Then everything crashed into her at once. She was at the Water Company with Finch. The crystal had been taken from her...and Angelo had been the one to shoot her at the Phoenix.

Her head swam with the force of it and she put her fingers to her temple and closed her eyes. Angelo's arms went around her waist, as if he could do something to help her.

She pulled away and looked up at him with a mixture of pain and anger on her face. "You're the reason I'm in here." She couldn't keep the bitterness from her voice.

His expression changed from hope to sadness. He took her by the shoulders and she struggled from his grasp. His grip tightened. "Bianca, this is very important. The room alarm sounded when you took the master crystal. How did you get out of the Water Company with it?"

The fog closed in on her again. "What?"

He shook her once, and forced her gaze to his. "Stay with me, Bianca. How did you get out before?"

"Passageways behind the walls," she said. "They run all through the building." Then suddenly, she wasn't sure. The labyrinth had thrown up another wall. She was blocked. Her brow furrowed. "What did I just say?"

He gathered her up and she let him. Her limbs felt weak. He pulled her onto his lap and crushed her to him, burying his face in the curve of her neck. "I'm going to fix this, Bianca. I swear. I'll get you out of here."

He released her and looked into her eyes. She smiled, reached up and touched his cheek. "Get me out of where?"

Chapter Ten

"Passageways behind the walls," Angelo murmured. Barefoot and wearing only the sweatpants he'd slept in, he walked from his bedroom into the bathroom. He turned the pure-water on in the sink, cupped his hands under the flow and splashed it over his face. Wearily, he rested on his elbows, bowed his head and allowed the pure-water to drip off his chin into the basin.

He had no idea what she'd been talking about. Within the last few days, between his duties, he'd tried every goddamn door, pushed on every panel in every hallway he could and had found nothing.

No, he'd been forced to figure another way out of the Water Company and he didn't like it—didn't like it one little bit.

He stood and stared at his reflection in the mirror. At some point he'd stopped shaving. He reached up and absently rubbed at the beginnings of the beard that shadowed his face. He stood there, shirtless, staring at his reflection for a long time. The expression in his eyes looked flat, dark circles marred the skin beneath them. He had not seen Bianca in forty-eight hours and it weighed heavily on him.

The computer link-up that connected all the rooms of the Water Company beeped loudly from his living room. He went to the small computer screen set into the wall near the door and pressed the incoming message key. Blue letters marched across a white screen, stating Finch's desire to see him in the observatory in twenty minutes.

He pressed the delete button and turned. Good. He could set his plan into action.

He'd thrown his uniform over a green upholstered chair in the living room. There had been a time he never would have done that. He would've hung it carefully in his closet, smoothed it over the hanger, made sure it didn't wrinkle, and treated it with the respect he'd thought it deserved. That time seemed eons ago now. He left it on the chair. For his plans he needed to give the illusion of perfect servitude and unwavering respect. He needed an unwrinkled uniform.

A perfectly pressed uniform hung in his closet. He took it into the bathroom with him and hooked it over the back of the door. After he shaved, he walked to the shower and turned on the water. He pushed his sweatpants down so they pooled at his ankles, then stepped out of them and into the white- and green-tiled stall. The water hit him hot and hard. He turned so it coursed over his shoulders and sluiced down his back. The pelt of the water massaged his aching muscles. He'd been training the guardians hard in the last couple days and he was sore from it.

A low groan of pleasure escaped him. If his plan worked, this was the last time he'd have running hot and cold purewater at his disposal. He closed his eyes and braced one hand on the smooth tiled wall. He'd better enjoy it. Tomorrow, with a little luck and a lot of preparation, they were gone from this place.

He soaped his hair and body, then rinsed and turned the water off. He stepped out, grabbed a towel and dried himself. Then he stood, naked, staring at the uniform that hung from a hook on the back of the bathroom door. Christ, he didn't want to put it on.

After pulling on a pair of boxers, he forced himself to walk to it and take the clothing off the hanger. He donned the dark blue pants, pulled on the starched black shirt and buttoned it, then slipped on black socks and shoes.

He went back into the bathroom and wiped the mirror. Using a comb, he slicked his hair neatly back against his head.

Looking at himself in the mirror, he declared himself the image of an obedient Guardian of Order.

His old self.

He locked the door behind him and headed down the corridor. Two guards stood at either side of the elevator. They nodded and said, "Captain."

Angelo grunted his acknowledgement and allowed the facial scanner in the wall to the left of the elevator to do its thing. On every floor there were scanners at both elevator and staircase, and at nearly every door. He'd noticed every fucking one of them since concocting his escape plan. The scanner beeped, glowed green and the elevator doors opened.

He punched the hundredth floor button and the elevator jolted upward. While he waited, he turned and looked out the glass back of the elevator, over the expanse of Sector Thirty. Down there were multitudes of people who relied on Finch to survive. In reality, Finch had control over every aspect of their lives, more so than the rest of the Essential Providers. Finch was like their God in a way, living inaccessibly high in the sky. Angelo now grasped the true meaning of that—the full potential nightmare of that. Finch possessed all the enhydro crystals. He alone possessed the complete knowledge of water purification. He held the lives of everyone in Sector Thirty in his hands.

The elevator stopped with a jolt and the doors opened. Angelo turned and walked straight into Finch's observatory. The glass walls showed a clear view of the Sector and the freysis-green expanse of Lake Michigan. Gray carpet spread underfoot and furniture made of shiny metal scattered the room. The whole place gleamed in metallic silver hues, broken only by the green true-plants, which sat at regular intervals along the walls and in the corners.

A guard decorated each side of the elevator and two more guards stood at the back of the room. Since Bianca had taken the master crystal and shown Finch that someone could breach the Water Company's security, Finch had not been taking any chances. He had at least two bodyguards with him constantly now, usually more. It was a serious hindrance to Angelo's plans.

Bianca sat in a chair on the right side of the room, staring out the window. Her body faced him, but her head was turned to the side. She did not acknowledge him as he entered. She sat straight, her slim body dressed in a long, blue silk dress that brushed her ankles. High-heeled shoes in the same dark shade of blue sheathed her feet. Her face was pale, as though her life force slowly leaked away with every day she spent at the Water Company. She had her hands folded primly in her lap and her ankles crossed like a lady. He wondered who had taught her to do that. Her silver-blonde hair was caught halfway up, halfway down. Careful curls spilled over her shoulders. Expensive-looking sapphire jewelry glittered at her ears and throat.

The doll was dressed and ready for her day.

Finch stood with his back to him, looking out the window.

Angelo stood at attention, like a good captain, his hands clasped at the small of his back, his feet spread apart, head held up, his face serious and his gaze confident. He cleared his throat and Finch turned toward him.

"You are dismissed," ordered Finch in a loud voice. Angelo knew he meant the other guards in the room, not himself. The guardians filed into the open elevator.

Finch drew a deep breath and let it out slowly before he spoke. "Angelo, I think the time has come for me to explain a few things to you. You are the captain here and, as such, my most valuable man. I chose you because you have certain abilities that the others do not possess and an unquestionable loyalty."

Finch paused, looked uncertain, and licked his lips. Gazing at Bianca, he continued. "I understand you spent a great deal of time with Miss Robinson before I retrieved her from you at the Phoenix. You were aware of her personality then as opposed to now, and I wondered if you might be wondering about anything."

Angelo remained silent for a moment, gathering his strength. He forced a smile, even forced it to his eyes. "You mean to ask me if I've noticed a change in Miss Robinson's personality?" He made it half question, half statement, and managed to keep all hostility from his voice. He was doing well.

"Yes. You see, she was quite...umm...unmanageable when she awoke. It became necessary for us to drug her to ensure she would not hurt herself or another. I have never told you about this drug I sometimes use because I didn't know how ethical you would think it. Only a few of the guardians are aware of it and they are sworn to secrecy."

"If you'll forgive me for saying so, I don't think it's wise you keep such secrets from your head of security."

Finch hung his head. "You're right, Angelo. It was foolish of me. I simply feared what you would think."

Angelo pushed all his hostility down and made his tone bland. "Miss Robinson was not so compliant or sweet when I was traveling with her. I suspected you'd given her something. Whatever you've done to her has calmed her." He forced a lie—one designed to comfort Finch and draw him out—past his lips. "It is an improvement." He was surprised when he didn't choke on the words.

Finch's shoulders relaxed, relieved at his reaction. Angelo wondered briefly what would happen if he stood in open rebellion. But then, he knew. If Finch felt threatened enough, he would override his authority as captain and have him taken into custody. That would leave Bianca and the crystal nowhere. No. As much as it pained him, it was better to satisfy Finch now, let him trust him. It would make the plans Angelo had devised all that much easier to execute.

Angelo's jaw clenched. With conscious effort he relaxed his muscles. "May I ask you to tell me of the drug now?"

"Of course." Finch walked around his desk, clasping his hands in front of him in an almost effeminate gesture. "The Kirans were experts at the manipulation of brain wave patterns, as you well know. In addition to alter-gun technology, they were masters at creating drugs which stimulate certain parts of the brain and put others to sleep." Finch paused and looked at him, as if to see if he was following.

"Go on, sir."

"They used a drug the French first identified in 2055 and named Oubliette. An Oubliette was a place they would imprison people long ago in France. It was a dungeon, or a deep hole in the ground. The word means *a place of forgetting*."

Angelo was not impressed with the history lesson. "You mean they'd lock people in the Oubliette they wanted to forget about." He managed to keep the fury from his voice. He was amazed at his self-control.

"Exactly, you understand the metaphor. In this case, we wanted to forget the old Bianca and create a new one, bringing more, uh, compliant and passive traits into her personality. Bring her a little more into line with who Calina had been."

"I see," he responded through gritted teeth.

"It makes the recipient lose time and have a very short-term memory. Basically, they lose themselves."

Angelo gripped his hands at the small of his back so hard pain shot up his forearms. He forced the muscles of his face to relax into a bland expression.

Finch continued. "Some people refer to it as 'being down the Oubliette'. You can see how highly useful Oubliette was to the Kirans. They used it on many important people in the beginning. Many politicians and others in positions of power were put down the Oubliette. Some suspect even President Thatcher herself was down it for a time in 2045."

Angelo spoke carefully. No anger, no hostility, just mild interest. God, how it cost him. "So instead of imprisoning her physically, you've imprisoned her within her mind."

"Not truly, Angelo. She is quite unaware she is being punished at all. Everything is perspective, after all." As if on cue, Bianca turned and looked at them with her blank eyes. Angelo wanted to scream.

"This way she knows nothing," said Angelo. "She is not aware she is being punished. She could be locked away like Dell is, imprisoned, aware of every tick of the clock's hand, aware of every day passing without the light reaching her face. This way she leads a pleasurable life."

Finch beamed as if Angelo was his son who'd just said daddy for the first time. "Yes, exactly. This is exactly how I look at it." He clasped his hands to his chest. "Oh, I'm so glad you see it this way, Angelo. I worried I'd lose the best man I had over this."

Now Angelo mouthed the speech he'd prepared the night before. "Of course not, sir. You know you have my complete loyalty and respect. You and the other Essential Providers wrote the New Covenant of Order, and according to it, you decide the fate of those who break its rules. You wrote it; therefore it is up to you to interpret it. I think you have done so in this case in a very—" he forced the next word past his lips, "—humane way."

"Excellent, Angelo!" Finch beamed at him. "Truly excellent. She feels no pain, you know."

"I must ask, sir. Have you secured the Kiran crystal she stole? I fear for its safety. I realize it is not of value, but since an attempt was made to steal it others may not have the same opinion."

"I have placed the crystal in my office safe for the time being."

"Good, sir."

"Did she-did she mention anything about the crystal to you?" Finch laughed. "I think she had some misbegotten notion the crystal could purify water." He laughed again, a little too forced. "That it was some kind of magic *water* crystal."

Angelo shrugged. "The girl was on the verge of insanity as far as I could tell, sir. Truly, I didn't pay attention to much of anything she said."

Finch clasped his hands in a gesture of satisfaction. "I'm so pleased with the outcome of this conversation. You've made me very happy."

Angelo gripped his hands tighter. "I'm so glad, sir."

"I've heard you've been running the men through many safety drills within the last couple of days."

If Finch only knew what was driving those safety drills, how he was changing the patterns of the Water Company to accommodate his escape plans. A genuine smile lit Angelo's face. "Yes sir, as recent events have shown, security here at the Water Company is sorely lacking. As captain, I have taken it upon myself to improve things."

"Excellent idea."

"I need to go over all the changes I've made with you. I'd like to arrange a meeting in your office tomorrow afternoon. It is imperative you are briefed."

"Yes, tomorrow afternoon would be fine."

"I'd like to meet around five, if that's all right. And you will not need guards in the room, sir. Some of the things I have to say are not for their ears." That wasn't even a lie.

Finch hesitated, and then nodded. "Very well. I'll see you tomorrow at five then," said Finch by way of dismissal.

Angelo unclasped his hands. They tingled as blood surged back into them. As he walked into the elevator, Bianca's distant, vacant gaze burned into him.

The crystal now lay in Finch's office safe. The safe could be opened only by Finch's secret voice command and a facial scan. If Finch looked or sounded under stress, the safe would not open and the alarms would sound. It was meant to discourage a thief from coercing Finch into opening the safe. And it *was* discouraging. But Angelo was just going to have to take the chance.

If the alarms sounded, a secondary plan of escape would have to be executed. Angelo did have a Plan B. He winced at the thought of it, but he couldn't stand one more day of her being trapped here. No more waiting. *No*. Tomorrow they would get out...with the crystal.

*****

The next afternoon, Angelo slipped his uniform shirt on over a white T-shirt and buttoned it up. Then he picked up the harness lying on the table beside him and placed it in the duffel bag with the other things he would need to break Bianca and the master crystal out of the Water Company successfully. He'd found all the equipment he'd needed in the training room. That had been the easy part. The hard part had been setting up the rest of his plan. But for better or worse, it was done.

Plan A was to get Finch to open the safe without tripping the alarm. Then Angelo would restrain Finch and he and Bianca would walk right out of the Water Company with the crystal in his pocket.

Plan B was beyond terrifying. The harness was for Plan B.

Angelo buckled his shoulder holster on, picked up the duffel bag and walked to the door. Casting a final glance around the apartment he would never see again and saying a silent goodbye to the life he'd known there, he shut the door behind him.

At five o'clock, he reached Finch's office, and the facial scanner admitted him. Finch was seated behind his desk, engrossed in paperwork. He never even saw the duffel bag, which Angelo dropped on the floor near the door.

Angelo scanned the room for Bianca. Inwardly, he breathed a sigh of relief when he spotted her sitting in the back of the room, a book propped open in her hands. He had worried this might be the one time she did not accompany Finch. She looked at him and smiled, but there was no recognition in her eyes. In fact, there was nothing in her eyes at all. Bland and cloudy, they stared in blue-green confusion from a pale face. Her hair was caught in a sleek twist and she wore a short dress of black silk and high heels. Not a practical ensemble for either Plan A or B. Especially not Plan B.

Two guardians stood on either side of the door. He'd hoped Finch would comply with his request that there be no guards present. Angelo turned to them. "Raymond and Mason, weren't you supposed to report for training in defense tactics for use in constrictive areas at five?"

"Yes, Captain Angelo, but Mr. Finch didn't want us to leave," replied Raymond.

Angelo suppressed his frustration. He didn't want them here. If they stayed, he'd have to delta them and that would cause the alarms to go off.

Angelo turned to Finch. "Mr. Finch, with all due respect, they truly do need further training in these defense tactics. They won't be gone for long, an hour perhaps, and I'll be here to protect you in the meantime."

Finch looked up from his paperwork and stared at him for a long moment. Then he waved his hand in a dismissive gesture. "Of course. I don't know what I was thinking. They're dismissed."

Raymond and Mason walked out the door.

"You have the men rappelling, I see," said Finch, with a gesture toward the window. Outside the large pane of glass, a rope hung. Angelo had anchored three rappelling ropes on the roof two days ago and had begun training some of the guardians on them. It was not work for the faint of heart. The building stretched one hundred floors high. That morning, Angelo had removed two of the ropes, but left one. Finch did not know how many there were originally and couldn't know he'd removed a couple of them.

"Yes, the building is controlled by the main computer. And computers, no matter how sophisticated, can be fallible. If for some reason the computer malfunctions one day and the tech team is unable to fix the problem, I felt it necessary that the guardians have an alternate means of leaving the building."

Finch nodded his head absently, seeming to lose interest in the subject. He looked down at his paperwork again. "Excellent.

So, Angelo, what other things are you doing to improve security?"

Now was as good a time as any. He drew his laser—not his alter-gun—and, flicking the safety off, leveled it at Finch. It made a soft whirring sound, powering up. Finch looked up at the sound with an expression of such complete shock that Angelo would've laughed if he weren't so angry. "I'm getting rid of the biggest thief in Sector Thirty."

Chapter Eleven

It took exactly two seconds for Finch to recover. He narrowed his eyes. "What do you think you're doing, Angelo?" he asked quietly. "All I have to do is give the command and the Water Company's security system will shut you in here." A look of realization crossed his features and he glanced toward the rope hanging outside the window.

He'd discovered Plan B.

Finch looked back at him. "You'd never make it out the window before the door unlocked and guardians come in."

Angelo smiled. "I have prepared for that small eventuality." He'd convinced tech they needed to temporarily program the computer to delay the opening of the door so he could conduct hypotheticals with the guardians — for training purposes.

"Computer—" started Finch.

Angelo waved the laser. "Stop! If you sound the alarm, I'll have no choice but to shoot you. After all, nothing will be stopping me then."

"You won't do that, Angelo," Finch bit off. "You care too much about the people of Sector Thirty to kill me. Who else would purify and distribute the water to your precious residents?"

Angelo smiled. "We'd figure it out, Finch, but who said anything about killing you? I thought I'd merely maim you. Shoot various parts of your body you're fond of. Laser fire is incredibly painful, you know. The skin burns and chars, the wounded tissue peels away like the layers of an onion, sometimes straight down to the bone. No, I won't kill you, but I'll make you wish I had."

Finch blanched. "What do you want?"

"Bianca and the water crystal."

"Why are you doing this?"

"Because you are not who I thought you were, Finch." His voice was calm, measured. It was low and dangerous-sounding to his own ears. "I thought you had the best interests of the survivors in mind. I thought that through you and the other Essential Providers, we could create a new society and build something truly great in the ruins of the war. But you stole all possibility of that away. You're worse than the Kirans. You've been sitting on something that could reverse the water poisoning simply to feed your own greed." His grip on the laser tightened and Angelo had to take a breath and relax his hand. "You and your father are responsible for the deaths of everyone who has died from freysis since you first learned of that crystal's true use."

"What about the woman? Why do you care what happens to her?"

His gaze flicked to Bianca. She sat, the book forgotten in her lap, staring at them both in curiosity. "That woman has more fire, intelligence and honor in her little finger than you will ever have." His voice rose. He couldn't master it any longer. "You took all that away from her, and I could kill you just for that. You will open that safe, Finch, and set these things to rights."

"I won't do it, Angelo."

He shrugged and flashed a cold smile. "Let's face facts here, shall we? I bet the alarm will sound when we attempt to open the safe. You're under a lot of stress and your voice and face will show it. I came into the room knowing that, and I'm not leaving without Bianca and the crystal. I have very little to lose, Finch. So maybe I should go ahead and shoot you now. I bet you'd change your mind about opening the safe if I used you for target practice. You don't need your right earlobe for anything, do you?" Angelo spread his legs, sighting a line of fire at the side of Finch's head.

Finch cringed and threw up his hands. "All right! All right! I'll open the safe."

Angelo lowered the laser and smiled. "Good."

Finch moved to the safe and Angelo followed him. He glanced at the back of the room and saw that Bianca was gone.

He whirled around, scanning the room for her. All he saw was one of the lightweight wooden chairs that sat near Finch's desk flying toward him. It hit him in the chest. A whoof of air escaped him only because he'd been surprised. The chair had been thrown with very little strength. He let it fall to the ground and pushed it aside. Bianca stood in front of him with a terrified look on her face, like she thought he planned to kill her.

Finch's arms wound around Angelo's waist in an effort to wrench him to the ground while he was off-guard. Angelo struggled with him, trying to retain his grip on the laser and keep Finch from drawing his holstered alter-gun or discovering Bianca's pistol, which he'd tucked at the small of his back.

"Leave him alone!" cried Bianca. Something large and heavy crashed against the back of his head. Angelo faltered for a moment, thinking he might actually pass out. He leaned on the side of the desk. Black spots dotted his vision. Only pure willpower kept him conscious. Chunks of broken blue vase littered the floor at his feet.

"See, I didn't take away all her fire," said Finch smugly.

Yeah, too bad she was employing it on the wrong side.

Finch grabbed for the laser. As Angelo struggled with him, it went off, blasting a smoking hole in the bookshelves. The smell of charred paper filled the room.

Damn. So much for Plan A.

The alarm went off and the heavy locks on the door slid home with a loud click. They were trapped. In a few moments every available guardian would be outside wanting in. Luckily, it wouldn't unbolt for ten minutes.

Angelo pushed Finch back and regained control of the laser. He leveled it at him and Finch's arms went up in a gesture of surrender. Angelo looked at Bianca, who stood a little to the side, looking terrified. "Bianca, get over by him. I have to treat you like the enemy, I guess."

She moved next to Finch.

"Why aren't the guardians in here yet?" Finch muttered.

Angelo closed the distance between them and motioned toward the safe with the laser. "Don't worry about that and open the safe. Try to relax."

He shot him a look of total disgust. "You point that laser somewhere else and I'll relax."

"Move!" Angelo ordered.

Finch moved.

Guardians banged on the other side of the door, trying futilely to open it. Ten minutes...ten short little minutes.

It took Finch five agonizing tries and three precious minutes to get the safe open. The crystal glimmered within on its small black velvet sack. Angelo reached in and took it, slid it into the pouch, then into his pocket. Just as he was closing the door, he spotted a syringe gun on the bottom shelf of the safe. He picked it up and let it lay heavy in his hand. "This is loaded with Bianca's next dose of Oubliette, isn't it?"

"No! Oh, God, no!" cried Finch. He took a step backward, his facial expression contorting in fear. Finch seemed far more afraid of the Oubliette than he was of the laser. In some deep primitive part of himself, Angelo found that very satisfying.

Angelo stalked toward Finch. He tried to escape him by going around the opposite side of the desk, but Angelo caught him by the shoulder. Without hesitation, he pressed the syringe gun to Finch's arm and squeezed the trigger. Then he released him and Finch took two steps forward and stumbled to his knees. His face went slack as the drug took hold of him.

Angelo glanced at his watch—six minutes and counting.

Bianca cowered in the corner. This next part would scare her but there was no time to worry over it now. Angelo pulled Bianca's pistol from his belt and she screamed. It was hard to imagine Bianca screaming at the sight of a gun, especially her gun, but she was doing it, long and loud.

He aimed the pistol at the floor-to-ceiling window and emptied the clip into it. The sound of the gunfire in the closed room near deafened him and the smell of hot metal and sulfur filled the air.

Mingled with Bianca's screams were the sounds of the guardians yelling and pounding on the opposite side of the door. He glanced at his watch — five minutes.

The bullets had weakened the window, but had not shattered it. He picked up Finch's heavy office chair and smashed it over and over into the glass, making sure the glass broke all the way down to the floor so they wouldn't catch themselves on any jagged pieces. Finally the window gave and the chair flew out to fall the fifty floors to the street below. Warm air rushed into the room, scattering the papers on Finch's desk. The rope dangled in front of him.

Shaking his head, the shards fell from his hair. Blood spotted his hands and arms from the tiny cuts caused by the shattering glass. He unbuckled his holster and tore off his shirt. Buttons popped and flew. He took the duffel bag from where he'd dropped it beside the door and brought it back to the window. After he'd ripped the bag open, he pulled out the harness. With fingers made sure from heightened awareness and adrenaline, he snapped the harness over his white T-shirt; pulling the straps tight and ensuring they were secure.

He went toward Bianca who watched him with wide eyes. She tried to twist away from him, but he caught her against him easily. There was no carefully aimed elbow to the solar plexus, no arm wrench. It was almost depressing. He dragged her to the window and the duffel bag on the floor in front of it. "You have to cooperate now, Bianca."

"My name is Calina!"

A dark part of Angelo wanted to turn around and shoot Finch just then—really shoot him. But Finch alone could purify the water for Sector Thirty, and who knew if the water crystal would really do what it was supposed to. He had to concern himself with getting Bianca out of there. He grabbed the other harness and turned her so her back was to him. He forced her into it. Every snap, every cinching was hard-won as she struggled against him. The harness wrapped around under her in a sort of seat made of straps, so he had to hike her skirt up to attach it. That drew outraged screams from her. She wore small black lace panties he noted, but had no time to appreciate them.

He reached into the bag, drew out a rappel device and carabiner and set them on a nearby chair. Webbing, to secure their harnesses together, came out next. He attached the length to himself, and then to Bianca, so her back was flat against his chest, and then double-checked all the attachments to ensure they were fastened. Last, he pulled out gloves for both himself and Bianca. It took precious time to get her hands into them.

He grasped the rope and pulled part of it into the room. Taking the rappel device and carabiner, he attached them to the rope. Then he clipped the carabiner to a hook centered on Bianca's harness at her chest. He would have to reach around her to control the rappel device, which would slow their descent and brake their fall.

Of course, there was going to be a whole lot more falling than rappelling.

He looked at his watch. Time was up.

The lock on the door clicked open, but he wasn't about to hang around and see what came through it. He wrapped one hand around the rappel device and the other around Bianca. He hurled them out the window just as the guardians pushed through the door.

They plummeted toward earth. He slammed on the rappel device to slow them and they fell back hard against the side of the building. Angelo twisted so he got the full impact against his back. He let up on the device and they fell hard and fast again. The wind rushed past them. The speed snatched Bianca's screams from her mouth. His heart, breath and blood flow took up residence in his nose.

Oh, fuck.

He slammed on the rappel device to slow their descent. Bianca no longer screamed, but breathed very quickly, probably in hyperventilation.

Laser fire whizzed past them and they both cringed. He looked down and wished he hadn't. They were about halfway, twenty-five stories from the ground. The dizzying height took his breath away—literally. He'd wagered the guardians wouldn't cut the rope since he had Bianca, their boss's intended wife.

God, he hoped they didn't cut the rope.

Angelo had an urge to let the rappel device go so they'd fall faster, but he worried about Bianca. "Are you okay?"

She didn't say anything, but she nodded slowly, shakily. That had to be good enough.

Laser fire ripped the air about six feet above their heads, hitting the rope. Angelo and Bianca both looked up to see the rope smoke and begin to fray. Bianca screamed. Angelo let go of the device. The rope would eventually snap under their weight. It was just a question of time. Their only chance was to make it to the ground before that happened.

The earth rushed up the meet them, whipping Bianca's hair into his face.

They were almost down, just a bit more. Hopefully, they'd beat the guardians out of the building. If not, well, then they had another problem.

The rope broke when they were about seven feet from the ground. They fell and this time Angelo's yell intermingled with Bianca's scream. They crashed to the ground, Bianca inadvertently using him as a full body cushion. A whoof of air escaped him, along with his breath. The rope came down around them.

Wasting no time, Angelo reached around to Bianca's harness, quickly finding the safety snaps and undoing them. They both struggled to their feet. Angelo's entire body screamed with pain, but he couldn't pay attention to that now. He caught Bianca fast by her upper arm so she couldn't run away.

He glanced around, noticing for the first time all the people on the street watching them curiously. They'd gathered a crowd of onlookers. No time to gawk at the gawkers though, the guardians would be out of the building and on them soon.

He started to lead Bianca away, but it was too late. The guardians were already down and out on the street. Their cries cut through the amazed murmurings of the onlookers. The crowd parted and Angelo saw a guardian leveling a laser at him.

Laser fire flashed, and white-hot pain seared his hip. He gave an agonized yell and went down, releasing Bianca.

Chapter Twelve

His hand went automatically to his injured right hip and he was immediately sorry. Pain speared him anew when he touched the wound. The flesh just above his right pelvis was split wide open, the wound red and glistening wet with fluid and blood.

The people on the street were screaming and running away. The commotion was actually a good thing. The crowd created a shield between themselves and the guardians. People gawked, others screamed and ran. The overall effect was chaos. Angelo glanced over and saw two guardians trying to push through the throng.

Angelo forced himself to take advantage of the diversion. He struggled to his feet, keeping his right leg extended. Bianca still stood beside him, looking at him with a mixture of shock, horror and pity on her face. He put pressure on his right leg and winced. Gritting his teeth against the pain, he grabbed her by the arm and ran, dragging her behind. Black spots dotted his vision and sweat beaded his forehead. It took supreme effort to stay upright and moving, but he had to get them hidden. They disappeared into the crowd and took a dark side street that Angelo knew had many hiding places.

They stayed in the shadows and moved cautiously down the street as fast as his injured hip would allow. Bianca didn't fight him. She merely followed behind. He didn't know why. Perhaps plummeting fifty stories had taken away what little will she'd had left. Or maybe her short-term memory didn't encompass her loyalty to Finch anymore.

They went from shadow to shadow, working their way out from the center toward the border. Angelo led them south, the direction Bianca had headed after she'd stolen the crystal. It was slow-going. Often they had to find a place to hide and let the guardians rush past them. Angelo took advantage of their confusion. They were hunting their very own captain for crimes against the Water Baron, and the Water Baron himself was insensible and would remain so for the time it took for the Oubliette to pass through his system. They had no solid leadership and Angelo knew they were disorganized. They'd follow protocol, however. They'd have the main thoroughfares along the border of the Center secured by late afternoon. That meant he and Bianca would have to be smart getting out of the Center.

They went to ground fifteen blocks from the Water Company. By that time he could barely walk. Adrenaline and willpower had sustained him until now, but they were fading fast. The only good thing was that the pain was so bad that his right hip and leg were almost numb. He pulled Bianca into an abandoned building in which he'd planned for them to take shelter.

He led her into an apartment on the second floor. Jagged shards of glass hung in the small windows facing the street, and the sad, decaying remnants of a dark green couch and loveseat dominated the living room. Paper and other refuse littered the floor. To his right, a small kitchen took up the back part of the apartment. The cabinets all stood open, and the shelving had been ripped out. Someone had squatted here in the not-so-distant past and they'd hung large pieces of multicolored fabric on the wall—for decoration? Angelo wasn't sure. It wasn't much, but they'd be calling it home sweet home until he recovered enough to travel on.

He turned his back on the kitchen and went to a closet in the opposite corner. Pulling open the door, he dragged out the duffel bag he'd stashed there yesterday. He'd packed extra clothing, a first-aid kit, a blanket, freysis boots for Bianca, and a freysis tent, canteens of water, nutro-wafers, sector credits and some candles.

He'd found an old, rusted crowbar way in the back of that closet when he'd put the stuff in there. Now, he picked up, walked to one of the walls and tore down one of the pieces of fabric. Every single movement was agony.

"Bianca," he breathed. "You're going to have to help me."

She walked over to him, her eyes wide.

"I'm about to make a big mess. Clean up whatever drops to the floor and hide it somewhere else in the building. Do you understand?"

She nodded.

He hefted the crowbar and his vision blackened with the pain. He paused and drew a deep breath. He had to do this now. The guardians would be searching for them and they needed a place to hide. Grunting, he swung the crowbar at the wall. The old drywall crumbled easily. He'd picked this place based on a few different criteria. One reason was the nice, thick hollow walls separating the living room wall from the outer hallway. They were just wide enough to hide someone.

He worked slowly, hacking away until there was a hole big enough that they could crawl into the wall, and made it low enough that he wouldn't pass out from the pain of his wound trying to get into it. Bianca busily cleaned up the chunks of plaster he dislodged and relocated them. Then he instructed Bianca to hang the fabric back up, covering the hole he'd made.

He stood back and surveyed the result of their efforts. "Okay," he breathed. "Good." He dropped the crowbar to the floor, staggered and nearly fell.

Bianca turned to him. "Are you all right?"

He shook his head. No, he really wasn't. "Will you help me get my clothes off?"

She looked uncertain.

"The material is irritating the wound, Bianca. I have to take my pants and shirt off."

She nodded. "All right."

He leaned against the side of the couch, carefully extracted the bag containing the crystal from his pocket, and placed it on the back of the couch. Then he unhooked his shoulder holster and dropped it to the floor. Bianca helped him get his boots off. He slid his T-shirt over his head and dropped it to the floor. It was soaked red at the hem. He unbuttoned his pants and gingerly pried the material away from where it clung to his skin, glued there by his own blood. Bianca knelt and helped him. Then he slid his pants over his hips, letting them drop to the floor. He wore only his boxer shorts. The waistband was low enough that it did not irritate the laser wound.

She stared at him but he was in too much pain to analyze it. "Could you find me clean clothes in the bag and the vial of fire salve that's in the first-aid kit?" His pants were ripped and burned by the laser fire. He'd have to change. They'd have to look as normal as possible to get out of the Center. Drawing attention to themselves would not be a good thing.

"Yes."

"Okay," he breathed. He couldn't stand any longer. He collapsed to his knees by the couch, and then lowered himself to the floor. At least there was a bright side. He couldn't feel the bump on his head made by Bianca's assault with the vase, or his back, which was a mass of bruises from the fall. His hip was a fiery black hole that sucked all other feeling away. It was his last thought before he passed out.

* * * * *

Finch rubbed at his arm where they'd injected him with the antidote to the Oubliette. He sat up from where he'd been laying on the couch in his office and shook his head to rid his mind of the last vestiges of the drug.

He looked around. Five guardians stood in the room. Raymond hovered over him with the syringe gun in hand and a worried look on his face. He never would have thought Raymond to be intelligent enough to remember the antidote. Finch was glad he'd been wrong.

"Did you catch them?" Finch snarled as soon as he felt confident enough to form words.

"Uh, no sir," answered Raymond.

He rubbed his aching head. "You mean all the guardians in the Water Company weren't able to catch *one* man and a near insensible woman?"

"They used a rope to rappel down the side of the building to the street, bypassing all the security. We've never trained for a situation like that. We couldn't get down and out of the building fast enough. Not to mention the men were confused since it was our own captain we were chasing. The leadership was fragmented."

"Excuses!" Finch roared.

"We did manage to injure Captain Angelo, sir. He could not have gotten far. We're searching a twenty-block radius very carefully and have set up blocks at the border of the Center."

Wounded Angelo? Well, that was something at least. "Don't call him captain. Don't think of him as captain. Think of him as *prey*, Raymond. Do you hear me?"

"Y-yes sir."

He raised his voice so the rest of the guardians in the room could hear. "I don't want any one of you thinking your loyalty lies with your former captain. Your loyalty only lies with Sector Thirty and me. Your former captain has betrayed me and betrayed the people of Sector Thirty. He will be dealt with most harshly."

"Yes sir."

"Good. Make that known to all the guardians. Now get me the keys to Dell's cell."

A few minutes later he walked down the hallway to the prison cells on the fourth floor, fingering a key. Fury built inside him like a bomb ready to explode. The master crystal and the twin were gone. Angelo, of all people, had betrayed him. His most loyal dog had bitten his hand when he wasn't looking, but that was no matter because now he'd put that dog down.

He slid the key into the lock on the cell door and he heard it click open. The small room was dark. He flicked on the light, revealing one narrow bed, a sink and a toilet. Even the prisoners got running pure-water at the Water Company. No one could say he was unkind. The man on the bed groaned and put his arm up to shield his eyes.

"Dell," Finch said.

Dell removed his arm and squinted against the bright light. Black hair furred his face. He hadn't been shaving. His nose was a myriad of interesting colors and puffy yet from his injury. "Mr. Finch?" he asked nasally.

Finch approached him. "I have a job for you, Dell. A really important one. If you do it right, you'll be captain."

Dell smiled, then winced at the pain it must've caused. "What happened?"

Finch told him the story. "You were right all along, Dell. And I didn't believe you."

Dell went still and looked stunned. "I was right?" he asked.

He nodded solemnly. "I apologize for not believing you."

A knowing look passed over Dell's face and he stood up, straightened his shirt and ran a hand over his stubbled chin. "They'll go south, the same direction the girl went the first time. I'll want a hovercraft."

"Anything you need, it's yours. But, Dell?"

"Yes."

"You make sure you kill Angelo. I'd like the twin back, but you have my permission to kill her too, if she causes you too much trouble. Get that crystal back at all costs."

A slow smile spread across Dell's face. "Hunting season is officially open then?"

"Yes."

* * * * *

Angelo opened his eyes slowly. Nighttime darkness met his gaze, cut by a soft light that flickered over him. Bianca had lit the candles he'd put in the pack.

He felt a warm, slim body pressed against his side. Raising his head, he first noticed Bianca's arm lying over his stomach, second that her short skirt was hiked up to the sweet curve of her buttocks, and finally, almost as an afterthought, the pain in his hip.

As soon as he noticed the pain, it slashed through him so intense it bowed his spine. An agonized groan accompanied his movement. She scrambled away from him.

She fumbled for the salve and came toward him on her hands and knees. She extended her palm, showing him the vial. "I found the salve in the first-aid kit." Her blank eyes were wide and frightened.

He reached out, caught her wrist and drew her closer to him. Reaching out, he cupped her cheek against his palm. "Bianca, are you in there anywhere?" Nothing. No reaction. Just a wide-eyed, blank stare. He sighed and released her.

She handed him the vial and he squeezed some of the cream onto his fingers, and then gingerly pressed it to his hip. He let out a sharp hiss at the pain and closed his eyes, fighting the unconsciousness that beckoned to him with heavy hands.

He fell back onto the floor and let the salve do its thing. Blessed numbness spread over the wound. He felt the soft brush of Bianca's hair against the bare skin of his upper arm and his eyes opened. She knelt beside him, looking down at him. Her sun-colored hair hid her face. "Are you all right? Does your wound give you trouble?"

He smiled. "The wound really hurts, but it's numbing now. Thanks for finding the salve." He struggled to sit up. In the soft light, Angelo saw that she'd cleaned the cuts on his hands and forearms made from the shattering glass in Finch's office and had dabbed disinfectant on them. "And thanks for this," he said, indicating his arms.

"No problem." Her gaze flicked down the length of his body and back up to his eyes. The look on her face took him aback. There was heat there, not feigned. This was real lust. She made no move to disguise it. Another side effect of the Oubliette, maybe? Pure honesty? Perhaps a deep part of her remembered the night at Hank's and the kiss in the bathing room of the Phoenix.

"You're the one who kissed me before, after dinner when you brought me to my room." Her hair had pulled out of its sleek twist long ago and was as mussed as ever. At least she looked like herself.

"Yes. Do you remember that?"

"I remember the kiss, not much more." There was a flicker in her eyes of the real Bianca.

It was enough.

He pulled himself to a sitting position and drew her near him. She scooted toward him and placed her hands on his upper arms. He wound his hand around the back of her neck, and let the other fall to the edge of her skirt and trace the line where it lay against her thigh. Something deep and dark within him wanted to push his hand up under it and feel the panties he'd had a glimpse of before.

He let his lips barely brush hers and trace their way over her cheek and down her neck. She shuddered and let her head fall back, exposing the perfect line of her throat. He lingered over her smooth skin, felt her pulse speed up under his lips. He kissed it and moved to the tender flesh under her ear, letting the tip of his tongue draw a gentle line there. Then he guided her mouth to his and tasted it. Coaxing her lips apart, he kissed her as if somewhere in her sweet mouth he could find the real Bianca and draw her out.

The real Bianca.

God, how he missed her.

With a groan he pulled away from her. She looked so confused and bereft that he wanted to crush her to him and kiss her again. Bianca hesitated for a moment and then reached out and touched his face, running her finger down the line of his jaw. Then she dropped her hand to his chest and ran her palm over it curiously, like a child who'd just discovered something new.

He hoped she didn't go any lower or she'd have a real surprise. Every part of his body was responding to her, and as long as she touched him like that, with that heat in eyes, it wouldn't abate. Despite his injuries he was hard for her. It was a testament to the power she wielded over him.

"Why don't you want to kiss me?" she asked. Pain shone clearly on her face even in the dim candlelight.

"Because you are not yourself, Bianca. I like and respect the person you are when you have not been altered by Finch's drugs. Right now you are someone I don't know. It makes it difficult for me to kiss you."

Her lower lip trembled. "Whoever I am," she said softly. "I want you to kiss me. I want more than a kiss. When you kissed me before strange things happened to my body. Things happened to make me want more than a kiss." She shook her head. "That never happened when Mr. Finch kissed me." She tilted her head to the side. "Why?"

Angelo's hands fisted at the mental image of Finch kissing her. He gritted his teeth and let out a slow, careful breath. "Because you and I share a powerful attraction," he replied.

"Yes," she said solemnly. She pulled her dress over her head.

His gaze slipped down over her body. She wore black, lacy panties and a matching bra.

Fuck.

He turned his head away and ground his teeth. Even under the influence of drugs she tempted and teased him. He leaned in toward her, ignoring the pain of his hip. The cream had numbed it up well, but it was still a little sore. His gaze caught and held at her lush mouth. "It wouldn't be right," he growled an inch from her face.

She shrugged. "None of this seems right to me. The only thing that does feel right is your hands on me."

He stared at her for several heartbeats and then pushed her down to the carpet beneath him. "Bianca," he shook his head. "You're incredible."

Her fingers went to the clasp at the front of her bra and undid it. The lacy cups lay over her breasts. One little flick of his wrist and... He pushed the cup off one of her breasts and watched the small pink nipple harden. Bracing himself above her, he dipped his head and laved it. With his other hand, he pushed the opposite cup off her breast and covered the mound with his hand. Her breasts were small, but sweetly curved. He could probably fit the whole of one in his mouth. He tried it and found he could. He sucked and licked her nipple like it was a piece of candy.

She bucked beneath him and let out a little sighing moan that made his cock go rigid. He couldn't make love to her, but he could explore her body with his hands and mouth. He could make her come for him over and over.

He wouldn't get any relief from it, but damn, he loved to her hear moans and cries. He wanted to feel her bare sex on his hand and tongue, if he couldn't feel it wrapped around his cock.

With one hand, he slipped her underwear down. She kicked them the rest of the way off and parted her thighs for him. He leaned back and took in the sight of her in lying there naked. Her pink pussy was plumped and aroused. She'd creamed up nicely for him, ready to take his cock. She lay there looking up at him, spread out like a five-course meal. He hardly knew where to begin.

He groaned. "Sweet heaven," he murmured. "That's what you look like to me." He leaned down and kissed the smooth skin above her navel.

"Your hip," she said with concern.

"Baby," he murmured against her as he worked his way down to her sweetest spot. "With your pretty little pussy so close to my tongue, I can't even feel it, believe me." He trailed his tongue through her short, curly blonde pubic hair and swiped his tongue across her swollen clit.

Bianca gasped and buried her fingers in his hair.

"Do you like that?" he murmured.

"Yes," she hissed.

He settled down between her thighs, resting his weight on his good hip. With his thumb, he spread her folds apart, examining all the beauty that was Bianca. God, she was so lusciously creamy. She wanted him badly. He licked her from her anus to her clit with long, sure strokes and pulled the small, aroused bundle of nerves between his lips, gently sucking. He groaned at the sweet taste of her spreading over his tongue as he lapped at her. Her engorged clit had pulled all the way out from its hood. It looked like a luscious piece of red candy and he sucked at it, treating as such. She arched her back, stabbing her nipples into the air.

"You want more?" he asked her, pulling away just long enough to speak. He pulled her labia into his mouth and massaged them between his lips.

"More," she panted.

He toyed with her clit, feeling it grow larger against the tip of his tongue. He circled it, drew it into his mouth and back out, enjoying the sensation of it against his tongue and enjoying her reaction even more. Her hips bucked forward, as though looking for something to impale herself on. He stroked a finger idly over her folds, rubbing and caressing them with his fingertip. Then he speared his tongue into her pussy, pulling out her cream and swallowing it down, fucking her with his tongue.

"Ah, yes," she moaned, tossing her head from side to side.

"You like that, baby?" he purred. "I know I do." He set once more to spearing his tongue in and out of her until she keened for him.

"Yes," she breathed.

He grinned at her carnal greediness and toyed with the entrance to her pussy, stroking over the sensitive skin there, while he sucked on her clit. Finally, he slid a finger into her.

Angelo threw his head back and groaned at the feel of her muscles gripping his finger. She was so hot and tight. Bianca had placed her feet flat on the floor on either side of him and spread her thighs as wide as she could. She whimpered and moaned as he drew his finger out and slowly pushed it back into her softness.

"You want more?" he asked hoarsely. God, this was killing him.

"More," she said plaintively.

He slipped another finger down and added it to the first. His fingers slipped in easily because of how wet she was, but her muscles were tight and clamped down around him. Her pussy was tight as a virgin's. His cock, not that he'd ever slide it into her, was longer and thicker than most men's. Hell, she might have trouble taking him she was so tight.

"Faster. Harder," Bianca gasped.

His mouth twitched. Or maybe not.

He drew his hand back and thrust into her. She dug her fingers into the carpet on either side of her. He set up an easy rhythm afraid he might hurt her. According to what she'd revealed at the Phoenix, she'd only had sex once in her life and that had been unwillingly.

He lowered his mouth to her clit and sucked it between his lips. Her body tensed and she cried out as she climaxed. The muscles of her pussy spasmed around his fingers and her hips bucked again. He stroked her clit until she quieted and pulled himself free of her body with regret.

His cock was so damn hard it hurt.

Angelo rolled to his back via his uninjured side and groaned in torture. Suddenly, Bianca was there, leaning over him, kissing him. He snaked a hand to the back of her head and crushed his mouth to hers. He parted her lips and let his tongue mate with hers. Her hand smoothed down his chest and rubbed at his rigid cock beneath his pants. He had her wrist in a flash.

She looked at him in surprise.

He shook his head. "Fuck, Bianca, you'll make me come in my pants. Please, no touching."

"Come in *me*," she said, confused.

He cupped her cheek in his head. "I wish I could, but that's something that can never happen."

She opened her mouth to say something else in the same moment he sensed them outside on the street. Their presence cut her response off.

Finch's hovercraft rose from the street below to hang like a vicious hummingbird in the air right outside the broken and grimy windows of the room they'd taken shelter in. The craft made a loud whirring noise and created a wind that blew the refuse around the room. The bright searchlight on the front of the craft lit up everything to the left of them in a searing glare.

Bianca screamed. Angelo covered her mouth with his hand and pulled her behind the couch. He'd bet his life there were guardians on the street outside.

The candles still stood, glowing in the center of the room. The duffel bag and clothing lay in a pile next to the couch. Why didn't he and Bianca just hang a sign on the outside of the building telling the world they were here?

The door to the building downstairs slammed open. "Spread out! Spread out! Search every room, every hiding place!" came a guardian's command.

Whoever operated the hovercraft, Dell probably, likely had the motion scanner engaged. But with so many guardians swarming the building, it'd be difficult to use. That was to their advantage.

The concentrated swath of light illuminated the room slowly from left to right. Before the candles and supplies were bathed in the searchlight, Angelo lunged out and grabbed them.

The pain of his wound seared him afresh. He gritted his teeth against it, extinguished the candles, grabbed the bag, their clothing and the crystal and pulled it all behind the couch just as the light reached him.

Angelo grabbed his alter-gun and the crystal and stuffed the rest into the duffel bag. Footsteps pounded up the stairs. The calls of the guardians grew nearer. Angelo eyed the wall where he'd made their hiding place, sweat breaking out on his forehead. They couldn't go for it until the light passed them over and they had the darkness to conceal their movement.

The guardians might reach them before then.

The men yelled to each other in the hallway right outside the apartment and Angelo gritted his teeth.

Chapter Thirteen

Breathing heavily, every second feeling like an eternity, they waited until the light trolled past them. Then he grabbed the duffel bag, took Bianca's hand and they ran to the wall. He flipped the fabric up so it draped them, slid the duffel bag in into the opening in the wall, and then lifted Bianca in. She remained naked and barefoot. That was regrettable, but there was no help for it. He hoisted himself up and into the hole. Pain from having to move this quickly and acrobatically ripped through him, even with the salve on his wound. He bit the inside of his lip so hard it bled against the pain. He couldn't pass out—not now. He had to get Bianca through this.

It was a very tight squeeze and it took him some considerable maneuvering to get down into the space. Bianca had some space to move, but he was wedged in. The wall compressed his chest with every breath he took. The fabric settled back gently against the wall, completing the illusion.

In the darkness, he felt the alter-gun, making sure it was set to delta. They would be gunning for him with more than an alter-gun, but he couldn't bring himself to kill any of his men.

Except Dell. Yes, he'd be able to kill him.

Bianca pressed herself to his side, her breath coming fast and hard. He shushed her and she quieted. If she hadn't been under the influence of the Oubliette she'd probably be holding her pistol right now, cocked and ready.

"Don't move," he breathed at her.

The sound of doors slamming open and furniture being tipped over filled the tense air. The guardians were like a tornado ripping through the building. He knew the drill, had helped to perfect it—three men to a room. One worked to the left of the entrance, one to the right, and one straight down the middle. Angelo had never had to work that way, however. All he'd had to do was ride his horse down the center of the street and sense the buildings, feel for the presence of the person they were searching for.

The door to their apartment banged open, startling Bianca. The guardians set about flipping over furniture and slamming open doors. He heard sounds that made him think they might be tearing the kitchen cabinets apart. Beside him, Bianca sucked in a breath and held it.

The thumping sound of guardian boots walking the perimeter of the room came dangerously close to their hiding spot. One the men brushed the fabric covering their hole and Bianca sucked in a breath. Unable to clap a hand over her mouth, Angelo squeezed her hand instead. She put a hand over her mouth and gave a tiny whimper.

Angelo held his breath and waited. The guardian moved away.

Long minutes passed. Finally, the guardians left their apartment. About twenty minutes later they moved to the next building, but Bianca and Angelo stayed hidden until long after they heard the hovercraft leave and the men move on.

After approximately fifteen minutes of complete silence, he deemed it safe to leave their hiding spot. With groans of pain ripped from the center of his soul, he pushed himself back out of the hole. The numbing salve had worn off.

He collapsed on the floor, breathing heavy. The apartment looked like a disaster zone. "Grab...grab the duffel bag, will you, Bianca?" He swallowed hard.

A moment later the duffel bag thumped to the floor beside him. He started pushing himself to his feet to help Bianca out of the hole.

"No," she said. "I can get out on my own. Rest."

She climbed out, fished her dress out from the bag and donned it. Then she knelt beside him. "Are you all right? You're bleeding again."

He glanced down. No big surprise there. It was worse that they were both covered in dust and grime, and dust and grime in his open laser wound wouldn't be doing him any good. The probability he'd contract laser fever was already high.

* * * * *

Bianca went for the bandages and the canteen of purewater in the duffel bag. The man's wound needed tending after he'd been crawling around in the dirty, dusty walls, and she was the only one there to do it.

She lit the candles and set out the water and bandages, then turned to him. "Please, lay down."

He came without protest and lay down in the circle of firelight. She doused the wound with some of the water. He sucked in a sharp breath of pain when it hit him. It trickled to the floor, tinged red from his blood. She winced for him. "Sorry. I don't know anything about tending a wound, but I'm guessing it needs to be kept clean," she said.

"With a wound this bad, there's a chance I could contract laser fever, Bianca. Flesh wounds made by laser fire are susceptible to infection. There's disinfectant in the kit."

She got the disinfectant and poured it liberally onto the wound. He let out a hiss of pain through a clenched jaw. She unwrapped the large bandages, removing their backing and carefully covered the wound with them. "This should help."

Bianca sat back on her heels and looked at him. He wore only a pair of dark blue boxer briefs. His legs, arms and chest were tightly muscled, not bulging—but with nice definition, revealing unquestionable strength. His flat stomach rippled with muscle. A long scar curled like a snake to rest on that perfect stomach, winding its way around from his back.

The scar was fascinating. "How did you get that?" She pointed to his abdomen.

"You don't remember having a conversation about this before, do you?"

She shook her head. "I don't even know your name. No, I don't remember any conversation, only a kiss. Three kisses now." Heat flooded her face and she looked away. "And the rest of what we did."

He sat up and leaned toward her. She returned her gaze to his eyes. "My name is Angelo, Bianca. You'll remember that soon enough. The scar..." he hesitated. Pain flashed across his features that had nothing to do with his physical wound. "I got it when I was young, about thirteen. There was a man who didn't like what I was and wanted to punish me. Actually, he wanted to kill me — nice and slow."

Bianca reached out and traced the scar on his stomach. He flinched, but let her do it.

"He used a whip," he continued. "He said he'd whip it all out of me or I'd die while he was trying. He said I was better off dead than being what I was."

"Whip what out of you?"

He went silent. She traced the line of the scar around his side and then removed her hand. She wanted to reach up and feel his chest. It had been hard and soft all at once under her palm before, also fascinating. Instead she folded her hands in her lap. She could see he wrestled with something. It was like he wanted to tell her some kind of secret, but couldn't bring himself to do it.

Finally, he spoke. His voice sounded low and ragged with emotion. "I don't know if you'll remember this conversation after you're out of the Oubliette, Bianca. I don't want to tell you."

"I won't hate you for what you are, Angelo. I can see you're a good man."

He made a scoffing noise. "That's the Oubliette talking. You thought Finch was a good man too—even tried to defend him. No, I'm not a good man. I have bad blood, the worst imaginable."

"But—"

"We should sleep now. We have a lot of traveling to do tomorrow."

Bianca reached over and snuffed out the candles. Angelo lay down and she tucked herself up against him on his left side, letting her hand rest over the scar on his stomach. "What are we doing running from Mr. Finch's Guardians of Order and hiding out in this building?"

"Nothing much, Bianca. Just trying to save the world."

* * * * *

Angelo awoke sore and stiff. Pain coursed through his body, but he was getting used to the sensation of constant pain now. The wound seemed more sensitive today than it had yesterday. He shifted in discomfort and accidentally woke Bianca.

She sat up and put a hand to his forehead. "You're warm." Her eyes were wide with alarm. "And you look like you're hurting. Aren't there any painkillers in the first-aid kit?"

He shook his head. "We've got to move out, get past the border today. Staying here is too dangerous." He pushed himself into a sitting position. Blood rushed through his body. He actually felt it flowing through his veins, and it left nothing but hurt in its wake.

He looked at the bandage. Around the edges of the wound, the flesh was an angry purple-red—a telltale sign of laser fever.

Bianca lightly touched the bandage and let out a gasp. "You need a medic."

"No time for that. Anyway, it's too dangerous." He placed a hand to his head where a headache raged. "We need a horse, Bianca. I won't be able to travel any other way."

He tried to stand up, lost his balance and sat back down. Pain shot through his hip at the impact. Bianca's cool hands went to his heated arms, helping him to his feet.

He searched out the extra pair of pants and clean white T-shirt that he'd packed and pulled them on. The waistband of the pants would've rubbed his wound if it hadn't been for the bandage. As it was, he'd have to be careful it didn't rub the covering away.

They'd have to obtain transportation first thing. He dug through the bag for the credits he'd packed. There would be no way he could walk the distance they had to travel.

Bianca packed up their gear as he struggled to get his boots on. When they were ready to leave, he took the bag from her and limped out the door with Bianca trailing. He took the stairs carefully, one by one. Climbing them the day before had been easier because of the adrenaline that had coursed through his veins. Finally, they reached the street and stepped into the sunlight.

He'd selected this building as a hiding place for their gear for strategic reasons. Not far away was a man who sold horses. That's where they were headed.

They walked down the sparsely populated street, passing people every once in a while. Angelo's awareness felt heightened to each and every one, watching for guardians on patrol. People passed them on their way to buy supplies at the market and children ran up and down the street calling to one another. The damaged sidewalk rose up in crumbling ridges they had to skirt from time to time. They passed a real-food vendor and the smell of roasted pure-turkey rolled out and covered them over. A small stand with a selection of pure-fruit for sale at unbelievably high prices stood just inside the establishment's double doors.

He'd thrown the duffel over his right shoulder and taken Bianca's hand in his left one. Here they were, just two young lovers headed down the street hand in hand. That's what he wanted the passerbys to see. He didn't want them to notice his limp, the feverish sweat that glistened on his forehead, or Bianca's black dress, dusty and ripped in places. Miraculously, she still had her small black sandals, though they were worn and scuffed now. Bianca wound her arm around his waist, and she coaxed him to put some of his weight on her.

They turned a corner and Max's business came into view. It had been an old gas station at one time. The pumps had been torn out long ago and the parking lot fenced in. The pavement had been ripped up and grass planted. Growing grass was a dangerous and highly expensive operation because you had to deal with tainted water to keep it healthy. Those that had enough money to afford the permit, and the massive amounts of pure-water it took, had small indoor patches of grass. Max's patch was large and outdoors, exposed to the rain. It was testament to how well Max did in his business. In this makeshift pasture, a number of horses roamed, pulling up grass made a vibrant green by freysis.

Angelo prayed the guardians had not notified the local horse dealers of the search. As captain, that would have been one of the first things he'd ordered. But he wasn't captain now, and he knew the ranks were confused. He was taking a chance, a big chance that this concern had been lost in the tumult and the power struggle that had undoubtedly ensued after his departure. He was betting on it.

He was betting a lot on that.

He approached the fence and saw Max discussing something with one of his employees near the small building that served as his office. Max spotted him and waved. A few moments later, he walked across the grass in his knee-high freysis-proof boots.

"Angelo, my God, I haven't seen you in a long time." His gaze swept over Bianca. "And with a woman, too. Careful, I'm an old man. You'll make me pass away from shock."

"Hi, Max," he answered.

Everything seemed all right. Max wasn't showing any outward signs of knowledge that he was a fugitive. He urged himself to ignore the pain of his hip and sound casual, normal, chatty...*Christ*. "So how's business?"

"Oh, same as always, fast and furious, making loads of credits. I think we're actually starting to bring the Sector's economy to something resembling stability."

"I hope you're right."

Max squinted, examining him. "You all right, Angelo? You aren't looking that great, downright flushed, in fact."

Definitely time for a topic change. "I feel great," he lied. "Listen, I came by because I need to buy a horse from you. I'm in kind of a hurry." He pointed to a chestnut-colored gelding that had a white slash down his nose. "I'll take that one, if he's available."

"Whoa, Angelo. What's the rush? Usually you ride a few before you plunk down the cash."

"Yes, like I said I'm—"

"—in a hurry."

"Yeah."

"In too much of a hurry to introduce me to this pretty thing hanging off your arm?"

He forced a smile. "'Course not, Max. This is Bianca. A friend of mine." No sense lying.

Max bowed. "You are one lovely woman, Miss Bianca."

"Thank you," she replied.

He winked. "You've stolen our captain's heart away. I can see it clear as day. Clear as day! And that, my dear, is a feat of impossible proportions. I thought our young captain would never find love."

Angelo shifted his weight impatiently. It was clear that deep in the Oubliette, Bianca didn't know what to make of Max's comments. It was just as well. He could only imagine what she'd have to say if the drug wasn't still in her system.

Max's gaze flicked back and forth between them, as if sensing he'd made them uncomfortable. "All right, enough fun and games. Let's get you that horse." He turned and walked into the pasture, took the horse by the lead and guided him to the gate.

Angelo suppressed a sigh of relief.

"This horse is named Jinx," said Max.

"Jinx?" He hoped it wasn't a prophetic name.

"You managed to pick out the only horse in the lot that isn't sold. The rest are already gone. I'm just holding them for the buyers. So it's either Jinx, or you wait until I get more stock in here. He's a fast one."

"I'll take him." He pulled a handful of credits from his pocket.

"You certain?"

"I'm sure. I'll take the gelding. I'll be needing tack too." He pushed some money at Max.

Max took it, counted some out and handed the rest back to Angelo. "All right then, one gelding named Jinx with all the tack coming right up." The old man turned and led the horse away to saddle it and slip a bit and bridle on.

Angelo leaned back against the fence and relaxed. Max knew nothing.

The old man returned a few moments later leading the horse and gave the reins over to Angelo.

"Thanks for the horse, Max. You take care." Angelo turned to lead the horse away. He didn't want Max to see him mount it. It was going to be excruciating. Bianca fell into step beside him.

"No, Angelo, *you* take care," Max called behind him.

Angelo turned and stared at him.

"Good luck to you," said Max meaningfully, then he turned and walked away.

Angelo led the gelding down the street. Perhaps Max had known.

*****

Bianca wound her arms around Angelo, who sat in front of her on the horse, in an effort to steady him. He'd grown worse as the day progressed. By late afternoon, they had reached a desolate stretch that, according to Angelo, formed the informal barrier between the Center and Out-Center.

Getting onto the horse had been incredibly painful for him, but he was on now and hopefully he wouldn't have to go through the pain of a dismount for a while. They'd traveled slow, kept off the main thoroughfares and in the shadows as much as possible. They'd seen some guardians, but had been able to avoid them every time.

Angelo's head dipped forward and she shook him anxiously, trying to prevent him from taking a tumble off the horse. He straightened. She couldn't count how many times that had happened in the last hour.

"Are we nearly there, Angelo?" She kept asking him that in an effort to keep his fevered mind on the task at hand.

"Nearly to Out-Center," he pushed out. "We'll find a place to hide soon."

"Do you want some water?"

"No. We're almost there…after…after we get into Out-Center. Then we'll stop."

The man needed water. If he didn't drink enough water, he'd pass out. She groped in the saddlebag for a canteen and pushed it into his hands. "Drink. If you pass out and fall from the horse we'll never get wherever it is you want to go."

"You're right." He took the canteen and tipped his head back. She peered around him and saw some of the precious water course from his mouth, trail down his face and wet his T-shirt. He didn't even have the motor skills to drink water. Pure willpower was likely the only thing keeping him going. Soon his body would override his mind and he would slip into unconsciousness. He handed the canteen back to her and she put it away.

They passed a park, the rusty play-set keeping lonely sentinel in large grassy area overrun with wild weeds and small animals. She'd noticed right away that weeds and animals had taken over parts of the Sector that were unoccupied.

Angelo reined the horse down a small sidewalk that led to a huge brown building. It stretched for several blocks. A sign out front proclaimed it a hospital. Half the roof and part of the front of the structure had collapsed. He led the horse through the broken down double doors, letting the weeds that hung across it slap his face, and making no move to push them away. Bianca ducked her head and hid her face in his back to avoid them, noting uneasily how heated his body felt against her cheek.

The horse's hooves echoed through the empty corridors. A feeling of suppressed energy, an echo of the former occupants, tickled her spine with ghostly fingers. The inside of the building smelled like a combination of mold, dust and growing things. Vines climbed the walls and grew through the cracked floor. Angelo led the horse through down a dark corridor and into a lobby.

The back door to the lobby had been ripped from its hinges. Angelo headed the horse through it, and they entered what had been a back parking lot. At the edge of the lot a tall fence topped with razor wire rose before them. No opening existed for as long as Bianca could see. Her heart sank.

Angelo swung his left leg over the horse's head before Bianca could stop him. He paused with both legs on one side, ready to dismount, and let a low, slow breath escape his lips. Then he slid off the horse and stumbled forward.

He ran his hands along the fence, searching for something. After a few minutes, he found a place where the fence had been cut and he bent it back carefully. The cut section was high enough that they could get the horse through.

"Smugglers use this to get into the Center," he explained. He walked back and led the horse through it. Bianca ducked low to the horse's neck to clear the opening. After he'd pushed the wire back he walked toward the horse…but he never made it.

He fell to his knees and then collapsed to the ground. Bianca slid from the horse and ran to him. His eyes were closed, his face flushed and he was unconscious.

Chapter Fourteen

The sun beat down on them with the ferociousness that only midsummer can bring. She shielded her eyes against the glare on the destroyed expanse of the concrete parking lot. A tree stood some distance away, providing shade. She grabbed him by the arm and pulled with everything she had, but he didn't budge an inch. Too heavy.

She had to find help. Bianca rose and whirled around, heading straight into what Angelo had said was Out-Center.

She reached the street on the opposite side of the hospital's lot and started calling for help at the top of her lungs. Her voice echoed down the deserted streets. She ran through the alleys, not realizing she was getting lost until it was too late. Soon, she stopped in the center of a lonely street and knew it with certainty. She would never be able to find her way back to him.

He was going to die because she'd gotten herself lost.

Tears crowded the back of her throat, threatened to rise and spill out. She drew a breath and calmed herself. She hadn't always been this way, had she? No, once she'd been capable. Glimmerings of a person she'd once known began to leak through and tease the edges of her mind. Was it herself? Mentally, she grabbed for them, but they eluded her like the wisps of a dream soon forgotten in the bright light of wakefulness.

She sat down on a street and breathed heavily through her nose. It was imperative she regain control of this situation. Angelo could not die because of her.

Drawing a breath, she stood up and again called for help in a voice fast growing hoarse. She didn't have to wait long before help appeared, but she wasn't sure it was the kind she wanted.

From around the corner of a building came an enormous man with long light brown hair. He wore a pair of old, faded jeans and a ripped red-checkered shirt. A week's worth of beard marked his face. He looked at her like she might be something really good to eat. The look in his eyes seemed to speak not of compassion, or aid, but of darker, more violent things.

"Hello, miss, are you in trouble?" His voice was low. He was trying to sound nice, harmless, but the hunch of his shoulders told a different story. It said one word—*predator*.

She put up a hand, palm out, as if to ward him away. "Uh, no, actually I'm just fine. Thanks."

He cocked one sandy-colored brow. "Really? I guess there's another pale-haired woman around here screaming for help at the top her pretty lungs, then? You can't stay around here. You better come with me, now, miss." He held out a hand as though he wished to calm her.

She wouldn't let this man fool her. She wasn't going anywhere with him. "No, I can't. I've got to see to my friend. He needs help."

He took step forward and she took a step back. She readied herself to flee.

"I'm not going to hurt you," he soothed.

She shook her head and tried a shaky smile. "Of course you're not going to hurt me. Uh, I have to go now." Her voice shook. She turned around and began to walk away.

"Miss, really," he said adamantly.

She turned around to face him.

"You can't wander around the Out-Center being a woman alone and looking like that." He gestured toward her dress and licked his lips at the same time.

It was an innocent enough gesture, but it did it for Bianca. She whirled and ran. He gave chase. Strong arms closed around her midsection and lifted her. Some primal, instinctive reaction took hold. She flailed her legs, the heels of her sandals striking true at his shins. She reached back and tore at his hair, yanking it forward. She came away with greasy hank of it in her hand. He bellowed in pain, but didn't release her. If anything, his grip became more vise-like.

He held her around the waist as she writhed and fought and simply carried her away. She kicked out in front of her and only succeeded in losing her shoes.

"I can't let you run from me. You run from me and you run straight to rape or death, maybe both."

Bianca ceased struggling only because she realized her skirt had ridden up perilously high. It was no use anyway; she'd never overcome this giant. He took her to a tall, mostly undamaged building, and carried her down a hallway that had been scrubbed clean. Even the cracked and crumbling drywall had been repaired.

She shuddered. He would probably kill her here in his lair.

At the end of the hallway, he kicked a door open. On the other side was a large room. Bianca scanned it while still in the giant's grasp. Two men. One was middle-aged with long, blond hair. The other sat on a long couch. He was younger and had brown hair. Movement caught Bianca's gaze. A woman with long red-blonde hair secured in a ponytail at the nape of her neck stood in a kitchen area in the back of the room. They all stared at her in surprise. The man set her on her feet.

"Don't try to flee," said the giant. "I just did you a good turn whether you believe it or not."

She looked up at him. Earnestness marked his features. Maybe she'd judged him by his impressive appearance too quickly.

"Little bird," said the younger man in a tone of surprise.

The giant turned and looked at him. "You know this woman, Gannon? I found her screaming her lungs out for help while walking around Out-Center. Doesn't even have a gun or knife on her. I brought her here before she got herself killed."

The older man stood and came toward her. "You, your name is Bianca, isn't it?"

"I don't know." She honestly didn't. Mr. Finch had called her Calina. Angelo called her Bianca. She just wasn't sure.

He took her chin in one hand and stared deep into her eyes. "You don't remember me, do you?"

"No," she said through the jaw he'd caught in his strong fingers. He wasn't hurting, but it was a steady pressure.

"I'm Quint." He released her, swearing under his breath. "You're deep in the Oubliette, Bianca. I can see it in your eyes. How long since the bastards last dosed you?"

Her brow furrowed. There *had* been shots, hadn't there? Memories, unless they were very special ones, seemed to fade so quickly. She concentrated. "Yesterday in the early afternoon." They'd given her one right before Angelo had come to Mr. Finch's office.

"You'll be out of the Oubliette by tomorrow evening, Bianca."

She shrugged. It meant nothing to her. "I need your help." She had to tell him where Angelo was before the memory slipped away. "I left a man on the other side of the Center's border, in the back lot of a huge brown building."

"Behind the hospital?"

"Yes. Please, he's injured and sick and he'll die if he doesn't get help. He's unconscious now." Tears welled in her eyes.

Quint touched her arm in a reassuring gesture. "It's okay, we'll get him and bring him here, all right?"

She nodded, trying to suppress the sob lodged in her throat.

Quint swept past her and motioned to the giant. "Dugan, you come with me." He turned to the younger male. "Gannon, you too. Come on, let's hurry." All three went out the door.

Bianca's knees went out from under her and she caught herself on a nearby chair before she collapsed.

The woman came toward her. "I'm Marie. Come and sit down." She smiled. "Better yet, you look tired. Would you like to lie down and sleep for a while? I bet when you wake up you'll know yourself again."

Genuine caring infused her voice. It undid Bianca completely and she didn't know why. Deep sorrow welled from some unknown source within her. She allowed silent tears to course down her cheeks. "No. I should stay here. I need to know if he's all right."

"He'll be fine. They'll bring him here and we'll do everything we can to help him. We even have a physician here. Now, you need to take care of yourself. You'll start to climb out of the Oubliette soon, and that is never a happy time. You fight for your personality over and over, but never truly get it back until you're out of that deep, dark hole completely. I know the experience well. Better that you sleep through it."

Marie led her out a door at the back of the room, and down a short hallway that had doors off either side. They entered a small room with a bed, a nightstand and some boxes of clothing in the corner. Bianca sank down on the mattress and the woman put her feet up, helped her to lay back and pulled a blanket over her.

Marie disappeared and returned a few minutes later with a cup in her hand. "Here, drink this."

Bianca lifted it to her lips and drank. It tasted bitter and she made a face.

Marie laughed. "It tastes horrible, but it will help you through the next little bit while you climb out of the Oubliette. Sleep now, and when you wake up you'll know which way is right again."

Bianca closed her eyes and fell asleep as Marie stroked her hair.

* * * * *

Angelo roused. He opened his eyes to see an old man with skin the color of deepest midnight, long wild black hair streaked through with white, and eyes the same color as his own.

He put a canteen to Angelo's parched lips. "There now, take a drink."

Cool water coursed into his mouth, drenching his dry tongue. His throat worked, but he couldn't swallow. He coughed and water streamed from the sides of his mouth. Every inch of his body alternated between hot and cold. The only constant was pain. He couldn't even feel his hip anymore. The agony had spread to every part of his body.

The old man laughed. "Slowly, slowly. A bit at a time."

Angelo leaned back against softness and looked through slitted eyes. He had no idea how he'd gotten here. It was a living area—an apartment in what had to be an abandoned building in Out-Center. It looked lived-in and loved. Where was he?

And where was Bianca?

Angelo lunged forward at the thought and caught the old man by the front of his vibrant blue and green shirt. "Where's Bianca?" he rasped.

The old man looked confused. He unhooked Angelo's hands from his shirt and pushed him back onto the bed. "I don't know who you are talking about. You need to be still and rest now. You've come close to death and still walk its edge."

He shook his head, panic scrambling at him. Gritting his teeth against the pain, he pushed himself toward the side of the bed, readying to stand.

"No! You've got laser fever as bad as I've ever seen," exclaimed the old man. "You'll just pass out again."

Angelo barely heard him. He had to find her. The old man struggled with him, trying to keep him still.

"Quint! I need help!" the man yelled.

Quint came through a door on the opposite side of the room. He crossed the floor with angry strides, his shoulders hunched and anger in his eyes. His long blond hair streamed behind him. Angelo watched him approach in confusion. He'd somehow ended up in Quint's home?

Quint pushed him back onto the bed. "Your name is Angelo. I remember." His tone held a note of restrained violence. "Listen, I know you don't want to be here. Truth is, we don't want you here, either. But even though you're a bastard, you saved my son's life and I owe you for that. So get back into bed and let Charlie treat you."

"Bianca. Where is she?" His voice was gritty, broken. His eyes were wild, and he knew it.

Quint didn't answer him.

Angelo fisted his hands in the blanket and he looked down. "I was stupid, Quint. I was blind. I didn't realize everything that was happening at the Water Company. I know now. I think I understand why you're out here, why you rejected the Center." He looked back up at Quint. "Where is Bianca, do you know?"

Quint's expression softened. "She's here and she's fine, sleeping in a back room. She's coming out the Oubliette and will be back to normal soon."

Angelo lay back on the bed, relief coursing through him. She was safe. "That's good news, Quint, the best in the world." Then the full impact of his words hit him. "How do you know about the Oubliette?"

"I've had some very up close and personal experience with it. Listen, you lay back now. Let Charlie treat your wound. The infection has spread throughout your body. Charlie needs to get the treatment for the laser fever into you. When you've recovered, we'll talk."

Panic struck him again. He'd been so worried about Bianca, he'd forgotten about the water crystal. "Where are my horse and saddlebags?"

"Your horse is out back. Your saddlebags are in the corner." He pointed to the left side of the room. "Don't worry. We didn't go through them." There was a heavy note of derision in his tone.

"I didn't think you did, Quint."

"Good."

Angelo pushed himself back up to the top of the bed and let Charlie remove his shirt.

Quint turned and walked toward the door he'd come through.

"Quint?" Angelo called.

He half-turned, tension still apparent in the way he held his body.

"Thank you."

"Yeah," he said, and then continued out the door.

Chapter Fifteen

Bianca roused and turned over, opening her eyes and taking in her unfamiliar surroundings with calm reserve. The dim light of either dawn or twilight filtered through a cracked window.

Closing her eyes, she searched her memory. What had happened to bring her here? She remembered being at the Phoenix, Angelo kissing her then Dell trying to drown her. She remembered being held close in Angelo's arms and feeling safe.

Then…Finch touching her cheek and Angelo shooting her with his alter-gun, in perfect obedience—the good little guardian following orders. He'd ensured her capture when he knew she'd rather die than become Finch's prisoner. Bitter tears pricked her eyes and sudden desolation threatened to choke her. She let a ragged sob escape her lips. Betrayal sliced her deeper than a sharpened knife.

She remembered throwing things at Finch and how he'd ordered his bodyguards on her. They'd shot her full of something…

She was in the Water Company!

She tossed the blanket back and sprang from the bed, then paused, disorientated. The room was old, clean, but old. This was not the polished luxury of the Water Company. She scanned the boxes of old clothing in the corner. Had they put her in the storage room?

Something moved in the doorway and Bianca turned. Her hand went to her waistband automatically, searching out her pistol on pure instinct. She groped air. In fact, she groped silk. She looked down at her body. What the hell was she wearing?

"You've slept all night and most of the day, Bianca. How do you feel?" A chiming voice met her ears, one that seemed on the verge of kind laughter. A tall woman with long reddish-blonde hair and soft green eyes stood at the door. Her face showcased high cheekbones full lips. She was beautiful despite the crow's feet at her eyes and the lines framing her mouth—laugh lines they called them. The woman smiled. She didn't seem to be an immediate threat.

Bianca knew then she wasn't at the Water Company. She took stock of how she felt. "Well, I feel like someone hit me over the head with a brick after they ran over me with their truck. Other than that, okay."

"You've been asleep for nearly twenty-four hours."

Her jaw dropped. "What?"

"So you know your name is Bianca now?"

The question took her by surprise. She almost laughed. What was wrong with this woman? "Uh, yeah."

"Do you know my name?"

"I have never met you before in my life. So, no, I don't know your name." She didn't mean to sound harsh, but what was with all the questions?

"My name is Marie."

"Hi, Marie. Where am I? Why have I been asleep for twenty-four hours? Who are you?" Now she was asking the fucking questions. Bianca looked down at herself—flimsy, silly little ripped-up black silk dress. The dress wasn't practical, not at all. There was nowhere to put a gun. She drew the neckline open and looked down the line of her body at the lacy black satin bra and matching panties. It got worse and worse. "And what the hell am I wearing?"

"You're in our home. My husband is Quint. You do remember a man named Quint, don't you?"

"The leader of the Southern Flot. Sure, I remember him. How did I manage to end up in his home?" She pressed the heel of her hand to her eye in a futile effort to banish her headache.

"You've been down the Oubliette, Bianca. The memories of the time that you spent there will come back. They came back for me, but it may take a little while."

"The Oubliette? Is that anything like the rabbit hole in that old story *Alice in Wonderland*?"

Marie smiled, but her eyes were tinged with sadness. "Very much, yes. You'll remember," she assured.

Bianca opened her mouth to ask what the Oubliette was exactly, when Marie spoke again. "You've got a man traveling with you. He was very worried about you, as you were for him."

She looked at Marie suspiciously. "Is he a tall, good-looking guy with deep brown eyes, short brown hair and body that stops your breath?"

Marie smiled. "His name is Angelo."

"Where is he?"

"He's in the room three doors down from this one, on the right. He's got a bad laser injury to his hip and took laser fever from it. He's being treated."

Her stomach tightened into a knot that had little to do with her hunger and a lot to do with her worry for Angelo. She squashed it down. He'd betrayed her, she reminded herself. "Is he okay? Is he well enough for me to see?" *So she could kill him.*

"Yes, his fever broke yesterday. The danger is past. He's resting now."

Relief coursed through her at Marie's words. The bastard was safe. She hated that she felt concern for the man who'd given her over into Finch's hands, but there it was.

Bianca brushed past Marie and headed down the hall, toward the room where he lay. The answers to the rest of her questions could wait for now. She had business with the handsome and deceitful Captain of the Guardians of Order.

She found him in a small room a lot like hers. There was a window in this one, too, overgrown with weeds on the outside, although the glass was miraculously unbroken. He leaned back against the pillows on a large bed. A thin, green blanket covered him from his waist down. He was shirtless, revealing the smooth, muscled expanse of his chest. That upper body looked perfect, even with the scars that wrapped him. His beautiful brown eyes were closed, his chest rising in a relaxed rhythm.

Again, relief flooded her that he looked unharmed. That relief was accompanied by the sharp desolation she'd felt when she'd remembered him shooting her with the alter-gun. She must've fallen literally into Finch's arms. She didn't stop to think. A set of emotions too complicated for her to unravel pooled in her stomach and compelled her forward.

She walked up and slapped him across the face—an openhanded slap, just like a girl. Normally she would've clocked him with her closed fist. Must be the dress and underwear, she thought with scorn. His head whipped to the side all the same though, girl slap or not.

He opened his eyes and stared up in surprise at her. "Bianca?"

"That's for using your alter-gun on me at the Phoenix." She knew she had tears standing in her eyes and she hated herself for it.

He touched his cheek. "I guess I should be happy you're out of the Oubliette and back to your lovable self. Do you remember anything that happened *after* the Phoenix?"

"I remember being at the Water Company, throwing things at Finch. I remember them shooting something into my arm. That's the last of it. No, wait—"

Maybe it was coming back to her like Marie had said. Images swirled like dust in her mind, but never settling. She closed her eyes and concentrated. "I remember you kissing me in the hallway at the Water Company, then making me kneel at Calina's grave." She opened her eyes and sat down on the bed from sudden shock. "I was at her grave," she said to herself, stunned.

"So you don't remember anything about me—oh, I don't know—abandoning my job, my home and risking my life to get you and the crystal out of the Water Company?"

He sounded angry. She was the one who was supposed to be angry!

"You don't remember doing everything you could to prevent that from happening?" he continued. "Including hitting me over the head with a vase? You don't remember plummeting fifty stories to the ground on a rappelling rope, me getting wounded by laser fire and subsequently contracting laser fever and almost dying yet again?"

Man, she felt really bad about slapping him now. "Er, no."

Bianca closed her eyes again and tried to remember. She fumbled around in a void for a moment and then a door opened. All the memories crashed into her at once, everything that had happened to her since Finch's hulking blond bodyguard, Raymond, had given her the first dose of Oubliette. Images and faces downloaded into her mind much as they had when her sister had died. Now she had even more experiences that were not truly hers. Since, in truth, in the Oubliette, she'd been an entirely different person. She gasped from the intensity of the memories.

"Well, all of those things happened, Bianca. So, tell me, do I get anything better than a slap for breaking you out the Water Company and getting injured in the bargain?"

She looked at him with what must have been an expression of complete shock on her face. "I remember," she breathed. It'd been like they'd raped her consciousness. Bianca had the sudden urge to take a bath, cleanse herself of the violation.

Finch had been in her head.

"You do?" asked Angelo. "Just like that?"

She nodded. She remembered what had happened in the apartment, too. How he'd hacked away at the wall to build them a hiding place while he'd been injured.

And how he'd pleasured her on the floor. Her body tightened at the memory. She'd begged him, once more, to touch her.

And, oh, how he had. Her whole body thrummed at the memory.

Bianca stood, crossed to the other side of the bed, crawled onto the mattress and went toward him on her hands and knees. He watched her with something akin to wariness in his eyes. A big, red handprint marked his cheek. God, she wanted to take it back.

She sat on her heels beside him, a breath's space away. "I remember...*everything*. Yes, you get something better than a slap," she murmured. She touched his hair and drew a gentle finger down the side of his face.

The crystal.

"Where's the crystal, Angelo?"

"Safe in the saddlebag," he said, indicating the corner of the room with a nod of his head.

She stared at him for several long moments, allowing her heated gaze to hold his. Everything she felt for him shone in her eyes. Bianca made sure of it. Her chest was nearly bursting with gratitude, relief...and passion. Then she leaned in closer and brushed her lips against his. His breath was warm against her lips and it made her own breath quicken. She spoke against his mouth, so he could feel as well as hear her words. "I'm so—" she gave him another lingering kiss, feeling his smooth, soft lips slide across hers, "—so sorry."

This time it was his breathing that quickened. The knowledge that she had made that happen sent a little thrill through her. "Uh, that's okay, Bianca." He smiled and she concentrated on every movement of his face. The way the skin around his eyes crinkled, the small dimple in his right cheek she'd never noticed before. "This makes up for the slap," he said.

"Really?" She drew back a bit and returned his smile. "Now I wish I'd clocked you." She lifted a brow. "Imagine what I'd have to do to make up for that."

He reached up and pressed a hand to her nape, crushing her mouth to his once more. He made a low sound in his throat and speared his tongue between her lips, taking her mouth in the possessive way he had. It made her body respond instantly. Made her cunt grow damp and plump with arousal. Made her nipples go tight and high. Made a moan escape her throat.

Angelo pushed a hand under her dress, found her breast and cupped it. He stroked his thumb over and over the hardened nipple through the material of her bra. Bianca shuddered against him and moaned out his name. Her clit felt huge and sent little fissure of pleasure through her where it rubbed her underwear.

She shifted to straddle him, careful of his injured hip. The press of his rigid cock felt hard against her cunt. She ground down against him a little and this time it was Angelo who groaned. He broke the kiss, tipping his back and closing his eyes.

She lowered her head and took advantage of his exposed throat, nibbling and kissing her way across it until he trembled beneath her. He caught her chin and tipped her chin up, making her meet his heavy-lidded gaze.

He reached up and stroked a fingertip down her cheek. "I'm sorry for using the alter-gun on you. At the time, I felt it was the only way to keep you from being hurt. I didn't realize then that Finch would never order you shot. I thought—"

She silenced the flow of words with her mouth.

He wrapped his arms around her and pulled her against him, keeping her safely away from his injured side. He pressed his lips to hers and she could feel his hard body under her.

She wondered how it would feel to have the naked length of him sliding against her bare skin. How it would feel to be able to explore every part of him from his head, down to his feet. To make him hers and allow him to make her his in every sense of the word. His cock to her pussy. Not just him giving her pleasure, but her making him groan and squirm.

He parted her lips and branded her tongue with his once more.

She melted. It was the only way she could describe it. She melted in a flood of hot desire pouring up her spine from some little known part of herself. Never had she wanted a man like she wanted Angelo. It excited her and scared her all at once. She realized then that the numbness she'd had since Calina's death had completely dissipated, leaving her defenseless. Angelo had thawed her emotions with his kisses until they were so much water, until they were fluid and giving, instead of hard and cold.

The knowledge slammed into her harder than the memories had.

She loved Angelo.

No, that couldn't happen. She couldn't love him. That was bad...*bad*. Everything she loved, she lost. It never failed. You gave your heart to someone and it got shredded. Always. That was the way of it. She'd loved her parents and they were gone. She'd loved Calina and she was gone.

No.

She pushed up and away from him. He looked bereft and confused as she slid across the mattress, putting distance between them. The look on his face almost made her say the hell with it and press herself against him once more, but she couldn't. She looked away from him.

"What's wrong, Bianca?"

"Noth—" she swallowed hard. "Nothing, Angelo." She tried a smile and failed miserably. "Here I am assaulting you with slaps and kisses and you're injured and beating off laser fever. I'm so selfish. How do you feel?"

"Better. My hip still hurts, but the fever is almost gone, I think. They have an old man here named Charlie. He's an incredible physician. They used a fortune's worth of water on me to bring my temperature down. I don't know how I'll repay them."

"They're repaying you, remember? You saved their son from Dell."

"I was just doing my job." Sorrow washed over his face, abrupt as a summer storm. Bianca knew he'd given up all his illusions. He'd lost himself. He'd never be able to recover his identity as Captain of the Guardians of Order. Now he would have to rebuild.

"Let's see your wound." She knelt beside him and drew the edge of the blanket back to reveal it. He lifted the edge of the bandage and she could see the wound biting deep into his upper hip. She sucked in an empathic breath. Laser wounds were vicious injuries, worse than third-degree burns. He'd have a scar there to match the ones on his back, side and stomach, no doubt about it.

"They've done all they can to it," he said. "It just needs time to heal now. Are you all right?"

She stood and smiled down at him. "Thanks to you, yes. I'm dressed funny and I have a headache, but other than that—" She threw her arm wide in a careless gesture. "I'm sorry, Angelo."

"For what?"

"For dragging you into all this. I'm sorry you're injured. I'm sorry you're disillusioned about the society in the Center. I'm sorry you're here with the Flot when I know you hate them. I'm sorry for slapping you."

"Bianca, my one desire is to keep the peace, to make this place better for humans than it was before the Kirans tainted the water. Seems like getting this crystal to Sector Twenty-Nine is the best way for me to do that."

"Yes." She hesitated. "Sometimes I wonder about that."

"About what?"

"Why you feel so obligated to help create a better society. I remember what you said to me the other night, about how you got your scars." She knelt beside him and laid a hand on his forearm, needing to feel him. He'd shared a painful memory with her and she was touched he'd confided in her, even though she'd been drugged. "I just wonder if maybe you don't feel guilty for something you have no control over."

"Yeah, well, I don't, so you can stop wondering."

Amazing how many secrets he wanted to keep.

She stood up and sighed. Fine. If that's how he wanted it. "You don't happen to have my gun, do you?"

"It's in the saddlebag."

She went to the corner of the room and dug it out, also making sure the crystal was there. It was tucked safely in its black velvet sack.

She stood and let the pistol lay in her hand for a moment, sighing in deep contentment as she became reacquainted with its comforting weight and the way it fit so nicely against her palm. It was like being reunited with an old friend. She went to slip it into her belt and realized there was nowhere to put it.

"Stupid dress," she muttered and stalked off in search of different clothing.

Chapter Sixteen

Bianca stood in the main room, remembering this was the room where Dugan had brought her after he'd found her in the Out-Center, where she'd been running around all crazed and half-suicidal. Embarrassed heat flushed her face. Dugan was not there now, neither was Quint nor his son. Bianca was thankful for that small mercy.

Marie handed her a fresh change of clothing, including a pair of gray pants and a solid black T-shirt, from a chest of drawers that stood in the corner of the large room.

Bianca took them. "Thank you. I'm sorry I was rude to you earlier, Marie."

The older woman smiled. "I understand. You were confused and worried about Angelo."

"I wasn't worried about Angelo. I was angry with him."

Her smile widened. "Angry, sure."

She opened her mouth to reply, and then closed it. If Marie wanted to think she cared about Angelo in that way, she could. It didn't make it true.

At least, she was going to force it to not be true. There would be no intoxicating chocolate-brown gaze for her, no dimpled cheeks or smoothly muscled chest. Nope. Angelo had no hold over her. They were going to get the crystal to Sector Twenty-Nine in a completely platonic fashion and then part ways. It was that simple.

A thudding sound on her left met her ears and Bianca looked over to see Angelo standing in the doorway. He'd propped himself up between two crutches, and was barefoot and naked from the waist up. His mussed hair stood up in tufts. She had an urge to run her fingers through it to smooth it down.

Damn.

"How are you feeling?" Marie asked him.

"Better." He smiled and looked at Bianca pointedly. "Much better."

Marie turned back to her with a secret smile playing on her rosy lips. "Well, I suppose you'll both be wanting a bath and some food. What would you like first?"

Bianca realized she should be hungry since she'd slept for so long, but all she felt was vaguely sick to her stomach. Her answer came fast. "I'd rather take a bath, Marie, if it's okay." She still felt dirty and violated by Finch's intrusion into her mind.

"Certainly. Would you like a bath as well, Angelo?"

"I wouldn't turn one down. Do you have enough purewater?"

"We do." Marie turned back to the chest of drawers, extracted fresh clothing for Angelo and handed it to Bianca.

"Let me lead you to the bathing room." Marie turned and walked toward a door on the right side of the room.

"You really have enough water for two baths?" Bianca asked. She didn't see how they could. "I'm not sharing mine." She gave Angelo an uneasy glance.

"Yes, we have some water left from a recent acquisition." She turned and walked out the door. Bianca followed beside Angelo, who hobbled along on his crutches.

Marie led them down a hallway, which emptied out into an old lobby. It was then that Bianca realized the building was actually a deserted school. They'd cleaned the place up well, and other people seemed to also reside in the building. The classrooms had been made over into small apartments. They went through another door on the opposite side of the lobby, which led into a large room. The sides were lined with rusty lockers and at the far end of the room were spigots from old showers. A series of bathtubs lined the center of the shower area. Connected to them by a series of pipes, was a huge cement tub.

Angelo hobbled over to the container and peered over the edge. "There's a lot of purified water here. Have you been ambushing water suppliers, Marie?" His voice had gone dangerously low. Bianca hoped he wasn't slipping into some kind of residual guardian mode.

"No. We bought the water legitimately and hauled it here," Marie answered.

Angelo's brow rose. "Really? You had to have a lot of money to buy so much water. How'd you come by so many credits?"

Bianca flashed a look of warning at Angelo. "Down boy."

"That's okay, Bianca." Marie lifted her chin. "Look. We don't have it easy out here beyond the relative civilization the Center affords, but we still have rules we don't break."

"Really," answered Angelo dryly.

Marie's eyes flashed. *"Really.* I'm not speaking for the whole of the Southern Flot, Angelo. I'm talking about Quint, Gannon, Dugan and myself."

"Okay. I can accept that. Why are you out here anyway, Marie?" asked Angelo.

"It's a long story. The short version is that once I was in position similar to Bianca's and Quint was in a position similar to yours. Quint was a master water purifier at the Water Company. And I, well, *I* was down the Oubliette." She sighed and suddenly looked older than Bianca had assessed. "I was one woman in a long string of them. After Quint realized I was being drugged on a regular basis, he rescued me. We left and have never looked back."

Bianca's mind stuttered. How many women had Finch imprisoned and drugged? *One woman in a long string of them.* She thought of Calina and grief choked her throat. Bianca glanced away in an effort to control the sudden emotion, swallowed hard, and focused on the other surprise. "Quint was Finch's master water purifier?"

"Yes. Although Finch, the greedy bastard, doesn't really need one. Finch could purify all the water of the world and hasn't done it. Finch has us right where he wants us, begging for every drop he has to sell."

Bianca and Angelo exchanged glances. "What do you mean, Finch could purify all the water of the world and hasn't done it?" asked Bianca.

"When I was down the Oubliette, Finch told me he had a master water crystal that would reverse the freysis poisoning. It was like I was—"

"His confessor," finished Bianca. Her hands clenched on the clothing Marie had given her, remembering all the things Finch had told her just in the short amount of time she'd been down the Oubliette...and all the things he'd told Calina.

"Yes, he told me about the crystal because on some level, I think he felt guilty about keeping it. He never told me where he kept it, or what it looked like."

Bianca glanced at Angelo. His face had gone tight with anger.

"I don't know if it's true," continued Marie, glancing between both their faces and looking worried. "But with Finch, I wouldn't doubt it. He stole five years of my life. A man capable of doing what he's done to women, I wouldn't doubt anything."

Bianca shivered. Five years down the Oubliette. Calina had been down about the same amount of time. Now Bianca knew why she didn't have any memories of Calina resisting Finch. They'd simply drugged her so she wouldn't.

"Well, I suppose you two want to bathe, right?" Marie asked. She turned her attention to the spigots on one of the bathtubs and flipped it open. Water poured into the tub. "We rigged up a way to heat it using solar panels. It should be warm enough for you."

Marie walked toward the door. "Come back when you're done and we'll get you something to eat and drink."

"Thank you, Marie," Bianca answered. Marie closed the door behind her.

Bianca set the clothing down on a nearby chair and looked at Angelo. She motioned at his crutches. "You need help getting into the bathtub, I guess." She knew she didn't sound enthusiastic.

Angelo hobbled toward her. She backed up until she pressed against a smooth, white-tiled wall beside one of the tubs. He stopped a heartbeat away from her. Bianca stared at his chest. She wanted to reach out and touch that smoothness, draw her hands over his shoulders and upper arms. God, he was beautiful.

He set one crutch against the wall and leaned on the other one. His gaze captured and held hers while he slid his hand up her outer thigh, under the edge of her skirt, all the way to her waist. His fingers rested suggestively on the waistband of her panties.

"What's the matter, Bianca?" he asked in a low, seductive voice. "Not too long ago you were more than eager to help me bathe. You were begging me to touch you." He brushed his lips across hers. "Eager to have me bring you. What's changed?"

Bianca couldn't answer. She was concentrating too hard on not licking the skin right above his left nipple. The entire lower part of her body seemed aware of every breath he took, every little move he made...not the least of which were the small, teasing brushes of the backs of his fingers on the bare skin of her hip.

"Hmmm?" he prompted.

She swallowed hard. "I-I don't know." That was a lie. She did know. She was out of her depth in her emotions for him. She risked drowning in them, in him.

One more loss would kill her.

The thing she needed most right now was distance from him and she'd fight to get it, to protect herself.

"Could it be that once things get serious…?" He leaned down and placed his lips featherlight against her cheek. His hot breath branded her skin and he gently drew the tip of his tongue down her jawline to her throat. He spoke against the skin below her ear in a tone that was more velvet caress than voice. "Could it be that once there are stakes, you can't handle it anymore?" He kissed her there and Bianca felt moisture soak her little black lace panties.

He eased his finger between her thighs and rubbed her clit. She gasped.

"What's making you so damn demure all of a sudden?" he murmured into her ear. "What happened to *please put your hands on me, Angelo*?"

"Angelo," her voice came out a sob. His strokes over her clit seemed relentless and she felt powerless to push him away. Tears pricked her eyes and she counted herself lucky he couldn't see them.

"What, Bianca?" he whispered. His breath had grown faster. "You don't know how much I love to put my hands on you. You don't know how much I love to make you come." He shuddered. "Your little cunt is heaven, angel-face. It feels and tastes like heaven to me."

A strangled gasp freed itself from her body. God, she was so weak when it came to this man.

"There's so much we could do, you and I," he purred. "There are so many things I fantasize about doing to your body."

Bianca closed her eyes. Ever since the first time he'd shown her that sex could be enjoyable, she'd thought a lot about all the things they could do. All the things she knew were possible, yet she'd never explored with anyone because of what had happened to her.

He dragged her earlobe gently through his teeth and goose bumps erupted over her body.

"Let me in," he murmured.

Swallowing a whimper, she allowed him to part her thighs a little. She grabbed onto his shoulders and held on, searching desperately for the strength to push him away and not finding it. He eased down and caressed her needy, aching pussy.

He groaned and slid a finger into her. "Heaven," he breathed near her ear.

Before he could make her completely senseless, before he could make her come yet again, she pushed his hand down and away. She gasped and slid to the side, twisting away from him.

She left him so fast that Angelo had to reach out a hand quick against the wall to keep from falling. She caught her breath before she spoke. Her eyes flicked to his lower body and she swallowed hard. He'd obviously liked the personal contact as much as she did since his erect cock now tented his sweatpants. "Look, I'll help you into the bathtub, nothing more."

He grinned. "I expect no more. I was just giving back a little of what you gave me, that's all."

"What's good for the goose, huh?"

His grin widened. "You bet."

"You keep doing stuff like that and you'll give me a heart attack."

The smile left his face. "I'm hoping to do something to your heart, Bianca. I really am."

He already had. That was the worst part about it. She stood staring at him for a moment, her hands dangling at her sides because she didn't know what to do with them. She suddenly felt awkward, and that made her mad. At least anger was a familiar emotion.

She stalked to the bathtub, leaned over the side and flipped the spigot off. Then she turned and pointed at his sweatpants. She wanted to get him into the tub so she could go hide. "Off."

Angelo shook his head. "I don't need help getting into the tub, Bianca. I crawled into a wall and got on and off a horse with this injury, I can get into a bathtub."

She gave him a look of uncertainty. "Are you sure?"

"I must have a hundred and twenty pounds on you, Bianca. What are you going to do if I fall?" He lifted a brow. "Catch me?"

She shrugged. "Good point."

"Awww, giving up so easily? And here I thought you wanted to get my pants off."

Embarrassed heat flooded her face and she looked away. "Are you sure you can get in and out of the tub on your own?"

"I can take a little pain. I can do it."

She still worried he'd slip and fall. "If you hurt yourself again, we'll be delayed leaving here even longer, and we have to get that crystal to Melvin. I'll stay in here just as long as it takes you to get into the tub, okay?" That, and she simply didn't want him hurt, but she couldn't admit that part.

"As you wish. Should I drop my pants now?" He didn't wait for her answer. He pushed his sweatpants down to his ankles.

She sucked in a breath at the curve of his ass and strong thighs. His cock was huge, long and wide. It was a beautiful organ, one that engendered an instant reaction in her body. Her mouth instantly went dry at the sight of it and the possibility of it sliding into her cunt. Her body primed itself and her nipples went hard at the mere prospect of it.

"Goddamn it, Angelo," she complained and turned her back.

He laughed.

She heard him move to the tub and climb the short stairs. Not being able to help herself, she peeked. His strong, smooth buttocks flexed as he lowered himself into the water. She bit her lip and suppressed a moan.

"It's safe to look." He made an appreciative groan and leaned against the side of the tub, intertwining his fingers behind his head in an action that showed his biceps to best advantage. He glanced at her and grinned. "Wanna join me?"

Bastard. He knew exactly what he was doing to her. She had to get out of there. "Uh, no. I'll catch the next bath."

"It'll conserve water."

"All the same." She nearly ran to get out of the room.

* * * * *

In the common room, Dugan and Quint stood by the table talking and laughing. They both went silent when she entered the room. Bianca closed the door behind her and wound her arms over her chest in a protective gesture, feeling like she'd intruded.

Dugan stood looking at her with round, blue eyes. She walked to him. "Thank you for helping me and Angelo. I'm sorry I feared you."

His loud, booming laugh filled the room. "Everyone fears me at first." He spread two huge hands wide. "I'm really just a kitten."

Quint took a step forward. "Marie told me you're finally out of the Oubliette."

She nodded her head.

He motioned to a round table in the center of the room. Pure-food scattered it, as well as plates and silverware. "Sit down. You must eat to regain your strength after going through such an ordeal. Nutro-wafers will keep you alive, but, psychologically, pure-food is more nourishing."

She sat down and looked at the bread, the remnants of a pure-chicken, ham, and apples lying on the table. While she salivated, Quint piled food onto her plate. She couldn't remember the last time she'd had pure-food. She went directly to the pure-chicken and ate as if starving. Quint looked pleased at her appetite.

After finishing off the chicken, she picked up a small apple and bit into it. The smooth, sweet fruit filled her mouth and she gave an appreciative little groan. She chewed and swallowed, savoring it.

"Why did Marie give me something to make me sleep for so long?" she asked.

"Coming out of the Oubliette is a nasty experience, Bianca. You regain yourself, only to lose yourself again. It's better to sleep through the drug working its way out of your system." He picked up an empty glass and filled it with pure-water from a pitcher sitting on the table. He held it out to her and she took it.

"Thank you for your generosity, Quint." She downed the glass in one lift to her lips, her throat working. She'd been far thirstier than she'd thought. Quint took her glass when she lowered it and filled it back up again. "You can't be too happy to be sheltering a Guardian of Order," she commented as she picked up a piece of bread Quint had piled with ham and took a bite.

"During the last two days I have come to see that Angelo is no longer a Guardian of Order. He is a man that wants only the best for his people and sometimes is blinded by the need to achieve that goal." He frowned. "It's almost as if he feels...*guilt*."

She rolled her eyes. "I know." Then she quickly lowered her gaze, not wanting to reveal what she suspected.

Dugan cleared his throat before speaking. "The doctor has been surprised at how quickly Angelo is healing, Bianca."

Bianca didn't say a word. She merely held her breath, the bread lying limp in her hand. Fast healing was a Kiran trait. She already suspected Angelo had some close tie to the Kiran. A tie he didn't appreciate very much. Was he, himself, actually a

Kiran? If so, he'd have to be part-blood. She'd never seen him consume freysis and Kirans needed the bacteria on a regular basis to survive. Could a part-blood live without freysis? She didn't know. But his tracking ability and now this healing ability, it made her suspicions even stronger. It would not be a good thing for Quint and Dugan to suspect what she did. Bianca didn't know how they felt about Kirans.

"Really?" she said finally, and took another bite of the bread and ham.

"Really," answered Dugan.

Just then the door opened and Angelo came through it on his crutches, dressed in the clothes she'd carried for him and with his sweatpants draped around his neck. "Bathing room is free if you want it, Bianca."

"Thanks," she said around a mouthful.

"Glad to see you're up and around, Angelo," said Quint. Despite what Quint had said about Angelo no longer being a Guardian of Order, a thread of tension hung in the air between Quint and Angelo. Bianca took another bite of bread and chewed carefully, her eyes on the two men.

Angelo hobbled over to the table. He smiled. "More or less. I'm up and around." He eyed the food on the table with interest.

"It's not stolen, if that's what you're thinking," said Quint defensively.

The room went silent and Bianca swallowed the lump of bread that had lodged itself in her throat.

Dugan cleared his throat as though uncomfortable, and then went for the door. "I have to get going, got lots of things to do this afternoon." The door closed behind him.

Angelo turned to Quint. "I would never insult my hosts, especially ones so generous as you, by assuming they stole their food. You saved my life as well as Bianca's. I don't think you're thieves."

Quint's shoulders relaxed. "I'm glad for that. Look, I didn't want to explain this to you while you were ill, but now that you're feeling better, I can. The Southern Flot is a society, like the Center under the Water Company is a society, but less, er..."

"Polished? Finished? Civilized?"

Angelo's suggestions drew a cold glance from Quint. "Something like that, yes. We have fewer rules and more freedom and therefore we have more problems. Members of the Flot *do* steal. They do sell illegal arms, pillage and hunt Kirans upon occasion for money. Dugan, some others and myself have formed a council to discipline those who commit these crimes. We have our difficulties, many of them, but we're trying to create a society where those in positions of power do not throw people into the Oubliette merely because they think them too headstrong, and do not prey upon thirsty and downtrodden people to make themselves rich. Most of all, we're trying to create a society where the pure-water is shared and not monopolized."

"It's very idealistic," said Angelo.

Quint smiled. "Look who's calling who idealistic."

Angelo laughed. "I think you might be even more an idealist than I am."

"Maybe so, but in any case, we could use some help out here. I know you were traveling out to Sector Twenty-Nine for some reason, but I'm inviting you to stay here, both of you, to help us organize and build this society. At first glance, I know it may seem unlikely that this could work, but if you'd take a closer look, Angelo, you might find it's exactly what you're looking for. We could use a man like you."

Bianca knew all about the creation of societies apart from the Center. Sector Twenty-Nine had one of their own. It was better than the Center and far better than the ragtag Southern Flot. But she didn't want to talk about Sector Twenty-Nine, since Kirans and humans in that community lived together. She didn't want to tell Angelo that until they got there, for fear he might not want to travel on with her. She wondered how Angelo was going to react once he knew.

She wondered a lot of things about Angelo. Too bad he wasn't more forthcoming with information. Apparently, she wasn't trustworthy enough.

"I admire what you're doing, Quint. I really do. Maybe after Bianca and I accomplish our goal in Sector Twenty-Nine, I'll come back here and help you organize the Flot. Our first priority is getting to Sector Twenty-Nine. We've been delayed far too long as it is." He leaned forward on his crutches and clasped Quint on the shoulder. "It means a lot to me that you would ask."

Something sharp twisted in Bianca's gut at the thought of Angelo leaving her, coming back here to help Quint without her. She squelched it, telling herself it didn't matter what Angelo did, or where he went after this was over.

God, she was good at lying to herself.

"It would honor me if you'd stay." He turned to Bianca. "If both of you would stay. But I understand if you must leave."

"Thank you, Quint," said Bianca.

"And now I must leave," said Quint. He glanced at the table. "Enjoy the food." He turned and walked out the door.

Bianca ate the last of the bread, chewed and swallowed. Suddenly, it was very quiet.

"Did you eat enough, Bianca?" asked Angelo.

"No, but I want a bath more than I want to eat right now." She stood and walked past him to get to the door leading to the bathing room.

He grabbed her forearm as she passed and pressed his mouth close to her ear. "If you've reconsidered and want to share a bath, I'd be happy to take another." His voice rolled over her like a seductive cloud and it made her shiver.

God, what was she going to do?

Chapter Seventeen

It had taken three days before Angelo could finally bend halfway at the waist and walk without crutches. It'd been too much time. They were delayed considerably. Angelo wondered how well Finch had spread his guardians over the Out-Center by now.

Angelo watched Bianca kneeling on the floor, loading the gear Marie and Quint had generously given to them into their packs. She folded up a freysis tent, which would protect them if it rained, and placed it inside. Marie sat on the couch and Quint and Gannon stood nearby, but Angelo's eyes were on Bianca.

Bianca wore a pair of jeans, given to her by Marie, and a tight white T-shirt without a bra. Her breasts were small, high and pert and her nipples pressed against the fabric every time she moved right. Loading the pack, that happened a lot.

Angelo could watch her load that pack all day long.

All he could think of was how sweetly her breasts filled his hands, how her tight nipples felt against his skin and his tongue. He'd loved teasing her in the bathing room, and could tell he was affecting her the way she affected him. He clenched his fists.

God, the things he wanted to do to her sweet body.

"It's done," announced Bianca, as she fastened the pack closed.

Quint took a step forward. "Your horse is ready and the skies look clear now, though I smell rain. I bet there's a good storm on the horizon, but you should be able to get far before it hits." He shoved his hands into his pockets. "You know our offer to you to stay still stands."

Quint had no idea they possessed the water crystal. He thought they were running from Finch because Angelo had rescued Bianca from the Oubliette, and they wanted to get to Sector Twenty-Nine because Melvin was Bianca's only living relative and could shelter them. They'd assumed all of that and Angelo had done nothing to dissuade them. It wasn't that he didn't trust them. It was simply too dangerous for them to know about the crystal—too dangerous for them and too dangerous for himself and Bianca. They couldn't afford to trust anyone right now.

"Thank you, Quint. You've been more than generous," answered Bianca.

"Our pleasure."

Bianca stood and Angelo stepped past her and lifted the heavy saddlebag. She protested, citing his injuries, and they had a short verbal sparring match, which he won. He might be injured, but he wouldn't let Bianca carry that heavy pack. She'd gone from being his prisoner to his partner, and he liked it better that way.

They walked out the door with Marie, Gannon and Quint trailing behind. Their horse was tied outside and ready to go. The gelding had been fed well on grain, hay and fresh purewater. Angelo had no idea how he'd ever repay Quint for his kindness. He'd tried to give him credits, but Quint had refused them, citing Gannon's rescue. Angelo couldn't believe he'd ever thought ill of him. He turned toward the other man when they got outside. "Quint, I—"

"It's all right, Angelo. I know you're grateful. I'm just happy to help out someone who's defied Finch and turned their back on the Water Company." He smiled. "Believe me, that's thanks enough."

Bianca hugged Marie, Dugan, Gannon and Quint each in turn while he secured the saddlebag and packs, and then mounted the horse. Angelo gave his farewells and they rode away.

Bianca rode behind him, with her hands clasped around his midsection. The sun beat down and he was growing hot. Especially with her body pressed up against his, but he wouldn't change that for anything. Quint had been right about rain being on the way. The promise of it hung heavy in the air and clouds accumulated in the western sky. That would probably cool things off, though it'd be a pain because they'd have to take shelter.

They traveled through Out-Center, and arrived nearly to the edge of the Wasteland by midafternoon. The buildings at the farthest reaches of Out-Center were all nearly demolished by time and the war. The horse walked on buckled and cracked pavement. Everywhere, freysis-enriched vegetation flourished. Vines climbed the crumbling walls of buildings, and grass grew out of the cracks in the street. Animals ruled here. This was their domain. Hawks and vultures circled the sky lazily and made nests on top of the buildings. Deer grazed openly and packs of wild dogs roamed. Carrying a gun in Out-Center wasn't just a good idea because of the human wildlife.

A bead of sweat trickled down his forehead and he wiped it away. He pulled his shirt off in an effort to seek coolness and laid it over the back of the horse's neck in front of him.

Bianca let out a sharp breath. He turned in the saddle to get a glance at her face. She appeared angry and somewhat afraid. He'd seen fear on her face more than once since she'd climbed out of the Oubliette. He wondered what was so scary about him.

"Do you have to do that?" she asked.

"Do what?"

She indicated his bare back with her hand. "That."

"Take my shirt off?"

"Yes."

He smiled. "Why should that bother you?"

"Now I feel funny about winding my arms around you."

He turned back around with a smile on his face. "Bare skin makes you nervous, huh? You want a double barrier between you and me—your clothes and my clothes. Anything less than that and you're afraid of what you'll want to do to me. Or maybe what I'll want to do to you." His mouth went dry as all those things, plus all the things he'd already done, flooded his mind.

"You know that's not true." She sounded angry, but the slight quaver in her voice betrayed her.

"It's not like I haven't touched you, Bianca," he said softly.

"That was bef—" She bit off the word.

"Before what?"

She didn't answer him.

"I love to touch you, Bianca. I could make a career out of it. You've got the prettiest breasts and pussy I've ever seen in my life and the noises you make when you come are so fucking sexy." His hand tightened on the reins as he remembered them.

"Please, stop."

"In the apartment you begged me to touch you. You spread your thighs as far as you could and bucked and moaned under my tongue and hands."

"Goddamn it, Angelo! Cut it out!"

He groaned softly at how hard his cock had gotten. The memories of how she'd responded to him made him want to take her into a dark corner and make love to her right now. She'd give in to him if he touched her the right way.

He gritted his teeth. A man had to have a will of pure steel to resist this woman.

A fine tremor vibrated up his spine. It meant someone was close. Were they friend or foe? He led the horse into the shade of a nearby building. "Bianca, someone is around."

Her arms came around his midsection. Bare skin didn't seem to be a concern just then. "How do you know that?" she whispered.

"I just do."

"Who is it?"

"I don't know. All I know is we need to get into the shadows."

Angelo led the horse through the wide, destroyed opening of what had once been a large building. The horse's hooves on the cracked marble floor echoed through the former lobby. Old papers, cans and other refuse littered the floor. A long, half-collapsed counter stood forlorn along the north wall. In the wall behind the counter hung a huge window, the glass almost completely knocked out of the frame by time and war. It looked like this had been a bank and that had been the drive-through. The ceiling had fallen in and a large pile of rubble dominated the left center of the room, opposite the ruined receptionist's desk. Behind the rubble stood a partially collapsed wall.

They felt the wind the hovercraft made before they saw the actual machine. Angelo glanced toward the opening above the receptionist's desk. They could make a run for it now, but the craft's motion sensor would likely register them. A horse would be hard-pressed to outrun a hovercraft.

He backed the horse up behind a pile of rubble to hide them. They watched through one of the broken-out windows as the craft floated down from the sky in front of the building next to theirs. The soft, gentle whirring sound was in direct contrast to the wind the craft produced. The paper refuse that littered the floor swirled around them and displaced old aluminum cans to slide along the floor, making a hollow ringing sound as they went.

Angelo swore loud and colorfully under his breath and backed Jinx up a few more paces, behind the remains of the wall.

"What are the guardians doing here?" asked Bianca.

He didn't have a comforting answer. "They're probably not really the guardians, Bianca. I'd make a guess that's Dell along with some muscle, acting for the Water Baron. What are they doing? Looking for us, of course."

"How did they know to look here?"

"This is the leading edge of the Wastes. I bet they've had Southern Out-Center under surveillance ever since we left the Water Company. I'm sure the border between the Out-Center and the Wastes is on their patrol. After all, they knew you were heading south before, Bianca. They probably figured we'd head south again."

"Great."

"Yeah."

The hovercraft inched its way to the left, toward their hiding place. The operator was definitely scanning the buildings in the area for activity. All they could do was hide behind the wall, stay as still as possible and hope the sensors didn't pick them up. They would, though, Angelo knew. They couldn't control the movements the horse made.

He fished Bianca's gun out from the saddlebag and handed it to her, and then he removed both his laser and alter-gun from his shoulder holster.

"Only use the gun if you're threatened, Bianca," he said. "Defensively, not offensively." If he could use his alter-gun, he would. The laser was a last resort.

The hovercraft's whirring became louder and Angelo knew it was in front of their building. "Don't move. Don't even breathe hard," he warned.

Bianca's arms tightened around him. Long moments passed. The papers swirled around them, the cans slid across the floor and their breathing was low and harsh in his ears. Still the hovercraft remained.

* * * * *

Dell eased back on the cyclet and let the hovercraft hang nearly motionless in the air.

One week and nothing. One week of roaming the Wasteland and the outer limits of the Southern Out-Center and nothing. Angelo and the girl had holed up somewhere, he was sure. They'd gone to ground, hoping to throw them off their scent, and it had worked.

All Dell could do was go back over the territory again and again, hoping to get lucky, hoping to come across some sign of them. Even now he awaited fifty more guardians and another hovercraft. They were trained on his craft's signal and should be arriving at any moment. Though he wasn't sure what good they'd do him. It was difficult when the one who you were tracking could sense you before you saw him. Goddamn Angelo was like a bloodhound.

Or a Kiran.

Dell leaned back and put his feet up on the console of the cockpit of the hovercraft. He'd suspected from day one that Angelo might have Kiran blood. A Kiran who hated Kirans. What a head case. He'd never minded as long as Angelo did his job and kept up his high Kiran capture rate. But now that he'd pulled this little stunt, well, now he'd have to die.

He'd enjoy killing the girl most of all. He could smell her sweet skin already, feel her fear coursing through him…and he would make her fear. He'd bring terror to those blue-green eyes before she died and love it. He'd feed from it.

Calina had been so easy to manipulate. Dell had told he loved her, and she'd believed him. He hadn't loved her, not really, but he hadn't wanted her to kill herself either. That had been bad. She'd been so sweet, so pliable. But Bianca, he could happily squeeze the life from her bones, and he would.

He flipped the switch for the motion scanner and looked at the craft's monitor with bored eyes. He had it set to look for moving things that were bigger than a breadbox. The beeping of the motion detector's alarm filled the cockpit.

"What the!" Dell's feet came down off the console and he sat straight up in his seat, squinting at the monitor. Something was moving in that building. It could be an animal.

But it could also be Angelo and the little girl.

Dell pressed the landing button and set the hovercraft down. He made sure his laser and alter-gun were holstered, and then left the cockpit. Two guardians sat at the small table in the passenger area, playing cards. They stood when he entered the room.

"Mason, Jacob, bring your lasers and stand guard outside the craft. I've got to check out something suspicious in that building."

They followed him down the ramp and out onto the street. Dell drew his laser and stuck close to the outside wall. He entered the building in proper, cautious guardian style, rounding the corner quick with his laser drawn and leveled, both hands on the gun's grip, and sighting a line of fire.

Nothing. There was only paper swirling in the wind made from the hovercraft and cans scraping along the floor. There had to be something larger. He edged his way over to the rubble pile, inching the long way around it, toward the wall. That was their hiding place, whoever they were. He would take them by surprise. He walked with his back to the wall, sliding along to the very edge of it, then rounded the corner, his gun out and aimed in front of him, still in a two-handed grip.

A massive fist came straight toward his nose. Pain exploded in blinding white flashes and then there was blackness.

* * * * *

Angelo stood over Dell, cradling his fist in his hand. He glanced at Bianca who still sat on the horse. A strange little satisfied smile played over her lips.

"Captain?" queried Mason from the doorway. He couldn't see Angelo around the pile of rubble and Angelo knew he asked after Dell, not himself.

"Yeah, over here." Angelo mimicked Dell's voice.

The guardians started inching their way around the rubble pile. Angelo could hear the soles of their shoes on the pavement, could feel their presence coming closer. One had taken the left side around, the other the right. They'd have their lasers drawn and Angelo wouldn't be able to punch them both at the same time. Angelo drew his alter-gun from his holster and made sure it was set on delta.

He glanced back at Bianca. She had her pistol in a two-handed grip. The barrel was trained on the edge of the wall.

Not good.

He caught her eye and made a slashing motion across his throat, then waggled the alter-gun at her. She lowered her gun to her lap with an air of disappointment.

Footsteps sounded on the opposite side of the wall. Angelo backed up against it, the alter-gun ready to fire. Mason came around the corner with his laser drawn and aimed at him. Angelo tagged Mason in the head before he could fire. He fell with a solid thump to the ground.

Jacob had gone silent, but Angelo could feel where he was in the room without hearing or seeing him. Angelo inched his way to the edge of the wall.

All his life, he'd fought his Kiran abilities. Even in times he could've used them, he'd denied the preternatural skills he possessed. Now, he chose to open himself to it. He closed his eyes and willfully tapped into his skill for the first time in his life. With his mind he scanned, feeling Bianca and the horse behind him, the unconscious forms of Mason and Dell on the ground and across the room, Jacob—the one he sought.

Jacob stood on the opposite side of the rubble. A wave of fear mixed with exhilaration hit Angelo square in the back. It took Angelo a second to realize the emotions came from Bianca behind him. He concentrated and found he could feel the emotions of every conscious being in the room...even the horse. They radiated out like waves of heat or energy.

Angelo tuned into Jacob. A steady current of ambition rolled off the man. He was determined to succeed where Dell and Raymond had failed. Purpose and enthusiasm coursed from him like the relentless waves of Lake Michigan against the beach, and were just as deadly.

Angelo could even hear the beat of his heart when he probed him, the very pulse of the blood coursing through his veins. He knew without a doubt that Jacob would kill him and Bianca without a second thought. Jacob wanted Dell's job. Jacob wanted only to please his boss, the Water Baron, and the Water Baron wanted them either captured or dead.

Listening closely, Angelo could hear a distant static hum, like white noise. With a jolt, he realized that if he tuned that hum in, he'd hear Jacob's thoughts.

The power of the connection jarred Angelo. He'd never realized he was capable of this. His hands shook and he took a deep breath. This was no time to let this affect him. He'd deal with his newfound abilities and what they meant later.

Jacob moved around the pile of rubble, closer to the wall, and into Angelo's line of sight. Angelo's hand tightened on the grip of the alter-gun. He rounded the corner, the gun aimed at Jacob's head. Jacob's gun arm went up wildly in surprise before he steadied it on Angelo. They fired at the same time. Jacob's shot went wide, hitting the wall and burning it with a crackling sound. The smell of charred drywall filled the air.

The alter-gun's stream caught Jacob in the temple and he went down where he stood, his laser flying from his hand and sliding across the floor.

Angelo holstered his alter-gun and walked to the fallen man. He took both his laser and his alter-gun, then divested both Dell and Mason of their weapons as well. He walked to Bianca, who still had a grip on the pistol. He placed the weapons into the saddlebag, but retained an alter-gun.

He reached out an empty hand, palm up. "Give me the pistol, Bianca."

She looked down at him, her mouth held in a tense line. Her grip tightened on the gun.

He placed a hand on her upper thigh and slowly rubbed his fingers across the fabric of her jeans, up nearly to the apex of her legs. His thumb brushed her intimately and sent a jolt of heat down his body to settle in his groin. Her breath quickened and her eyes widened.

"Give me the gun, Bianca," he said in a low, purring voice.

She handed it over to him without a word of protest. He gave her the alter-gun in exchange. She looked at it like it had suddenly grown hair and a pair of wings. "What do you expect me to do with this? I don't know this thing works."

He kept his hand on her thigh, not to discomfit her, as he'd meant to before, but merely because he liked touching her. "If you would be the least bit patient, I am going to show you. But remember, you only use the alter-gun if you're sure you can hit your target's head. Otherwise, use your pistol or a laser."

"Okay, but move your hand from my leg."

"Leg?" He moved his hand up a dangerous inch. "I thought I was touching your thigh. Your upper thigh, in fact."

She grabbed his hand pushed it away. "Leg, thigh, whatever! Just don't do that!"

He smiled slyly. "Ah. It's kind of like taking my shirt off, isn't it?"

She made a frustrated sound and showed him the back of the gun where the different settings were. "Teach me how to fire this damn thing." She glanced at the unconscious Dell and shivered. "And let's get out of here."

He raised a brow. "I was thinking we'd take the craft. It will fit a horse and get us where we're going a whole lot faster."

"Well." She smiled. "It is unmanned and unguarded, isn't it?"

"Sure is."

Just then the wind picked up, buffeting their hair and sending tendrils whipping into Bianca's face. An additional soft whirring joined that of the hovering craft in the street. Bianca looked at him in disbelief.

"A second craft," said Angelo. "More guardians."

"How many more?"

"No way to know."

He made a command decision. He mounted the horse behind Bianca in one smooth movement, wound his arms under hers and grabbed up the reins. Angelo dug his heels into the horse's sides and aimed the horse straight for the receptionist's desk. He nudged the horse harder, into a run. The gelding jumped the remains of the desk and out the window behind it. Bianca gave a full-throated scream.

The horse hit the street outside and slipped on the pavement. Angelo loosed the reins and let the horse have its head. It managed to keep its feet and not dump them off. When the horse had steadied itself, he dug his heels in and the horse jolted violently forward into a gallop, and then a flat-out run.

Angelo leaned down over Bianca, pressing her as close as he could to the horse's neck. He didn't guide the horse, Jinx would find his own way to safety. He glanced back. No hovercraft followed behind. He hoped they hadn't been seen. Most likely the second craft was merely meeting the first and weren't after them…yet. The guardians would disembark when they couldn't raise Dell on the craft's communication system. When they did, they would find Angelo's handiwork. Then they would search for the perpetrators. But by that time, he and Bianca would be long gone and in hiding. Hopefully.

The horse took them straight out of Out-Center and into the Wastes. Angelo let the horse stop at the edge of a grassy field, marked at either end by rusted and broken goal posts. Abandoned houses dotted the area in the distance. They'd encounter few buildings and even fewer people from here on out.

Bianca looked at the sky, and he followed her gaze. The sun dipped in the sky and storm clouds gathered on the darkening horizon. "It's almost night."

"Yes, we need to find a place to sleep."

She glanced behind them. He knew she was wondering where that second hovercraft was. "And to hide."

Chapter Eighteen

They found a house that had a roof that wasn't completely collapsed and dismounted. Angelo kicked the door open, and Bianca led the horse within. They couldn't risk the horse being seen from outside. If the garage was suitably undamaged, they'd put him in there for the night.

Angelo closed the door and turned. Hot blood trickled down his leg, and he knew he'd opened his wound back up. Vaulting onto the horse had done it. She glanced down and saw it, and then touched his leg where the blood had seeped through his pants.

"Angelo," she said softly, her face clouded with worry.

"It's not that bad."

"It's bad enough to disinfect," her tone sounded final. She fished out the first-aid kit and situated by him by a window, where she had light to work by. While he drew his pants and boxers down low enough on his injured side, Bianca grabbed a blanket from the couch and wiped the grime from the glass.

She knelt in front of him and by the waning light of day, cleansed his wound with gentle hands. He sucked in a breath that had less to do with the pain of his wound and more to do with the touch of her.

She stilled and looked up at him with an expression of concern. "Am I hurting you?"

He smiled and shook his head. "Not hurting." She only had to drop her hand down and over a little to see what she was doing to him. The slightest intimate brush of this woman's hand made him hard as a rock.

She finished cleaning the wound. While she replaced the first-aid kit, he drew two candles from the pack, lit them and placed them in holders. He gave a holder to Bianca, and then held out a hand to her. "Come on." He led her deeper into the house.

The structure was surprisingly undamaged, even most of the windows were intact. A thick layer of dust had covered over everything. They moved carefully, in order not to displace it. The house was like a museum; as if out of all the houses in this neighbourhood, this one had been untouched by the war and had only been ravaged by time. An overstuffed couch and two chairs sat in the living room, in front of large television set. Off the living room was a dining room with a long table and six chairs. Bianca followed him into the kitchen. Two bowls, a petrified carton of milk and a box of cereal sat on a small round table.

Angelo stood and stared at the ancient place settings. It looked as if the residents of the house had been ready to sit down to breakfast when something had happened to alter their lives forever. What horror had driven them from their home in such a hurry? Had they still been wearing their pajamas?

Bianca walked to the table and touched one of the bowls. She shivered and the candle she held quavered and threatened to extinguish. "My God." Her voice broke.

Angelo walked up behind her, set his candle on the table and placed his hands on her shoulders. She jumped, startled, and he hushed her, rubbing his palms over her upper arms and pressing his chest to her back. He didn't have anything to say. It always jarred him to find things like this, such deeply touching evidence of the horror of the war. This was partially his fault.

He turned away from her, his hands clenching in anger.

"What's the matter, Angelo?"

Turning, he found her looking at him with curiosity shining in her blue-green eyes. He wanted to tell her. He wanted to tell her everything. He wanted to tell her that his father had been a Kiran, his mother human, wanted to scream that he was a Kiran half-breed, shunned by the whole world. Wanted to explain that he and his sisters were rare things; Kirans did not often consort with humans. Half-breeds were uncommon. His mother had always told him his father had loved her, loved his children.

As if a Kiran could love.

He opened his mouth to do it, to tell her everything. It would be so nice to have someone share his burden. But he closed his mouth because he wouldn't be able to stand the shock and horror in her eyes. He couldn't bear to have her hate him. She stood there now in the candlelit kitchen with that damned stubborn tilt to her chin. That tilt had become endearing. No, Bianca's hatred would be worse than death, because standing there, looking at her, he realized something.

A Kiran could love.

"Nothing." He shook his head. "Nothing. It just bothers me, that's all."

She looked doubtful. "Okay, Angelo. If you ever want to tell—"

He picked up his candle, turned and walked out of the kitchen. "Let's see how the bedrooms look."

* * * * *

Bianca walked behind Angelo and tried not touch anything. She felt like an intruder here, like the occupants would be back at any moment and find them invading their privacy.

They passed a small hallway table where a vase of long-dead flowers stood. The desiccated petals had fallen to the table and onto the floor, so only brittle stems stood in the container. They passed the entrance to a small bathroom. Two closed doors stood at the end of the hallway. Angelo opened the first and found a bedroom, filled with debris from where the roof had fallen in at one corner. The weight of it had collapsed the bed and broken a long dresser. Bianca looked up at the sky where stars now shone. He closed the door and went to the next one.

That bedroom was as undamaged as the rest of the house. A large, four-poster bed stood in the center of the room. A dresser with a cracked mirror stood along one wall and a tall wardrobe dominated the opposite wall.

Angelo stepped into the room and motioned toward the bed. "Only one."

She stood outside the doorway, in the hall. "Guess so."

"I'll get you a blanket to put over this bed and you'll be able to sleep here very comfortably." He walked out the door and past her.

She caught his arm. "Where are you going to sleep?"

He shrugged. "On the couch in the living room."

She shivered. "No, Angelo, please, I don't want to sleep in here alone."

He raised an eyebrow. "Are you saying you want me to sleep with you?"

"Yes." Her grip on his arm tightened. "But just sleep, nothing else."

"Of course, Bianca. That's all I want, too." He pulled away from her and he walked down the hallway, probably to get the blankets from the pack.

Did that mean he wasn't attracted to her? She bit the pad of her thumb, suddenly thrown into a maelstrom of thought. She gave her head a sharp shake. Why should she care whether or not he was attracted to her?

But she did care.

He came back and only then did she enter the bedroom. She felt very uncomfortable in this house, especially here. The bedroom was the most intimate of rooms—where a person became most vulnerable to their partner, both while sleeping and making love. It was the room in the house where a person was the most exposed. Bianca felt vulnerable and exposed now.

While Angelo covered the bed with the blanket, Bianca reached out and brushed a woman's black robe that hung on the back of the door, sending up a cloud of dust. She sneezed.

"It's ready," said Angelo. "I'll sleep on the floor."

"No. Sleep on the bed with me. It's okay. I mean, unless I'm so unattractive that it would make you sick to sleep in the same bed with me, or something. I wouldn't want to make you ill." She'd tried not to sound hurt, but there it was—screaming hurt all through her voice.

He looked surprised. Yep, he'd heard it. She wanted him to want her and she'd just announced it plain as anything. Damn. "Get on the bed, Bianca," he said in a low voice.

"Angelo."

"Get on the bed before I come over there, pick you up and put you there."

Bianca blew out the candle and set it on the dresser, and then she walked over to the bed and crawled onto it. She rolled onto her side, facing away from him. She didn't want him to see her expression, which she knew was some conglomeration of dismay and hope. Bianca had never been good at dissembling, never had any skill at schooling her expression. She'd learned how to do it in order to survive, but Angelo had rendered her unable to don her mask.

The room went unbelievably dark when Angelo blew his candle out. Bianca had to admit she was glad for Angelo's presence. This house felt especially creepy. The bed creaked under his weight as he sat down on the mattress. With an exhausted groan, he lay on his side and pressed against the length of her body at her back. She felt the strong pressure of his chest against her, his thighs against the back of her thighs. He cupped himself against her in a way that said protection, telling her nothing would hurt her now. She snuggled against him, making a satisfied sound that came from somewhere deep in the center of her. His arm came over her waist and she pulled it against her like it was a teddy bear. She couldn't resist laying a kiss on the back of his knuckles.

"I want you, Bianca. More than anything. Remember that." His voice was a low whisper near her ear and the words rumbled through her bones. "You ought to know that by now."

She shivered and his arm tightened around her. The words, *I want you too*, almost tumbled from her lips, but where would that leave them? Would she roll over in the strong circle of his arms and would he kiss her? Would it go further than that? Would they make love here in this bed? If they did, what would happen tomorrow? Bianca knew. She'd be lost, lost in him, lost to him, even more than she already was. When the time came for him to leave her—and they always left—her heart would break again and shore itself up with another coating of ice. This time it'd be too thick to ever melt. Better to protect herself early and not allow that to happen.

She tried for bored and flippant and knew she'd failed before she even opened her mouth. "Great, that's good to know, Angelo. Why don't you go to sleep now?"

He sighed, but said nothing. Soon she heard his breathing deepen and knew he slept. Bianca lay in his arms and didn't sleep until early morning.

* * * * *

He'd taken his shirt off sometime during the night. That was the first thing Bianca noted when she opened her eyes. The second thing she noticed was the intimate tangle their legs made. They'd shifted easily while they'd slept, like they were lovers. He laid on his back and she on her side. Her head lay in the crook of his arm, half resting on his chest, and her arm draped over his upper stomach. One of his arms twined around her waist, the other thrown wide. He gripped a laser in the hand of the latter.

She lifted her head and pulled away from him. His arm tightened around her, pinning her against him. His breathing changed and she knew he was awake.

"Where do you think you're going?" he asked in a sleep-roughened voice, without opening his eyes. A small smile, the smile of a predator, curled his lips.

Her breath caught at the combination of the view of his chest, his arm around her and his sexy, sleepy voice. Heat flooded every inch of her, tightening her nipples and things lower down. She hated that he affected her that way.

She jerked away from him, saying at the same time, "Let me go!"

He let her go and she rolled off the bed to the floor with a thump, sending up a cloud of dust. She came up on her hands and knees, and sneezed.

Angelo leaned over the side of the bed. "Are you okay?"

She sneezed again. "Just great," she muttered. She stood and brushed dust from her jeans. A dull, gray-colored light filtered in from the cracked bedroom window. "Looks like a stormy day," she said, walking toward it.

"Yes, but we can't stay here. After that episode yesterday, they might search these houses."

She nodded. "We need to get as far from here as possible. I know a way that's not out in the open and not a direction they'd think we'd take."

"They don't know where we're going. Dell only knew you'd head south, not specifically what your destination was. I don't even know where we're going."

She turned and looked at him. He lay on the bed, propped up on one elbow, the other arm resting on his side. The laser lay on the blanket behind him. She'd been cradled in his arms all night long. Desire coursed through her as she imagined his hands tangling in her hair, moving over her bare skin, his lips moving over hers, his tongue demanding entry. A shudder ran through her as she remembered his mouth on her pussy, the way he'd sucked her clit between his sensual lips and made her come.

"Good thing too," she said, looking away. Fear flicked through her. Christ, what was she going to do?

"Are you afraid of me, Bianca?"

She looked back at him and lifted her chin. "No. What makes you say that?"

"I can feel fear radiating out from you."

"What do you mean, 'you can feel fear from me'?"

"Yesterday, when I was trying to pinpoint Jacob's location in the room, I felt his emotions, and your emotions. I can feel your emotions now too. They're mixed up."

She blushed. Could he feel her lust?

He cleared his throat, glancing sidelong at her.

Yep, he could.

"Mostly, it's fear, intense fear," he continued. "In fact, you are more afraid right now than you were yesterday, when you were facing possible death. Which means you fear being in my arms more than you fear dying."

"That's ridiculous."

"I wish it was."

They remained looking at each other and not speaking for several long moments. Then he rolled off the edge of the bed and stood. He walked toward her and she backed up until she was against the dresser. It reminded her of what he'd done in the bathing room at Quint's. He obviously liked backing her into corners, but he was about to find out that when you trapped things, they usually lashed out to protect themselves.

His mouth came down on hers so unexpectedly it literally took her breath away. One hand cupped her cheek, the other the nape of her neck. The hard length of his body brushed against hers. He parted her lips with no pretense, no subtlety, and plunged his tongue within.

She melted against him, giving up her fight for a moment under the erotic onslaught of his tongue on hers. Desire rose up from the depths of her and raced along her spine, surprising a low sound from her throat.

She knew that if he got her to the bed, it'd be over. There'd be no way she could tell him to stop. Once his hands were on her, she'd be his.

She bit his tongue. Not hard enough to draw blood, but enough that he made a surprised sound and broke the kiss. Then she pushed him back. Hard. Her fists clenched and she shook. "Don't." She drew a breath, her chest heaving. "*Don't* do that, Angelo."

He touched his tongue with his finger. "What are you so afraid of? I can feel desire from you, along with the fear."

"Look, I never gave you permission to take any kind of a look into my emotions, into my-my heart! Just stay out of there!" Tears stood in her eyes.

He stood looking at her. "You're right. It is an invasion of sorts. I'm sorry, Bianca." He took a step toward her with his hand out, to calm her, probably.

She took a step to the side. "Don't touch me!"

He dropped his hand and looked hurt. Her heart twisted. "All right." He turned so she couldn't see his expression. "Let's get going before the rain hits us." He took the blanket, his shirt and laser from the bed and walked out of the room.

* * * * *

The first fat drops of rain began to fall in early afternoon. They'd traveled as fast as Jinx could carry them without fatiguing the already tired beast. Bianca looked around anxiously but there was nothing, no shelter in view—only trees and rolling hills, dotted through with abandoned houses too dilapidated to trust in the rain.

Bianca tightened her grip around his midsection. "Angelo?" she asked. She knew he'd understand just by the tone of her voice. They had to find shelter and fast, preferably something other than the freysis tent. She didn't want to be in such close proximity to him. She scanned the horizon for rain-worthy shelter, but saw nothing in sight.

Angelo led the horse under a stand of pine trees; at least they'd be hidden if Dell were out with his hovercraft searching for them from the sky. He swung down off the horse and ripped open his saddlebag, groping within for the tent. The rain pelted them harder now. Bianca swung down from Jinx and went under the horse, trying shield herself.

Angelo popped the button on the tent and it burst forth, inflating and opening. The rain pounded down now. He grabbed the blanket out of the saddlebag and dove inside. Bianca watched him do it all without moving. She was not getting in that tent with him. No way. No how. Not after what had happened that morning.

His head poked out. "Get in here, Bianca! You're risking your life."

She huddled under the horse, staring at him balefully.

He muttered something under his breath, then louder, "I've never met anyone so stubborn!" He lunged forward, grabbed her arm and yanked her stumbling into the tent.

It was tight in the tent, too close. Bianca didn't want to be that close to him. Her guard might slip. She might do what she wanted to do — fall into his arms and never leave them.

"Take off your clothes," he ordered.

Chapter Nineteen

"Excuse me?" She knew she had to take them off. Goddamn it. She knew she did, but she didn't want to.

"It's not like I haven't seen you naked before, Bianca and this is no time to suddenly get modest. You can't stay in those wet clothes. Get them off now. Otherwise the freysis will soak into your blood. Your toxicity level will go up, maybe dangerously high."

He pulled off his boots, shirt and then his pants. He stood before her only in his boxer briefs, which didn't leave much to the imagination—washboard stomach, strong thighs, the outline of his... She blushed, looked away, and just stood there shivering.

"Bianca," he said with a warning in his voice. "If you don't take them off, I will."

She looked back at him. "You're getting a little territorial there, aren't you?"

"This is a serious situation. I'm not joking."

"Neither am I."

"Bianca."

She hesitated for a moment too long. Angelo stepped forward and grasped her shirt, starting to pull it over her head. She pulled away from him but there wasn't anywhere for her to go. The tent was too small. Filled with sudden anxiety, she plunged out the doorway and into the pouring rain. Angelo's arms came around her waist immediately and pulled her back in.

"Your stubbornness is going to get you killed!" He sounded as angry as she'd ever heard him. She faced him, shivering with the cold and staring up at him through her wet hair. His chocolate-brown eyes flashed with warning.

"All right! All right! Fine!" she said, holding up a hand, half in surrender, half to warn him away from her. "Get under that blanket and turn the other way."

He raised an eyebrow. "I can remember a time when you couldn't wait to undress in front of me."

"Do want me to do this or not?"

He spread the blanket on the floor of the tent, got under it and turned away.

Bianca drew her shirt over her head and tossed it to the side. Then she slipped off her shoes, socks and jeans. Her bra and panties were damp, but she didn't want to take them off. She wore the black lace set, freshly laundered by Marie. She stood, shivering, her wet hair clinging to her face, back and shoulders. She wasn't sure what to do now. Angelo had the only blanket.

He made a frustrated noise and flipped over. "Bianca, what are you doing?" She heard his breath catch and she felt herself blush. "Christ, you're beautiful," he breathed. "Every damn time I see you, I want you almost more than anything else in the world."

She rolled her eyes. "I don't believe this."

"Okay, I'm sorry. I'm turning over now, all right? But come under this blanket. You need to get the hair off your shoulders and you're going to get sick standing there near almost naked."

Bianca stood there watching his back for several long moments, her skin turning to gooseflesh. Then she knelt, picked up the edge of the blanket and tucked herself under it. Instantly, she felt enveloped in his heat. A sigh of pleasure escaped her.

Angelo turned over and she shot him her best look of warning. He motioned to her hair. "Just let me."

"Fine."

He propped himself up on his elbow and used his free hand to gather her hair off her shoulders and spread it out around her head in a fan. That way it wasn't touching her skin. She tried her best to ignore how good it felt to have his hands on her. Jesus, she wanted so badly to hate him.

After he finished arranging her hair, he hovered over her and ran the edge of his thumb down her cheek. She closed her eyes against the feel of his warm breath on her face.

Angelo must have taken the sigh she'd let out for acquiescence because he moved closer to her, brushing his body against hers. He felt warm and soft and hard at the same time. Her breath caught and her body quickened in that way that was now so familiar, pleasure pulsing down low between her legs.

God, she was fooling herself. What did it matter if they had sex or not? She *loved* him. Whether or not she allowed herself to express that love physically wouldn't change that. He already possessed her heart. She was already lost. She was already past the point of being able to protect herself.

Somewhere, between here and there, she'd completely given herself over to him. She'd feared losing another she loved, but what she suddenly realized was that whether or not they made love didn't matter. It would hurt just as badly to lose him if they never consummated what lay between them.

She opened her eyes and saw him staring down at her with heat in his eyes.

"Angelo," she breathed. "I—"

He didn't let her finish her sentence, probably afraid of what she might say. He lowered his head to hers and stopped the flow of her words with his mouth. He barely nipped at her lips and warmth flooded every inch of her. She wanted to push him away. She wanted to get up and run screaming from the tent, but Christ, he felt so good.

He applied more pressure to her lips and she parted them. His tongue sought hers and asked to dance. She didn't refuse. When his hand grazed the swell of her breasts where they peeked from the top of the bra and went lower, she shuddered in pleasure and anticipation. His hand came to rest on her stomach and stroked once, his fingertips grazing the edge of her panties like he was asking for permission. It drove all thoughts of denial and escape from her mind. Anyway, she was boneless now. The thought came sluggishly...a girl can't run when she doesn't have any bones.

He broke the kiss and looked down at her with a gaze that made her pulse quicken. "Bianca." He said her name in a way that seemed to stroke the innermost parts of her. It was half entreaty, half dark promise.

She reached up and touched his chest, letting her fingers trace the smooth muscle and soft skin. She ran them over his nipples, met his scar where it wrapped his side, and traced it to his stomach. Her fingers found his treasure trail and followed it below the waistband of his boxers. When she found his cock, her eyes widened. She'd never touched a man before, not even Adam, and the feel of Angelo against her palm was different than she'd expected. It was like a length of silken steel, soft and incredibly hard at the same time. She stroked him, loving the feel of him.

He shuddered at her touch and groaned low. His eyes went dark with undisguised need and his hand slid over the swell of her breasts, catching at the front clasp of her bra. He wanted to undo it, but she knew he wouldn't. Not without her permission, never without that. She opened her mouth to give it, and then closed it.

They were entering the realm of no return.

"Angelo—I'm—" she swallowed hard, not knowing how to even say the words.

"What?"

"I'm—" She dropped her gaze and stared at his chest. "I'm afraid. Last time I was with a man like this, so intimate...bad things happened. I know we've touched before, but the first time was with clothes all on and the second, well, I wasn't really myself."

He dropped his head and kissed her. "No, Bianca. It wouldn't be that way between us."

"It-it wouldn't hurt?"

Angelo brushed his lips along her hairline. "Oh, no, angel-face. It wouldn't hurt, I promise. Do you want me to show you a little of what it can be?"

His hand dropped lower, rubbing against the silk of her panties at the apex of her legs and stroked her clit. It seemed to throb harder with every pass against it. He moved his finger over it in a circular motion. A moan caught in her throat, and then broke free. His fingers closed around the elastic waistband of her panties and he looked at her. She held his dark gaze and nodded once, giving permission.

He slid them over her hips and down her legs, a whisper of silk sliding across her skin. She pushed them off and away with her feet. His open palm slid up her leg, drawing a line of fire from her calf to her thigh, then past her hips to her bra. One twist and the front clasp gave way and her breasts spilled out to his hands.

He propped himself up on an elbow so he could look down at her. She heard his breath catch in his throat and Bianca responded in kind, half from self-consciousness and half because the look on his face was so dark, so passionate. She turned her head to the side, away from him.

He caught her chin and forced her gaze to his. "You're beautiful, Bianca. My God, you're the most beautiful thing I've ever seen." The look in his eyes told her what he wanted to do to her before he dropped his head and did it. His mouth closed over her right nipple and he laved his tongue over it.

The feel of his tongue against her and the sight of his dark head bent over her body in such an intimate act drove a small helpless sound from her throat. His fingers trailed over her abdomen and went lower. He urged her thighs apart and she complied. She felt exposed, like he had stripped her armor away.

He touched her soft, folded flesh with slow movements, slipping a finger inside her. She let out a quick hiss of breath, ending in a soft moan and arched her back. Bianca reached up and wound her fingers through the silky hair at the nape of his neck.

He moved from her breast, caught her lips against his and parted them, sliding his tongue in and brushing it against hers. Then he moved his finger and tongue within her in a synchronized rhythm and let the pad of his thumb rub over her clit. The combination drove all thought from her mind until she was a merely a bundle of sensation.

The pleasure grew and grew. The slow buildup of it drew small sounds from her throat, and caused her to knead and rub her hands along his upper arms and back. When he brushed against her side with his pelvis, she felt the long, thick length of his cock. He wanted her and the thought of him coming within her, thrusting inside her the way his finger did now, caused the building pleasure to breach its limit and wash over her. She arched her back against the intense climax. It stole her breath so she couldn't even moan. Bianca held her breath and bit her lip, closing her eyes while pleasurable spasms racked her.

Angelo stared down at her with that same dark desire burning in his eyes, but now it was even hotter than before. His brown eyes were dark, nearly black.

Bianca caught her breath. She wasn't sure she could speak without her voice shaking. She reached up and pressed her palm against his cheek. "You never take anything for yourself."

He dipped his head and kissed her. "Making you come is something I enjoy, Bianca."

She rose up and pushed him down to the ground. "I want to make *you* come. That is something *I* will enjoy."

His pupils dilated.

She leaned down and kissed him. He pressed his hand to the nape of her neck and crushed her mouth to his. His tongue tasted hot and delicious as it rubbed against hers. She pulled away and grinned at him, then proceeded to kiss her way down his throat and chest. She laid a couple quick tongue swipes to his nipples and moved down, eager to do what she had in mind. Later, she'd explore every last square inch of his incredible chest at her leisure. Now there was pleasure-giving to be done.

Bianca took his cock in hand and stroked it. He let out a low, sexy groan at her touch. She studied its soft crown and the heavy veins that ran down the shaft. He groaned again when she took his balls in one hand. "Um, I've never done this before, so I'm sorry if I screw it up or if it's bad."

He raised his head. "What do you—oh, hell!"

She'd licked the crown and then engulfed it in her mouth.

Angelo tipped his head back, showing his Adam's apple, and groaned out her name. "Give me some warning next time."

She closed her eyes and licked up the shaft, enjoying the way he'd twined his fingers through her hair. When she slid her lips down him again, his body tensed and his hips jerked.

She smiled a little, wanting to purr with pleasure.

What she lacked in skill, she tried to make up for with enthusiasm. She took note of the areas she touched that drew the biggest reaction from him, learning his body as she went. She took joy in the feel of him against her tongue and the slide of his cock in and out from between her lips. She took even more joy in the way it seemed to affect him. His breath came short and raspy in the tent and he gripped her hair gently but firmly.

"Bianca," he growled.

"Mmmmm?"

"Fuck." His hands tightened in her hair. "Bianca, I'm going to come. Back away."

No way.

She thrust him far down into her mouth and stroked the base of him as she sucked him in and out. His body went rigid and his balls felt tight and hard. His hips jerked forward, forcing his cock past her tonsils. She made an effort not to gag.

"Aw, hell, Bianca," he groaned.

She felt his cock jump in her mouth as he released himself. His cum shot down her throat and she swallowed every bit of it. "Bianca," he breathed.

When the waves of his climax had passed, she rolled over onto her back. "So that's what that's like. I always wondered."

He let out a bark of laughter. "You're incredible." He leaned over and pulled her close. Together, they listened to the rain pelt the tent's roof. Thunder crashed in the distance. "For your first time that was…uh…"

"Was it bad?" She wrinkled her nose.

He tipped her chin up and kissed her. "Are you kidding? You sent me to heaven," he murmured. "What other things have you wondered about?"

She drew line with her finger over his chest. "Lots of things. I'm inexperienced but not innocent. Try stuff and find out."

"So now I have carte blanche on your body? This morning you almost bit my tongue off for kissing you."

She half-shrugged. "A girl's entitled to change her mind."

"So I'd better take advantage while I can, in other words." He rolled her beneath his body and pressed his cock against her leg. "Imagine what I would do with carte blanche," he growled.

She sighed and snaked her hand between their bodies to stroke him. "I can only pray you'll do your worst," she answered solemnly.

He pulled her over on her side and slid his hand down her thigh, hooking it over his leg. "You skin is so damn soft, Bianca," he murmured as he rubbed his palm over her back, massaging the muscles. With heat-stopping slowness and tenderness, he stroked his hand down over her hip and buttocks, to her sex.

She hissed out a breath at the feel of him stroking over her folds. She was still wet there, still powerfully aroused by how he'd come in her mouth. He caressed her clit, using some of her cream and she felt it plump once more, again hungry for stimulation. When he slipped his finger to her anus, her hips bucked in surprise. He circled it, awakening nerves she hadn't known existed there. Her pussy wept anew.

"How about this?" he purred near her ear. "Have you wondered?"

"Uh," she gasped as his finger slipped into the tight ring of nerves. "Oh, God," she moaned.

"Is that a good *oh, God*, or a bad one?"

"Good," she breathed. She'd never known that part of her body could feel that way.

He dipped his fingers down, coating them in more of her slippery juices, and then rubbing them over the tight entrance of her ass. He thrust the tip of his finger back in and out slowly.

"I have wondered," she answered. "I just never knew…it, ah, would feel like that." Her nipples were like hard rocks tipping her breasts and her pussy was creaming hard in arousal.

"I can take you here, but nowhere else. Not now, at least. It will be good, Bianca. I'll be gentle. You'll like it. I know you will. It's your choice."

The thrust of his finger deeper into her anus made his words a little muddled in her mind. Her body tensed to climax and her fingers sought the blanket for something to grip. He could take her from behind, he'd said. "Why, Angelo? Why can you only take me from behind?"

"I thought you were curious." He leaned forward and kissed her. "Are you frightened?"

He stroked his finger in and out gently, making her breath catch and her senses leave. Pleasure skittered up her spine. He hadn't really answered her question, but that seemed of little consequence. She just wanted him inside her, however he wanted to come. "No. I'm...intrigued."

He pulled free of her body and rolled over to fish something out of his bag. He came back with a small vial. "The doctor gave me this. It's a lubricant. He used it to lessen the friction between the bandage and my skin, but it's organic. It can be used internally."

"Internally?" she said hesitatingly.

"Get on your knees, angel-face. Let me show you how it would feel."

She rolled to her stomach and pushed up. Part of her was scared, but most of her was curious and turned on.

"What a beautiful sight," Angelo groaned behind her. He stroked her ass, delving his fingers between her cheeks to tease her labia. "I can't wait to be inside you." He stroked down her back, reaching his hands around to her front to catch and knead her breasts. He rolled her nipples between his thumbs and forefingers, making her moan.

"Mmmm, I like you in this position," he murmured.

His hands disappeared and she heard him squeeze some of the lubricant out onto his fingers. He rubbed it into her pussy. It was slick and warm from his skin. He rubbed his finger over her anus and her hips bucked and a jolt of uncertainty went through her.

"Say the word and I'll stop," he said softly. He slid his other hand down her front, letting it disappear between her spread thighs to tease and caress her clit. In the same moment, he pressed a finger straight into her nether hole.

"Oh, God," she cried at the dual sensations.

His finger thrust in and out of her as his other hand stroked her clit. She felt ready to climax at any moment. "You want more?" he asked her.

"More?" she gasped. "There's more?" She slurred her words like a drunk. God, it was good.

He gave a low, masculine chuckle. "Oh, yeah, there's more, angel-face." He added a second finger into her rear, widening her muscles back there. Slowly, he thrust his thick fingers in and out of her.

She balled her fist and hit the floor of the tent with it. "Yes," she hissed.

"Does it hurt?"

She nodded. "A little, but it's okay."

"I can't wait to take you here," he groaned. "You're opening up for me. You're relaxing back here enough for me to fit. You're going to be so damn hot and tight around my cock. You're going to be so fucking sweet and perfect."

He slipped his other hand down and speared her pussy with his fingers so that he took her in both places at once. Bianca bucked against his hand and lowered her head to raise her ass up, offering herself to him without restrictions. "Angelo," she gasped. "That's so good."

"You like that?" he rasped.

She nodded. In this position she felt completely at his mercy, in total submission to him. She was happy to give up control, to trust him with her body. She did trust Angelo…with everything she was.

Angelo shifted the hand working her pussy so that he stroked some spot deep inside her that felt extra-sensitive. Bianca wanted to sob she was so turned on. She wanted to beg him to take her. A climax flirted hard with her body.

"Come for me, Bianca. Come on, baby. I want to feel you drench my hand."

His words, spoken in a needy, strained voice, were her undoing. She climaxed and her muscles clenched and unclenched around his fingers. She cried out, her hips bucking as the hardest climax she'd had so far ripped through her.

"Ah, that's what I wanted," Angelo purred as the waves racking her body were receding. "Are you ready for the rest of me? Are you ready to take me into your sweet little ass?"

"Yes!" she sobbed.

She felt his hard chest brush her back and as he leaned over and bussed his lips across the nape her neck. Bianca stilled. She'd said she was ready to take him, but Angelo was by no means a small man.

Hell, he'd rip her to shreds.

She heard the lubricant bottle opening back up. "Uh, Angelo?" she asked softly.

"It's all right, angel-face. I'll fit. Do you trust me?" He pressed the head of his cock to her, and she bucked involuntarily.

"Y-yes."

"I'd never do anything to hurt you, Bianca. Never."

She took a deep breath and relaxed. "I know."

He grabbed her hips, holding her in place, and then brushed the head of his cock across her opening and she felt her muscles relax for him. "Ah, fuck," he groaned. "Your body is so ready for this. You're nice and aroused, nice and open."

"Come inside me," she murmured. "I can't wait to have you within me."

"The crown will be the worst," he said through gritted teeth. Angelo put one of his big hands on her shoulder and placed the other on her hip. The head of his cock pressed into her, breaching the tight ring of muscles of her anus. She inhaled at the sharp mixture of a pleasure and pain. He pressed inside her slowly, oh, so *very* slowly.

"More," she gasped. She pressed back, trying to impale herself.

He groaned and slapped both hands to her hips, stilling her movement. "Hell, Bianca. You're going to make me come before I'm even all the way in." He eased her back against him and slowly thrust the shaft of him deeper into her. "You're so damn sweet and tight. Just like I knew you'd be."

Finally, he seated himself within her to the base of his cock. "Ah, Angelo," she moaned and hit the floor with the flat of her palm. "It's so good." Her muscles clamped down on his cock and she gritted her teeth at the painful pleasure. Part of her wanted to ask him to pull out, but most of her wanted him to fuck her.

He did the latter.

His hips pulled back and thrust forward as he set up a relentless rhythm. With every thrust the penetration grew easier. "I can't hold back," he groaned as he picked up speed, pushing her harder with each piston-like movement. "You feel too good around me."

"Don't stop," she moaned. "Don't you dare fucking stop."

He slid his hand around her front, stroking his fingers through her pubic hair. She bucked her hips when he returned to thrust two fingers into her creaming pussy. She moaned out his name when he ground his palm into her clit and finger-fucked her there, even as he took her from behind. Such pleasure surely had to be beyond the laws of nature. The sensation of him filling up both her orifices that way wiped her mind clean of thought. Her whole world narrowed to Angelo and Angelo alone.

"God, you feel so good," Angelo groaned. "I can't get enough of you."

He extracted his fingers from her dripping pussy and slicked her cream over her clit as he worked the sensitized bundle between two fingers.

The muscles of her body tensed and shuddered as another intense climax racked her. Her vision grew black and for a moment she feared she'd pass out.

"Bianca." Behind her, she heard Angelo's deep groan as came. She felt him fill her up, his cock jumping and his body shuddering against hers.

They collapsed onto the floor of the tent, breathing hard. The rain fell in a slower rhythm now, though Bianca was too tired, too sated to care. "So that's what that's like," she said with a short laugh. "Now I know."

"There are lots of things we can do together without me actually taking your pussy."

His words made her still. A memory from when she'd been down the Oubliette came flooding back at her. She'd asked him to come in her and he'd said he wished he could, but that would never happen.

Huh? *Why?* Obviously, his cock was working just fine. The delicious soreness of her ass was a testament to that very fact.

"Why wouldn't you want to take my pussy?" she asked. She rose up on her elbows and laid her lips against his. She spoke with their mouths touching and her eyes closed. "I want you within me, Angelo. I want you moving inside me more than I've ever wanted anything else."

His free hand moved from her stomach and slid around to the small of her back, supporting her. He pressed her to him, deepening the kiss, his tongue sliding in and branding hers, quick and hot. "I want you more than I can tell you, Bianca."

"So why can't you have me? I'm not stopping you." She lifted a brow. "*Au contraire.*"

He groaned and pressed his face into her neck, muffling his words. "We can't. Not without protection."

Bianca let herself fall back to the ground. "Protection? Protection against what?" Then it dawned on her. She hadn't even thought of the possibility of pregnancy. In truth, she'd never really thought about having children at all. There was currently a law against having more than one child per couple. As a society, they walked a fine line between having to repopulate a diminished world, and not bringing too many thirsty little mouths into it. Despite all that, looking up into Angelo's brown eyes, knowing the kind of person he was, the only thing Bianca could think of was how much she'd love to carry his child. There were many children in the Valley, both

Kiran and human. She loved each one and watched them often for their parents.

"You're afraid you'd get me pregnant?" she said finally, understanding dawning.

He nodded. "There are ways for us to prevent pregnancy without any formal protection. But they aren't foolproof."

She raked her eyes down his body, from his strong arms and chest, to his narrow stomach, and finally to his long, wide cock that now rested flaccid on his thigh. "Yes," she murmured. "You definitely *could* get me pregnant. There's no doubt about that."

She reached up and cupped his cheek in her hand. "In case you haven't noticed, we're running a little short on people here on Earth. In any case, I'd more than happy to carry your child. I'd be…proud." The truth. All of it. She hoped he did make her pregnant. That way she'd always have a little part of him if she lost him.

He touched her cheek. Indefinable emotions chased across his face and he rolled away from her.

Bianca wrapped the blanket around her and sat up. Angelo went to the door of the tent and drew the flap back. It had stopped raining. "Angelo, what's wrong? Did I say something to upset you?"

He had his back to her and didn't turn around. "I'm going out to get the other saddlebag. We have dry clothing in it."

She watched, mute and wondering, as he slipped on his boots, went out to the horse and came back with the saddlebag in hand. He placed it on the ground, opened it and pulled out an old pair of faded jeans. He pulled them on.

"Angelo, please talk to me. What just happened? Is the thought of me having your child that terrifying to you?" She used anger in her tone to cover the hurt she felt, but she knew she wasn't doing a good job of masking the pain in her eyes. He could probably feel it anyway.

He zipped up his jeans, but left the top button undone. Then he stood there, shirtless, staring down at her with a dismayed look on his face. "No. I mean, partly, but not in the way you think."

Her answer was swift, her tone like steel. "What other way *should* I think?"

He sighed and dragged a hand back through his hair. "I really don't want to talk about this. It's not you carrying my child that upsets me. It's..." He trailed off and looked away.

She went on her hands and knees and crawled toward him. The blanket slid off her, leaving her naked. She rose up on her knees, hooking her fingers in the waistband of his pants and looking up at him. "It's what then?"

He looked down at her and his eyes filled with desire. It chased the last of the fear away. He placed his hand to the top of her head and trailed his fingers down through her hair. Then he knelt, taking her in his arms and pushing her backward. He crawled over her and pressed himself down on her. Her legs came around his waist and pressed against him. Only his clothing separated them and Bianca could feel his aching hardness as he thrust against her slowly in a teasing semblance of the actual act. It sent fine waves of excitement up her spine.

God, she wanted him filling her so much. She'd enjoyed what they'd just done, but she wanted him in her pussy. She wanted him like this, intimately connected and sharing each other's breath. His mouth came down on her breast, and then traveled to her collarbone, her throat, her chin, and finally, her mouth.

He rubbed himself against her clit with the perfect amount of friction and in the perfect place. "Angelo," she gasped.

He didn't answer her. He only dropped his head and laved and sucked at her nipple as if it were the best thing he'd ever tasted, all the while sliding the length of his hard cock sheathed by his pants relentlessly over her clit.

Her head fell back as another climax ripped through her. How many times could the man make her come?

She lay, gasping for air. "Angelo, please. I want you inside me so bad," she said, finally.

He let out a ragged groan and pushed up, leaving her bereft. "No," he said in a low growl. "We can't do this." He went to the saddlebag, grabbed a sheer blue summer dress that Marie had packed for her and tossed it to her. It landed on her stomach. "Put this on before something happens that we'll both regret."

She winced as though he'd struck her. *Regret?* His actions had thus far been in direct conflict with these words. What was going on? "I wouldn't regret it, Angelo. I'm sorry you would." Sorrow filled her up now, and it bled through her voice.

He stayed silent.

What was it? What wasn't he telling her? Could it have something to do with the possibility that alien blood ran through his veins? Bianca rose up on her elbows, letting the cool, soft fabric of the dress rest against her stomach and breasts. "Why don't you trust me enough to share your secrets, Angelo? Why won't you let me help carry the weight you so obviously bear?" She softened her expression. "There is nothing, *nothing*, you could tell me that would make me think ill of you."

"Don't be too sure of that, Bianca. You don't know everything I might reveal."

The self-hatred that shone in his eyes astounded her. It wounded her that he wanted to keep such secrets from her. It hurt her that he didn't trust her, and that he didn't want to build any kind of deeper relationship with her. Worst of all, it hurt her that he hurt and she didn't know why.

She sat up and drew the dress over her head. "Fine," she snapped. "Keep your secrets. But you won't be able to keep your secrets and me at the same time. You're going to have to make a choice about which you want the most. Secrets won't keep you warm at night. Secrets won't—" She snapped her mouth shut and gritted her teeth. She'd almost just admitted she loved him. That wouldn't do, especially now.

He stared down at her and she up at him. Finally, he moved. He shoved their wet clothes in the waterproof part of the saddlebag designed to carry them and stuffed the blanket into the main part of the bag. He stalked out the tent opening. "Put your boots on. Let's get going."

Bianca sat there with tears stinging her eyes.

Chapter Twenty

Angelo shifted the reins to his opposite hand. They'd traveled for two days in near silence. Now they were deep into a place that had once been called *Indiana*. Swollen, heavy clouds hung in the sky. They almost looked painful, as if they wanted to shed their load, but couldn't. He looked up at them, squinting against the glare. Or maybe he was simply projecting his own troubles onto them.

Yesterday, he and Bianca had ridden until it had been too dark to see. The heavy cloud cover had hidden the moon and forced them to stop for the night. Neither knew what to say to the other at this point, but they'd been so exhausted they'd fallen right to sleep, so it hadn't mattered.

Having Bianca beneath him, responding to his touch had been heaven. Taking from her behind had been one of the most erotic experiences of his life, yet he wanted to stake a claim to her pussy. He wanted to make it his and he couldn't. That pained him badly.

And not only did he want her with his body, but with his heart as well. Unfortunately, he'd realized long ago he couldn't have a relationship like that with a woman. He'd never condemn Bianca to life with a half-blooded Kiran who never wanted children. It wasn't fair to her.

The terrain was growing hillier and there were many trees, fewer and fewer abandoned houses and communities. They'd lost the guardians. That was one good thing. He worried they'd lost themselves as well, but Bianca seemed to know where they were going. Angelo could track a person through unknown territory, but not a place. Bianca had said little about their destination, only that it was called the Valley.

They passed an enormous sinkhole at the base of an elm. It exposed the elm's root structure. It was not the first they'd seen.

"What causes that?" he asked, almost to himself.

"Those in the Valley think they're being caused by the freysis. It's alien bacteria, after all. There are bound to be some side effects."

"Maybe the freysis is changing the soil, making it unstable." He'd never seen it in the Center, or the Sectors where his family had lived. But those places were cities with less open ground.

"Yes, that's what they think. I saw it in the Out-Center, on the way to the Water Company. It's not just happening in the country."

Angelo rubbed a hand over his chin, considering her words. Apparently, even though the foliage thrived on the freysis, Mother Earth did not.

The sun, what you could see of it behind the clouds, anyway, was sinking fast. It would almost be time to seek shelter again. "Bianca, do you know of a place we can spend the night?"

"We're almost there."

Angelo looked around. For as far as the eye could see there were only trees and rocks. Occasionally, there was an old building, but beyond that, it was only Bianca, himself and the occasional squirrel, rabbit or deer.

"Really?" he asked. With his mind, he reached out and felt for people and found them—lots of them.

"Wait until we reach the top of this hill. Then you'll see."

They lapsed into one of their frequent silences. When they reached the summit, he could see what Bianca called the Valley. Small houses and larger buildings, all made of split logs, with black solar panels on their roofs dotted the lush, green carpet of grass. They were nestled under a stand of large trees, which shaded and concealed the community from the air.

"Welcome to the most-populated section of Sector Twenty-Nine—the Valley," said Bianca. "It's hidden very well from hovercraft. The founders did that strategically to guard against the guardians and bounty hunters sent to hunt K—ah—captured persons who have escaped. The Essential Providers sometimes will send guardians out in hovercraft, but then, you know that. The area is also hidden well by those traveling on foot or horseback, since it's out here in the middle of nowhere. Also, we have scouts who tell us when people approach. I'm sure they've already been notified of our presence."

"What do you do in the winter when the leaves are off the trees?"

"Pray. Well, and there are a lot of evergreens. But guardian patrols are far more limited in the winter anyway, as you know, because of the snow. Makes the world a very hazardous place, even with freysis suits."

"Yes."

People walked along neatly kept packed stone streets, almost like cobblestone. No refuse littered the area. It looked clean, neat and very civilized. It looked like everything Sector Twenty-Nine was not supposed to be.

"Just follow the path. It will lead you straight into town," said Bianca.

Angelo saw a path leading down the side of the hill. He guided the horse onto it.

When they reached the edge of "town," as Bianca had called it, a little girl with two black pigtails came running up to the horse. "Bianca! Bianca!" she cried. "I thought you were never coming back!"

Bianca slipped from the back of the horse, knelt and scooped the little girl into her arms. "Now you know that's not true! How could I go away and not see my Sianna anymore?"

The little girl laughed and hugged Bianca and Angelo stared. He'd love to see a child of his own in her arms, but he never would.

Sianna caught sight of him and cowered in Bianca's arms. "Who is that?" she whispered fearfully.

Bianca glanced up at him. "That's Angelo. I don't know why he looks so scary all of a sudden." She gave him a piercing look. "Normally, he has a very *nice* expression on his face."

Angelo relaxed the muscles of his face, realizing he'd been scowling. He forced a smile that probably looked more like a grimace. "Hi, Sianna."

"Hi," she said shyly, then buried her face in Bianca's neck.

A crowd gathered around them. Angelo dismounted and held the horse's reins in his hands.

People of all ages, wearing clean, patched clothing, came up to Bianca, hugging her, welcoming her. A low-level buzz started in his ears. He knew what it was from and it made his blood run cold. There were Kirans here, and a whole lot of them if the level of buzzing told the truth. All Kirans could recognize each other this way. Upon first meeting, their brain wave patterns recognized each other's by emitting a low range frequency pattern that went away a few moments after initial contact.

The enemy surrounded them. He forced himself to remain calm.

He watched as she greeted them with genuine warmth. Didn't she know some of them were Kiran? Were they trying to hide themselves among humans? Unconsciously, his hand went to the laser in his shoulder holster. Fingering the grip, he readied to draw. He could take all these Kirans into the Center and imprison them. Then he shook head, realizing he wasn't a guardian anymore.

An old man with long white hair parted the crowd with a scowl on his face. "Let me through!" he demanded. Everyone stepped out of his way.

The man walked straight to Angelo, and placed a gnarled, blue-veined hand on the back of his. The buzzing peaked when the man touched him. Angelo tried to pull away, but he held him with surprising strength.

"It's all right," the old man said. "We're all friends here." The old man looked into his eyes and Angelo looked back into his steely blue ones, and they knew each other for their shared Kiran blood.

A small part of Angelo felt exhilarated, happy. Surprised and appalled by his reaction, he tamped it down, pushing it far within him. The Kirans were cause of all their woes.

The crowd had gone quiet. They all stood looking at him. Slowly, he moved his hand from the laser. He had to get Bianca alone and tell her these people weren't all human, but how would he explain how he knew that?

Bianca took a step toward the old man, an apprehensive look on her face, as if she didn't know whether he would hit her or hug her. If he hit her, the man was going down. "Melvin."

Melvin turned and opened his arms to her. "Bianca, I worried you'd never return to us."

She let him draw her into his arms for a brief hug. She remained visibly stiff, but closed her eyes and sighed, as if relieved he'd not turned her away. She pulled away from him and motioned with an open hand toward Angelo. "Angelo, meet Melvin. Melvin, Angelo."

Angelo inclined his head. "Nice to meet you," he said stiffly. An older woman took Bianca's arm and she turned away from them.

Melvin reached out and grasped his hand in his bony, wispy ones. "We have much to talk about, my boy. I do believe we have some things in common."

He pulled his hand away. "We have nothing in common, old man." Steel backed the words. Having a Kiran touch him, say they had things in common. It was too much.

Anger flashed in the old man's eyes and Angelo became aware of a harshness, an instability even, roiling under his seemingly calm, kind exterior. "You have much to come to terms with, *Arapass*," Melvin hissed under his breath. Arapass was the name used for a fellow Kiran. It was not considered an insult, but for Angelo it was the gravest of them.

Angelo went rigid and his jaw locked. He looked at Bianca, hoping she hadn't heard.

Melvin followed his gaze. "I understand," the old man whispered. "You are ashamed of your blood and do not wish Bianca to know of it. That look you just gave her speaks volumes. Your secret is safe with me, Arapass."

Bianca turned toward them again, extricating herself from the grasp of those who seemed so happy to see her. "Melvin, we need to get home. We have urgent things to discuss."

The old man crooked a finger. "Come."

He and Bianca followed him out of the crowd, Angelo leading Jinx. They walked down a narrow street lined on each side by split log homes, each separated by large yards and fences. Barrels planted with fresh flowers stood on some doorsteps.

Angelo couldn't help but stare. "You've built these homes by hand."

Melvin glanced back at him. "Instead of taking the leftovers from the war, we decided to start again, start new. We built our own places to live, created our own community."

"Where do the humans get their water?" There was hostility he couldn't mask in his voice.

Bianca turned and looked at him with surprise on her face. Either she knew many of these people were Kiran and was surprised he knew it too, or she didn't know they weren't all human and was surprised by his phrasing of the question.

Either way, he and Bianca were due a long talk.

"There's a natural source," Melvin answered. "A very deep and plentiful well of water in a cave nearby that hasn't been contaminated by freysis. We keep it carefully capped and draw water from it. It's what determined the location of this place. We have covered greenhouses where we grow pure plants and vegetables. Covered barns where we keep livestock on purewater and feed. It might look simple, but this is no unsophisticated operation, boy."

Bianca didn't look at him. So she did know.

They turned a corner and walked down the street. Woods stood at the end of it. The very last house had windows with panes of unbroken glass and yellow flowers planted outside in neat, even rows. Black solar panels stretched above the roof.

Melvin turned and took Jinx's reins. "I will make sure he gets water and feed. He looks exhausted. You've traveled long and hard."

Angelo rubbed the horse's muzzle. The gelding huffed with pleasure. "Yes, and the horse didn't live up to his namesake, thankfully."

Melvin disappeared around the side of the house with Jinx, and Angelo reached out and ran a finger down one of the unbroken panes of glass. He turned to Bianca with the question in his eyes.

She shrugged. "We scrounge and salvage what we can from Out-Center. That was one of our primary jobs, Calina and I."

"Why would they send two beautiful young girls to Out-Center? That isn't safe."

She shrugged again. "We lived for years in the Out-Center and knew it well, Angelo. We were already fifteen by the time we came here and knew how to survive in the Out-Center. So, we volunteered for the job in order to earn our keep." Clouds of dark emotion passed through her eyes. "Anyway, what do you think? Life is supposed to be safe for young girls? I think Calina has proved that's not true."

Angelo took a step forward and ran a finger down her cheek. She didn't step away and he was glad about that. "You've proved it too."

She looked away. "You want to go in?" She turned and pushed the front door open. They entered the house and the first thing Angelo smelled was fresh-baked bread. Christ, was this place for real, or was he dreaming?

Handmade wooden furniture dotted the living room to their right. A rocking chair made of heavy branches stood next to a couch made of spilt logs with cushions laid on it. A red and brown woven rug lay on the floor in front of a huge stone fireplace. On the mantel were small crystal figurines of animals, interspersed with what Angelo recognized as Kiran crystals. Straight ahead of them lay a small hallway with several doorways opening into darkened rooms. Angelo assumed they were bedrooms.

To their direct left sat a round wooden table with four chairs. In the back left corner was a cooking area. Another smaller, stone fireplace stood there. A pot hung from a hook over a small fire lit within, and above that was a metal box with a door set in hinges—an oven, maybe? Several tall tables that probably served as countertops lined the walls, along with two large tubs with four spigots coming out the walls, which Angelo surmised constituted sinks. He walked over to take a closer look. Why were there two?

"We have running water here. Each house has a large water containment unit in the back. It's filled with water that can be used throughout each individual house. We even have flushing toilets and showers. All houses have solar-powered water heaters as well."

Angelo turned with amazement on his face.

She smiled that same smile that never reached her eyes. "Necessity is the mother of invention." Her smile faded. "But, if we are to stay here with Melvin, special water arrangements will have to be made."

Angelo narrowed his eyes. He knew what she meant, but he wanted to hear her say it. "What do you mean?"

"I didn't want to tell you earlier because I was afraid you wouldn't come here with me. I know you know now, though, that Melvin is Kiran."

"So are a lot of other people here."

She cocked her head to the side. "How do you know that?"

"Never mind how I know. The point is, I do."

She sighed. Fatigue had painted smudges beneath her blue-green eyes. "In any case, the water in the tank is freysis-tainted now. Please don't use it. Because Calina and I lived here, Melvin has two tanks in the back—one for freysis water, the other for pure-water. That is why you'll see four spigots, not just two. I'd imagine the pure-water tank was emptied after I left. We don't waste it or let it sit. We have strict laws regarding pure-water usage here, just as they do in the Center. The well is plentiful, drawn from an underground source, but bringing the water up and getting it into the tanks is back-breaking work."

Little did she know he probably could use the tainted water. He'd never tested the theory, but it was likely he could metabolize freysis like a Kiran, even though he was only a half-blood. He didn't need freysis to survive like a full-blooded Kiran, but likely it wouldn't harm him either. He'd just never wanted to test it out.

"You've been planning to give the water crystal to a Kiran, Bianca?" he asked too softly. Would she hear the subtle rage in his voice?

She shook her head. "You don't understand. Melvin lives to right the wrongs of the Kiran leadership. There is a whole contingent of Kirans here who have been looking for ways to reverse the water poisoning."

"How can you be so trusting?"

She took a step toward him. Her voice rose in anger. "I've lived with Melvin since I was fifteen. I'm not saying we're close, or that he's like a father to me, but I do know I can trust him with the water crystal. All you have to do is trust me. Do you think I'd go through everything I went through merely to give it over to someone who would make it disappear?"

"No."

"Do you trust me, Angelo?" Her eyes glittered with tears. Angelo could feel a mixture of anger and sadness coming from her. He tried not sense her emotions, tried not to intrude, but they were so strong.

"Yes."

"All right then."

Melvin walked through the door and glanced at Angelo. "Your horse is with mine in the back munching happily on feed. I wish I could offer you refreshment, but I have little here." He gave Bianca a pointed stare, which made her look away. "I did not know my wayward fosterling would return to me today."

"I'm sorry I left so suddenly, Melvin."

Melvin stalked up to her faster and with more leashed strength in his body than Angelo thought was possible for a man his age. It was a hint of the man he'd probably been when he was younger. He came within a breath's space from her, his thin frame looming over her, his posture and the look on his face menacing.

Angelo was there, taking him by the shoulder and wrenching him back away from her. Melvin spun around from the force of it and grabbed the edge of a rocking chair to balance himself. "Don't touch her," Angelo growled.

"Angelo!" Bianca said in alarm. "It's all right!"

Melvin drew a breath and laughed. It rattled loose in his chest. "I'm too old a man to hit people, boy, but if I could, I'd hit you right now. Leave alone what is between Bianca and I."

Melvin didn't even try to mask his Kiran accent. It was heavier when he was angry. To have a thick accent like that he must have come here from Kira, rather than been Earth-born, like most of the others. He was old enough that he'd probably been here when the poisoning occurred. He may even have been a part of it.

Bianca touched Angelo's upper arm. It calmed him and he realized he'd been standing over the old man with his shoulders hunched, an expression of anger on his face. "Melvin's behavior can be a little off sometimes," she said. "But he's never raised a hand to me, never."

Angelo took a step toward Melvin. "Even so, you won't try to intimidate her, not while I'm here. I don't care who you are."

Melvin looked around Angelo at Bianca. "You've chosen well, child. This one really cares for you."

She let out an audible breath, but said nothing.

Melvin's gaze traveled to Angelo's eyes. His voice grew harsh. "I care for her as well and she left here without so much as a goodbye. I lost the first twin and didn't want to lose the second. I feared for her safety. I didn't know where she went. I still do not know where she went." His eyes narrowed. "All I know is that between here and there, she picked up a stray."

Bianca brushed past him and hugged the old man. Melvin looked surprised, then folded his arms around her and stroked her hair.

"I'm sorry I left like that, Melvin. Something happened and I-I had to go. I didn't think, didn't do much of anything except act. We have much to talk about. I know what happened to Calina. She's dead, Melvin, but I know what happened to her before she died."

Melvin pulled away from her and looked at her with wide eyes. "She's...dead?" he asked, grief thick in his voice.

Angelo shook his head. Theirs seemed to be a complicated relationship, but what relationship wasn't? He turned and went out the front door, giving them some privacy.

Angelo walked down the street to a small park that had wooden benches and swing sets made from logs, chains and plastic pieces for seats. A slide stood to the right of the swing set, made from twisted and pounded metal. He found a bench and sat down. In the distance he could see the inhabitants of the little village going about their business. A couple walked together and laughed. A woman carried a basket full of clothes into her house, calling out a greeting to her neighbor. Two men worked to repair the roof of one of the houses. The place seemed so ordered, so calm. Angelo never would have dreamed a place like this existed in the Wastes.

A low-level buzzing started. A small boy, maybe about six or seven came up on his right and touched his shoulder. "My name is Xavier. I saw you come in with Bianca," he said.

"Hi, Xavier. I'm Angelo."

"You're like us, aren't you?"

"What do you mean?"

"You're a Kiran too."

Angelo sighed. "I try not to think about it too much, Xavier."

"Why? Don't you like being Kiran?"

His answer was swift. "Nope, I sure don't."

"Can't help it, though, can you?"

Angelo went silent, at a loss for words. The boy left and went to the swing set. He pumped his legs back and forth, making the swing go higher, his dark eyes always on Angelo. The chains made a creaking sound against the thick wooden beam they were bolted into.

He could sense Bianca at his back before she was there. She sat beside him and he could feel her like a wave of calmness hitting him. When he'd opened himself to sense Jacob back in the Out-Center, he'd opened the floodgate on some empathic ability he hadn't known he'd had. Now he seemed unable to completely control it or shut it off. They sat for a long while in silence.

Angelo finally spoke. "You should have told me about the Kirans in this place before now."

"I know. I'm sorry. I was just afraid you'd refuse to come and Melvin is the only one who can figure out the crystal."

"Did you give to him?"

"Yes. He thinks that with a little time and research he'll be able to figure out how it works."

"What role did Melvin play in the poisoning?" He tried to keep the bitterness from his voice and failed.

"You know little of Kiran history, I'm sure, but Melvin made sure Calina and I were educated. Let me give you a little history lesson."

Angelo turned to her. "I'm all ears." He was angry, angry that he was here surrounded by Kirans and suddenly forced to confront his own blood, and angry she had kept a secret this large from him.

But then, he was also keeping secrets, wasn't he?

"Not all the Kirans wanted to introduce freysis into the water. Some of them wanted to approach Earth's governments with their plight, ask for sanctuary, ask for a piece of the planet to call their own and not poison all the water."

"That never would've worked."

Bianca shook her head. "No, probably not. In any case, the Kiran top brass, those in charge, didn't like that idea. They thought their only shot at continued existence was to take Earth from the humans. They figured they were more evolved and it was survival of the fittest. Before the poisoning there was a faction that came from Kira. They'd been trying to terraform another planet to meet their needs. It was working, but there wasn't enough time to complete the process before Kira's sun burned out. This faction came to Earth right before the poisoning, in order to plead with their leaders not to carry it out."

"Let me guess, Melvin was in this faction."

She nodded. "He was one of the ones in charge of terraforming the other planet. The poisoning was done against Melvin's will. As you know from our own history, many times—" her lips twisted, "—almost all the time, leaders don't listen to their people. Then the war started and all hell broke loose."

"But the ones who didn't want the poisoning to occur must have been a small minority."

She shook her head. "You'd be surprised, Angelo. You'd be surprised how gentle and good the Kirans can be. Just like there are good and bad humans—"

"There are good and bad Kirans."

"Definitely. I won't lie to you, there are Kirans here in the Valley who were for the poisoning, but they understand now what their avarice and superiority wrought them, because by coming to this foreign planet, the virus developed. They view the virus as cosmic payback, some kind of karma. Really, I think Earth was just trying to protect herself. The freysis may be good for the plants and not hurt most of the mammals, but you've seen what the freysis does to the Earth in the form of those sinkholes." She shook her head. "It's a worry for the future if we can't reverse the poisoning. I just hope that you don't hate me for bringing you here."

He turned and caught her face between his palms. "I could never hate you, Bianca. Never worry about that."

She closed her eyes, and when she opened them, her steady gaze held his. "No, you only hate yourself, right?"

He released her and turned away. "What would make you say that?"

"I don't know, Angelo. You tell me."

Angelo shot up from the bench and walked away.

Chapter Twenty-One

Branches cracked and leaves crumpled under Angelo's freysis boots as he walked away from the Valley into the woods.

Hate himself?

He raked a hand back through his hair. Deep in thought and distracted, he nearly tripped over a fallen log. He stumbled, caught himself and then decided to sit down on it. The trees concealed him from the view of those in the town, while giving him an excellent view. He watched them as they walked down their little streets and talked and laughed with each other.

Kirans and humans living together with apparent ease. It was more than he could get his mind around.

He, his mother and his sisters had first lived in a quiet community in Sector Thirty-Two, but when it had been discovered they were Kiran spawn, his mother had moved them to a different community. The place they'd settled in had been crude and urban. It had been a tough environment to grow up in, but it had been home.

Rex Collins had been the community's elected mayor and had dated his mother for a time. To this day, Angelo didn't know how Collins had found out, but he had. Collins had been the one to take the whip to him. Rex Collins had outed them to the community and soon they'd been shunned. After that, the community had denied his mother the right to buy pure-food, making them live on nutro-wafers. They'd barred access to community buildings and all but the bravest few had stopped talking to them.

Fearing for their safety after they'd received death threats, they'd relocated to Sector Thirty-One and found yet another community. They stayed there and managed to hide their secret.

Angelo not had seen nor communicated with his mother or sisters in months. After this was done, he'd visit them. Why hadn't he done it sooner? Why had he stayed away for so long? Angelo sighed. Avoidance, maybe. Being with his sisters and mother only reminded him of his heritage. Alone, with full-blooded humans, he could ignore it.

Now he was being slapped in the face with it.

* * * * *

Bianca curled her legs underneath her and huddled into the blanket she'd wrapped around her shoulders. Melvin had instructed those in charge of water to fill up the second tank with pure-water. After she'd taken a bath, she'd dressed in a pair of soft light blue pajamas. She felt much better now, though the bath had not washed away the lump that had been in her throat ever since parting with Angelo that afternoon.

Melvin busied himself in the kitchen, baking a loaf of pure-bread. He hummed to himself and would peek out of the kitchen every once in a while, as if to assure himself she was still there. He actually seemed happy she'd come back. Bianca had not been sure what his reaction would be. Melvin had an inconstant personality, sometimes warm and loving, other times angry and harsh. Living with him had been a challenge. She'd never known which Melvin to expect.

Bianca had always figured he'd taken them in simply to assuage his guilt over the poisoning. But when Calina had been abducted, Melvin had moved heaven and earth to find her and had genuinely mourned when they couldn't. Now, the way Melvin was acting—almost like a caring adoptive father—it made her think he'd actually missed her. The old coot, she could never read him.

There were those in the Valley who said that being unable to stop the poisoning combined with the loss of his family to the virus, had made Melvin unstable—a little insane even. Bianca wouldn't go that far, but Melvin was different, that was for sure.

He'd opened the cottage windows and the cool valley air blew inside. It smelled of pine trees and fresh flowers. It was twilight and even in the summer, night air could be cool in the valley. She tightened the blanket around her shoulders and sighed. Overall, surprisingly, she was happy to be here. She'd always felt safe here, if not always at home. It was a far cry from the ratholes she'd lived in with her sister before this community had taken them in.

She'd be even happier if Angelo would come back. Just to make sure he hadn't taken off, she'd gone out several times to make sure his horse was still there. Each time it had been placidly pulling up grass outside the small barn Melvin had erected for his own horse.

Melvin laid a steaming hot loaf of bread on the table and took a knife to it. "Tell me more about this stray you've brought home."

Bianca wiggled down to lay her head on the cushioned armrest of the couch. She didn't want to talk about Angelo. She sighed. "There's nothing more to say."

Silence ensued. When she looked up, Melvin's blue gaze penetrated her. "You look like you've been hit by a train," he said. "Don't tell me there's nothing to say. I recognize love when I see it. Love will hit you like a locomotive every time, leave bloody tracks across your heart."

No sense denying it. She did love Angelo and there was no way to undo it. "How do you get a person to stop hiding from himself, Melvin?"

"You find him yourself, then give him a mirror."

"What happens if he closes his eyes?"

Melvin shrugged. "You wait for him to open them."

But what if he never opens them? A knock sounded on the door, startling her.

"Come in," called Melvin.

Angelo walked through the door, and threw a glance at Bianca. She sat up and ran her fingers through her still damp hair self-consciously.

"Ah, we were wondering when you'd rejoin us," said Melvin. "You are free to take a bath if you desire it. I laid out some fresh clothes that may fit you. We have only two bedrooms. You are welcome to the couch if you would like." He hesitated. "Of course, Bianca is a woman grown, and I'm not her father. Therefore, you are welcome to sleep wherever you wish." He brushed by Angelo, headed out the door, but paused before closing it behind him. He looked at Bianca. "I am going off in search of some pure-butter for that bread I just baked, and some more clean clothes that will fit the stray."

"My name is Angelo," he said through gritted teeth.

"Forgive me…Angelo." He tipped his head with a little smile on his mouth, and then closed the door behind him.

An uncomfortable silence grew in the room until it was nearly unbearable. Angelo stood looking down at her and she up at him. There seemed to be worlds unsaid between them, but neither would make the first move. Tears pricked her eyes.

Finally, she stood. "I'm going to bed now. I'm very tired."

"Have you eaten?"

She nodded. "A nutro-wafer from the pack and some smoked pure-ham a neighbor brought over. It's in the kitchen. It would go well on the bread Melvin baked. Feel free to help yourself. We'll get more pure-food tomorrow, a chicken, some vegetables, even some milk and cheese."

She walked past him and he touched her arm. "How did you end up in Melvin's care?"

She shivered and drew a breath. It wasn't something she liked to talk about. She couldn't remember much of that night and hoped the memories never came back. "I-I've been told our parents died in a fire caused when the military attacked a suspected Kiran encampment. Needless to say it wasn't a Kiran encampment; it was human. We were about eight when they died. Calina and I lived in the Out-Center for many years, dodging the Flot and scavenging. We grew up hand-to-mouth, stealing and finagling pure-water and avoiding those who wanted to abuse and exploit us. When Melvin found us we were like wild things. He had to track us down a few times, coaxed and tamed us like we were feral cats, but eventually, he won our trust and brought us to live here." She tried a weak smile. "We were strays too."

"I'm sorry," he murmured, rubbing a strong hand up and down her arm.

"Me too. It was hard, but we made it. What about your father? How did he die?"

His eyes clouded with pain and something else that seemed unidentifiable. She wanted to reach out and touch his face. "Shot, I'm told." He looked away.

She did reach out then. Gently, she traced his jawline with her index finger. "Will you please sleep with me tonight?"

He looked back at her. Heat flashed in his eyes. "If you'll have me next to you."

"Definitely."

"Then I'll be there." He walked past her, into the bathroom and closed the door.

She walked into her bedroom. Once there had been two beds in the room, now there was only one. Shelves ran along the wall filled with little things she and Calina had gleaned from Out-Center, a plastic horse with a broken leg, a frayed teddy bear with one eye. A dresser stood at the opposite of the room, filled with clothing, blankets and towels. A small table stood to the right of the bed. She turned off the lamp, which stood on the nightstand, and crawled into bed. She didn't close her eyes until she felt strong arms wrap around her and hold her close.

She turned over in the circle of his arms, breathing in the clean, spicy-citrus scent the soap had left on his skin. His damp hair brushed her cheek. She snuggled down against his bare chest and let him hold her. For now she would forget his inability to trust her. Just for tonight she would pretend he loved her and wanted to share himself with her. Just for tonight she'd pretend everything was all right between them.

* * * * *

Angelo woke wrapped around Bianca. His chin rested on the top of her head and he'd folded her into his chest, with her back against him. He sighed happily and tightened his arms. She yawned and turned over, bringing her mouth close to his.

He couldn't resist, he leaned in and pressed his lips against hers. When he pulled away, her blue-green eyes were open and had a wary look he didn't like. He felt that caution come off her in waves mixed with desire. A searing shot of wanting came from her and it only fueled his own.

"Good morning," he murmured and smiled. "I could get used to sleeping like this."

"So could I." But she didn't smile.

He leaned into her, catching her lips once again. Her arm, the one that wasn't trapped beneath her, came to rest briefly on his upper arm, then traced over his shoulder to the back of his neck. He parted her lips and that searing shot of want became a steady wave. Reading the emotion that radiated from her, and knowing she wanted him as much as he wanted her, he found the edge of her pajama top and pushed under, finding the soft, warm mound of her breast and closing his hand over it.

She took a sharp breath against his mouth, and then deepened the kiss. He kneaded and massaged, finding her nipple and running his thumb over it until it pebbled. Bianca moaned deep in her throat, and then fell silent and went still.

Abruptly, she let out a soft hiss of air and tugged on his wrist, pushing his hand down and away. She sat up. Her face was flushed and her long silver-blonde hair was sleep tangled around her shoulders.

He sat up. "I don't want to make love, Bianca. I just want to touch you, give you pleasure."

"That's the whole problem, Angelo. Why don't you want to make love to me? Am I so repulsive—"

He leaned forward and kissed her, then leaned his forehead against hers and let out a long, slow breath. "God, Bianca, you know I don't think that. Please remember the tent."

She reached down; sliding her hand past the waistband of the soft pajama bottoms he'd worn to bed and found his hardened cock. Biting her lower lip, her breathing coming as hard as his, she stroked him until he groaned. He took her wrist and pulled her hand away, then took her other wrist and pressed her back onto the bed and straddled her.

"Please don't do that," he said, his lips just above hers.

She struggled upward, pushed off the bed, and stood. "If I can't have you—all of you—then, I'm sorry, Angelo, but I don't want any of you."

He sat on the edge of the bed. "You wanted me to sleep with you last night."

"I did. I love to have you near me, but at the same time—" she made a frustrated sound, "—I want to mean enough for you to…" She trailed off and choked up. "I-I want you to mean enough to yourself…" She trailed off again, gave her head a vicious shake and walked over to him. Pressing her lips together, she reached out and touched the scars on his abdomen, tracing them around his side to his back. "Tell me about these."

"I already have."

"No. I mean tell me *all* about them. Why and when you got them. What exactly that man was trying to whip out of you."

He didn't know what to say. She must know, or at least suspect, that he had Kiran blood. Clearly, she wanted him to acknowledge it, to hear him say it, to tell her all his awful secrets. "You mean so much to me, Bianca, more than I've told you. But I don't know if I can give you what you're asking for."

She touched his cheek in a tender gesture. Love filled her eyes. "You are the bravest, strongest, gentlest man I've ever known. At the same time you're so scared of who you are. I want nothing more than to embrace every single bit of you, and all you want is to run away from yourself."

He looked at her in silence, realizing she loved him. Not only that, she loved the part of him he hated. She loved him regardless of his blood. It jarred him, made him speechless. It held him in awe that Bianca could suspect what he was and actually still love him. The look in her eyes, coupled with his realization, rendered him bereft of words.

Bianca got up from the bed, grabbed the clothes she'd laid out for the day and left the room.

Chapter Twenty-Two

Angelo stepped out of the cottage and walked down the street that led to the heart of the town. The day had dawned brilliantly clear. Blue, cloudless sky stretched as far as he could see between the branches overhead. The green trees of the valley created a canopy over the town, reaching up toward that magnificent blueness.

Melvin had been in the cottage when he'd arose, but the old man had been bent studiously over the water crystal, surrounded by books, and had only grunted distractedly at him when Angelo had said good morning.

It seemed everyone in town had disappeared. There wasn't a single person in sight. He passed a large building that had a sign hung on the outside, The Exchange. He wondered if maybe they used some sort of bartering system here to get things they needed from each other.

The door was open and he peeked his head within. Various stalls displaying different items lined the walls. One showcased rich, homespun rugs, blankets and clothing. Another had small jars of jams, honey and other foodstuffs. Yet another displayed well-made furniture made of heavy branches and polished wood, the same kind Melvin had in his home. Yes, it looked like they did barter to obtain the things they needed. It was an interesting arrangement and it impressed Angelo. He was impressed with this community, period. It was the most organized and peaceful community he'd ever seen, despite the fact that it was full of Kirans.

He stepped out of the building and continued down the road, toward the opposite end of the town. A two-story building made of white birch stood in the center of the town square, flanked by spilt-log homes in a circle around it. The sign outside declared it Town Hall. That was where they held their meetings, made their laws and passed judgment on those who broke them. Bianca's rapist had stood some sort of scrutiny within those walls and had been sentenced to banishment.

Angelo hands fisted. He would've sentenced him to something much more severe than that, although, banishment—especially if he'd been human—was a very harsh punishment.

A strange sound met his ears, carried by the sweet late summer wind, a voice, then tinkling laughter.

And not just anyone's laughter, Bianca's.

He followed the sound around the side of the town hall and between a couple of houses. In a lush green field, he found Bianca surrounded by a group of children. A low buzzing sounded in his ears and he knew many of them were Kiran. He scanned the group. Xavier was there. The brown-haired boy chased Bianca through the tall grass and she slowed deliberately, allowing him to catch her. The boy tagged her and she feigned disappointment, as if she'd truly tried to outrun him. She laughed again and the sound of it warmed him. Her smile actually reached her eyes, lit them up with an inner glow that was positively irresistible. Angelo wanted to be the one to put that smile on her face and that glow in her eyes.

Only half realizing he did it, he took a step toward her into the tall grass. She turned his way and spotted him. The smile on her face died and was replaced by something complicated, a mixture of hope, love and sorrow.

Something in his chest squeezed.

She took two strides to the right and tagged a little girl with a blonde ponytail. The little girl squealed with laughter and ran away. "I'm taking a time-out," Bianca called with her eyes on him. She walked toward him. Soft-looking black leggings hugged her, topped with an aquamarine shirt the same color as her eyes. The top several buttons were undone, revealing her collarbones. Soft black freysis boots sheathed her feet and came up to mid-calf.

She didn't say anything as she approached. Wariness dominated her expression.

"When I first met you, I never would have pegged you for someone that liked kids," he said.

She gave him a sharp glance. "When you first met me, I was in shock from my twin dying and emotionally numb. Not to mention, I was intent on reversing the water poisoning with an object that you confiscated," she accused without heat.

He pushed a hand through his hair. "Good point."

"I love kids. I love animals, too," she finished softly. Her voice rose, "But that doesn't make me soft."

He raised his hands in a gesture of surrender. "I would never think you were soft, Bianca." He lowered his hands and smiled. "And I like that you love kids and animals."

She looked down and away and didn't respond.

"Where is everyone?" he asked.

She glanced up at the sky. "It's a beautiful day. The sun has burned all the dew off the grass, making it safe for humans." She shrugged. "Most everyone is out and about. Some are taking advantage of the weather to work in the fields or go hunting. Some went down to the river to lie in the sun and relax. Pretty soon it will be winter and when it snows, as you know well, humans have to stay inside unless they have the gear to protect themselves." She shrugged. "Everyone's soaking up the sun while they can."

He nodded. The children laughed and ran around in the field behind them. He eyed the children at length. Some were Kiran children, carrying on the heritage. What were their parents thinking, creating more of them? "So you're left to baby-sit?"

"I can see the unsaid in your eyes, Angelo. Yes, I offered to entertain the murderous alien children." She flung an arm wide to encompass the giggling kids. Xavier ran up to the little girl called Sianna and tugged at one of her black pigtails. Sianna turned, laughing, and chased him. "They're such a threat, you know. We have to keep our eyes on them all the time, for fear they'll rise up and try to kill all the humans in town." Her voice dripped with sarcasm.

"That's not what I meant."

"Oh, yes, it is." She looked at him angrily, then her gaze softened and she glanced away. "They're not all Kiran kids. Some are human. Sianna is human. But they all play together anyway. They're being raised to accept and love each other, despite their differences and despite the past. There is nothing we can do about all that. What's done is done. We only have the future to think of now. Survival to think of. Our future includes Kirans and humans existing together, whether we like it or not."

Angelo opened his mouth to respond but his remarks were cut off by a child's terrified scream, followed by a chorus of them. Bianca whirled and together they ran into the clearing, toward the source of the screams, which had now transformed into frightened whimpers and sobs.

The children gathered around something on the ground. Angelo and Bianca ran up to them. Beside him, Bianca gasped. A portion of the earth had simply collapsed into a hole filled with mushy, powdery earth approximately thirty feet in radius.

Bianca glanced around at the children. Under her breath, she took inventory. "Where's Xavier?"

Tearfully, several of the children pointed at the sinkhole.

Fear seized Angelo's heart. He immediately jumped down into the hole and sank in to his upper thighs. It had the consistency of quicksand. He didn't know how stable the earth was, but he had to find Xavier before he suffocated. No time could be lost. He was careful to stay on the edge of the hole since he didn't know where the child had been buried, and stepping on the boy definitely wouldn't help matters.

Bianca made ready to jump in too, but Angelo held up a hand. "No! Stay out, Bianca. It's too unstable. The earth in here is almost like quicksand."

"But, it's so big! How will you find—"

"I'll find him. It's all right." He hoped he sounded more confident than he felt.

The other children had gone silent. They gathered around Bianca and she reached out, trying to touch them all in a comforting way. Stark fear blanched her face.

Angelo went still and reached through the top layer of the earth with his mind, searching for the boy's presence. He found him almost right away, buried approximately four feet under the earth. Angelo felt for the child's emotion, and got none. That likely meant he was unconscious.

With effort, Angelo waded through the earth slowly over to the far left part of the sinkhole. He plunged his hands into the earth, searching for Xavier, and felt soft skin and the fabric of the boy's shirt. Feeling further, he found Xavier's torso. He dug in, slipped his hands under the boy's armpits and pulled him out. Relief flooded Angelo as he cradled Xavier's slight weight in arms. Balancing him carefully, he brushed the dirt away from the child's eyes with a free hand. Xavier was unconscious, as he'd presumed.

Bianca ran around the edge of the hole and helped him climb out, while he still held the boy in his arms. He was loath to lay the child down anywhere near the sinkhole. He didn't know how stable the ground was around it. Together, they ran away from the hole, close to the outer edge of homes near Town Hall. He laid the child on the ground, listened for breathing and found none. The children and Bianca stood around him while he started CPR.

A tense minute later Xavier coughed, turned to his side and spit out dirt. Then he drew a shaky breath and began to cry. Angelo looked up at Bianca. Relief sung through her, matching his own. She smiled.

Angelo cradled the boy in his arms and let him wail. Bianca knelt and smoothed Xavier's hair, making soft crooning sounds. The child wrapped his arms around her neck and she extracted him from Angelo's arms.

"How did you know where he was?" she asked over the child's tears.

"I told you. I just know where people are sometimes."

The child was covered in dirt from head to toe. Bianca used one hand to shake his hair free of some of it. Angelo slipped his own T-shirt off and used it to wipe the dirt from Xavier's legs, arms and face.

"I need to blow my—my nose!" Xavier wailed. Angelo and Bianca laughed and looked at each other, sharing the knowledge that he would be just fine.

Angelo gave the boy his T-shirt and he used it to blow his nose. Xavier handed it back to him with a whimper when he was finished.

"Uh, thanks, Xavier," said Angelo, holding a hand up. "But you can keep it. Maybe you'll need to use it again."

When he was all cried out, Bianca brushed his hair to the side. Xavier, exhausted from his ordeal, buried his face in her neck, his small hand clutching Angelo's T-shirt.

"Let's go find your parents, Xavier," said Bianca.

Xavier nodded sleepily.

They all trooped out of the field and through a small copse of trees. All the children followed behind. Angelo walked beside Bianca, who held the boy close to her, his legs dangling over either side of her hips.

"Is he heavy? Do you want me to carry him?" asked Angelo.

She shook her head.

He kept stealing glances at her; with every stolen look thinking how much he wished Xavier were their own child. He jerked involuntarily, remembering that Xavier was full-blooded Kiran. Even more Kiran than he was.

Sianna came up on his right side and the little girl with the blonde ponytail, a Kiran, came up on his left. They both reached out, wanting to hold his hand. Angelo reached out tentatively and took their small hands in his.

Bianca looked at him sidelong. "You jumped in that sinkhole, not knowing how stable the earth was, to save a boy you don't even know." She paused. "A Kiran boy no less. Thank you very much, Angelo. I don't think I could have gotten to him in time if I'd been alone. This child owes his life to you."

Angelo shook his head. "Don't thank me, Bianca."

"I saw fear on your face. You truly didn't want him to die."

Angelo extricated his hand from Sianna's and reached out to lay his palm on the top of the sleeping boy's head. His hair was downy soft and his head felt so fragile under his hand. "Of course not. Do you think I'm some kind of monster?"

"But he's full-blood Kiran," she said with a question in her voice.

He sighed and removed his hand. "I'm aware of that."

They passed out of the copse of trees and into a large field where the tall grass had been thrashed and laid in the sun to dry.

"Hay for the horses," Bianca explained, seeing the questioning look on his face. "The Kirans harvest grain as well. It's not dangerous for them to do it, after all. They can stand the dew in the morning and the irrigation it takes."

"Who makes the pure-food for the humans?"

"There are four families who keep pure-vegetable gardens and livestock on pure-water. They barter their crops in the Exchange. The Exchange is—"

"I saw it, actually. It's very impressive." He frowned. "And also wide-open. Aren't they afraid of people stealing?"

Bianca laughed. "You'll always be a guardian, Angelo."

He raked a hand through his hair. "A part of me, yes."

"If someone is caught stealing, especially food, they can be sentenced by the town council to banishment. Believe me, that's not a fate most wish to endure."

"That is how they punished the one who—"

She interrupted him before he could say the word. "Adam? Last I heard he had headed west, out to Sector Fifty-Four."

"Was he Kiran, or human?"

She glanced at him. "Does it matter?"

He shrugged.

"Human. What he did to me, r-rape, is highly chastised and very unacceptable in Kiran culture, even in times of war. Rape by a Kiran is a very rare thing."

They reached the edge of the hay field and went through another small area of trees. Then they walked through a large open area. They passed first a large greenhouse, then a barn.

The sounds of laughter and splashing water drifted on the summer air. Low buzzing sounded in his ears.

They passed through another stand of trees with the children. Families lined the banks of the freysis-green lake and children splashed at its edges. Just another day at the beach for the Kirans. Revulsion tightened low in Angelo's stomach. The children that had followed them ran to their families, or friend's families, Angelo presumed.

* * * * *

Bianca shifted Xavier on her hip and stole a glance at Angelo. The look on his face was angry. His pupils were dark. Melvin said to give him a mirror. He definitely had one here, all right.

Her gaze dropped to his bare chest as it had about thirty times since he'd taken his shirt off. Christ, she couldn't think straight when confronted with that strong, muscular expanse. All she wanted to do was run her hands and tongue over it.

Xavier's parents spotted them and came toward them with worried looks on their faces. Xavier was still covered with dirt. Bianca handed the boy over to his mother, and Xavier made a sleepy sound and wound his arms around her neck.

"What happened?" his father asked.

Bianca told him about the sinkhole. "Angelo found him. If it wasn't for him, I'm not certain I would have reached the child in time to save his life."

Ellsatha, Xavier's mother, looked up at Angelo with tears in her eyes. "Thank you," she said in a quavering, breathless voice.

"Thank you seems so inadequate," said his father.

Angelo drew a shaky hand through his hair. He seemed unable to look Ellsatha or her husband directly in the eyes. "It's fine," he said in a gruff voice. "You don't need to thank me. I'm just glad I got to the boy in time."

The man shuddered and held out his hand. "My name is Maren. My wife is Ellsatha."

"Kiran names," Angelo said.

Since the Kiran had planted roots so far back in Earth's history, those generations of Kirans that had grown up on Earth had simply adopted Earth names and much of Earth's culture. But those Kirans—along with their descendants—that had arrived right before or during the poisoning had retained their Kiran names.

"Yes," answered Maren. "You have not yet been formally welcomed into the Valley. But I welcome you now, into our home, whenever you wish to visit us. Please, I ask that you and Bianca both come for dinner soon." He looked at Bianca. "We will, of course, provide pure-food."

Angelo opened his mouth to speak. Bianca could tell he was searching for a way to decline the offer.

Bianca interrupted him. "Thank you, Maren." She looked at Angelo. "I think it would do us both good, especially Angelo, to have dinner with such fine people as yourselves."

"Speaking of welcoming," said Ellsatha. "My husband and I are on the Town Committee and have planned a formal welcoming for you this afternoon. I trust that Melvin told you about it?"

"Well," answered Bianca. She flicked an uneasy glance at Angelo. "No, he didn't."

"Well, that old coot," muttered Ellsatha. "Can you come, or should we reschedule it?"

"Ah—" started Angelo.

"Yes, he can. We will both attend," interrupted Bianca.

"Oh good. We'll send someone to escort you around four," said Ellsatha. "Now we're going to go home and clean Xavier up. He needs some time to recover. We'll see you this afternoon."

Bianca watched the family retreat into the trees, headed back to town.

"What's a formal welcoming?" asked Angelo. Confusion and anger warred for dominance on his face.

"Whenever an outsider arrives, one they know doesn't have anywhere else to go, has no home, they formally welcome him into the community. That means you can stay and live here should you choose. If you decide to stay, a house would be built for you, and a water tank erected. If the person is a human, they happily share their pure-water and the work it takes to maintain it."

"They just welcome you in, build you a house, Kiran or not, no matter what?"

"Yep. You're expected to abide by the town rules and if you don't, one of the protectors will find you and bring you before the town committee for judgment and possible sentencing."

"Protectors?"

"Yes, they're sort of like the guardians. They make sure everyone obeys the rules and hunt down those who don't."

"Amazing."

She laughed. "Not really, Angelo. You're just surprised we could be so organized out here in the Wastes."

"I'm surprised by a lot of what is out here in the Wastes."

Bianca glanced around and saw that all the children had either found their families, or had found a friend's family to stick close to. She started back toward the town and Angelo followed her.

"Did you see Melvin this morning?" she asked him as he fell in step beside her. She pushed the bough of an evergreen out of her way with her free hand. It sent up a fresh scent, which she eagerly inhaled. It was then that she decided to veer from their path.

"He was bent over the water crystal with an intent look on his face, muttering to himself in Kiran."

"Yes, he says he thinks he knows how the crystal works. He just wants to make sure. It would be a pity if we did the wrong thing with it and ruined it."

"That's the understatement of the century."

They continued on through the thickening woods in silence. The sunlight overhead dappled the ground, making patches of brightness on the pine needle and leaf-strewn floor of the woods. Bianca remained vigilant. They had to be extra careful of wild animals now that humans were no longer a major threat to them. It seemed they grew bolder and more confident with every passing year. They'd even had a bear ransack the Exchange two years back.

"Where are we going, anyway?" asked Angelo.

She turned and gave him a slow, secret smile. "You'll see in a minute."

As they climbed a steep slope, Angelo took her hand and helped her up it. At the top they walked through the tree line. The top of the bluff showed the valley and the green trees for miles and miles. Green met the blue, blue sky and the contrast was startling. Directly below them was a huge lake, glittering an intense freysis-green in the bright sunlight.

He took a few steps toward the bluff, his attention on the horizon. "It's beautiful," he breathed.

She walked to him and wound her arms around him, so her breasts pressed against his back. She peered around his upper arm. "This is my absolute favorite place in the world."

"I can see why."

He turned and caught her in his arms. She laid her head against his chest, right above his left nipple and rubbed her cheek against the smoothness of his skin, breathing in the scent of him. He smelled of soap and leather. Not able to resist, she laid a lingering kiss against his skin and looked up. His eyes had gone dark with barely banked passion.

They needed to assuage the taut edge of tension stretched between them. One right move and it would snap, and he'd give in. Bianca could feel that. He was on the edge.

He touched her lips with his fingertips. She parted them as he ran the pad of his thumb back and forth over her lower lip. The passion heating her gaze answered what she saw in his eyes. She took his hand and slowly kissed his fingertips one-by-one.

"I want you, Angelo," she murmured. "I want you to make love to me. I want your cock inside me. I don't care about anything else right now. I only want you."

She stepped back away from him, her hands going to the buttons of her shirt. One by one she undid them as he watched. His hands fisted at his sides as if he wanted to make himself stop her, but couldn't. The last button came undone and she gripped the edges of her shirt, showing the white line of bare skin that ran from her throat, between her breasts and down to the waistband of her pants. Slowly, she slid the shirt back over her shoulders, let it slip down her arms to pool at her elbows, revealing her bare breasts.

"I love you, Angelo. I want to show you I love you. Please," her voice broke, "make love to me."

Chapter Twenty-Three

The warm breeze buffeted his hair as Angelo let his gaze slide over her perfect, bared breasts. Her nipples tightened as he watched her and he felt his cock get hard in response. She let the shirt drop to the ground and took step toward him. Any hope he'd had of keeping his cock away from her sweet pussy had slipped away with her shirt to pool on the ground, already forgotten. It had slipped away when she'd told him she loved him with that deep look in her beautiful eyes.

She'd brought him up here to seduce him. To break his resolve. He could see it in her eyes. She looked unsure of exactly how to do that, but sure she'd do it all the same.

Angelo knew right now she'd get what she wanted. He was sick of fighting it.

She walked toward him, her eyes flicking down the length of his body. Her gaze traveled down the line of fine brownish-black hair that disappeared past the waistband of his black jeans. It caressed him below the belt, where his cock strained against the material.

He stepped forward, closing the small distance between them, and enveloped her in his arms. She sighed. His bare skin rubbed against her soft breasts, and he shuddered with pleasure. "I can feel your desire, Bianca. It's feeding mine."

She looked up at him, raised an eyebrow and let her hand trail down to rub him through his jeans. "I can feel your desire, too, and I don't even need any preternatural ability." She grinned.

He scooped her up in his arms and she made a surprised squeal. Searching the landscape, he found a patch of thick green grass, laid her down, and knelt beside her. His gaze raked her body, lingering at her small rosy-tipped breasts and the curve of her waist. Angelo ached to touch her, but hadn't yet. They were going to do this right. He'd prolong and delay as long as he could, until she was screaming for him.

She touched his face. "I love you, Angelo. Do you hear me? I love you no matter what, and I want you—all of you."

He looked into her eyes and saw the truth of her words there. She loved him despite everything he hated in himself. She loved him no matter what he was.

"I love you too, Bianca. I think some part of me deep inside started loving you the moment you tried to blow my head off."

She shuddered. "Thank God I missed."

He grinned. "Yeah, I'm kind of happy about that, too. Now, relax."

One by one, he took off her boots and socks, making every motion count. He rubbed her arches with strong fingers until she closed her eyes and moaned. Then his hands went to the buttons of her pants. He heard her catch her breath and swallow hard.

How good would it be to feel her sex enveloping his cock, to sheathe himself inside her warmth and her love and stay there for as long as possible? He wanted her moving under him in a cloud of pleasure, and to drive every thought from her mind but those of him and all the things he was doing to her.

* * * * *

With deft fingers Angelo unbuttoned her pants. Bianca concentrated on every movement his fingers made and the look of desire in his eyes. She lifted up from the ground, helping him get her pants over her hips and off. Her underwear came with them and she lay there completely naked, but she wasn't cold. Not at all. Not with his warm gaze taking in and holding every square inch of her. He was on his knees beside her now, but she wanted him within her. Couldn't wait for it.

Unable to stay still, she sat up and put her hands to the buttons on his jeans. She fumbled and she laughed nervously. Finally, she got them undone.

He tipped her face up to his with his index finger. "Patience, angel-face. We're alone here and we have all afternoon. There's no reason to hurry. Slow." His eyes went dark. "Slow is better." He lifted off her and she heard his boots come off, thumping against the ground. She looked up to see him sliding his pants and underwear off. He kicked them aside and stood in the sunlight.

He knelt beside her once more. He lowered his mouth to hers and kissed her, his lips sliding warm and soft over hers. Then he parted them and his tongue slipped into her mouth. With a sigh of pleasure, she explored every inch of his torso that she could reach. She drew her hands up his arms, over his biceps and shoulders, down to his back.

Angelo wrapped one arm around her waist, placed his other hand to her nape and kneaded the muscles there with strong fingers. When he pressed her up against him, she felt the hardness of his chest against her nipples, his bare skin next to hers.

Holding her against him, still kissing her, he tipped her back and laid her onto the grass. When he pressed his hands flat on either side of her head and straddled her hips, she fought the urge to pull him down on her and whimper. Angelo was taking his time, making every moment, every breath count.

He slanted his mouth to the side and deepened the kiss until she could feel only his lips on hers, his tongue in her mouth. At first, he sipped from her, and then drank like a thirsty man. With a groan, he broke the kiss and drew a hot, wet line with his tongue down her chin, to her collarbones and laid a kiss.

Her breath caught when his mouth closed over one nipple, laving it and biting gently. At the same time, his fingers found her other breast and caressed it, running the callused pad of his thumb over the nipple. She arched her back and let out a small moan.

He lifted his head. The smoldering look in his eyes heated her blood to the boiling point. "Touch yourself for me, Bianca," he murmured.

"Touch myself?"

He nodded. "I want to see you arouse yourself before I fuck you boneless."

A fissure of lust ran up her spine at his words. They were coarse, and they excited the hell out of her.

"Show me where you want me to touch you. Show me where you want me to make love to you," he said.

She bit her lip, watching him take his cock in his hand and stroke himself. She slid her hands up her sides to cup both breasts. His pupils dilated at the sight. Tentatively, she plumped her breasts, unsure of what he wanted.

He groaned. "Awww, Bianca, that is so damn exciting." His cock jerked in his hand. "Give me more."

More confident now that she understood the game, she rubbed her fingers over her tight nipples. Pleasure shot out from her breasts and she gasped. She'd never touched herself before. She rolled her nipples between her forefinger and thumb and arched her back, moaning.

"Spread your thighs for me," Angelo said in a rasping voice. "Bring your feet up and show me everything."

Now completely aroused and creaming hard for him, she did as he requested. She bent her knees and brought her feet up to touch her butt, letting her thighs open. In this position, she was utterly and completely exposed to him and she loved it.

Angelo ran his gaze over her sex, groaning. "Your pussy is all pink and plumped up for me, baby. You're all creamy and delicious-looking and your perfect little clit is excited and has come out to play. It's begging to be sucked."

"Touch me," she moaned as she kneaded her breasts and writhed.

"I will." He shook his head. "But not yet. I want to see you touch yourself."

She flicked her hard nipples with her fingernails, enjoying the little bit of pain that seemed to make pleasure seem all the sweeter. She closed her eyes. "I'm imagining you touching me."

He made a little growling sound in his throat. "Show me how you want me to fuck you, Bianca. You show me where with your fingers and I'll do it with my cock. Sink your fingers into that lovely, creamy little pussy, Bianca."

Her breath caught in her throat at his words. God, he was turning her on. She wanted to drive him as crazy as he was driving her. She stroked her hands down her breasts a last time and slowly, oh, so very slowly, down over her stomach to her pubic hair. She stared at him staring at her hands. The expression on his face appeared strained. He was holding himself from her with effort.

He had the control here and she'd given it up to him with pleasure. Yet, in reality, she was still the one with the power. His cock jumped in his hand and he stroked himself, waiting for her to touch herself. She threaded her fingers through her short blonde pubic hair and dipped down to stroke her clit.

"Oh, God," she groaned, her hips bucking.

"That's it, angel-face. Is that good?"

"Uh, huh." She gathered some of the moisture seeping from her pussy and used it as lubricant on her clit. Fissures of pleasure racked her body as she teased herself. She'd make herself come way too fast that way and she had more teasing and arousing to do. She slid both her hands down and spread her labia apart, showing the entrance of her pussy to Angelo.

"This is where I want your cock, Angelo," she said breathlessly. Teasingly, she ran her fingertip over herself. She whimpered as she imagined him fucking her there. Her hips thrust forward.

"You want me to take you there, angel-face?" he asked. "You want my cock filling up your sweet little pussy?"

"Oh, God, yes," she breathed.

"You fill it up first. Show me how you want me to take you."

She rubbed two fingers around the entrance of her pussy, then slipped them inside of her. She gasped at the feel of her muscles clamping down.

"How does it feel?" he asked in a strained voice.

"Like I want a cock. Your cock."

"I bet it's so hot and tight," he murmured.

"Why don't you come on in and see." She drew her fingers back out and thrust them back in over and over while he knelt beside her, watching avidly and stroking his cock. With her other hand, she caressed her clit, running the pad of her finger up and down it. Her body tightened as climax approached. She tossed her head back and forth. "Oh, God, Angelo. I'm going to come."

"Let it go," he purred.

Her hips bucked and her back arched as pleasure spread out from her sex and consumed her world. She felt Angelo move her hands away and his hot, hungry mouth come down on her while she was in the grip of her orgasm. His lips and tongue worked her fast and hard, as he sucked in her clit and speared his fingers up inside her, fucking her fast and hard with them. Bianca screamed as another, harder climax slammed into her body. Under the onslaught of his masterful hands and mouth, she couldn't resist it.

Her pussy still tingled when it was over, when the spasms of her double climax were finished. He hovered over her, a needful look in his dark eyes. "Angelo, please, *please* make love to me," she murmured.

He pushed his cock at her entrance. "Nothing in the goddamn world could stop me."

"Ah, yes," she cried out as the wide crown of his cock pressed into her. He was huge. She'd felt that when he'd taken her from behind in the tent. He stretched her muscles so deliciously. He slid into her inch by mind-blowing, delicious inch. He did it slowly, carefully, as though afraid he'd hurt her.

She reached up, panting, and met his gaze. "I'm not made of china," she whispered. "Don't treat me like I'm fragile. I want to feel you."

Holding her hips and her gaze, he thrust forward, impaling her. He slid all the way in.

"Yes," she hissed, throwing her head back. She felt completely possessed by his shaft, totally filled up. Every square inch of her pussy seemed touched by him. Slowly, so she could feel every little vein of him, he slid out, and then back in. She writhed beneath him, tears stinging her eyes at how good it felt to have him inside her.

He dipped his head down and kissed her as he moved slowly in and out of her. Her lips parted in wonder at the look of love in his eyes and the intimacy of this act, having him within her and face-to-face. He parted her lips and mated his tongue with her. She tightened her hands on his shoulders and whimpered in the back of her throat at the perfectness of the experience.

He brushed her hair away from her face and held her gaze as he shafted her leisurely. "I haven't been this happy in a long, long time, Bianca. I never want this to end."

A tear squeezed from the corner of her eye and he kissed it away. His motions became surer and longer and harder with every stroke he made. Bianca let a moan rip from her throat as she arched her back. She could barely form a coherent thought. Her entire reality had narrowed to only feeling him.

He placed a hand to the back of her knee and hooked one leg over his hip, changing his angle and deepening the penetration. This position caused him to move back and forth over an especially sensitive area deep within her. She braced her other foot on the ground and thrust her hips up at him, driving him harder and deeper inside her.

"Fuck, Bianca," he breathed.

She went to pieces beneath him as a climax washed over her. She moaned out his name, clutching his shoulders as the muscles of her pussy milked his cock.

He answered in kind. Angelo groaned and she felt him spill within her.

Breathing heavy, he rested on top of her, bracing his arms on either side of her. He buried his face in the hollow of her neck and laid a line of kisses to her skin. She wrapped her arms around him and smiled happily, never wanting him to leave her body.

They stayed that way for a long time, basking in the aftermath of their shared pleasure. She kissed his shoulder and inhaled close to his skin, reveling in the musky male smell of him. Bianca hoped the scent of him stayed on her, had worked its way into the pores of her skin. She wanted to be marked as his—completely and totally.

Part of her was happy and sated beyond belief, but another part was afraid. Would he resent her now that she'd deliberately seduced him into making love to her? Her arms tightened around him. Would he regret it?

He wound his arms under her and rolled over, pulling her with him so she lay on top of him. Her legs trailed down between his. She laid her hands flat on his chest and rested her chin on them.

Her face must have betrayed her thoughts, because he reached up and pushed her hair away from where a few tendrils had fallen over her eye. "Hmmm. I'm not sure I like that look on your face after I've made love to you."

"Are you sorry? Sorry we just did that?"

He laughed. "Sorry? No, Bianca. I'm definitely not sorry."

"What about not wanting to make love to me because you were so afraid to get me pregnant? I assumed you were afraid to carry on that bad blood you told me about before." She rolled off and sat beside him, drawing her knees up to cover her nakedness. Suddenly, she felt very exposed.

"Let's not dance around the subject, angel-face. You already know my secret." He lay on his side beside her.

"I want to hear you tell me, Angelo."

"Fine. It's past time I did. I'm Kiran, Bianca. There, I said it."

Relief flooded her. He'd said it out loud. He'd admitted it. That was a step in the right direction. She shook her head. "You've got to be only part Kiran. I've never seen you consume freysis."

"You're right. I'm half-Kiran. My father was a full blood. I've never exposed myself to freysis because I don't know how I would react, like a human or a Kiran."

She shuddered, leaned toward him, and kissed his forehead. "Let's not test it out anytime soon, okay?"

* * * * *

Angelo stared up at Bianca. One long tendril of her hair was swept over her shoulder, and the end had curled around a delicious-looking pink nipple. Unable to resist, he reached out and leisurely stroked his thumb over it, feeling it harden under his caress.

They were completely naked, and he was revealing secrets about himself to her that he'd never told anyone. Secrets that even he and his sisters had been loath to discuss together.

And it was all right.

In fact, it was more than all right. It felt good. He felt relieved at finally being able to share his darkness with another person.

"We ran from community to community," he said. "We were threatened, tormented. I've never seen a community like this one, where Kirans and humans live together."

She reached out and cupped his cheek against her palm.

"We never belonged anywhere," he continued. "We were never accepted."

"I'm sorry."

He shook his head. "You can't blame humans for hating the Kirans."

"The Kiran leaders have much to atone for. You'll find that all the Kirans here in the Valley are very ashamed and are willing to do anything they can to right their wrongs. If this crystal does what we think it does, they will want us to use it."

"How can you be so sure? If the water crystal does reverse the bacterial process, where will they get their freysis?"

"Melvin's been contemplating this situation for years now. He says if the water crystal is successful, the Kirans will have to band together in one community." Bianca shrugged. "Before the poisoning, Kirans lived among humans and survived. There were methods they used to store and consume freysis-tainted water. The freysis will have to be carefully contained, as the pure-water is now. They knew before the poisoning that there were ways—though complicated—that humans and Kirans could share this planet. That truth remains, doesn't it?"

"But there are lots of Kirans who like things the way they are. Won't they simply find a way to poison the water again?" Angelo asked.

"Melvin said that if—" She shook her head. "Let's wait and see what Melvin discovers about the crystal. First things first."

He reached out and ran his fingertip over her nipple, moving her hair away. "And second things, second," he said in a low voice. His gaze caressed her body.

She shivered and closed her eyes as he lazily ran his fingers over her pussy. "Angelo," she said breathlessly.

Pleased with her reaction to his touch, he sat up, leaned forward and tasted her lips, while simultaneously running his hand lower, over her flat abdomen, headed for sweeter, warmer places. Maybe he could get an even better reaction.

"I've only got one thing on my mind right now. Want to know what that is?" he asked, his lips hovering over hers.

She kept her eyes closed and nodded. At the same time his hand found the entrance to her slick sex, and she opened like a flower for the sun. He slid inside her and drew out the mixture of their cum and spread it over her sex. He rubbed her clit with slippery mixture and she moaned loud and long, spreading her thighs for him.

"You excited again, angel-face?" he asked.

She licked her lips. "You know my body is yours. You can do anything to it you want."

He raised an eyebrow in speculation. He loved it when she surrendered herself that way to him, gave him carte blanche. His cock twitched as he gazed down at her well-loved pussy and her heavy, swollen breasts with their little lickable nipples. "What do you want to me do to this sweet body of yours?"

She flashed him a wicked smile and rolled over onto her stomach and pushed to her knees. She lowered her head and thrust her ass into the air. "Anything. Just touch me." She grinned. "I'll even beg for it, if you want."

He reached out and covered her dripping sex with his palm. Her clit was begging for a good sucking, exposed and aroused the way it was. He settled for stroking it with the pad of his finger over and over, softly, slowly, until he wiped the grin off her face and her expression was one of slack-jawed lust.

"Anything?" he growled. He scooped some of the cream that coated her sex and spread it over her lovely little anus. He teased it, then slipped a finger inside. "How about this?"

Her hips bucked up against his hand and he smiled. His little angel enjoyed it when a man took her from behind and that was good since it was one of his favorite things to do to a woman. That, and use his tongue. He added a finger to her ass and she moaned.

"Hmmm, I think you like that just fine," he said. He slipped two fingers of his opposite hand into her pussy and thrust in and out, in time to the way he finger-fucked her ass.

Bianca keened for him and the sound hit him straight in his cock. He stared at his fingers ramming in and out of her, possessing both orifices at once.

"I want you inside me," she cried. "Take me from behind, Angelo."

He stilled, his cock twitching at the prospect. He pulled his fingers free of her body and coated his cock with the cream from his fingers. He set the head of his cock to her anus. "Here?"

She pushed back at him in an effort to impale herself. "Yes, please." The crown of him breached the tight ring of muscles and she hit the ground with her fist. "Oh, yes."

Angelo bit his lip to keep from slamming into her. It still amazed him that her body could take his cock this way. He pushed in slowly, inch by inch. Her rear engulfed his cock bit by mind-blowing bit and her muscles clamped down on his shaft.

"Fuck," he swore under his breath. Her little ass would make him raw it was so tight. "I'm not hurting you, am I?"

"A little," she breathed.

He stilled.

"But it's good! Please, don't stop now."

His breath hissed out of him as he pulled out and thrust back in. Her hips wiggled, driving him crazy. He clamped his hands on her to keep her in place. "God, you're hot and tight."

She whimpered and rocked her hips back, forcing him another inch.

"How do you want it? You want it fast and hard?"

"Yes! God, please! I'm not delicate, Angelo. I can take it. I want it."

"Hell, Bianca, you feel so unbelievably sweet around my cock," he murmured as he slipped his hand down to stroke the pad of his finger over her distended clit. Her hips bucked against him. "That good?"

"So good," she slurred.

"This will be better." He slicked his fingers of the hand he'd already used to tease her pussy over her wet labia to the opening of her slit and speared within. He finger-fucked her there as he started to shaft her from behind.

"Uh, Angelo," she moaned.

He found the little bundle of nerves in her pussy, the backside of her clit, and rubbed over it. Bracing himself on the grass with his other hand, he set up a punishing pace behind her, thrusting in and out of her in long, easy strokes. It was an awkward position, but worth it to hear her go crazy beneath him.

"Oh, God, I'm coming," she yelled.

She came undone beneath him with a hoarse cry. Her cream drenched his hand and she felt the muscles of her anus clamp down around his cock and her pussy convulse around his fingers.

He tipped right over the edge of his own climax. He buried himself balls-deep inside her and felt his cock erupt. He groaned and gripped her hips, holding her in place as he filled her.

When they'd both descended from their erotic highs, he pulled free of her body and collapsed with her to the ground. He pulled her close, breathing hard, kissed her all over her face and throat. "You're going to kill me," he murmured.

"Mmmmm," she sighed.

They lay tangled there, stated and happy.

Angelo had never been more content in his life than he was with Bianca in his arms. He pulled her close, and murmured that he loved her.

He'd never let her go. Not for anything. She was his now.

* * * * *

They finally left the bluff and went back into town. Bianca held on to Angelo's hand and felt truly happy for the first time since she couldn't even remember.

She ached in very intimate places from their afternoon of lovemaking, but it was a good ache. One she wouldn't trade for anything. Even better than the lovemaking, which meant it was really, really good, was the fact that Angelo had finally confided in her. He'd finally trusted her enough to reveal that secret part of himself.

She shivered. And he'd told her he loved her.

She was loved.

Was there anything better than that?

Nothing could chase away the warm glow that had begun within her. Hell, she couldn't even wipe off the all-too-stupid grin that had spread across her face.

They walked between a couple of houses and headed toward the town center. People were beginning to file into the town hall for the welcoming ceremony already. Ellsatha and Maren would probably be at Melvin's shortly to escort them.

They hurried down the street leading to Melvin's cottage. When they opened the door, Melvin stood inside the living room, his arms crossed over his chest.

They closed the door behind them and turned to meet his critical gaze. Melvin took a step forward and picked a dead leaf out of her hair. "Where have you two been all day? And what is that smile on your face, girl?" He shook his head impatiently. "Scratch that, I don't want to know."

Bianca tried to stop grinning, but just couldn't.

"The welcoming ceremony for Angelo begins soon, but I must discuss the crystal with you before then," Melvin continued. His hands shook visibly. "Right now."

Angelo moved to her back and put his hands on her shoulders. She knew her smile was suddenly gone. "Have you discovered if the crystal does what is claimed?" she asked.

Melvin nodded, a smile blooming on his mouth. "Yes, I have."

"Well?"

"It does."

Angelo's grip tightened on her shoulders. His voice rumbled through her back as he spoke. "And have you figured out how to use it?"

Melvin's smile grew wider as he nodded again. His eyes glittered with excitement.

They all three stood there, suddenly mute, in a state of mingling fear and hope. Someone knocked on the door, startling them all.

Melvin walked to it and threw it open. "What do you want?"

Ellsatha took a step backward in alarm. "It is nearly time for the ceremony, Melvin. I came for Angelo."

"We'll be there in a few minutes," he replied and shut the door in her very surprised face.

Bianca caught Angelo's eye and they shared a look. Yes, Melvin was off a bit.

Melvin turned around, gleefully rubbing his hands together. "I consulted many Kiran books I have on the subject of crystals." He turned to Angelo. "Boy, I'll bet you don't even know about the power of Kiran crystals, do you? You should, you know, it's your heritage." Melvin cast a guilty look at Bianca.

"It's okay, Melvin. I told her," said Angelo.

"Good. She was going to find out anyway, you know. The whole damn town knows you're part Kiran." Melvin walked to the crystals on the fireplace mantel and picked up a small crystal wand. Holding his hand out, he walked toward Angelo. "Take it."

Angelo reached out and took it, then gasped and nearly dropped it. "It thrums. It's like being shocked with energy."

Melvin nodded, and then jerked his head toward Bianca. "She can't feel anything when she holds them because she's human. But for a Kiran, a Kiran with the right abilities, that is, a properly charged crystal will sing. It recognizes our blood and our brain wave patterns. You can do a lot with these crystals. A Kiran with empathic ability can even heal with them."

Angelo looked down at the crystal wand in the palm of his hand.

"Yes, we can heal as well as kill, boy, create as well as destroy."

Angelo looked up at him but didn't respond.

"You've got a lot of ability," Melvin continued in Kiran, a language Bianca knew. "I felt it the first time I touched you, but it's all unformed and wild. You've not been trained and you've got a lot of learning to do."

Again, Angelo seemed unable to reply.

Melvin nodded jerkily. "Come back here after you use the water crystal and I'll teach you, boy. I'll teach you to see the beauty in your heritage, as well as respect the darkness. I'll teach you how to embrace yourself if you'll meet me halfway with your willingness."

Angelo handed the crystal back to him. "Yes, I can meet you halfway."

"Good." He walked the table where the water crystal laid amid stacks of books and papers. "Now, let's talk about this crystal."

Angelo picked up a book and looked at the writing on the spine.

"It's a book about the nutritional benefits of freysis," said Bianca.

Angelo looked at her in surprise. "You can speak Kiran?"

Melvin waved his hand. "That is not important at this time. But, yes, I taught the twins to speak it when they came to live here." He held the crystal out. "This, my children, is going to redeem the Kiran their wrongs against the planet Earth." He smiled. "I'm only happy I get to play a small role in this. If you choose to undertake this task, you two will realize it."

"How do we do that?" asked Bianca.

"This is basically an enhydro crystal, Bianca, but a very special one. Somewhere near the heart of planet Kira, normal freysis-killing liquid was trapped and the crystal formed around it. What makes this crystal different from other enhydros is its age. This crystal is probably somewhere near three million years old. Over all that time, the liquid transformed itself into a very potent and powerful powder."

Angelo took it from Melvin's hand. "So, I'm assuming the powder, like the liquid in the enhydros, kills freysis?"

"Yes. The enhydro liquid, if you didn't already know this, contains microorganisms that eat the freysis in the water, removing them. The microorganisms hibernate within the enhydro. When a crystal is opened and a drop of the liquid is secreted into freysis-laden water, the microorganisms wake up, so to speak, and quickly spread, reproducing at an unbelievably fast rate until all the freysis has been consumed."

"The liquid only kills a limited amount of freysis. How much freysis will this powder kill?" asked Bianca.

"The microorganisms in the powder, though hibernating, have evolved into a very powerful creature over the years. They are called *chimra* in this state. If the chimra are released correctly, they will use the hydrologic cycle to spread, just like the freysis did." Melvin smiled. "These little creatures are powerful enough to reproduce at a rate fast enough to kill all the freysis on planet Earth."

Hope surged through Bianca in such a powerful rush that she was sure Angelo must have felt it.

"You must take this crystal while it is still warm outside, my children. The chimra will reproduce faster when the temperature of the water is high. You must put the powder into the right-sized body of water. Lake Michigan is the only lake around here that is large enough. The hydrologic cycle and the chimra itself will do the rest."

Bianca stared at it. "But it's so small. How can it do all that?"

Melvin made a frustrated noise. "You humans. Why do you always think something has to be big to be powerful?"

"But once this is done, what's to stop the Kirans from re-poisoning the water?" asked Angelo. "You can't be so naïve as to think they wouldn't try."

Melvin shook his head. "With the chimra in the water, they wouldn't be able to release freysis. The chimra will continue to live in the water, so they would simply eat it as soon as it was introduced."

"Then how will the Kirans survive?" asked Bianca.

Melvin beamed. "Ah, my girl, did you think I hadn't considered that? The chimra will take at least two years to spread worldwide. It's not a lot of time, but perhaps it will be enough. We will have send word that the poisoning will be reversed to the other Kiran communities. We've kept up a good system of communication over the years. Freysis will have to be cultured in intensive quantities. Chimra-laden water can be infected with freysis, if the water quantity is small and the freysis count overwhelming. But a global-scale freysis poisoning would not be possible. We can repair and use the old water treatment plants to prepare water for the Kirans."

"This is incredible," Bianca breathed.

"I think it would be better to send only a couple people on this errand," said Melvin. "More than that would be detectable to the guardians. Better a mouse sneaking into the house than an elephant. So, the question is—do you want to do it?"

"Yes," answered Bianca and Angelo in unison.

"We've got the most invested in this," continued Bianca. "Anyway, who best to outwit the guardians than the captain himself?"

Angelo eyed the crystal speculatively. "How do we get the crystal open without spilling any of the chimra?"

Melvin shivered. "Spilling the chimra would be bad, my boy. Don't do that." He walked into his bedroom and came back with a small instrument in hand. It was a small, with a black handle and a beveled edge made of sharpened crystal. "Stand back," he said.

Melvin picked up the instrument and pressed something on the end of it. A brilliant blue light flickered out from the edge. Melvin lowered the instrument to the edge of the table, so the light touched the wood. It burned a fine line there, sending up the scent of scorched wood. He released the button and the light flicked back inside the instrument. "This is used to cut enhydros. But be careful not to burn any of the powder with the laser cutter. Be careful with the danged thing, period. It works like a super-fine laser and can injure you."

"Why would the Kirans have brought this crystal here?" Angelo asked. "I can see why they brought the enhydros since they only purify small quantities of water and perhaps they had need of that, but this crystal—" he shook his head, "—it's like a nuclear bomb. I don't get it."

"Enhydros were treated as toxic waste on Kira," said Melvin. "They were disposed of very carefully. Someone brought the enhydros and this crystal containing the chimra here to Earth for a reason. Maybe they feared something with the poisoning would go badly and it would be needed. Perhaps they took it in case my team had success terraforming the other planet right after the poisoning and they would want to reverse it. I am unsure."

Bianca fisted a hand at her side. "At any rate, Finch's father must've have gotten his hands on it early in the war, along with the enhydros, and hidden the water crystal so he could have the glory, power and prestige of being the sole water-giver."

Melvin sighed sadly. "That sounds like a possible scenario, my child." He gave the instrument to Bianca who slipped into her pocket. He turned to Angelo. "And now, Arapass, we go to welcome you to the bosom of our community." He quirked a brow. "I believe Bianca has already welcomed you to her bosom in her own way. Go put on a shirt."

Bianca felt heat rise to her cheeks. She watched Angelo go into the bedroom and return wearing a dark blue shirt.

"We go!" announced Melvin as he went toward the door. "Give me a day to further consider things. You two can leave first thing the day after tomorrow."

Chapter Twenty-Four

Angelo leaned against the doorway of Bianca's bedroom and watched her with hunger curling slowly through his body. She wore a pair of shorts and a thin T-shirt. Her breasts, he'd noticed earlier, were bare beneath. A book lay open in front of her and she seemed to be completely engrossed in the story.

She hadn't even noticed it when Melvin had muttered something about needing to take a walk and had left the cottage. It was the first time they'd been alone all day.

He watched her idly swing one long, lean leg back and forth and rotate a slim ankle. He let his gaze travel over the luscious swell of her ass and the bit of exposed skin at the small of her back where her T-shirt had ridden up.

He was insatiable for her. She was all he thought about. His cock hardened at the mere scent of her skin. Since they'd made love yesterday, all he wanted was more of her. His Kiran heritage be damned. Everything else in the world be damned.

He had it bad.

He moved toward the bed. "Bianca," he murmured.

She looked up at him, seeing the expression of need on his face. Her pupils dilated and she smiled. It nearly stopped his heart. She set the book on her nightstand and sat up. "Angelo," she replied, heat infusing her voice.

Without another word, his hands went to the edges of her shirt. He pulled it up and over her head. He knelt his head and brushed his lips over the swell of one breast. She sighed and curled her fingers through the hair at his nape. "What about Melvin?"

"He's gone for a while."

"Mmmm, well then."

He gave one last swipe to her nipple, feeling it pebble beneath his tongue, and crushed his mouth to hers.

She broke the kiss and slid down the bed to the floor. He followed her until they were both on their knees, facing each other. She slid her hands down the front of his chest, undoing each button of his shirt one by one, and kissing and licking each bit of flesh that was revealed. Finally, she pushed the shirt off his shoulders. She laved one of his nipples, making him groan.

"You have the finest chest of any man I've ever seen," she said breathlessly. "The sight of it makes my clit pulse."

He smiled. "Really." He slipped a hand to the small of her back and pulled her up flush against his chest. At the same time, he lowered his mouth to her throat. She arched her back, pressing herself against him, and gave him the full expanse to kiss and nibble.

"God, Angelo, I want you," she exclaimed breathlessly. "I want you all the time."

She blindly fumbled at the button and zipper of his pants, finally getting them undone. His pants slipped down and he kicked off his shoes and socks. She wrapped her hands around the base of his cock and pumped him.

He groaned. "Fuck, Bianca. You're going to kill me."

"I don't want to kill you, I want to make you come," she answered.

Angelo gritted his teeth as she continued to stroke him and unbuttoned her shorts. They were loose enough that he could get his hands into them to stroke her clit.

She pushed his hand away, shaking her head. Her eyes went dark. "No. I want you in my mouth, Angelo."

He gripped his cock and pumped it once. Her eyes followed his movements. "It's all yours, Bianca."

She pushed him back and leaned down, licking the drop of pre-cum that had pearled on the head. She moaned against him and Angelo closed his eyes. Her hand slid up his cock, using his foreskin to pump him.

He groaned, tipping his head back. With eager fingers, she explored every last ridge and inch of his shaft and balls. "Holy hell," he murmured, his hips jerking forward. "You're teasing."

"Mmmm…isn't it good?" she breathed.

He groaned. "I'd rather have your lips around it."

She engulfed him in her mouth.

He fisted his hands in her hair and blew out a hard breath. The hot, velvet interior of her mouth was unlike anything he'd ever felt. He fought the urge to hold her head and fuck her sweet, hot mouth. He fought the urge to rip her shorts off and sink into all that promising warm silk he knew existed between her slim thighs. She'd probably be so deliciously wet for him by now.

Instead, he watched his shaft disappear into her mouth and reappear, over and over. His cock was slick with her saliva. "You're going to make me come, baby."

She intensified her efforts, sucking him down the back of her throat and caressing his balls at the same time.

"Aw, hell!" He couldn't take it anymore. He held her head in place as he fucked her mouth gently, sliding himself down her throat. She held still, allowing him to do it.

Hot cum shot out of him and into her as pleasure enveloped his body. She swallowed down everything he gave her. He tipped his head back and groaned. "Bianca."

He pulled his cock free from her mouth. She'd rocked back on her heels. Her breasts were heavy looking, the nipples hard and red. Her shorts had slipped down a little, exposing some of her silky blond pubic hair. The look in her eyes and on her face was completely carnal. Making him come had turned her on.

His cock twitched. Even though he'd just ejaculated, he felt himself getting hard again. It had been so long since he'd had sex, his libido was doing overtime.

"Take off your shorts and get on the bed," he commanded in a guttural voice.

She raised an eyebrow and moved slowly, deliberately driving him insane. She stood and pushed her shorts off, then turned, giving him a nice look at her shapely ass, and climbed onto the bed.

He stood, watching as she lay down on her back. His gaze ate up every part of her naked body. She stretched like a cat and he groaned. Bianca knew how gorgeous she was and was trying to tease him with it.

She needed to be teased a little.

"Remember how I asked you to touch yourself before?"

Her eyes darkened. "Yes."

"That excited you, didn't it?"

"Yes," her voice had gone breathless.

"Do it again, angel-face. I want to watch you make yourself come again."

She bit her lower lip and lowered her eyes. "I've never done that before."

"All the better. Go on. Touch yourself. Start with your breasts."

She slid her hands up her sides to cup both breasts. With unsure movements, she plumped her breasts.

"That's right," he encouraged. "Perfect. Stroke your nipples for me."

She brushed the pads of her fingers over her hardened nipples. Her back arched and she panted. After brushing them a few more times, she rolled them between her fingertips and closed her eyes.

"Is it good, Bianca?"

She nodded distractedly, drew her knees up and let her thighs fall apart, exposing her whole aroused, creamy little cunt to him. The motion was so fluid and natural Angelo doubted she even knew she'd done it. His breath escaped him as he let his gaze trail over her swollen labia and the moisture that glistened on them. His fingers curled into fists at his side. All he wanted was to jump her, but it wasn't time yet for that.

She ran the pads of her index fingers over her rock-hard nipples, first brushing across them, then slowly circling the pebbled peaks. Her hips thrust forward, looking for something to fuck, and she moaned.

"Your clit is swollen, begging to be touched and licked."

Her fingers faltered at their work on her breasts, slipping down on their own over her stomach toward her pussy. With her eyes still closed and her breath coming faster, Angelo knew she was caught in a deep net of physical need.

Angelo watched her brush her clit. She shuddered and moaned.

"That's right, stroke yourself."

A tremor shook her body at his words and she opened her eyes. She stared up at him with a heavy-lidded gaze and caressed her clit. He watched a pearl of her cream slide down her inner thigh and resisted the urge to lean down and lick it away.

"Do you like it?" he asked hoarsely.

"Yes, but I'd like it better if you were touching me."

"I will be soon. After you bring yourself so I can watch."

He watched the rotation of her fingers around her swollen clit. The muscles at the entrance of her pussy pulsed and contracted. Her hips thrust forward again.

"You want me to make love to you, angel-face? You want my cock inside you?"

"Yes," she breathed.

"Slide your finger inside your sweet pussy. Tell me how it feels."

She hesitated a moment, but then slid a finger down and rubbed it over her entrance. His cock went ramrod straight as she pushed it inside and moaned.

"How does it feel?"

"Tight and hot."

"I can't wait to be in there, Bianca, but right now I want to watch you bring yourself. Make yourself come while I watch."

She added her middle finger to the first. Her body went rigid and her back arched as she slid them both in then pulled them out. With her other hand, she caressed her clit, running the pad of her finger up and down it.

Angelo fisted his hand so hard his nails bit into flesh as he watched her fingers thrusting into her pussy. His gaze traveled from her breasts with her suckable hard nipples to her pistoning fingers.

"Are you going to come for me, baby?"

"Yes." She cried out and groaned, her back arching. Her body trembled and the room filled with her moans. Her body shuddered and her hips bucked as her climax enveloped her.

Finally, she quieted and lay panting.

That was it. He couldn't take any more. "Bianca, baby, get on your hands and knees," he commanded in rasping voice.

She opened her eyes and smiled a little, then flipped over and did as he asked.

Her reddened, glistening sex hung between her spread thighs, begging for his cock. Angelo fell on her like a beast, covering her body and guiding his cock inside her without preamble. He groaned at the feel of her tight, hot muscles gripping his shaft. There was nothing, *nothing* like being within this woman.

Bianca lifted her hips in offering and moaned low as he slid himself inside her to the hilt.

He groaned. His fingers bit into her waist.

"Take me hard," she gasped. "I want to feel you hard and fast."

Angelo was all too ready to oblige. He grabbed her hips and gave her what she craved. He pulled back and slammed into her over and over. Bianca bucked and moaned beneath him.

He shifted his hips and drove into her at a different angle, so the crown of his cock rubbed over her G-spot with every powerful forward thrust of his hips. She gasped and lowered her head to the bed, tipping her hips up and offering herself completely to him.

She came in a frenzy. She gripped the comforter and cried out. He felt the muscles deep within her ripple, then spasm as she came. He thrust balls-deep into her and his cock jumped within her. He groaned. A hot stream of cum filled her.

They collapsed on the mattress, both breathing heavy.

"Damn it, Bianca," he groaned, running a hand over his face.

She laughed and pulled herself against him.

He heaved her over onto her back and kissed her deeply. "Bianca, I love you," he murmured against her lips.

He felt her smile against his mouth. "I love you, too."

* * * * *

Angelo wrapped his arms around Bianca. They stood in the backyard of Melvin's cottage, awaiting Melvin's final instructions before they began the journey back toward the Center. Contentment filled him as Bianca pressed her back against his chest and rubbed her cheek against his chest where his shirt was open.

"Come on, come on. I swear, don't you two ever stop touching?" asked Melvin as he brushed past them. "It's enough to make an old man lose his breakfast."

Angelo let Bianca go reluctantly.

"We're coming, Melvin," she called after him. "We're all packed and ready to go. Angelo just needs to saddle the horse."

As Angelo did so, Melvin brought feed in a bag that they could strap to the saddlebag. They'd travel light, just a couple changes of clothing, a first-aid kit, pure-water, a tent, air mattress and nutro-wafers.

When the horse was ready, Angelo took the crystal from Melvin. He'd wrapped it in a small bit of blue fabric. Melvin grasped his shoulder. "You carry the future of this planet in your hand, Angelo. It's not a light responsibility, but you and Bianca are strong enough to see it through. You are truly a guardian, Angelo. The guardian of the planet. When this is through, come back here to live and make Bianca happy."

"Thank you." He glanced at Bianca, who stood near the house. "That's definitely in my plans."

"I have wrapped a healing crystal in with the water crystal. I know you don't know how to use it and hopefully you won't have occasion to try. If you do, simply follow your instincts. Follow your blood, Arapass."

"Follow my instincts." Angelo twisted his lips. "Easy for you to say." He'd spent his entire life suppressing those inclinations.

"It will come naturally to you, I swear."

"Why weren't these crystals used to cure Kirans of the virus?"

He patted his forearm. "Good question. I pray the opportunity does not arise, but if it does, you'll understand why not. Arapass, half-brother, I have confidence in you. You have much ability for a half-breed." Then Melvin clapped him on his shoulder and left him. Angelo wondered if he'd just been insulted.

Melvin went to Bianca and wrapped her in an embrace. He whispered something her ear that Angelo could barely hear. "You have been like a daughter to me these past years. Though I've never told you so, I love you like one. Stay safe, my girl. I am very proud of you."

Bianca hugged him and told him she loved him too. When she turned to Angelo, she had tears in her eyes. "Let's get going," she said brusquely.

Angelo swung onto Jinx and helped Bianca to mount behind him. "Prepare the Kirans for a drastic change, Melvin," said Bianca.

He nodded. "We'll begin to make ready for the transition and send messengers to the other Kiran communities."

They traveled out fast under the new morning sunlight. They had a long trip ahead of them.

At midday, when the bright yellow sun was high in the sky and they were far from the Valley, he dismounted and handed Bianca an alter-gun and her pistol.

"You remember everything I told you about the alter-gun, right?" he asked as he slipped on his shoulder holster. He'd given Bianca a lesson on how to operate the weapon while they'd been in the Valley.

"Yes." She slipped her pistol into the waistband at the small of her back and put the alter-gun in the top of the saddlebag, within easy reach.

"Remember, only use the alter-gun if it's a Guardian at close range. If you don't think you can hit them in the head, or if it's Dell or Finch—"

"I'll use the pistol."

"No question, angel-face."

"I got it, Angelo. Don't worry."

"I am worried. They're going to have the shore of the lake staked out."

"I know. They'll be patrolling with the hovercraft. We're going to have to be really careful."

He mounted again and let Bianca wind her arms around him. The stakes were higher now. There was no way he'd lose Bianca to them.

Two nights ago at the welcoming ceremony, nearly every member of the community had greeted him with open arms. Some of them viewed him warily because they knew he was formerly a Guardian of Order and did not trust him. But most of them came up to him, human and Kiran alike, and clasped his hand or his shoulder and spoke words that warmed Angelo's heart. *You are welcomed into our community. Come as you are. Stay as you are.*

Unconditional acceptance.

They had offered to help him build a home and had requested his assistance as a protector. When they'd asked him if he intended to stay among them, he'd hesitated. He'd been thinking of Quint and his community, and visions of possibly fusing the two had danced through his head. Also, he dreamed of bringing his mother and sisters here. This is where they needed to live, a place without fear.

Bianca's face had grown guarded as he'd hesitated and he'd felt a quick flash of deep sorrow, quickly supplanted by false aloofness. Had she worried he'd say no? Did she think he'd leave her? When he said he'd stay, her face and emotions had relaxed.

Last night he'd spent the whole night showing her just how much he wanted to be with her. With his hands, lips, teeth and body, he'd done his best to drive all thoughts of his leaving from her mind. They'd been quiet, but thorough, and when Bianca had writhed, moaned and lost herself beneath him again and again, he thought she knew.

He wasn't going anywhere.

They rode until late into the night, then finally stopped by a water source for the horse and put the freysis tent up under a willow tree. They hadn't forgotten that Dell was still searching for them. It was best to place the tent under trees, to conceal themselves from patrolling hovercraft. By tomorrow evening they'd be at the edge of Out-Center, far to the south of Lake Michigan.

Angelo let Jinx drink some water and graze in the grass. After the horse was secured for the night, he went into the tent where Bianca waited for him, all warm and cozy on the air mattress Melvin had given them. He couldn't think of anywhere he wanted to be more than in her arms. He flipped open the tent flap and she was exactly where he'd imagined her, except she appeared to be nude. The smooth skin of her arms and her incredibly kissable collarbone were exposed to the sweet-smelling night air. Her skin was bathed by the gentle glow of the solar-lantern. She certainly looked all delicious and bare, but he couldn't know for certain until he felt her. And, wow, did he want to feel her.

He raised an eyebrow. "Are you wearing your pajamas, angel-face?"

She smiled bright and beautifully. It reached her blue-green eyes, lit them up. Angelo knew the smile was all for him, caused by him. It made his heart swell.

"Why don't you come under here and find out?" she said in a low, sultry voice.

He was already pulling his shirt off. "I was just waiting for an invitation."

* * * * *

The Southern edge of Out-Center was nearly deserted when they arrived. Coming back near the Center was always suffocating for Bianca after being in the lushness of the Valley. She'd grown up in the Out-Center — struggled to survive there for seven years — but it always took her a couple of days to get accustomed once again to all the cement, the scent of old death and the many ghosts that seemed to cling to the buildings.

They passed through the suburbs, keeping as close to structures as they could, and ready to take cover at the first sign of a hovercraft. The damn things were near silent and that made it difficult.

At the leading edge of Out-Center, the buildings were taller and placed closer together. Patches of grass grew less frequently and the cement spread out, bowed and cracked in places, fallen in completely in others where the soil had caved in beneath it.

The buildings lined the street, playing silent sentinel. They looked down with broken eyes and gaping mouths as they passed. Almost all the doors were kicked in, broken down. It made the buildings seem like they were screaming.

She shivered. She was letting her imagination run away with her. The Out-Center seemed more desolate now only because she knew Dell was out there somewhere, watching for them. He'd kill Angelo, if he had the chance. She knew that without a doubt. Finch would want Angelo dead. She didn't know what Finch wanted to do with her if he caught them, keep her drugged and caged, or kill her. It better be the latter, because there was no way she was going back to the Water Company alive.

"Are you okay?" asked Angelo. "I just felt despair come from you in a wave."

She was still growing accustomed to Angelo's newfound abilities. It could be disconcerting to have him suddenly tell her how she felt. She could forget ever hiding anything from him now. "I'm fine, Angelo. Really."

"My gorgeous little liar."

She tightened her arms around him. "I am," she insisted. "I'm with you, so I'm great."

He rubbed the back of her hand. "Remember what I said about keeping you safe from Dell? It still stands."

She rubbed her face along his back and breathed in the scent of him. It made her head swim and everything from her throat to her knees tightened with desire. She hadn't had enough of him yet, and doubted she ever would. "And I believe you, too."

"Good. We need to find shelter for the night. We're not far from the lake. If we were to keep going we'd reach it, but it's almost dark and there's no moon tonight."

She cringed at a sudden mental image of them fumbling in the dark and spilling the chimra. "I'd rather cut and deposit the crystal in the light."

"Yes. Less chance for error. If we used lanterns, we'd be easily spotted from the air. Anyway, I'm exhausted. This has waited close to forty years, another six hours won't make much difference."

They traveled until night fell. Bianca looked up at the black expanse of the sky that sparkled with twelve million little glittering lights.

Angelo tipped his head up. "It's beautiful, isn't it?"

"You could get lost looking at all those stars. Completely lose your sense of even having a body. The most amazing part is, Angelo, a part of you is from those stars. That is a beautiful thing."

Angelo was silent for several long moments and Bianca thought maybe she'd pushed too hard. Finally, he spoke. "My mother says she loved my father and he loved her back, but I never thought it was possible that a Kiran could love." He paused. "But then I met you and I found out they can."

If she'd been a cat, she would've purred. Instead, she tightened her hold around his waist and kissed his back.

Soon they reached an old church that looked stable enough to use for shelter. Angelo led the horse in through the broken-down double doors and tied the horse off in the lobby. Jinx had drunk from a water source not long ago and they'd fed him on a recent break. Bianca sat down on a half-broken step and watched Angelo take the saddle off and rub the animal down.

She looked around her. Every noise they made echoed through the cavernous room. The ceiling, at least in this room, was intact. It rose in a point above them. She noted that the walls likely used to be white. Now they were a smoky gray color in places. In other places, they were yellow, showing the wear and tear of the war and the simple passage of time. A large crucifix hung on the back wall of the room, half broken and looking forlorn.

Angelo took her hand. In his other, he held the solar-lantern. The air mattress was tucked under his arm. "Come on, let's get some sleep." His voice echoed through the place.

Broken pews marked the main part of the church. The ceiling sloped into an arch above them here, as well. She could almost hear the voices rising in song and in prayer and it made her shiver.

He set the lantern down on the steps of the elevated area at the front of the room and pressed the button that inflated the air mattress, and then laid it down in the area where Bianca supposed the priest would have given his sermons. Angelo unbuckled his holster and slid it off, then took off his shirt and lay down. He stretched, reached his arms back, resting his head on his hands and closed his eyes. Naked from the waist up, he looked good enough to lick.

She took the pistol out from its resting place at the small of her back and placed it on the floor near the blanket, within arm's reach, and then laid down beside him on her side. Her head rested on his chest and the entire length of her body touched his. She sighed happily and rubbed against him. He let one arm come down around her back and they found that perfect position, the one that allowed them to touch as much of the other as possible while still being incredibly comfortable.

"Mmmmm, nice," murmured Angelo. The solar-lantern flickered, running out of juice, and then went out. "Perfect. Now we don't even have to move. Except to do this." He rolled over, slid his hand under the bottom her shirt and leisurely stroked her nipple into a little peak. Her breath caught and she immediately creamed for him. He was always doing that, always touching her breasts possessively, always petting and caressing her. It kept her constantly aroused.

"Angelo," she murmured. "You keep that up and we're going to have a problem." She shifted her hips restlessly, her arousal growing.

He stopped stroking her nipple long enough to set her hand on his cock. It was hard. "Mmmm…we already have a problem." He pushed her shirt up and started sucking and licking away at her breast as if he owned it. She shuddered with desire, her clit growing and her pussy readying itself for him.

"Should we, uh, be doing this in a, uh, church?" she asked in a breathless voice.

He growled around her breast and slipped a hand down her pants to rub the pad of his finger over her clit through the fabric of her panties. "I love you more than I have loved anyone, Bianca. I don't think showing you that in a church is a bad thing." He set to laving over her aching nipple.

She threaded her fingers through his hair and sighed happily. He pushed under the waistband of her underwear and slid a finger into her. Bianca closed her eyes and moaned. That was it. She was lost to him completely now. Lost to his hands and mouth. He thrust his finger in and out of her and she moved her hips, helping him do it. That now familiar feeling of a drugged haze came over her. When he got her like this nothing mattered but their bodies and how they fit together, how many different ways they could bring each other pleasure.

They removed each other's clothing bit by bit as they kissed and greedily nipped and licked at the each other's bodies as they were exposed to the cool air.

Bianca was a panting bundle of need by the time he lowered her to the blanket and parted her thighs aggressively with his knees. Angelo eased her hips up higher than normal, set the head of his cock to her entrance and impaled her with one long, smooth stroke straight downward. They groaned in unison. He pulled out and thrust down again, balls-deep within her. In this position his cock reached deeply within her.

He stayed thrust up as far as possible within her and stared down into her eyes. "This is how I feel the best, Bianca. I feel totally at peace when I'm a part of you." He kissed her long and slow, his tongue stroking up against hers as he stroked in and out of her pussy. He shafted into her slow, so slow it made tears sting her eyes at the delicious, wonderful torture of it.

Then he took it even slower. All she could do was feel him. The rest of the world and all their problems seemed to fall away.

Their breathing and murmurings filled the church as Angelo stared down at her with a smoldering look in his eyes. She twined a leg over his waist and canted her hip to bring him deeper inside of her. He cupped her buttocks, lifting and spreading her, and picked up the pace of his thrusts until she came, creaming all over him. She tipped her head back and cried out.

"You feel so good, Bianca," Angelo rasped. His motions were becoming faster and harder now. He jackhammered down into her, sending her straight from one climax and into another.

He came down on her exposed throat, kissing and nipping it lightly with his teeth as he lost himself inside her. "Bianca, I love you so goddamn much," he gasped against her collarbones.

She hugged him to her, twining her arms and legs around him to keep him inside her. "I love you, too," she whispered.

Afterward, he pulled her close and draped the blanket over their still nude bodies. Bianca traced a pattern on his chest. "When will you go to see your family?"

"Soon. If we get out of this alive, that is. Maybe I'll bring them back to the Valley with me. Do you think that would be okay?"

"Definitely. I can't wait to meet them."

"I can't wait for them to meet you, too." He sounded tired, his words slurred.

"Angelo?"

"Uh-huh?"

Yep. He was already half-asleep.

His breathing deepened into sleep and Bianca sighed. One of them should really stay awake to play lookout. She could stay up a while longer. Her eyelids drooped and she forced them open. Her eyelids drooped again and sleep's heavy hands grasped her so tightly she couldn't get away.

* * * * *

"They will have figured out the crystal by now."

Dell stared at Finch. His boss's voice was dangerously low. Usually people started to die when Finch spoke like that. Dell shifted uncomfortably in his seat in the passenger area of the hovercraft and delicately put his fingertips to his bruised cheek. It was still green and yellow where he'd taken Angelo's punch. And, goddamn it, he'd lost a tooth.

"So what does that mean, Dell?" asked Finch, his eyes narrowing.

Dell narrowed his eyes at him, trying to figure out if it was rhetorical question, or if he really wanted an answer.

"Well? What does it mean?" Finch yelled suddenly.

Every day the crystal was gone, Finch became stranger and less predictable. The proof was that he was out here with him, instead of ensconced in luxury at the Water Company. It was a testament to how worried Finch was.

"It means we need to start scouring the outer edges of Lake Michigan, sir. The southern edge is most likely where they'll head," answered Dell.

"Yessss," he hissed in response. "Good answer."

"It's a big lake, sir. And we've only got ten hovercraft."

Finch went silent in response. His steel-blue gaze bored into him.

Dell sighed. "I'll keep the hovercraft patrolling the southern shore of the lake, sir. Since that's the most likely place they'll head. We'll find them. I swear."

"Not only will you swear, Dell. You'll stake your life on it. Because if we don't find that crystal, I'm going to take my displeasure out on your hide." He leaned forward with a cold smile. "Believe me, Dell, I'd be so displeased I don't think you'd survive it."

It was hard to cower in fear from such a squat, effeminate man who couldn't even get it up. But Dell knew Finch would order him subjected to intense pain and eventually death by much scarier people than himself and that was a terrifying prospect.

"I want to catch them just as much as you do, sir," he replied, "though maybe for different reasons. Angelo, I want to see dead. There's no doubt about that. I want to kill that little girl too, sir, but I want to do it slow, painful, and I want Angelo to watch."

Finch's eyes narrowed again. "Why do you care so much about the twin, Dell?"

Ah, here he'd have to be careful. He couldn't tell him the truth—that she'd threatened him, mocked him and broke his nose—because Finch would ask why she'd done those things. Finch thought Angelo did his nose. The damn thing was healing crooked. He was missing a front tooth and had a crooked nose now because of those two.

A light bulb went off. He quickly formed a proper response. "She caused me trouble with you, sir. Not mention caused you worry and heartache. She made you doubt my loyalty to you. For that, I want to see her dead and I wanna do it slow."

Finch narrowed his eyes. "How do you know I don't want her back?"

He raised an eyebrow. "Do you, sir? After all the face you've lost because of her? The other Essential Providers are wondering why you can't keep a woman. They all suspect Calina committed suicide just to escape you and now they think Bianca has run away. It's not very good for your virile image, is it now, sir?" Virile illusion, more like.

Finch's small hands clenched in rage. Dell knew he'd hit a sore spot. "She's yours," he ground out. "They're both yours. I can find another woman, so she's yours and she's dead, however you want to do it."

Dell smiled slowly. "That's what I wanted to hear, sir. That's what I wanted to hear. You're motivating me well, sir, very well."

Finch rose from his chair and pointed at the cockpit door. "Now get in there and go find them. Don't come back to me until you've got one or both of them in your possession, or you have the crystal!" He turned and walked out the main door of the craft, down the gangplank and out of sight.

Dell stared after him with loathing, then got up and headed to the cockpit. Finch was getting on his last nerve. He'd find them, but he'd do it to satisfy himself, not because Finch ordered him to do it.

He engaged the hovercraft and lifted off. It was almost dawn. He'd do one last sweep of the houses around the southern tip of the lake, and then he was going to hand over the controls to someone else and get some sleep.

It took no time at all to get to his destination. He angled the craft's camera down and stared at the monitor, then he put his feet up on the console and yawned. Christ, another night of no sleep and no reward for his labor.

He kept his eyes on the monitor's screen, knowing full well if they were holed up somewhere down there, they'd be safely tucked away in an abandoned building, hidden from the seeking eye of the craft's camera.

It was tedious work. Every building he came across, he had to stop and scan with the motion detector. And there were a hell of a lot of buildings in the Out-Center, a lot of them filled with small animals that tripped the detector's sensors. He wished he could use the detector when it was moving. It'd make this job go a lot faster.

He came to a large abandoned building and stopped over it. Irritated, he flicked the motion detector on with the toe of his boot and settled back into his chair with a sigh. Seconds ticked past without the telltale beeping of the detector's alert system. He was just about to flip it off when the alarm went off. It was something big, like a deer...or a horse, maybe.

Like maybe Bianca and Angelo's horse?

This he would have to check out. Dell's feet came down off the console and he hit the land mechanism on the control panel to bring the craft down a ways from the building. This time he wanted the element of surprise. He guided the craft down into the middle of the street, grabbed his laser and exited the craft. Sticking to the shadows and with his laser at the ready, he made his way down the street and into the building.

The first floor was a layer of dust and debris. A long hallway stretched before him, with doors off each side. It had perhaps been an office building once-upon-a-time. He stifled a cough at the rank odor of the place. He let the arm holding his laser drop as his hope sank. It wasn't likely they'd picked a place like this to stay in.

Something in the room to left of him rustled. He raised his laser and went on high alert. Hooves clopped on the floor and a deer appeared in the doorway. It froze and blinked big brown eyes at him.

Disappointment and rage made him shake and flush red. "Goddamn it!" he yelled. Startled, the deer took off down the hallway, leaping over the piles of debris.

He aimed his laser and took a shot, but missed and only managed to blow a hole in one of the walls.

"Great...that's juuuust great!" he raged. An ancient trash can stood near him, filled to overflowing with refuse. He kicked it hard and it tipped over. The sound echoed down the corridor. "Angelo is on his way to the goddamn lake and I'm out here playing with the goddamn wildlife!" he yelled down the corridor to the deer.

Muttering to himself, he left the building and headed back to the craft. Finch had deployed all the craft he had and all his men. They'd split up to cover the most ground in order to make it more likely that they'd find Angelo and the little bitch. But he wanted to be the one to do it.

God, how he did.

He did a double take at a mark on the ground. "What's this?" he murmured as he knelt to examine it. It was a perfect print of a horse's hoof. Not a deer—a horse. One carrying quite a heavy load, too, from the looks of it.

Could it be? Could he be so lucky? Only one way to find out. Follow them.

Maybe he'd see terror in that little girl's blue-green eyes yet.

Chapter Twenty-Five

Bianca awoke first and turned on her side, still under the arm Angelo had draped over her. He'd thrown the other arm wide. Early dawn light spilled in through the holes in the walls of the building and bathed him in golden and rosy hues. He still slept deeply and there was no reason to wake him yet.

She extricated herself from his hold, and grabbed her gun. Rolling to her feet, she stretched, dressed, and then went for the exit, tucking the pistol in at the small of her back as she went. Nature called, but she wouldn't answer unarmed, not in Out-Center. Stopping in the lobby, she untied the horse and led it out with her. She needed to find it water. Last night they'd spotted a small pond not far from the church. That had been one reason they'd stopped there to sleep.

The sweet and fresh early morning breeze bathed her face as she walked out of the musty-smelling church. Rain wafted on the air. A storm was on the way.

With the reins in one hand, she picked her way around the huge fallen sign in the front of the structure and went the side of the building, headed toward the pond. The water source was nestled between two houses. It actually looked like a sinkhole that had filled with rainwater. Staying carefully away, she allowed the horse to go to it and drink.

She walked to the trees bordering the pond and answered Mother Nature's urgent call.

It would be wonderful if Angelo's brought his mother and sisters to the Valley to live. A pang of uneasiness went through her. She hoped they liked her. Either way, she wanted to see Angelo make up for lost time, for all those years he stayed away from them. He hadn't told her he'd avoided them, but Bianca suspected it. He'd stayed away because they were reminders of his Kiran blood.

Bianca wasn't sure how he was dealing with that issue overall. He had years of denial and shame to rinse away and it wouldn't go so easily, she knew. Although he seemed to be on the path to self-acceptance now, and she knew that she had no small role to play in that. His visit to the Valley, a place where he was accepted despite his alien heritage, had probably helped immensely.

He'd certainly embraced making love to her. Nope, he showed absolutely no hesitation in that area at all anymore.

She stepped out the trees and went back to the horse that had wandered away from the pond to placidly pull up grass. "Come on, we've got grain back at the church for you," she knelt and crooned to the horse, rubbing its smooth muzzle. She wanted to get back. Angelo was probably awake by now.

When she stood, she felt two hands close around her shoulders. The grip was hard, harsh. She knew right away it wasn't Angelo. "Hi, little girl, long time, no see," came Dell's raspy whisper, intimately close to her ear.

Fuck. She dropped the horse's reins, trying to twist fast out of his grip. One hand went to the small of her back, groping for her pistol. He gave her one powerful shove forward and she went down on the dew-soaked grass, her cheek flat against the freysis-drenched earth. He pushed his hand to the back of her neck, so she couldn't lift up, and ground his knee into the small of her back. His knee hit her gun. He swore, and then removed it.

He whistled low. "My, my. I see Angelo gave you your pistol back. Shame on him." He laughed. "'Course I'd make a bet Angelo has given you *lots* of things since we parted ways," he said in a low, silken tone, the words laden with insinuation.

Bianca concentrated on breathing. The hand on the back of her neck clamped down harder. She winced.

"What's the matter? Did I surprise you that much? At a loss for words? Now, that has got to be a first." He released his hand from the back her neck and her vision swam momentarily. She gasped at the relief.

He pulled her hands to the small of her back, and she felt cold metal touch her wrists. One click and then another announced the presence of handcuffs. He flipped her over to her back. The action twisted her arms painfully beneath her. Now he straddled her upper thighs, impeding the movement of her legs. Cold fury squeezed her stomach. She was completely at his mercy. He patted her down, looking for additional weapons and found none.

He leered at her and patted her down again…this time his touch was more intimate. Bile rose in her throat. She choked it down.

"I'm not going back to the Water Company, Dell," she rasped. "I'm not going back down the Oubliette. You might as well kill me right now."

He produced a gag and secured it around her mouth, tying it painfully tight at the back of her head. He leaned down until his long black hair obscured his face, until she could smell stale nutro-wafer on his breath. "You'll go anywhere I say you'll go, little girl. But don't worry, I *want* to kill you."

He sat back, a speculative look on his face. "Unless forcing you down the Oubliette would be even worse than death for you." He went silent, as if in thought, then he shook his head. "Nah, I wanna kill you." He leaned down until a tendril of his hair brushed her cheek. He placed his mouth to her ear. "You, and your boyfriend too," he whispered. "'Cause he is your boyfriend, isn't he? No way those sparks between you two didn't turn to flame at some point."

She struggled at that, tossing her head back and forth and kicking her legs as much as possible. He just laughed.

Dell stood and picked her up by her upper arms, causing sharp pain to shoot down to her fingertips. He threw her over his shoulder like a sack of horse feed. She kicked her feet, aiming for his groin, but he held her legs against his chest. "I don't think so, little girl. Anyway, I knew enough to put on a nut cup before I came after you."

He walked her straight into the hovercraft, which was hidden behind a nearby house, and up the gangplank. The solid, silver door closed with a final-sounding click behind them.

* * * * *

Angelo roused and stretched, his hand searching for Bianca and groping only cool morning air. His eyes came open and he saw that she was nowhere near. He rolled off the air mattress and looked around. "Bianca?" he called. Only the name, echoing through the abandoned church, was his response.

He dressed and walked out to the lobby. The horse was gone. Assuming she'd taken him to the pond to drink, he stepped outside. There were dark clouds on the horizon. A storm was moving in. Damn, that could delay them.

He glanced around and saw the horse in the far side of the church's yard, grazing in the tall, flattened down grass and weeds. Alone. Sudden fear settled in his stomach like a rock. Something was very wrong. He reached out with his mind, searching for her, but she was nowhere near. He felt nothing.

Angelo ran back to the saddlebag and quickly extracted the water crystal. He searched the church for a suitable hiding place and finally found it. In the far corner of the lobby, the floorboards had come loose. He reached under as far as he could and placed the crystal within. If Dell were behind this, he'd have to be free of the worry of the crystal in order to get Bianca back. He went back to the mattress and gathered up his holster and shirt and put them on. Then he saddled the gelding. He might not be able to sense her presence in the immediate area, but he could track her.

He threw himself up into the saddle at the same time his spine thrummed. He reined Jinx around in the direction from which the presence emanated. Raymond's hulking form, sitting on a horse, met his view. In one meaty hand, he held a laser.

Angelo drew his laser and Raymond shot, grazing his forearm. Pain ripped up his arm and he dropped the laser to the grass below. "Don't," Raymond warned. "I was sent to fetch you, not injure or kill you. Don't make me disobey the commands."

Angelo held up his hands, wincing at the wound on his arm. "Where is she?"

Raymond shrugged broad shoulders. "Dell has her. He took her first so he had leverage to use on you."

Leverage? Oh yeah, Dell had leverage all right. "Is she okay?"

"Yeah, she's okay. Restrained, at Dell's mercy and scared, but physically she's fine."

"Bring me to her."

He nodded, and his blond hair fell into his face. "That's what Dell wants. He wants you to come so he can play with you and Bianca before he kills you—"

Hmmm. Sounded like fun.

"—and he wants the crystal," Raymond continued. "You got the crystal?"

Angelo thought of the crystal, safely hidden away, and of the healing crystal that looked a lot like it in his saddlebag. He smiled. He had leverage too. "I have a crystal, yeah."

Thundered rolled. Raymond motioned with the barrel of the laser. "Then bring it." Angelo spurred the horse toward him. Raymond held out his hand. "Give me your weapons, all of them. Don't hold out and make me search you, Angelo. There's a time limit for the woman."

Angelo's mouth went dry. He handed over all his weapons. Raymond reined his horse around and Angelo followed him. Eventually they reached a tall, abandoned building in Out-Center.

They dismounted and tied their horses off. Angelo unlaced the saddlebag and brought it in with him. Outside in the street were two hovercraft, signaling the presence of guardians. He could feel the area trembling with humanity. Finch had broken out the forces in a big way. There were so many, the skin on the back of his neck tingled so hard it almost hurt.

He opened himself up mentally, searching for Bianca, but caught all the guardians instead. Low-level emotion coursed toward him, rolling in waves from every direction. He could only catch snippets of each individual thread, before they blended back together. He caught boredom very strongly. Most likely they were bored. They were probably reclining in the hovercraft and throughout the building, playing cards and waiting for their orders. He couldn't sense Bianca at all.

The inside of the building was musty-smelling and damp. Drywall crumbled from the walls onto the floor and the wallpaper peeled off in flakes and had settled into faded pools of color on the floor. Many footprints imprinted the dusty floor, all leading down the hall and through a doorway.

Raymond walked behind him with the muzzle of the laser pressed between his shoulder blades, ready to shoot him if he bolted. Raymond could put the damned thing away, he wasn't going anywhere without Bianca.

Angelo stepped through the door at the end of the corridor. Overturned furniture, half-smashed boxes, loose paper and other refuse littered the room. Dell stood with his back to him, looking out the dirty, cracked window.

Dell turned. "So glad you could join us, Angelo."

Rage threatened to overwhelm Angelo at the sight of the cocky, superior expression on his face. He needed to keep it leashed. "Cut the damn cheesy drama, Dell. Where's Bianca?"

"That is no concern of yours at this moment."

Angelo dropped the saddlebag and crossed the room in a few broad strides, caught Dell by the collar of his shirt, and pressed the man back against the wall. Raymond was there in a flash, pressing the muzzle of the laser into his temple. Angelo's eyes never left Dell's. "Where is she?"

"Desist, Raymond!" ordered Dell, then he shifted his gaze to Angelo. "He's not going to hurt me, not when I'm the only one who knows where the little girl is." A slow, confident smile spread over his mouth.

Raymond backed off. Angelo grabbed fistfuls of Dell's shirt and slammed him to the floor, sending up a cloud of dust. "Don't be too sure about that, Dell," he said in a low voice. "Don't you remember? I can track."

Angelo felt Dell's fear flicker through him. It was quickly replaced with confidence. "Kill me and the girl dies, Angelo. You'd never find her in time."

"In time for what?"

Dell just smiled a cold, cruel little smile.

Angelo shook him, slamming him back against the floor again. Dell coughed. "In time for what?" His temper was close to growing out of control.

"You'll find out soon enough," Dell snarled.

His grip on his shirt tightened. A muscle in his jaw worked. "I swear to God, Dell. If she is harmed in any way, I'll make you pay for it. You mark my words now and consider it a warning. If she is injured, you die."

Dell laughed. "Big, bad Angelo. Take a number and get in line. Everyone wants a piece of me."

Angelo stared down at him, putting every once of the contempt and hatred he had for him into his eyes. Then he pushed off him and stood. "Take me to her."

Dell picked himself up off the floor and dusted off his pants and shirt. "Give me the crystal and you can see her."

Angelo raised his eyebrows. "You think I'm just going to hand the crystal over to you? What makes you think I even brought it with me?"

Dell rolled his eyes. "You didn't have much choice, did you? I have Bianca."

Angelo stared at him in silent challenge. Fear rippled through him. What the hell had done with her?

Dell gave a harsh laugh. "That look on your face is great. Tells me all kinds of things. Not only are you sleeping with that bitch, you've gone and fallen in *luuuve*. Awww. Ain't that fuckin' sweet. That's gonna make all this twice as fun to watch." He took his laser from his holster, pointed it at Angelo and snapped his fingers. "Raymond, search his saddlebag."

* * * * *

Bianca came awake slowly, keeping her eyes squeezed shut. Her head pounded. She placed her palm to her temple and realized at the same time her hands were unbound. Bianca moaned and curled up into herself, rolling over onto her side. Keeping her eyes squeezed tightly shut against the pain that shot through her head and breathing in through her nose and out her mouth, she explored her last memories.

Dell ripped the gag from her mouth and she worked her jaw, trying to relieve the pain of the material cutting into her skin.

He reached one hand out lazily and fingered the top buttons of her shirt, undoing two at his leisure. His eyes ended up on her mouth.

"Touch me and you'll regret it, grease boy," she said.

He slipped a finger over her collarbone and rubbed slowly. "Oh, I highly doubt I'd regret it. But we don't have the time. Too bad, in another life you and I could have made beautiful music together."

"More like discordant crap."

He leaned down until his breath caressed her lips. She fought a gag reflex only because he had her pinned against the wall and any forward movement would only bring her lips against his. That was the last thing she wanted. "I don't think so, my silver-gold flower." He smiled. "That's what I used to call Calina. She believed everything I told her, every lie. Every single bit of imaginary hope I threw at her she grasped like a life raft. She was so gentle, so gullible, so sweet...so unlike you."

Bianca tried to kick him and only ended up throwing herself off balance because of her bound wrists. She slid down the wall to rest on her side. Silent rage rolled through her and tears pricked her eyes.

Dell laughed. "Awww...poor thing, so helpless when you're cuffed." He leveled the alter- gun at her head and fired.

Bianca opened her eyes slowly, seeing a rusted chain-link fence in front of her. Thunder boomed in the distance. Alarmed, she rolled to her back and looked up...more chain link. She sat up, groaning at the pain of her head.

Glancing around, she saw that she was imprisoned in a cage—an old, rusted-out chain-link cage. There was nothing within it except tall grass, flattened from its own weight. There was nothing to shield her from the rain that would surely fall from the dark clouds rolling nearer and nearer. There was no shelter from it either. No escape. She stood up too fast and almost passed out. Thunder boomed in the distance and she forced herself to stay conscious.

The first few drops of rain began to splatter her like big, fat teardrops from heaven. She ran to the door of the cage and saw the padlock on the outside of it. She wound her fingers into the chain-link and pushed back and forth yelling, "Help! Someone let me out of here!" It was desperate attempt. She knew all too well she was alone.

She gasped, remembering the laser cutter she'd stuffed into her pocket. Dell hadn't recognized the small tool as a weapon when he'd searched her. Frantically, she dug for it and aimed it at the fence. The light shot out and she guided it around in a large square in an effort to cut a door for herself. When she was finished, she stuffed in the pocket of her coat and ran to the fence. She gripped it and pushed.

It didn't give. The metal was smoldering and burned, but it hadn't cut.

"No! Oh, God! No!" She leaned her head against the fence as the rain started to come down harder. She tipped her head back and screamed. Her voice echoed out into emptiness and then was overtaken by a roll of thunder. She fell back and sat down with a thump on the grass. She was going to die just like her sister, but instead of suicide, it would be murder.

Her thoughts turned to Angelo and her chest tightened painfully.

* * * * *

With every raindrop that hit the windshield on the cockpit of the hovercraft, another knot tightened in Angelo's stomach.

Dell rolled his head toward him, a lazy, almost bored expression on his face, but his cold gray eyes were shiny and bright, betraying how much he was enjoying this. Angelo didn't even have to sense his emotion to know that. "We're almost there, lover boy." He whistled low. "I wish I would've had the time to taste her. I bet she's good, really good. All fire and sweetness in the sack."

Angelo's fists clenched. "Watch it, Dell. Touch her and I'll take your head off."

Raymond's laser whirred up, getting ready to fire. Angelo's gaze flicked to him. He'd been standing silent sentinel at the back of the cockpit ever since they took off.

"Don't worry," said Dell. "I didn't touch her and never will, because pretty soon it will be too late." He shrugged. "I'm not much into necrophilia."

Angelo came off the chair toward Dell.

"Shoot him if he touches me!" yelled Dell.

Angelo's hands found the armrests of Dell's chair at the last second and squeezed. The action pained the laser wound on his forearm. He didn't touch Dell. If he was wounded, he might not be able to help Bianca.

Dell held his gaze. "He can always watch his beloved die while he's wounded by laser fire. That's fine with me."

"You bastard."

Dell used an index finger to push Angelo at the place where his collarbones met. "Back off and go sit down, Angelo. We're almost there."

He did not sit down. He stayed standing at the cockpit's window, watching with growing horror at the scene unfolding before his eyes. The cage that came into view shone like dull gunmetal in the gray storm light that filtered through the clouds. Angelo's hands spread on the hovercraft's console as he saw Bianca's slim form sitting in the middle of the cage, the rain beating down on her.

Fear coursed through him, quick and hard, followed by fury. "Let her out of there!" Angelo roared. He saw Raymond steady the aim of his laser on him. "You have the crystal. There's no reason to kill her!"

Dell set the craft down and smiled. "Pleasure. That's a good reason." He held Angelo's gaze and pressed the button that opened the cockpit door. The cool metal slid open and Angelo could see the door to the hovercraft also slide open. The gangplank descended automatically. "Go on, go say goodbye. You better hurry." He glanced outside. "It's raining, but you can stand a little freysis can't you...*Kiran*?"

Angelo looked back at him with a flicker of disbelief, but he had no time to analyze his comment or react to it. Bianca was out there dying. He didn't think past her. He simply turned and left the hovercraft.

He ran across the grass in the pelting shower, his boots slid in the slick grass and he struggled to keep his footing. "Bianca!" he yelled, but got no response. When he reached the door of the cage, he wrapped his fingers around the wire and pounded it back and forth, trying to loosen it. She knelt with her eyes closed and her head thrown back, like she was accepting her fate, accepting her death.

No!

He knelt. "Bianca." His voice came out a rasping whisper. He cleared his throat and tried again. "Bianca," he said louder.

Her eyes flickered open and she tipped her head forward, the rain streaming down her face. Her gaze was calm, but then recognition crossed her face, as though she realized who knelt in front of her on the grass. Her expression tightened with fear. "Get out of here, Angelo! Go find shelter!" She crawled to the fence on her hands and knees.

"Not without you, I won't." He pressed his hand against the fence's mesh and pushed his fingers through to try and touch her. She placed her palm to his palm on the other side, winding her fingers through his.

She shrugged and smiled. "A little rain never hurt anyone." She coughed.

"But whole lot can kill you."

She laughed sadly, and then coughed again. It rattled in her chest, one of the signs of freysis poisoning. Soon, soon it would be too late. "I love you, Angelo."

His fingers tightened over hers. "I love you too, Bianca. You saved my life."

"And destroyed it."

"More like rebuilt it."

Bianca shifted her gaze to somewhere behind him. Her expression tightened and grew cold. Footfalls squished in the grass and Angelo turned. Dell and Raymond both wore freysis suits. Raymond still pointed a laser at him. Too bad the laser was no longer very much of a threat to him. Angelo was feeling desperate. He wouldn't lose Bianca. He couldn't.

"Now this is what I call a touching scene," said Dell, his voice muffled under the freysis gear.

"Angelo," Bianca said breathlessly. The hold she had on his fingers slipped. He looked back at her. Her eyes fluttered shut and she tilted back for a dangerous moment, almost passing out.

He tightened the grip on her fingers. "Bianca!"

"Oh, she's done for, Angelo," said Dell with glee in his voice.

Her eyes opened. She stopped swaying and her gaze focused on him once again. Bianca winked at him, then groaned and fell back onto her side. Angelo gripped the wire so hard he cut his finger and felt his blood run. "No," he whispered hoarsely.

Then she struggled back up and placed her hand back to the mesh against his as she'd done before. He felt something hard held against her palm and realized all that had been a ruse to get this object out from her pocket. Angelo discreetly took it from her, slipping it between his fingers without Dell noticing. It was the laser-cutter for the water crystal.

A weapon. One Dell probably wouldn't have recognized as anything beyond harmless.

The rain slowed, then stopped. But Angelo feared it was too late for Bianca. She was so pale he could see the veins running beneath her skin. Her eyes couldn't focus and her jaw was slack.

"Kiss her goodbye," said Dell. "Her life is slipping away even as we stand and watch...doing nothing."

Angelo wasn't paying attention to him. He was watching Bianca. Her pupils were blown—now huge and dark, another sign of freysis poisoning. He thought for a minute he could see the night sky in them, dotted through with stars. Then she swayed, lost her grip on his fingers and fell back onto the grass.

This time it wasn't a ruse.

Chapter Twenty-Six

"Bianca!" He couldn't touch her. He couldn't hold her. All he could do was watch in impotent rage as she lay on the grass.

And rage it was.

Angelo stood with the laser-cutter concealed in his hand. He fingered the bottom button, ready to fire. Without warning he turned and caught Raymond in the wrist. It burned through the freysis suit like butter. Raymond yelled out in pain, then took a step back and slipped in the wet grass. Angelo didn't waste the opportunity. He took three strides forward and grabbed the laser from his hands. Then he swung around toward Dell, who was struggling to extricate his laser from its holster, impeded by his glove-covered hand.

Angelo shot him with a steady stream in the chest. A killing shot. Dell fell to the ground and writhed, moaning in pain. The smell of burned rubber and flesh mixed with the earthy smell of the wet ground. Dell went still.

He pointed the laser at Raymond. "Get up and get the key to that padlock, now!" Raymond did as he was told. Unzipping his freysis suit, he extracted the key and threw it to Angelo.

Angelo walked toward Raymond with the laser leveled at his chest. He reached into his open freysis suit and pulled out his alter-gun, then took a couple steps back, taking aim. "Please don't, Angelo."

"Can't have you trying to hinder me, Raymond." Angelo waggled the laser at him. "It's this or the alter-gun." Angelo shot him on delta.

He threw down his weapons and raced to the cage. In his haste, his fingers fumbled with the key, but he got the padlock undone.

He gathered Bianca into his arms, feeling for a pulse. There was one, but it was faint and slow. She felt cold and stiff. *Too late...* He rocked her for a moment, running his hand down her sodden hair. Then he lifted her and brought her into the hovercraft.

Her lips were turning blue and her pulse—when he could even feel it—was like a fragile bird fluttering against his fingers. He stripped her freysis-soaked clothing off and laid her in a chair. With that accomplished, he went into the cockpit to draw up the gangplank, close the door and lock it.

By all rights, if he couldn't metabolize freysis, he should've passed out like Bianca had. He guessed he now knew he could metabolize it like a Kiran.

Hell of a way to find out.

He slammed the door open to the emergency freysis shower that Finch had installed in the craft and turned the water on. It held eighty gallons of pure-water. Angelo picked her up from the chair and walked to it. Fully clothed, he stepped into the shower. The cold water hit his back and he gasped. Slowly, it began to warm. Sinking to the bottom of the shower stall, he let the water run over them. He settled her in his lap and rubbed her skin vigorously to get as much of the freysis off her as possible. But he knew it was an exercise in futility. The bacteria had infiltrated her system long ago.

After he'd finished getting as much of the freysis off her skin as possible, he sat there with her in his lap for a moment and let the water course over them both. His head bowed, he watched Bianca's hair flow over his arm like golden waterfall. He'd give his own life to heal her.

And, so, he would try.

Angelo stood, turned off the water and stepped out of the shower, letting the water run from Bianca and himself onto the carpeted floor of the hovercraft in a steady stream.

"Computer, set the bed." A bed slid out of the wall on the opposite side of the room. He laid her on it and spread her hair out in a fan around her head. His hands trembled as he opened a drawer that contained the blankets and towels. He pulled a blanket out and covered her with it.

The radio in the cockpit emitted static and a voice. It came in gravelly, then clearer. "Dell, we've picked up your signal and we're coming to meet you," came Finch's tinny voice. There was a long-suffering sigh. "When we get there, you better have the crystal."

There was a final-sounding click, static, then silence. Angelo was already in the cockpit, pulling back on the cyclet. The last thing they needed was company. The hovercraft lifted off the ground, sending the grass and tall weeds beneath to shifting and brushing over the two figures that lay on the ground.

Angelo shut down the comm links that connected the hovercraft to other craft and flipped off the tracking device. He brought the craft up high enough, and then engaged it as fast as it would go. It slammed Angelo back in his seat and he worried for a moment about Bianca, but knew she'd only been pressed into the pillows of the bed.

Angelo set the craft down in the center of a long plain in the middle of the Wastes. He needed time and no interruptions to do what he was planning to do. The healing crystal lay on the console in the cockpit, where Dell had set it. Angelo grabbed it up and went back to Bianca.

There was no time to be afraid, no time to think about what would happen if he failed. All he could do was focus on this moment and on drawing the freysis out of Bianca before it killed her. He looked down at the crystal lying in his palm. It thrummed with energy.

Melvin's words came back to him… *Simply follow your instincts. Follow your blood, Arapass.*

Instincts. Did he have any? He was just a Kiran half-breed. Angelo found himself wishing something he never thought he'd wish for—that he was a Kiran full blood.

Water Crystal

He looked at the healing crystal. Then he looked down at her ashen face and knew he was going to have to come up with some instincts damn quick. Her skin was pasty and her lips near white. He couldn't even make out the rise and fall of her chest. Her body was fighting the freysis and had completely shut down to use every last bit of strength and energy to obtain that goal. But it was a losing battle. Without some kind of aid, she'd die for certain.

He closed his hand around the crystal and concentrated. Shutting his eyes, he felt only the smooth, jaggedness of the piece in his hand.

Nothing.

Silently crying out for the aid of his bloodline, he thought of Kira, the home of his father. Abruptly, his body faded from his awareness and he saw space. He hurtled through the darkness, the stars whizzing by him at the speed of light until he stopped.

A large planet loomed in front of him and he knew with his heart and a measure of his soul that this was Kira. Behind it loomed the sun. Just the barest flickering of heat emanated from the star. It was far too cold now to provide any life to Kira. The planet of his ancestors felt cold and dead. Soon Kira's sun would begin the process of becoming a giant red star and would expand out, engulfing Kira within it.

He felt the immenseness of the planetary object—its death and destruction surrounding him, becoming a part of him. He knew by some unexplained instinct that he could share himself with whatever might remain of Kira within that huge red orb. He could transform that death and destruction into life and creation.

Something he could only describe as silver energy glimmered within him. His hand tightened on the crystal. Concentrating on that silver energy, he directed it toward his forearm. Suddenly, he was back in his body, back in the passenger room of the craft. Warm, tingling silver-colored energy reached out from the crystal and wound around his palm, stretching up his arm to his shoulder, then down his chest, slowly enveloping him in sparkling, glittering comfort. It smoothed over his arm like rich velvet, repairing, regenerating.

He gasped and dropped the crystal onto the bed. He looked at his forearm in amazement. The shallow wound was completely gone, replaced by smooth, unmarred skin. "God," he breathed.

Not wasting time, he stripped all his clothes off and laid down next to Bianca, drawing her into his arms. He picked up the crystal and put it between them, nestled between their chests.

He wrapped his arms around her, closed his eyes and concentrated on the crystal once more, this time thinking only of Bianca. First, there was nothing and a flicker of despair touched him. Then a spark of silver warmth came from the crystal. It grew until it covered over them, brushing the length of their bodies with something that felt like liquid silk. It smoothed over his skin, wrapping them in that same velvet comfort.

They became one. Her heart, sluggish and inconstant, was his own. The rush of her blood sounded in his ears. The darkness that had enveloped her mind was also his. For a brief moment, his head swam with it and it threatened to steal his consciousness. He fought it and, with a sheer act of willpower, pushed it back and retained awareness.

He explored her body from the inside out, pushing and pulling through the heavy, thick freysis that filled her. Catching him off-guard, he felt something that was out of place—something bright in the cloying gloom. Way deep down was a spark of life, a flicker of potential, imbued with a bit of his soul and a piece of hers. Unexpected, jarring happiness rushed through him, followed quickly with despair.

Bianca was pregnant.

There would be no way the tiny life could survive this onslaught. He caressed the spark with his mind, sending it the warmth of his hope and love. Then, with heavy regret, concentrated on healing Bianca.

He acted as complete empath to her and felt the freysis like she'd felt it before she'd passed out. It was a ravening, marauding mass of intrusion throughout her body. It attacked every organ it could and there was nothing to stop it or slow it. The alien bacteria would simply eat away at her until there was nothing left. Angelo also felt the displeasure of the freysis at finding him within her, because he was an entity that would fight and reject them.

Even though what he felt were phantom sensations and not caused by anything affecting him physically, he still gasped from the pain of it. His vision clouded black momentarily and he blinked to clear it. Instincts told him that in order to save Bianca, he had to draw the freysis from her body into his own.

Pushing his consciousness further into her, he reached out to the freysis, inviting them into him. He pressed his mouth to her unresponsive lips and kissed her, pressing his body along the length of hers, making sure as much of their skin touched as possible. The crystal dug into them both.

The freysis left her in a stream, coursing from her pores and into his. He took them until his head pounded with pain, until his stomach clenched and his vision darkened. His back arched into a near spine-breaking position and his eyes opened. He let out an agonized yell and then knew no more.

Chapter Twenty-Seven

Bianca did not wake gently. She gasped, her eyes coming open in a blur of pain. Nausea gripped her stomach. Carefully, she breathed in through her nose and out her mouth until she felt stable enough to focus her vision on something around her.

Her vision cleared and what met her eyes was disorienting. She lay on her side in a strange place...again. A soft blanket covered her and she realized with a start that she was naked. A mountain of pillows cushioned her head and two comfortable-looking easy chairs sat on a carpeted floor in front of her. It was luxurious, wherever she was. Panic gripped her. Was she at the Water Company?

She sat straight up and pain shot through her head and shoulders. Nausea threatened to overwhelm her. She bent over the side of the bed and found a trash can. Was someone expecting her to throw up? She aimed for it and dry-heaved.

Her cheeks flushed and her head pounding, she went limp over the side of the bed and contemplated different escape possibilities. Too bad she felt too wretched to pursue any of them. She touched her forehead. Heat radiated out and hit her palm. What did she have, the flu?

With great care for her head and sore muscles, she settled back into the pillows as the memories flooded her mind. Not the flu. She had freysis poisoning. She was lucky she wasn't dead. She frowned, remembering all that rain. Why wasn't she dead?

She closed her eyes as tears pricked them. What had happened to Angelo? If he hadn't escaped Dell, she didn't care where she was. A cool wet cloth came to rest over her forehead. Her eyes fluttered open and Angelo's face came into focus. "Hi, angel-face," he said.

She tried not to throw herself into his arms and spare herself the agony of the motion, but she couldn't resist. Her fingers closed over his bare shoulders and she gripped him, assuring herself that he was truly there. Burying her face in his neck, she held on to him and sobbed. His hands slipped around her waist and he sat down on the bed, lifting her onto his lap. She let him wrap the blanket around her and push her hair away from her face.

"Glad you're so happy to see me," he said, emotion thick in the words.

"Where—" Her voice came out a croak and she cleared her throat and tried again. "Where are we?" This time her voice was no more than a rasping whisper, but understandable.

"In a hovercraft, far from Finch and Dell."

She gaped at him, and then cast a furtive glance toward the small room that looked like the cockpit. "You hijacked one of Finch's hovercrafts?"

His lips twitched. "I think stole would be a more appropriate description of what I did."

Worried agitation flooded her. "Can they track us? Follow us? Where's the crystal? What happened to Dell?"

"Shhh." He lifted her gently and laid her back into the pillows, making sure she was adequately covered to keep her body heat. "Rest," he murmured.

She looked up at him with what she knew was indignation on her face. She wanted her questions answered!

"Rest now, Bianca, relax. Your body is still recovering from a major trauma." He put a hand to her cheek. "You came really close to dying, you know."

"I did? How—"

He quelled her question with a look and she fell silent. "I'll bring you something to drink and some food."

She watched him leave. He wore only a pair of loose-fitting blue drawstring pants. His chest and feet were bare. After a minute, he returned with a piece of bread, a bit of dried meat, a couple nutro-wafers and a plastic container that she suspected stored pure-water.

"I raided the first-aid kit and the craft's galley. There's lots of food in there." His lips twisted. "Only the best for Finch. We'll start with this and later, when you're feeling better, you can have more." He uncapped the container and held it to her lips. "Drink this. It's for freysis poisoning. The label says it will help replenish what the freysis took from your body."

Grasping the container, she let the cool, sweet liquid slide down her throat. She closed her eyes and let her throat work. When she was done, Angelo took it from her and gave her the bread and dried meat. "Eat, then sleep. Soon you'll feel better." He grinned. "I'll have a treat for you later."

"You still haven't told me what happened." Her voice sounded better already.

He settled back into the pillows beside her and told her while she ate.

"So the crystal is hidden at the church?" she asked when he was finished.

"Yes. It's safe there. Raymond has awoken by now and Finch must think we have the crystal. They won't be searching for it." He paused. "As much was we want and need to empty the chimra into the lake, we're going to have to stay here for a while, to make sure you're recovered and also to give them time to search the area for this hovercraft and move on."

"Then we can go back in and get the crystal."

"Yes."

She went quiet for several minutes, assimilating the information. "Is Dell dead?"

"I think so. I don't see how he could've survived a wound like I gave him, but I don't know for certain. I was more concerned with you than him at the time."

She rolled over on her stomach and laid her arm over his stomach. She pressed her face to his side so it muffled her words. "You embraced your Kiran blood to save me."

"Yes, I guess I did."

She shuddered. "I'm so happy you can metabolize freysis."

"Me too." He drew a breath. "Now I know why the Kirans didn't use the healing crystals for the virus."

She raised her head. "The healer would've died, wouldn't have been unable to handle absorbing the virus. They would've contracted it themselves."

He rubbed his palm over her bare back down to just above her buttocks, then back up. He worked his magic fingers over her muscles, relaxing her. "Yes."

She closed her eyes, reveling in the feel of his hand on her and drifted off to sleep.

When she awoke, she felt almost back to normal. Aside from some residual aches and pains, her body appeared to have repaired itself during her rest.

Angelo slept beside her. She pushed up into a kneeling position and stared down at him sprawled across bed, one hand flung back above his head. She reached out to touch him, but pulled her hand back. He needed to sleep as much as she did. He, too, had put his body through a great deal of stress. She got up from the bed, settled the blanket over him, then went to explore.

Finding the shower, some soap and a tube of toothpaste, she cleaned herself up, and wrapped herself in a fresh towel when she was finished. Her clothes were hanging up near the shower and had dried. She fingered them, but she just couldn't bring herself to put them on right now. Those were the clothes she'd been wearing in the cage. She shivered and turned away.

She couldn't find a comb and had to settle for untangling her wet hair with her fingers. She walked to the main room and found Angelo had left the bed. The sound of a door shutting met her ears and Angelo emerged from the galley with a smile on his face. He held up his booty. "There's practically a feast in there."

She examined the item he held. It was—amazingly enough—a peach.

"A pure-peach?" she asked hopefully. She'd had one once, long ago when she'd been a child. Her mother had bought it for her and her sister on their birthday. They were hard to find and almost unreachably expensive. It represented good memories—memories of being pampered and loved.

He smiled and nodded. "A ripe pure-peach."

Words seemed insufficient. "Wow," she breathed.

He walked to the bed and she followed, completely entranced.

Following his lead, she slid onto the mattress. He set the peach to her lips and she bit. The smooth skin rent under her teeth and she swallowed the juice that ran sweet and warm into her mouth. Then her teeth passed into the flesh and took a mouthful. She closed her eyes and savored the flavor. Delicious rapture consumed her. "Mmmmm."

"You can say that again."

She swallowed and opened her eyes to find Angelo staring at her mouth. She played it up by giving him a sultry smile, looking at him coyly out of the corner of her eye and lowering her voice. "That's even better than sex."

He raised an eyebrow. "Now I have a piece of fruit for a rival. What am I supposed to do about that?"

"I don't know." She looked at him sidelong. "Maybe take up the challenge?"

He didn't reply. Instead, he took the peach from her fingers and put it on a nearby table. Then, never taking his eyes from hers, he licked the juice off her fingers with exquisite slowness and care. Her breath caught in her throat as his hand found the place where the edge of her towel tucked in and pulled it free.

Water Crystal

The gentle air hit her bare body like a velvet caress. He dragged her up against his chest and kissed her long and deep, driving any residual thoughts of the crystal or of peaches from her mind. With a groan of wanting, he pressed her back onto the bed with only his mouth on hers for pressure. Desire for him flowed over her skin and pooled between her legs like molten gold. She needed to feel him, needed to have become a part of her.

He ran his hand over her breasts in that deliciously possessive way he had, then dragged his fingers down her flesh and cupped her sex. He pulled his mouth away from hers and swore under his breath. "You're sick, Bianca."

She put her hand over his at her pussy. "And you inside me will be very healing. Not made of china." She raised a brow. "Remember?"

"I want you all the damn time," he murmured. "You're my ultimate weakness." He kissed her.

She sighed against his mouth as he dragged his fingers up her pussy to caress and tease her clit from its hood. Bianca relaxed into his embrace, enjoying the feeling of his hands roaming her body and exploring every hollow and curve. His hand brushed over her stomach, her side and her sensitive nipples. She reached down, her knuckles brushing minutely over his muscled abdomen, and fumbled blindly with the drawstring of his pants. When she couldn't get the knot undone, she gave the waistband a tug. "Off," she growled into his mouth. "Now."

She felt him smile. He reached down, untied the knot and slid the pants over his hips and down his legs, freeing his gorgeous cock to her touch. With a contented sigh, she wrapped her hand around the shaft and stroked until it drew a ragged groan from his throat.

Taking her by the waist, he rolled her over him until she was on top, straddling him. "I want to watch you, Bianca. I want to see you moving over me."

She shivered at the dark look of arousal in his eyes and the intricate play of emotion on his face. "Okay," she whispered, suddenly overcome by her own feeling of love.

She positioned herself over him and felt him push against her. Then she lowered herself down on his cock, inch by inch, until she was impaled. Closing her eyes, she threw her head back and let a long, slow breath escape her. When she felt him rise up and lay a line of kisses from her breast to her throat, she tipped her head forward.

"Move for me," he said near her ear in a low, barely controlled voice.

He lowered himself back onto the bed. His hands strayed to her buttocks, helping to push her up and slide her back down him agonizingly slowly. The action drew sighs from her. With every stroke he brushed some little known spot deep within her that felt exquisite. She took over and quickened the pace. He met her downward movements with small thrusts of his own until he brought her and she cried out her pleasure to the small cabin.

He rolled her beneath him and dragged her wrists over her head, pinning them to the bed above her. She remembered the first time he'd touched her intimately, how he'd pulled her pants off and licked her until she'd come. She shivered and closed her eyes at the delicious memory.

Passion marked his features and eyes and he drove into her until sweat sheened his chest and forehead. Her whole world narrowed to the feel of his cock driving in and out of her, the feel of his chest rubbing her stiff nipples and the sound of his harsh breathing as he worked over her.

"Bianca," he groaned. "I love being inside you so much. I love the way you feel around me, the way your pussy grips me like you don't want to let me go."

"I don't, Angelo," she gasped. She braced her feet on the bed and thrust her hips up, meeting his strokes and driving him harder and deeper inside her. They moved in unison, the sound of their breathing and the slap of their flesh the only sounds in the room.

He pushed her over the edge again and her pussy spasmed around his shaft. The thrust of her hips faltered and she spread her thighs as far as she could go. He released her wrists and slid his hands under her buttocks, lifting and spreading her as he moved piston-like in and out of her.

He swore softly and thrust all the way in. His cock jumped inside her and let out a low groan as he came, and rasped her name.

He collapsed on top of her and she panted, her eyes wide open. Again, as was with the pure-peach, words seemed wholly insufficient. He'd made love to her like that before—had even brought her several times during a session of lovemaking. But there was something about now, after she'd almost died, after she thought she'd lost him forever, that had made it extra special, extra satisfying. "Wow," she said breathlessly.

Propping himself up on an elbow, he idly stroked her nipple until she shuddered and felt her cunt pulse with interest. "Better than the peach?"

She lifted up and kissed him. "Definitely. No competition."

After they finished off the rest of the peach, he enveloped her in his arms and they slept once more.

* * * * *

Bianca twisted the edge of her shirt in nervous fingers as Angelo angled the hovercraft around to land not far from the church. They'd waited until just after twilight to come back in, wanting to use the cover of darkness.

There had been no sign of Finch and she fervently hoped it remained so, but Finch knew they had one of his crafts. They'd be watching for it. On their way back in, they had flown over the cage and Dell and Raymond had been gone, of course. Not so much as a mud streak in the grass had marked their presence.

The hovercraft came to a halt, hovering over the overgrown lawn of a dilapidated house. Angelo opened the door and let the gangplank descend.

He turned to her. "I want you to stay here, okay?"

She looked at him like he'd grown a horn in the center of his forehead. "Are you crazy? Where you go, I go."

Angelo gave her a look of exasperation and, for a moment, it felt like old times. "Even if where I'm going is incredibly dangerous, huh, angel-face?"

"Especially then." A smile curved her lips. "Someone's got to protect you, after all. You didn't happen to get my gun back from Dell at any point, did you?"

He went over to a small cabinet and opened the door. Two lasers, two alter-guns and her pistol lay there. "I saw Dell put it in here when we left Out-Center. I'll give you an alter-gun too. You sure you don't want a laser instead of your pistol?"

She shook her head. "I like bullets better than that intangible laser fire."

His lips quirked in a half-smile. "It isn't so intangible when it hits you, believe me." He handed her the pistol and the weight of it felt good in her hand. "If it should come up, shoot to kill, though. None of that missing stuff like you did with me and Dell when we first apprehended you."

Indignation and wounded pride rose up. "I only missed you because your eyes were so...so..." He cocked his head to the side and smiled. "So nice," she blurted. "And I didn't miss Dell, I grazed him."

"Yes," he drawled out. "Grazed him."

"Leave me alone!" She pushed past him with the pistol in hand. "You ought to be happy I missed you."

"I am. I just don't want you to miss Dell again, or anyone else who means you harm."

She turned back to him, popping the cartridge out to make sure it was still loaded, and then sliding it back in with a click. "This time, I won't miss. Don't worry."

They edged their way through the yards and the debris-strewn back alleys until they made it to the church. Keeping to the shadows, they entered the building. The fetid darkness of the church hit her like a slap to the face.

Angelo turned the solar-lantern on and headed for the place he'd hidden the crystal. He came back with it in hand. Mission accomplished, they turned to leave. They walked to the door and almost made it before she felt him stiffen. He pulled her into the shadows. "Someone's here," he whispered.

"Damn. Couldn't be easy, could it?" she whispered back as she drew her pistol.

"They're coming into the church." He flipped off the lantern and darkness enveloped them.

Two figures moved through the door and both of them flipped solar-lanterns on. They split up without a word and began to search the building. The first man stayed in the lobby and the second one went into the main part of the church.

"Someone has been here," the second man called. He'd found their abandoned air mattress and blanket. The first man went toward his voice.

Angelo motioned to Bianca that she should get up and move toward the door. She stood and inched her way forward. Something cracked beneath her feet.

The first man turned toward them, a gun-shaped something in hand. Angelo whirled with his laser drawn. "Don't move, or I'll shoot," said Angelo.

Great, just what they needed, a standoff.

"Hey, all right. I'm not moving," said the man.

Bianca sucked in a surprised breath. "Gannon?"

The man, young man actually, held the lantern up to his face. A smile spread over his mouth. "Little bird! We keep running into each other. I wonder if it's fate saying we're slated to be together."

She laughed shakily. "You're a little young for me, Gannon."

"Awww…just by a few little years," Gannon replied.

Angelo turned his lantern on and turned back to Gannon. "What are you doing out here?"

"What?" asked Quint from the doorway. "Do you think stuff goes down in Southern Out-Center that I don't know about? I think not." There was a smile in his voice. "There's been patrols all over this area for the last week. Then a couple days ago there were reports of a lot of activity around here, hovercrafts flying all over the place. Finch himself has been spotted roaming around, and I've been told by a reliable source that Finch's right-hand man, Dell, is dead." He paused and his voice lowered. "Wouldja' know anything about that, Angelo?"

Beside her, she felt Angelo tense. Dell deserved everything he'd got, after all he'd done. But at the same time, it couldn't be a nice feeling to know you'd killed someone. "I might, Quint. I just might," replied Angelo.

Quint walked toward them. "So I figure it's got to be you two out here, causing them to rip up my territory. I figured you two would be ass-deep in trouble, like I always seem to find you." Affection rang through his voice. "So I brought some men out here to see what was going on."

He stopped in front of them and they could finally see his face. He cocked his head to the side and smiled. "So, tell me, Angelo. Why are you bringin' Finch back into my life, and do I have a shot at getting a piece of him?"

* * * * *

"Hank's Special," said Quint, pulling a flask from the inside pocket of his denim jacket. Angelo got glasses and set them out.

They were sitting around the table in the hovercraft with the crystal lying in front of them. During the last hour of intense discussion, Angelo had laid it all out for Quint and Gannon.

Quint reached over and poured Special into the glasses. Angelo almost reached out and stopped him from giving Bianca any, but there was no way the baby had lived through the poisoning. No use holding out hope. Sorrow twisted in his gut as he stayed his hand and looked away.

"Are you okay?" Bianca asked him, laying a hand over his knee under the table.

He turned back to her. "Yeah, I'm fine. But you're not going to be once you taste that." He indicated her glass.

She smiled at him and picked up the glass. "Wouldn't be the first time I entertained a death wish."

"To the downfall of the Water Baron and the reversal of the poisoning," said Quint, raising his glass.

Everyone raised their glasses and repeated the toast. Then they tipped their glasses up. The Special washed through Angelo's mouth and burned its way down his throat, leaving a sweet-sour trail behind. He felt it hit his stomach and spread out, warming him through.

He looked at Bianca. Her eyes were wide and her cheeks full. She turned her head and sprayed the Special out of her mouth. She sputtered and coughed and Angelo laughed, rubbing her back with the flat of his hand.

Quint laughed. "What's the matter, Bianca? Is the drink too fine for you?"

She swallowed and cleared her throat. "That-that-drink will put hair where I don't want it."

"Where Angelo doesn't want it too, I'd make a guess." Quint winked, then stood. Gannon followed suit. "We'll go to the lake in the morning to release the chimra. My men and I will meet you at the Southern edge by the old planetarium. We'll be there just in case Finch shows up."

"Finch has a lot of territory to cover. He doesn't know where or when we'll dump the chimra. I'm not expecting him."

Quint went for the door. Angelo got up and opened it for him. "You never know, my friend. I'd leave this area for the night."

"Don't worry. We're planning on it," answered Bianca. "Quint, why don't you and Gannon stay with us for the night? It's not big in here, but there's plenty of room for two more."

Gannon smirked. "Awww...little bird, does that mean you've finally given in to me?"

"Thanks for the offer, but I'm sure you want some privacy." Quint smiled. "And anyway, I've got my own lady's arms waiting for me." He walked down the gangplank.

Gannon shot a parting grin at Bianca. "You get sick of him—" he indicated Angelo with a jerk of his head, "—you come find me, okay?" He turned with a teasing wink at Angelo and left.

Bianca laughed. "Gannon is quite a character, isn't he?"

Angelo pulled up the gangplank, closed the door and pulled back on the cyclet to bring the craft up to cruising altitude before replying. "Oh yeah, quite a character." He pushed the cyclet forward to full velocity and they were both slammed back in their seats.

Chapter Twenty-Eight

The plan was simple. Angelo would wade into the lake and dump the chimra, to make sure it got a good start in shallow water, the way Melvin had told them to do it.

They opened the door and extended the gangplank. Bianca drew a breath. She had deep misgivings about this. Something niggled at the back of her mind, something telling her all was not well. "You know what they say about the best-laid plans," she commented.

Angelo had cut the crystal the night before. It had been an excruciating process. He'd done it like he was cutting a diamond. Sweat had sheened his forehead. He'd drawn deep laser marks in the craft's table, but that was of no matter. In the end, he'd cut the crystal neatly around all sides, burning precious little of the chimra within.

Angelo eyed the door. "Yeah. I'd tell you to stay here, but I know you won't."

She grinned. "I'm not going to miss this for anything."

They walked down the gangplank together and toward the lake. The round, rusted planetarium rose on their left. Quint stood by the side of the structure with some of his men. Dugan stood to his right. "Angelo, Bianca," Quint called.

Her steps faltered. Was there a note of nervousness in his voice? Or was she imagining it? Well, of course he'd be nervous, she reasoned. They were all nervous.

"Quint? Where's Gannon?" answered Angelo cautiously. He went still, then he stiffened in that way Bianca was beginning to recognize meant he sensed others were near. "Why, Quint?" Angelo breathed only loud enough for Bianca to hear.

Dell, with about twenty guardians, all with drawn lasers, walked around the side of the planetarium. Dell's chest was wrapped with white bandages that were seeped through with blood and fluid. His face was a mask of pain, and he wore a gruesome smile.

"They captured him last night, Angelo," said Quint. "Marie too. They caught us right after you left the area. They suspected I knew you and where you were going. They said if I didn't make the Flot help them they'd kill Gannon, and Finch would take Marie back and put her down the Oubliette again." He dropped his head. "I'm sorry."

A soft whirring filled the air, accompanied by a breeze. Bianca turned to see the other hovercraft set down beside the first.

"No, no, Bianca," Dell called in a singsong voice laced through with pain. His voice went low and dangerous. "Look over here. I want you to be watching when I shoot lover-boy."

"Don't shoot! He's holding the cut crystal!" she called. "The crystal that will reverse the freysis poisoning and return the water to its original, pure state." She yelled it, so the all guardians could hear.

Some of them lowered their weapons and glanced at each other in confusion. Just as she suspected, they didn't know why they were there. They were just following orders. Encouraged, she continued, "This is the crystal Angelo, the honorable Captain of the Guardians of Order, risked his life to obtain. The one Finch has been hiding from us all, even though he knows the contents will kill freysis on a global scale."

"You are *such* a pain in the ass," said Finch, walking across the grass toward them.

Dell leveled the laser at Angelo. "Why would that stop me from shooting Angelo, little girl? I can just as easily pry it from his dead fingers."

"Because he'll drop the damn crystal on the ground and if it's cut, the contents will spill. I don't know what that will do. So hold your fire, Dell!" ordered Finch.

Dell didn't lower his weapon. "I'm getting really tired of taking orders from you, Finch."

Finch stopped, drew his own laser and pointed it at Dell. The image jarred Bianca. She hadn't assumed he even knew how to use one. "Put it down, Dell," he ordered.

"Hey, Finch, I know something you don't know," said Bianca.

Dell's gun swung toward her. "Don't."

Bianca closed her eyes and spoke in a rush. "Dell took Calina's virginity and was her lover when you couldn't do it yourself."

Finch took in a surprised gulp of air.

"That's right," Bianca continued. "He slept with her over and over, enjoying her body in ways you never could."

"Goddamn you," Dell said. He shot and Angelo pushed her to the ground, causing the laser fire to arc above them. He pressed the crystal into her palm and closed her fingers around it. Then he got up and drew his laser. Angelo rounded on Dell, aiming, but Finch beat him to it. A stream of laser fire hit Dell in the chest, right in his original wound. Dell let out an agonized sound, crumpled like a rag doll and went still.

Angelo rounded on Finch. They were at a standoff. Bianca looked up from her sprawled position on the grass with growing horror. The guardians, for the most part, appeared confused.

Unexpectedly, Quint gave something between a strangled groan and a battle cry and the Flot attacked the guardians. There were a series of laser fires and a scrambling of bodies as they engaged in combat.

"Give me the crystal, Angelo," said Finch.

Angelo stood with the laser leveled at him and his hand in a fist, feigning that he still held it. "I'm not giving it to you."

Bianca crawled forward on her hands and knees. Finch thought Angelo had it. That meant she might be able to get to the lake and dump it in.

"I bet you'd give it over for her. I'll shoot her, right in her side, right in a major organ. Raymond! Get the twin," he called.

Bianca looked up and saw Finch pointing his laser at her and Raymond ambling across the grass. Everything began happening too fast for her to register. She acted out of instinct, pure and simple. Events started to flow past her in series of little pops. Bianca looked up, staring at the expanse of the lake not far away. Her objective. Then she scrambled to her feet and bolted. Laser fire shot past her and she altered her course, never looking behind her. She knew Raymond was back there, right on her heels.

She stopped up short at the shore and the freysis-green water lapped at the toes of her boots. Underhanded, she lobbed the crystal into the water. With a plop the crystal went in and almost instantly the green began to be transformed to blue. It was the most beautiful shade of blue she'd ever seen. It spread out slowly as the chimra replicated and fed off the freysis.

"Amazing," she breathed.

Something hit her from behind and blackness closed in.

* * * * *

Her head swam as she regained consciousness. Strong arms held her. Angelo. She squinted up into the light and saw Quint staring down at her. "Bianca," he said.

"Where's Angelo?"

He drew a shaky breath and didn't answer.

Bianca struggled to sit up. "Quint," she said carefully. "Where's Angelo? Tell me."

"Bianca, there was a battle. Finch got away and went for the hovercraft. Angelo followed him in another…" Her head ached, but she tried to focus. Bile rose from her stomach. She knew what he was going to say, heard it in his voice before he said the words. She only caught snippets, "Crash over the lake…explosion…Angelo…gone."

Gone—not dead—but she knew that's what he meant.

He'd left her after all.

Numbness rocketed through her and blackness sucked her under once again.

Chapter Twenty-Nine

Bianca sat in the darkness on the grass, holding her knees tight against her chest. She couldn't cry. Yet, she wasn't numb as she had been after her sister's death. No, the grief that washed through her was nearly overwhelming. Angelo had taught her how to feel every emotion without exception. Now she wished for the numbness.

When she'd come to again, Quint had explained what had happened more clearly. The crafts had collided over the lake. There'd been an explosion and they'd plummeted into the water.

Bianca shivered. Quint had tried to make her come with them when they'd finally left to rescue Marie and Gannon. He didn't think she should be on her own, but she'd refused. The only thing she wanted now was to be alone.

The guardians, upon realization of what exactly was happening to the lake and how Finch had tried to stop it, had changed their tune quickly and stopped fighting. Even Raymond, apparently after hitting her over the head with the butt of his laser, had realized the error of his ways and rescued her from the still partially freysis-tainted lake water she'd fallen into. She felt the back of her head and winced at the lump.

Quint had sent Jinx back to her via one of the Flot, again with an entreaty to join them, but she'd refused angrily. She didn't want anyone near her and she didn't want to leave the lake. Angelo was out there somewhere. Somehow, she'd find Angelo's mother and sisters and bring them to the Valley. That was her next task. But that was for later. Now she kept vigil, though for what she didn't know. All she knew was that lake called to her in some strange way, kept her there.

Her thoughts strayed to Quint. Maybe, eventually, the Southern Flot and the Valley could be merged somehow. Angelo had been thinking of trying to do that.

There was a splash and a moan. A black shape rose from the water at the edge of the lake, and then collapsed. She went still, tamping down the hope that suddenly rose within her. Hope now was a bad thing, a potentially crippling thing.

What if it was Finch? She shook her head. No, there was still freysis in the lake. Even if he'd survived the crash, he wouldn't survive the freysis.

Hope rose up again.

Another splash and moan brought Bianca to her feet. She ran to the shore and splashed into the water. "Angelo?"

"Bianca," he rasped. "Get...out...of the water." With that, he collapsed onto the shore.

"Angelo!" She tried to roll him over, but he was too heavy. She pushed and pulled at him until he finally roused. He picked himself up and crawled out of the lake, onto the sand and dirt edge and collapsed again.

"Angelo?" He was passed out cold. Bianca wanted so much to examine him, see if he was whole, make sure he was all right, but there was no light to do it by. Not even the moon shone down.

She would have to wait, to hope, that he was okay. With hope beating strong in her chest, she curled up around him, heedless of his wet clothing, and held him in an effort to at least keep him warm.

* * * * *

Angelo awoke with a throbbing headache and aching muscles. His thigh pained him badly. He turned over and realized he was pinned down by something...something warm, sweet and loving. "Bianca."

She roused, her blue-green eyes coming open with numbness and sorrow — the way her eyes used to look. But instead of a cynical mask, pure joy transformed them. "Angelo," she said, her voice was a low purr of pleasure and it warmed him all the way through.

He shifted onto his back and sat up. Pain shot through his stomach. A long, angry red and bloody slash ripped across his abdomen. His lips twisted. "Another scar to add to the collection."

She jumped on him, kissing his face all over, then finally finding his lips. "You're perfect. No matter what, scars and all, you're beautiful and perfect and mine."

"I'm yours, definitely, Bianca. No doubt about that."

She rocked back on her heels. "What happened?"

"I ejected before the crash. I ended up far out in the lake and had to fight my way back to this shore. I cut myself on a piece of the wreckage."

Bianca bent her head and examined the wound. "Looks like a trip to Quint's is in order, Angelo. It needs to be cleaned."

"Are Marie and Gannon all right?"

"As far as I know, yes. Marie is probably very shaken. Being with Finch again likely didn't do great things for her mind."

He reached up and touched her face. The sun had come up and the morning light filtered through her hair like a halo. She looked like an angel. An angel with dirt smudged on her forehead, but an angel all the same. He rubbed at the dirt with his thumb. "The only thought that kept me from drowning last night was you. The only thing in the world I wanted was to be back here with you."

Bianca went green, scrambled to her feet and ran into the bushes. Once there, she bent over and promptly lost whatever had been in her stomach. Wincing, Angelo got up and limped over to her. She stood shakily, holding a hand to her abdomen.

"Er, I wasn't really expecting that kind of reaction," Angelo said. "Are you okay?"

She nodded, and then went green again.

"Do you want to sit down?"

She nodded and they sat. Angelo drew her into his arms.

"Freysis poisoning?" she managed to push out.

Angelo shook his head and threw an arm wide. "Look." The expanse of Lake Michigan was a startling, clear blue as far as they could see.

She looked up and caught her breath. "Oh…my."

"It's the beginning. According to Melvin within two years most the freysis in the world will be gone. The chimra will evaporate into the air and then fall down with the rain, spreading all over the world."

"Well, what is it then?" She fingered the back of her head. "Maybe I have a concussion or the good old-fashioned flu."

"Or maybe it's morning sickness."

"What?" She looked at him with hope in her eyes, and then looked away, shaking her head sadly. "You wouldn't like that."

He turned her face to his and set his forehead to hers. "It's all I want, angel-face. Think the Valley can handle another family?"

"Definitely…many more." She frowned. "But there's no way a baby survived all I've gone through."

"You'd be surprised how much abuse life and love can take and still find a way to survive." He brushed the hair back from her shoulders.

"Yes." She smiled, and that smile reached all the way to her eyes.

Enjoy this excerpt from
And Lady Makes Three
*© Copyright Anya Bast, Nikki Soarde,
Ashley Ladd, 2005*

All Rights Reserved, Ellora's Cave Publishing, Inc.

An Excerpt From:
Prism

© Copyright Nikki Soarde, 2005.

All Rights Reserved, Ellora's Cave, Inc.

He breathed a sigh of relief, and flopped back on the pillows. He hadn't slept as long as he thought, and still had an hour before he was due down at the Audi dealership. He was just mulling over the clients he was scheduled to see that afternoon when a loud snort from the other side of the bed demanded his attention.

He propped himself up on his elbow and looked down at the man beside him. He smiled and shook his head. Dax slept like he did everything—with gusto. His long wavy hair was fanned out across the pillow, his arms and legs flung wide. He had a knack for taking up almost three quarters of the available space on the bed, and his snores could rattle the windows at fifty paces. He worked hard, and played harder, his rugged physique and deeply bronzed skin, attesting to just how much time and energy he devoted to his passions. He gave his all in every situation, and he never turned his back on trouble. Or on a friend.

Barring the occasional forgivable one-night stand, and one catastrophic stab at the suburban white-picket-fence myth, Dax and Clay had been together almost since graduation and Clay had never once regretted his decision. They were good together. They were good friends, and God knew the sex was great.

So what was going wrong?

Clay knew he'd overreacted the night before, but he didn't know why. He also didn't know why they'd been arguing more lately, picking fights over everything from which brand of coffee they should buy to escalating long distance bills.

He lay back on the pillow and stared at the ceiling as he considered the events of the past few months. Had something changed and they just couldn't see it? If so, how did they figure out what *it* was, and when they did, what did they do about it?

But the more he thought about it, the more certain he was that *nothing* had changed.

Everything in their relationship was exactly the same as it had been a year ago. Two years ago. *Five* years ago.

And then it hit him. At last he knew exactly what was wrong. How could they have missed it? How could they have been so blind?

He closed his eyes and groaned. Now, if only he could figure out what to do about it.

An Excerpt From:
Twilight
© Copyright Anya Bast, 2005.
All Rights Reserved, Ellora's Cave, Inc.

"Are you all right this morning?" Dai asked. Her moods seemed so unknowable. He felt like he was constantly dancing on the edge of her temper.

"I-I'm fine" She shot him a glance. "I'm just fine."

He waited a heartbeat and then knelt beside her. "I think not. Tell me what is troubling you."

She turned to him. "*Why* could I feel you coming down that path? Why can I sense you in ways I've never been able to sense other people before?"

"I think you know the answer to that."

She sighed, stood, and walked to the tree line. He followed. Twyla whirled on him. "What do you two want from me?" Tears stood her eyes.

"You know the answer to that, too."

"You both want my body."

"Your body, yes. We're healthy males who have waited a long time for you. That goes without saying, but we want more than just your body."

"What, then? You want my emotion, my love, my-my *soul*?"

Dai smiled and shook his head. "Nico and I already have your soul, love. It's already intertwined with ours. We want the rest, though. Most of all, we want your love, freely given."

She stood there, looking up at him with large, tear-filled eyes. The way she looked now, she could almost fool him into thinking she was vulnerable. Maybe she was. He took a step toward her, wanting nothing more than to pull her into the circle of his arms and hold her.

"I don't have any love left to give," she whispered hoarsely and turned away from him.

He reached out and touched her shoulder. When she didn't jerk away, he pulled her to his chest and wrapped her in his arms. She let out a long, ragged sigh and relaxed against him. Closing his eyes, Dai inhaled the scent of her. His heart sung. To have her in his arms was better than all his imaginings. "You do," he murmured insistently into her hair. "Let Nico and I show you."

She turned in the circle of his embrace and tipped her face up toward his. Tears made tracks down her cheeks. "Kiss me," she whispered.

An Excerpt From:
Pirate's Booty
Copyright © Ashley Ladd, 2005.

All Rights Reserved, Ellora's Cave Publishing, Inc.

Keir's warm breath tickled her neck. "Something troubling you, Princess?"

Her hand grasped her throat in shocked alarm.

"I have a name. Would it hurt you so terribly to use it?" She exhaled slowly as she turned to find him barely kissing distance away. Lifting her lashes slowly, she gazed up at him. Not as tall as his colleague, he was the perfect height, his nose level with the top of her head. His lips rested at her eye-level and from this distance, they looked ideal, too. Usually, she couldn't see them for his full beard, but at this distance, she could see them very clearly.

"Melena." Keir caressed her name as no other had before him. It rolled off his tongue like the richest Synkethian milk chocolate.

Mesmerized by his dark, sultry voice, a minute gasp escaped her lips. Quivers of lust racked her, and a strange twinge resounded between her legs. It might not hurt him terribly to use her given name, but apparently it made her ache. But it was too late to take it back now.

Realizing she stared as if he were her last supper, she cursed silently and forced herself to act nonchalant. She was chained by a thousand different prisons and had no right to quiver at his nearness or devour his lips with her gaze. Too late to act as if everything was sunny when she probably looked as if she were about to go nova so she confessed to the partial truth.

At least, he wouldn't hear a lie in her voice. "What if we're never rescued?"

Swallowing the lump in her throat, she swept her gaze wide in an all-encompassing arc around the glade where they'd moved their camp. Lifting her chin high, she tried to sound confident, but her voice emerged strangled. "What if we spend the rest of our days on this planet, completely alone, except for the three of us?"

Keir raised his hand as if to stroke away the stray wisps of hair from her heated face, but it hovered mid-air and then dropped limply to his side. "We have to be optimistic. We can't give up hope."

If it were only the two of them, she and Keir, it could be paradise. But three? She worried her bottom lip between her teeth. Someone would be the odd man out and that spelled trouble.

Uncomfortably hot, bored, and frustrated, she glared. "Why? Shouldn't they have found us by now if they were searching? My people must think me dead from the explosion. They may not have launched any missions of rescue."

Keir slid a finger under her chin and forced her to look him square in the eye. His were deep, murky pools that she could happily drown in. "Because we'll go crazy if we give up. Because you're much stronger than that. We're not just going to lie down and die…"

About the author:

Anya Bast writes erotic fantasy and paranormal romance. Primarily, she writes happily-ever-afters with lots of steamy sex. After all, how can you have a happily-ever-after WITHOUT lots of sex?

Anya welcomes mail from readers. You can write to her c/o Ellora's Cave Publishing at 1056 Home Avenue, Akron OH 44310-3502.

Why an electronic book?

We live in the Information Age—an exciting time in the history of human civilization in which technology rules supreme and continues to progress in leaps and bounds every minute of every hour of every day. For a multitude of reasons, more and more avid literary fans are opting to purchase e-books instead of paperbacks. The question to those not yet initiated to the world of electronic reading is simply: *why?*

1. *Price.* An electronic title at Ellora's Cave Publishing and Cerridwen Press runs anywhere from 40-75% less than the cover price of the <u>exact same title</u> in paperback format. Why? Cold mathematics. It is less expensive to publish an e-book than it is to publish a paperback, so the savings are passed along to the consumer.

2. *Space.* Running out of room to house your paperback books? That is one worry you will never have with electronic novels. For a low one-time cost, you can purchase a handheld computer designed specifically for e-reading purposes. Many e-readers are larger than the average handheld, giving you plenty of screen room. Better yet, hundreds of titles can be stored within your new library—a single microchip. (Please note that Ellora's Cave and Cerridwen Press does not endorse any specific brands. You can check our website at www.elloracave.com or

www.cerridwenpress.com for customer recommendations we make available to new consumers.)

3. *Mobility.* Because your new library now consists of only a microchip, your entire cache of books can be taken with you wherever you go.

4. *Personal preferences are accounted for.* Are the words you are currently reading too small? Too large? Too...**ANNOYING**? Paperback books cannot be modified according to personal preferences, but e-books can.

5. *Instant gratification.* Is it the middle of the night and all the bookstores are closed? Are you tired of waiting days—sometimes weeks—for online and offline bookstores to ship the novels you bought? Ellora's Cave Publishing sells instantaneous downloads 24 hours a day, 7 days a week, 365 days a year. Our e-book delivery system is 100% automated, meaning your order is filled as soon as you pay for it.

Those are a few of the top reasons why electronic novels are displacing paperbacks for many an avid reader. As always, Ellora's Cave and Cerridwen Press welcomes your questions and comments. We invite you to email us at service@ellorascave.com, service@cerridwenpress.com or write to us directly at: 1056 Home Ave. Akron OH 44310-3502.

MAKE EACH DAY MORE *EXCITING* WITH OUR

Ellora's Cavemen Calendar

www.EllorasCave.com

THE
☥ ELLORA'S CAVE ☥
LIBRARY

Stay up to date with Ellora's Cave Titles in
Print with our Quarterly Catalog.

TO RECIEVE A CATALOG,
SEND AN EMAIL WITH YOUR NAME
AND MAILING ADDRESS TO:

CATALOG@ELLORASCAVE.COM

OR SEND A LETTER OR POSTCARD
WITH YOUR MAILING ADDRESS TO:

CATALOG REQUEST
c/o ELLORA'S CAVE PUBLISHING, INC.
1056 HOME AVENUE
AKRON, OHIO 44310-3502

Cerridwen, the Celtic Goddess of wisdom, was the muse who brought inspiration to storytellers and those in the creative arts. Cerridwen Press encompasses the best and most innovative stories in all genres of today's fiction. Visit our site and discover the newest titles by talented authors who still get inspired - much like the ancient storytellers did, once upon a time.

Cerridwen Press

www.cerridwenpress.com

Ellora's Cave

Discover for yourself why readers can't get enough of the multiple award-winning publisher Ellora's Cave.
Whether you prefer e-books or paperbacks, be sure to visit EC on the web at www.ellorascave.com for an erotic reading experience that will leave you breathless.